SURRENDER

"Who are you, Susannah Fitzgerald? What you try so hard to appear . . . or something else?"

For an instant, the truth hovered on the tip of her tongue. The mere temptation to speak was terrifying. She put a hand to his chest as though to push him away.

That was a mistake. The instant of contact with the hard, broad surface of his chest seared her. On a thin thread of sound, she murmured, "Oh . . ."

Rand felt it too. The unwelcome, unwanted, but completely undeniable attraction that now, this moment in the scented garden beneath the cloud-draped moon, could no longer be held at bay . . .

Praise for **MAURA SEGER**'s previous novels

PERCHANCE TO DREAM

MAURA SEGER

AVON BOOKS ◆ NEW YORK

AVON BOOKS
A division of
The Hearst Corporation
105 Madison Avenue
New York, New York 10016

Copyright © 1989 by Maura Seger
Cover illustration by John Ennis
Inside cover author photograph copyright © 1983 by Leslie A. Beran
Published by arrangement with the author
Library of Congress Catalog Card Number: 89-91268
ISBN: 0-380-75338-3

First Avon Books Printing: November 1989

Author's Note

This is a different kind of historical romance, one that deals not with events as they actually happened but with the far more tantalizing question of what might have been.

The story takes place in 1876, fourteen years after the South *won* the Civil War. This is not as outlandish as it might seem. The South actually did come very close to winning the war at the battle of Antietam in 1862.

What if it had? What would the consequences have been? Not only for the famous people of the day whose lives would have been drastically changed, but also for a man and woman thrown together under extraordinary circumstances.

You are about to meet Susannah and Rand. They may seem like characters in a particularly fictitious novel. But who is to say that somewhere out beyond the twists and turns of time, on a branch of history apart from our own, they aren't as real as you or I?

Prologue

Richmond, Virginia
April 1876

I t had been raining for several days, a cold, unseason-
able rain that alternated between a steady drizzle and
an outright downpour. The tulips and irises that had
optimistically sprouted in the city's flower beds had long
since bent to the ground. The magnolia trees, late to bloom
because of the cold, had lost their pale pink-and-white
flowers within a matter of days. Richmond's citizens looked
up at the leaden sky, shivered, and pulled their mantuas
and greatcoats more snugly around themselves. Social traf-
fic in the fashionable parts of the city all but ground to a
halt. Anyone who could remained inside close to the fires
that served, to some small degree, to hold the chill at bay.

By evening, the city streets were virtually deserted.
Only a few solitary carriages creaked over the rain-slicked
cobblestones, sending up showers of muddy water in their
wake. Anxious eyes watched the James River, hoping it
would not rise far enough to threaten the newly strength-
ened levees. Foam-flecked water swirled around the wharves
and set the ships docked there to rocking wildly.

A dank, biting wind whipped off the river, around the
corners of the two-story red brick warehouses where tobacco, coal, rice, and cotton were stored, and moaned

down the darkened lanes of ramshackle wooden buildings where gas lamps cast their yellow glow. Here, in the part of the city no one would ever call fashionable, life continued as usual.

Shouts, laughter, and tinny music could be heard from the flash houses that occupied almost every corner. Silhouetted against the shadowy light, burly men clustered around the bars, throwing down mugs of beer and shot glasses of raw whiskey, lunging after the dollymops who shrieked and giggled while figuring what price to ask for a tumble on the rumpled beds upstairs.

Scuffles broke out like flash fires in tinder-dry woods over a turn of the dice, a woman, or simply an ill-aimed glance. The random episodes of violence usually ended with one or more crumpled forms propped up in a corner to sleep off the effects of alcohol and fisticuffs.

In the shadow of one of the flash houses, a small, slender figure paused. Dressed in homespun trousers, a shirt, and a rough jacket, it looked little different from the scores of young boys who haunted the docks of Richmond's Rocketts section looking for work or, if they were less scrupulous, likely prey for a quick robbery. Indeed, the cap pulled low over the small figure's eyes and the quick glances the figure cast back and forth along the deserted street suggested something was amiss.

Shivering in the chill rain, Tad—as the figure was known in certain quarters—suddenly stiffened and pressed closer against the side of the building. The door of the flash house flew open and banged against the outside wall. Air warmed by unwashed bodies struck the night breeze and seemed to coagulate, hanging motionless for some moments like an evil-smelling miasma. The bitter odor was compounded by sour drink, ancient sawdust, and the nameless effluvia of hopelessness.

A man emerged, roughly dressed and with several days' growth of beard obscuring his face. His large, scarred hand was clenched around a leather leash, at the other end of which strained a snarling pit dog. The dog turned reddened eyes in Tad's direction and growled deep in its throat.

"Shuttup, Sheba," the man ordered. "Ye've 'ad yer fill t'night. Twenty rats and no mistake. Good dog, yer are. Gotta nice bone fer yer at home."

Sheba did not want a bone, nor was she apparently interested in killing more rats, in the pit or elsewhere. She wanted whatever was hiding in the shadows. Her fangs gleamed whitely in the rain-washed light as she tugged harder on the leash.

"Damn ya, bitch!" the man snarled. He raised his free hand and sent it crashing down against the side of the dog's head. Sheba staggered and whimpered. Her owner dragged her off down the street, muttering to himself.

Tad drew a long breath and let it out slowly. His stomach heaved, but there was no time to be thinking about that. The moment the coast was clear, he darted out from the shelter of the building and quickly crossed the street to blend against the shadows on the other side. The speed with which he moved did not conceal a certain lithe grace that might have given an observer pause.

Safe on the other side, he paused for breath. Rain trickled down the collar of his shirt, assaulting the smooth, bare skin beneath and making him grit his teeth all the more firmly.

Tad was afraid as well as physically uncomfortable, but neither sensation was unusual. Though he had barely seen his eighteenth year—and looked even younger—he had experienced far more of life's dangers than most people his age. And having experienced them, he knew how to persist in the face of any difficulty no matter how great.

Stepping lightly over the treacherously slick cobblestones, he paused again near the corner of the warehouse and checked once more up and down the street. Rising high above the opposite side of the river was the darkly shadowed hulk of Church Hill, one of the seven hills on which the city was built, which caused its proud residents to liken it to Rome. Muted by distance and by the steady downpour, the midnight tolling of the church bells nonetheless reached Tad. He stiffened and immediately began to run.

Half a block away he found the door he was looking for and knocked on it urgently. No sound or light emanated from within. Breathing raggedly, he knocked again while staring down the street. The church bells had barely rung out their last peal when the sound of booted feet moving purposefully, despite the hour, reached him.

Since the war, Rocketts had been patrolled by a nightly watch more notable for tenacity than intelligence. The members of the watch could not be faulted for their determination to seek out wrongdoers and bring them to justice, but it had apparently never occurred to them that by keeping to the same schedule night after night, they made it possible for someone who was clever to avoid them.

Tad was counting on doing exactly that, except that he had gotten a late start and been further delayed by the weather. Now, as he pressed against the door, he wondered frantically if he should knock again and take the risk of the watch hearing him or if he would be wiser to seek some concealment elsewhere. He was about to do the latter when a peephole in the door suddenly opened and a single, bloodshot eye peered at him.

"Banks," he whispered tensely, "open the door, quickly!"

There was a moment's hesitation, then the bolts grated loud enough to make him wince. The door gave way abruptly, and he all but fell into the darkened room as the door was shoved shut behind him.

"Quiet," a man's voice admonished.

The warning was hardly necessary. Tad could hear for himself the watch passing by immediately outside. He waited, his senses straining, until the last booted footfall had faded away before he whispered, "What took you so long? Another moment and I would have been caught."

The man, who had struck a tinder to a small oil lamp set on a wobbly wooden table, turned and glared at him. "I had to be sure it was you, didn't I? Besides, you're late."

Tad smothered a sigh. He was accustomed to a certain amount of surliness from those who, like himself, were afraid, and he understood the emotions that drove people like Zachery Banks to express their fear through anger. That understanding did not, however, make them any easier to deal with.

"Let's get this over with," he said curtly. "I have to get back."

"You think I want you around any longer than necessary?" Banks demanded. He was a short, squat man with the thick chest and arms of a docks bale loader, which, indeed, he had once been before he climbed his way up to become foreman for the company that owned the warehouse in which they were meeting.

Tad distrusted him instinctively. Banks had made it clear from the outset that he did what he did strictly for the money. Indeed, he was at that very moment holding out his hand.

"The package first," Tad said.

Banks's red-rimmed eyes narrowed. "Why you . . ."

"We have this argument every time. There's no point to it. The package first."

"You've not much sense, have you?"

Tad didn't bother to answer. He knew Banks was trying to intimidate him and was equally certain he could not allow that to happen. Having decided the outcome in advance, there was no question as to his response.

Silence made Banks nervous. He bounced back and forth on the balls of his feet and glared at Tad. When that failed to cause any reaction, he laughed sarcastically. "I could snap you in two, I could. Take the money and dump your carcass straight into the river. Nobody'd ever be the

wiser. Fact is, I can't think of any reason why I shouldn't.''
He took a step toward the boy, pausing when he realized
that Tad still showed no sign of fear.

Quietly, so that Banks had to strain to hear him, Tad
said, ''If you want to be hunted down and killed, go right
ahead.''

Banks laughed again, this time uneasily. ''You think
your friends are that tough? Then why do they have a boy
coming here on a man's job?''

''Maybe they just don't think what you do is very
important, Banks.''

The older man flushed. He liked the money he got, all
right, but he also liked the sense of importance his clandestine activities gave him. ''What do you mean by that?''

Tad shrugged. ''Only that you're a small cog in a very
large wheel. So am I, for that matter. But my friends
would still avenge me, make no mistake about that. It's a
matter of principle, you see.''

''Principle . . .'' Banks rolled the word off his tongue
as though he had never encountered it before. His scowl
deepened. He knew little about the boy or the people he
worked for. But he knew they had money, they took
chances, and if Tad was anything to go by, they were very
confident. Not good people to have against you.

''All right,'' he snarled, thrusting a small, flat package
at Tad. It was about the size of a ladies' reticule and was
wrapped in canvas to protect it from the damp. Brown
twine secured the plain wrapping, which indicated neither
the package's origin nor its destination. ''Take it,'' Banks
urged. ''The less time it's here, the happier I am.''

Without hesitation Tad slipped the package into his
jacket and removed the small pouch holding Banks's payment. As he handed it to him, he warned, ''There'll be a
reply in the usual place.''

''Isn't there always,'' Banks grumbled. He weighed the
pouch in his hand and looked sidelong at the boy. Determination to have the last word made him careless. ''Though

why those two have so much to say to each other is beyond me.''

Tad had turned toward the door but at those words he froze and looked back at Banks. ''You aren't supposed to know who this is from or where it's going.''

The older man gave him a derisive look. ''Think I'm a fool, do you? I'd have to be deaf, dumb, and blind not to know that those two old men are up to something.''

''Perhaps they are, but you'd be wiser not to mention it.''

Banks hesitated. He was a hard, tough man who stood for no guff from anyone, let alone slight, beardless boys. But there was something about this one that made him think twice about lashing out as he would normally have done, and it wasn't merely the matter of the friends and how they might react. The boy's physical presence was not imposing in the least, yet he gave off a sense of steely strength coupled with an absolute determination that marked him as at least potentially dangerous. Banks hadn't survived as long as he had by courting unnecessary risks. ''I haven't said anything,'' he muttered.

Tad stared at him for a long moment. His eyes beneath dark, slanting brows were an unusually striking shade of green. Banks found that he could not tear his own gaze away. For the space of several very uncomfortable heartbeats he felt pinned by the boy's scrutiny. Just as he began to think he was going to have to say or do something, Tad shrugged. The gesture released Banks.

''See to it that you don't,'' Tad said as he gestured at Banks to cover the light.

Banks obeyed quickly, more anxious than ever for his visitor to go. A moment later, Tad was back out on the street, hurrying through the rain, a small, wraithlike figure who blended easily with the shadowed buildings until he seemed to vanish entirely.

1

Susannah Fitzgerald paused in the midst of studying the contents of her Moroccan leather jewelry case. She looked over her all-but-bare shoulder at the stern-faced black woman behind her. A smile lifted the corners of her soft, full mouth. "Don't fuss, Sukie. This gown's perfectly proper."

Hands on her hips, brow furrowed, Sukie replied, "It's perfectly disgraceful, if you ask me. Why if that neckline was cut any lower, your bosoms would be hanging right out. What your daddy's going to say I just don't know."

"You're presuming he'll notice," Susannah said as she turned back to the mirror with a pair of diamond drop earrings in her hands. She held up the earrings and tilted her head this way and that, trying to decide whether or not she liked the effect. "Which is highly unlikely given how preoccupied he is these days. But if he does, I'll just tell him it's the fashion—which, as you know, is true."

"Wicked French fashion," Sukie informed her, still shaking her head. "Why in your mama's day—"

"Necklines were cut every bit as low. I know because I've seen the old fashion magazines. Not only that, but I've peeked at her dresses that are in the trunks in the attic." At her maid's chagrined expression, Susannah

8

laughed. She fastened the earrings in place, glanced in the mirror again, and nodded her satisfaction.

"Besides," she said as she rose, "I'm eighteen now. It's time I started looking like a woman."

Sukie's brow furrowed as she surveyed the girl before her. Susannah was of barely medium height, but her slenderness and the natural grace with which she carried herself made her appear taller. Her bearing and the tilt of her small chin hinted at stubbornness, but few men ever noticed that. They were far too taken with the classically beautiful features framed by ebony hair arranged in a tumble of silken curls that fell from the crown of her head halfway down her back. Most riveting of all were Susannah's eyes, which could vary from the emerald softness of a forest glen to the cool, surging depths of the sea awash in sunlight. Framed by thick, dark lashes, they were a constant mystery as well as a challenge.

"You look any more like a woman than you do right now," Sukie said bluntly, "and you'll have those fine Southern gentlemen pawing the ground and snorting, if not something else."

Susannah's gaze was all innocence. "Why, Sukie, whatever do you mean?"

"Never you mind, missy. You just remember your manners tonight. You may think your daddy's wrapped right around your little finger, but there are limits to what even he will stand for."

"I know," the girl said gently. "The last thing I ever want to do is hurt Father."

The expression on Sukie's broad face softened. She reached out a workworn hand and patted Susannah's arm gently. "You've got a good heart, child. I just wonder sometimes if that's enough to protect you in this world."

Something flitted behind Susannah's eyes: regret, wistfulness—Sukie could not tell. In a moment, it was gone, replaced by a smile. "You've done a wonderful job," the girl said as she looked at herself in the full-length mirror set near the floor-to-ceiling windows. The spring twilight had already faded, but at least that evening there had been a spectacular sunset. The rain was finally over, though the dampness lingered. Gas lamps in gilded brackets along the damask-covered walls filled the spacious room with a warm, soft light that revealed the truth of what Susannah said.

Her gown was of white faille silk embroidered with tiny rosebuds and worn with an underskirt of emerald taffeta. The softly puffed sleeves were off the shoulder, and as Sukie had said, a generous portion of her high, firm breasts was revealed by the low neckline, which plunged even more deeply in the back. Skirt and underskirt alike were caught up in a flounced bustle that fell away into a ribboned train. With the gown she wore not only the diamond earrings that had been her father's eighteenth-birthday present to her a few months before, but also the magnificent necklace of baguette-cut diamonds and emeralds that had once belonged to her mother.

Few women could have failed to look lovely in such raiment, but Susannah, blessed by remarkable beauty, was almost too entrancing. She epitomized both the sensual fascination of a woman and the tender innocence of a young girl. It was an irresistible combination that drew men to her like the proverbial bees to honey and assured her disfavor with the Richmond mothers seeking to launch their daughters in a society Susannah seemed destined to dominate.

No thought of that was in her mind as she smoothed on her long white evening gloves. Sukie's large, blunt fingers were surprisingly adept at fastening the tiny pearl buttons that reached well above the elbow. Susannah picked up her lace-and-ivory fan and her small beaded reticule. She looped both over her wrist before giving Sukie a quick hug. "Now don't you wait up for me. I'll probably be late."

The black woman sniffed disparagingly. "I'll sit up like

I always do. If I happen to nod off, you wake me up, you hear?''

Susannah laughed. "I hear." She picked up her skirts with her free hand and wafted out the bedroom door, trailing the scent of jasmine behind her.

Her father was waiting in the entry hall below. Jeffrey Buchanan Fitzgerald looked elegant as always in a black tailcoat, black trousers with braided side seams, and a white satin waistcoat. His silver hair, still as thick as many a younger man's, was brushed back from his high, broad forehead. He had a modest mustache and sideburns as well as bushy brows set above large gray eyes. Those eyes, as he looked up the staircase at his daughter, were filled with love.

Yet his voice was gently teasing. "There you are at last. I was beginning to think I would have to go on alone."

"As though you would," Susannah chided him as she sailed down the steps, her gown floating gracefully around her. "Besides, I'm barely five minutes late. That hardly counts at all."

"Actually, it doesn't," he agreed as he took the velvet evening cape a servant proffered and held it for her to slip on. "If you're serious about being a belle, you'll have to learn to keep people waiting longer."

Susannah fastened the cape at her throat and drew the silk-lined hood up over her hair, settling it lightly in place. "I don't think I could stand that. I'm usually far too impatient to get wherever I'm going to want to delay."

"Don't change. Being a belle is highly overrated."

Susannah raised her eyebrows in mock surprise. An elderly black man opened the front door for them. "Did you hear that, Zebediah?" she asked as she swept past. "Father doesn't want me to be a belle."

Zebediah smiled gently. "He just wants you to be happy, miss. Same like everybody else."

"Is that true?" Susannah asked as her father handed her into the brougham that waited at the curb. The high, lace-spoked wheels reflected the lingering dampness on the cobblestone streets, but the dark sky above was cloudless. "Will you be satisfied if I am merely happy?"

Jeffrey settled himself on the broad leather seat across from her before he replied. "Merely happy? I wouldn't put it that way. Happiness is a great accomplishment in this world."

Susannah looked at her father. His strong, steady features seemed to her to have changed little over the years, but she could hardly ignore the signs of strain that had lately come upon him. The lines around his eyes and mouth appeared deeply etched, and there was a weariness about the set of his shoulders that worried her. He was, as far as she knew, in good health, but he was also badly overworked, a condition for which there appeared to be no remedy in sight.

"You know," she said softly, "we didn't have to go tonight. We could have stayed home, had supper together, perhaps"—she dropped her voice to suggest wicked indulgence—"played a few hands of piquet."

Jeffrey laughed, eyeing his daughter fondly. He doubted there were many young girls in Richmond who would rather sit home with their fathers on a spring evening than attend what promised to be one of the most glittering events of the social season. Yet he didn't doubt for a moment that Susannah meant exactly what she said. For all her remarkable beauty and vivacity, there was a down-to-earth streak in her that kept her from being overly impressed by pomp and circumstance.

As unobtrusively as he could manage, he stretched his right leg more comfortably before he replied. "If I had kept you home, I would have incurred the wrath of every young buck in the city. I hope you're prepared to dance the evening away, because I don't think you'll be allowed to sit down for a moment."

Susannah affected not to notice her father's discomfort even as she wondered how much trouble his old wound was giving him. She lifted one small foot clad in a white silk evening slipper and laughed. "Sukie told me that Mother considered an evening to have been a failure unless she came home with her slippers in tatters."

A reminiscent look flitted across her father's face, his stern expression softening with love. "She danced divinely, as though she moved on air. I remember the first time we waltzed together. It must have been the spring of fifty-seven. It was considered very improper for an unmarried girl to waltz, yet when the music began I found myself at your mother's side. She didn't hesitate to accept my invitation. That same evening I proposed to her, and we were married a few months later."

Susannah had heard the story before, but she nonetheless listened avidly, as she always did when her father spoke of her mother and of the past. Both fascinated her. Her mother had died when Susannah was barely four, taken by a typhoid outbreak Elizabeth Fitzgerald was attempting to stem among the slaves on the family's Tidewater plantation, Belleterre. Susannah scarcely remembered her, but she cherished the small painting she had of a beautiful, gentle woman whose soft voice still sometimes haunted her dreams.

"How I wish she could have lived to see all that has happened."

"She would have been extremely proud of you," her father said softly.

Susannah wondered if he was right. She couldn't discount the possibility that her mother would have disapproved of certain of her activities. On the other hand, perhaps she would not have, for Elizabeth Fitzgerald had been a woman of action who did not wait for events to happen but rather took a part in shaping them.

The carriage was turning up Broad Street toward Capitol Square. Susannah caught sight of colorful Chinese lanterns waving gently in the night air, their illumination revealing the wrought iron gates that stood open to admit a steady

stream of guests onto the Capitol's grounds. The original
Greek-style building that had stood there had recently been
replaced by a large, domed edifice considered more suitable to its purpose. Susannah had preferred the earlier
structure and considered its successor overdone, but she
kept her sentiments to herself.

However, as her father handed her from the carriage,
she could not resist a rueful comment. "Surely Caesar
would have felt at home here. All that marble and gilt sets
a definitely imperial tone."

"I gather that was the idea," Jeffrey replied. He tucked
her hand into the crook of his elbow, and together they
ascended the monumental stone staircase leading to the
portico. "Some suggested that the veterans might find this
entrance difficult, if not impossible to ascend, but practicality was ignored in favor of magnificence."

Susannah glanced up. Ahead of them, over the Capitol's
entrance, hung an immense flag, illuminated with an almost unearthly light that no gas lamp could produce.

"How . . . ?" Susannah murmured in surprise.

"I believe it has something to do with electricity," her
father explained. "A gentleman named Edison from New
Jersey convinced the Congress to try his invention."

"It is . . . very impressive. One could believe that night
has been turned into day."

Indeed, it did appear that was the case. Surely no shadows lay over the fourteen white stars set on crossed blue
bars against a red background, the hallowed emblem of the
Confederate States of America.

President Robert E. Lee was speaking. He stood, an
elegant figure in a pearl gray frock coat and snow-white
beard, his manner cordial, relaxed, but with that ineffable
air of resolution that had not failed him in all his sixty-nine
years. He did not bother to raise his voice, but then he
didn't have to. All of the two hundred odd people at the

tables set beneath the Capitol's dome hung on his every word.

"My friends," he said, "I hardly need tell you that we are gathered here to commemorate a momentous occasion. The events at Fort Sumter some fifteen years ago today began the conflict which resulted in the birth of our nation. Begun in bloodshed, we have prospered in peace."

Here he was interrupted by spontaneous applause that continued for several minutes. There was a self-congratulatory tone to the clapping. Most of the people in Lee's audience gave themselves no little credit for the Confederacy's success. Any among them who had been less than enthusiastic at the outset of the War of Secession had long since forgotten that fact. They were all loyal sons and daughters of the South who could be forgiven a certain complacency because it had been hard earned in a bloody struggle.

At length, Lee went on. "We are far stronger today than when we undertook to separate ourselves from the Union. We have proven beyond question our ability to exist as a sovereign nation. However, as I contemplate the beginning of my fourth term as your president, I am conscious of the dangers of presuming that the future will simply be a continuation of the present."

Halfway down the head table, Susannah listened closely. Unlike most of the people gathered around her, she had some idea where President Lee was heading with his speech. Her heart beat more urgently as she waited for the words she knew were coming.

"All of us here, I am certain, have as our most fervent hope that our children will never know the horrors of war. But as an old soldier who loves his country, I am saddened to say that I see the shadows of those horrors gathering on our horizon. There are those who see in the division of a nation its weakening, and who seek to profit by that. To them I say that we are not a small or petty people. We of the Southland pride ourselves on the largeness of our spirit. For myself, and I believe for you ladies and gentlemen, when we look to the North we see not hated enemies but vanquished brothers to whom the hand of forgiveness is not ill put.''

At the surrounding tables, heads nodded. Susannah smiled to herself. Though she had been only a small child when the War of Secession ended, she was well aware that many of those Lee addressed had virulently hated the Yankees. But with victory had come tolerance, if not the actual forgiveness for which he asked.

"To those who seek opportunity in weakness," Lee said, "I repeat the words of that great son of the South, Mr. Thomas Jefferson, who allowed that though he had become an old man, he was still a young gardener. So am I, my friends. I pledge to you that my fourth term will be a time to reap the harvest of these many years and to store it up safely for those who come after us."

Sustained applause erupted as the company rose to its feet. He had momentarily disconcerted them with his reference to change, but reminders of their glorious heritage were always soothing. Only a few in the audience pondered the mention of weakness and its relationship to disunity, but that was enough.

The seed had been planted. Lee, as great a gardener in his own way as Jefferson, did not doubt that it would ripen. The president inclined his silvered head graciously. His eyes met Susannah's briefly, and he gave her a small, private smile.

An hour later, as the orchestra played and couples whirled around the circular marble floor, which had been cleared for dancing, Susannah remembered that smile and felt a faint tremor of concern. She knew she had to speak with Lee before the evening was out, but she wasn't certain how that would be arranged. Meanwhile, she had Thurston to contend with, and he never failed to set her nerves on edge.

"You're looking particularly lovely tonight, my dear," her partner said as his hand tightened on her narrow waist.

She felt his fingers even through the layers of fabric and whalebone separating her skin from his. "But pearls would be a better accompaniment to your beauty than diamonds and emeralds. I look forward to the day I may give them to you."

Susannah suppressed a flicker of irritation. She glanced up at the young man through the thick fringe of her lashes. His narrow face with its sharp nose, small mouth, and receding chin was, as usual, set in an expression of pompous solemnity.

He took himself very seriously, Thurston did. She could count on one hand the number of times she had seen him laugh, and then it had always been at somebody else's expense. His gray eyes were actually well set and might have been appealing except that they lacked any hint of warmth. His brown hair was invariably well cut and combed but still appeared lank.

He dressed meticulously well, almost too much so, as though he was so concerned about outward appearances that he had neither time nor interest to spare for what went on inside. Indeed, as she well knew, only superficialities mattered to Thurston, which at least made him relatively easy to manage.

No hint of her thoughts showed as she tossed her head prettily and smiled. Dimples appeared at each corner of her full mouth. "Aren't you being just the tiniest bit forward, Thurston? After all, nothing has been settled between us."

His mouth tightened further as a shadow of impatience moved behind his pale eyes. "I realize, Susannah, that in our society a beautiful young woman such as yourself has a certain obligation to be, shall we say, a coquette. I have no objection to that, so long as you do not attempt to take it too far."

"Why, Thurston, I have no idea what you're talking about." As she spoke, she glanced around, trying to locate Lee. She spied him finally at the center of a group of men

standing on the edge of the dance floor. Her father was
also among them. He looked in her direction and smiled.

Susannah smothered a sigh. Although her father had
never spoken to her directly about Thurston, she had the
impression he approved of him. She hardly had to wonder
why. Heir to the immense Sanders lumber-and-mining
fortune, Thurston was one of the most avidly sought after
catches in the entire Confederacy. At that very moment,
Susannah was conscious of numerous pairs of eyes watching their progress across the dance floor. At the first sign
of discord between them, ambitious mothers would be
racing to make the most of it. Which would have been fine
with Susannah except that she hated to disappoint her
father.

The problem was that she didn't particularly care for
Thurston, finding him self-centered and more than a little
pretentious. There was also something about him—she
couldn't precisely figure out what—that faintly repulsed
her. To the best of her admittedly limited knowledge she
was a perfectly normal young woman with all the requisite
emotions and responses. Yet she did not like to have
Thurston touching her, not even in the impersonal manner
required on the dance floor.

"I do believe my poor feet are about to drop off," she
murmured as the music ended. "Would you think me
absolutely terrible if I hid in the cloakroom for a little
while?"

"If you hadn't insisted on dancing with every man
present, you wouldn't be in such discomfort now."

"Surely not *every* man," Susannah said with feigned
lightness. His rudeness annoyed her, but she was bound
and determined not to show it. "Half of them, perhaps."

Thurston's hand tightened again, this time actually hurting her. "Sometimes I believe you go out of your way to
provoke me."

"No," she corrected him coldly as she removed his

hand from her waist and stepped away, "I do not. Now please excuse me."

Before he could reply, she turned and walked off the dance floor, not caring if her actions displeased him further or fueled the hopes of ambitious mothers. She had used up her patience for that night. There were far more important matters to deal with.

A large room on the second floor had been set aside for the use of the ladies. Half a dozen young girls, Susannah's age or thereabout, occupied the mirrored dressing tables. They leaned close to their reflections, smoothing away stray wisps of hair, dabbing powder on their noses, or simply studying themselves intently. The pretty ones looked satisfied and confident, and their plainer sisters were either miserable or resigned.

As Susannah entered, a petite blonde rose from one of the tables and turned to view herself in the full-length mirror. She made a moue of displeasure. "I declare, if my waist gets any bigger, I'm going to look like an absolute cow." As she spoke, she placed her hands around her waist, which had the effect of calling attention to its narrowness. "I told that no-good Tessie to lace me tighter, but she just won't listen."

Beside her, a pale, quiet girl murmured, "You look absolutely beautiful, Lucy. It's hard to imagine how you could possibly be any lovelier."

Lucy, eyes still on the mirror, saw in it a reflection of Susannah standing near the door. Her gaze narrowed even as she smiled. "I will say that at least I look like a lady, unlike certain other people I could mention."

Around her the other girls tittered and cast sidelong glances at Susannah to see how she would react. Lucy warmed to her audience. "Well I declare, it's bad enough to show up in a dress you're practically popping out of, but wearing all those jewels. That's just not done. And then the way she acts with Thurston, that just absolutely makes me sick."

"Then why don't you console him?" Susannah asked lightly. She walked farther into the room, found a place for herself at one of the dressing tables, and sat down. As she removed a small silver compact from her reticule, she added, "I'm sure he'd appreciate it."

Lucy glared at her. She was nineteen, the daughter of a wealthy Tidewater family, and an acknowledged beauty. She and Susannah had known each other in a casual way since childhood. Susannah didn't feel one way or the other about Lucy, but she was well aware that the other girl considered her a bitter rival, and not without reason. Were it not for Susannah, Lucy would have been Richmond's reigning belle. Susannah would gladly have ceded the honor to her except that there was, of course, no way to do so.

Had gentlemen been present, Lucy would have bitten off her tongue before giving vent to her feelings. But in their absence, she made no pretense of even rudimentary courtesy. "You're so full of yourself, Susannah Fitzgerald. You think you're so all-fired special. Well, let me tell you something—it isn't true. Thurston's willing enough to dally with you now, but when the time comes for him to choose a wife, he'll think twice. He'll want a proper lady, not some . . ." She waved her hands as though she couldn't quite think of the word.

"Hoyden?" Susannah suggested helpfully.

"Yes, hoyden! You think it's funny, but it isn't. It's a disgrace for any Southern woman to be so forward."

"I'm sorry you feel that way," Susannah said softly. She rose, lightly adjusted her bodice at the shoulders, and turned to go.

"Is that all you have to say?" Lucy demanded. "You don't care what we think of you, do you?"

Susannah hesitated. She was tempted to merely shrug and let it go at that, but for once in her life she couldn't.

Since childhood she had lived with the knowledge that she was different from other people, partly because of her upbringing, which had endowed her with healthy self-esteem and confidence in her own ability to make a difference, but also because her mother's early death had left her without anyone to ease her entry into feminine society in such a way as to lessen the inevitable resentment of her beauty. Her Aunt Miriam had tried to help, but she was no more skilled in such areas than Susannah herself and was, if anything, even less interested. Susannah had grown so accustomed to fending for herself that it was something of a shock to realize how much she still regretted the lack of friendship of girls her age.

With quiet dignity, she said, "You're wrong, Lucy. I would like to have the good opinion of all of you. That's only natural. What I won't do is turn myself inside out in order to get it."

"What's that supposed to mean?" one of the other girls demanded.

"Only that I think nothing is more important than being true to yourself. In comparison, going to balls, being popular, and catching a husband are all inconsequential."

"Easy for you to say," Lucy muttered.

"You think so? There are times when I'd like nothing better than to be like the rest of you. I just can't manage it, that's all."

Before any of them could comment, Susannah left the cloakroom and closed the door firmly behind her. She heard the sudden upsurge of voices on the other side but did not linger. It had shaken her to reveal even that much of her inner feelings, but she did not regret it. She was not one to indulge in self-recrimination in hindsight. That was one of the benefits of always acting with sincerity.

She paused for a few moments on the balcony that ran along the entire inner curve of the Capitol and afforded an excellent view of the hall below. She could see Thurston looking ill at ease as two young ladies tried to make themselves pleasant to him under the benign smiles of their chaperones. Several more waited their turn. Susannah suppressed a smile and looked elsewhere. Her father was still in conversation with the men who had been attending Lee, but the president himself was gone. She scanned the hall quickly to make sure, then turned and hurried away.

A narrow back staircase led from the Capitol's second floor to a small cluster of rooms tucked under the dome. Few people knew they existed, and fewer still would have been using them at such an hour. Yet as Susannah reached the top of the staircase, she caught the faint glow of a single gas lamp. Without hesitation, she slipped past the door that had been left open and stepped inside.

Lee was sitting at a plain wooden desk. He stood up as she entered and inclined his head cordially. "Good evening, my dear. I'm sorry to have kept you waiting so long, but it was impossible to extricate myself any earlier."

"Please don't apologize, Mr. President," Susannah said as she shut the door behind her and walked farther into the room. "I'm only glad to be able to get this to you."

From a hidden pocket in her gown she withdrew a small, flat package wrapped in canvas and tied with brown string. Lee took it eagerly. His strong, gnarled fingers snapped the string and undid the wrappings in the same motion. Within was a plain envelope across which was written his own name.

"I am tempted to ask how you received this," Lee said with a smile, "but I have the distinct impression that I might not care for the answer."

Susannah shrugged lightly. "There's no reason to concern yourself with the details, Mr. President."

"But I do, Susannah." He looked at her for a moment, his brow furrowing. "Please sit down."

She did so with some reluctance, having the distinct suspicion she was in for a lecture.

"Now, I'm not going to lecture you," Lee said. At her quick, rueful grin, he laughed. "Well, only a little. We've talked about this before. I think I can be excused for worrying about you."

"There's no reason. I'm not in any danger." She spoke with perfect honesty, having long since come to the conclusion that danger, like beauty, was in the eye of the beholder. Lee, for instance, had been known to say that he had never felt personal danger on the battlefield. Undoubtedly, that was true. The fact that on several instances his life had hung in the balance apparently did not concern him. So it was with Susannah, who always had her eye fixed so firmly on her objective that she barely noticed how she got there.

"If your father knew what you were up to, and that I allowed it, I daresay he'd have my hide."

"We agreed some time ago that there was no reason for Father to be informed."

"That was before . . ."

"Before what?"

Lee lightly hefted the packet in his hand. "Before the stakes became quite so high."

Susannah's gaze held his. "Tell me something. If you were in a battle and you had soldiers who had been fighting long and hard to win it, would you remove them from the field short of the victory? Or would you allow them to remain and savor what they had won?"

Lee stroked his beard as a rueful smile spread over his countenance. "Young lady, there are times when I am grateful that the laws of this state and our nation forbid the seating of women in our Congress. I would not wish to have to debate you."

Susannah's mouth twitched at the corners. "You know my opinion of those laws, Mr. President."

"I do, indeed, and I confess to sharing it more often than not. But to return to the matter at hand, the conduit you established for getting clandestine messages between here and the North is a tremendous help. Indeed, I wonder how I managed without it all these years. However, it is not so important that I would place you at risk."

"If I were a man, you would not hesitate to do so."

"True," Lee admitted. "But you are not."

"Then it is just as well that I am not asking you for a more active role in our organization. What I do is little enough, merely carrying messages back and forth. Truth be told, I enjoy the game."

"Is that how you think of it?"

"What else? It's like dressing up and playing pretend. Besides, don't you know that every woman loves having secrets?"

Lee was not by any means easy to fool, but he had a vested interest in believing Susannah. Slowly, he nodded. "All right, if you're convinced there's no danger, we'll let it go. But should the situation change, I want you to inform me immediately. Understood?"

Susannah nodded. She did not mistake an order when she heard one; she merely thought that change was a matter of interpretation. She sat with her hands folded on her lap, her eyes courteously averted from the president as he opened the packet and read what was inside. With a sound of delight, he turned to her, the letter in his hand. At that moment, he looked like the young man he had once been, eager and full of hope, instead of the weary leader the years had made him.

"He has agreed to all my suggestions. We have made substantial progress."

At his urging, Susannah took the letter and read it quickly. By the time she reached the bottom of the page, she was smiling broadly. "This is wonderful news. It seems we are within striking distance of all we desire."

"Now, my dear," Lee cautioned, "I wouldn't go quite that far. There is still a great deal to be worked out. But at least we have begun." He gestured at the letter that Susannah still held. "I had every confidence that we would. He is a wise and perceptive man. His countrymen would have done well to value him more."

Susannah glanced again at the letter and its scrawled signature. In bold if slightly shaky letters was written the name of the man she knew Lee admired above all others; his erstwhile enemy and longtime friend, Abraham Lincoln.

2

By the time Susannah returned to the dance floor, Lee's response carefully hidden in her pocket, the orchestra had taken a break and the guests were milling about chatting. Thurston was standing in a corner, into which he had apparently been backed by several eager females. He caught sight of her and looked relieved, a fact she conveniently ignored as she pretended not to notice him.

Her father was on the opposite side of the room, still conversing with several men. She made her way through the milling crowd to join him. His friends felt comfortable with her and did not, as men so often felt compelled to do in the presence of women, change the subject to some trivial matter. Instead, they continued discussing the issue that gripped them all.

"If the Yankees invade Canada again," Philip Haley said, "there can be no question but that the British will be forced to act. After all, it is their province."

"Then they had better stand ready to defend it," Jeffrey said. "Since the North made that peculiar decision to buy Alaska, they've been casting covetous eyes to what adjoins it."

"So long as they don't look South again," William Eden muttered. Unlike Philip Haley and the others, he was

26

too young to have fought in the War of Secession. Like all the men of his generation who had missed out on glory, he was perpetually resentful. Another war would have suited William Eden very well, provided, of course, that his side won.

"I don't think there's any danger of that," Jeffrey said. "President McClellan learned his lesson well enough not to forget it."

"That popinjay." Haley snorted. "He was a braggart back in sixty-two when he boasted he'd take Richmond, and he's a braggart now. They would have done better to elect Mr. Greeley. He may be only a newspaperman, but at least he understands the workings of power."

"Perhaps they will reconsider with their next election," Eden suggested. "At any rate, it is not our concern."

"I disagree," a deep, firm voice said. "Like it or not, North and South are still entwined."

Susannah glanced absently at the new arrival, looked away then back, her attention suddenly caught. A shock of what could only be called awareness reached to the very core of her being. This man, whoever he was, made all her senses come acutely alive. In one instant, his features were imprinted on her memory for all time. But more than that, every facet of his appearance intrigued her. Every subtle nuance of his presence captured and held her.

It was, for example, clear that the other men were not enthused to see him. Her father did not appear particularly put out, but the others viewed him with thinly concealed wariness that, if he stooped to recognize it at all, evidently did not disturb him.

Certainly there was no hint of distress in the clear amber eyes that looked back at Susannah. Nor was there any mistaking the smile that played on the firmly masculine mouth. It was a smile that at once fascinated and annoyed her. Before she could stop herself, she said, "You're very bold in your opinions, Mr. . . ."

"Cabot, miss," he replied, the smile deepening as he

surveyed her frankly. "Rand Cabot. I don't believe we've had the pleasure."

A warm flush spread over Susannah's high cheekbones. She was intensely aware of being looked at more thoroughly than ever before in her life. His tawny eyes lingered on her delicate features before sweeping over her generously exposed breasts to take in the narrow span of her waist and the slender curve of her hips. His appraisal was saved from impropriety by its lack of calculation. There was nothing assessing in his glance, no attempt to judge her as men did women and fit her into some neat category. On the contrary, what she sensed was an overwhelming surprise and a wariness that was not so very different from her own.

Susannah felt a rush of blood to her midsection, as though someone had dealt her a blow there. She breathed in sharply and tried to still the sudden shaking of her limbs, then looked again at the tall, leonine man who stood before her.

He was very handsome; she had to give him that, though his looks were hardly classical. She guessed him to be in his late twenties, with a blunt, square face that showed his years and was surrounded by golden hair slightly longer than fashion dictated. His eyes were deep set, his nose could most graciously be described as assertive, and his mouth . . . She preferred not to think about his mouth.

He was elegantly dressed, though there was no hint of foppishness about him. His perfectly tailored tailcoat could not conceal the wide breadth of his shoulders and chest. His waist was trim, his legs long and solidly planted. He looked like a man who would be as at home on the deck of a ship as on land. Moreover, he appeared to be one of those men who knew how to hold their own wherever they went.

Rand had recovered enough to appear amused by her scrutiny. He smiled as her father said, "Allow me to present my daughter, Susannah. My dear, as you've already learned, this is Rand Cabot. We do business with him.''

Now that she thought about it, Susannah distantly remembered the name. It had cropped up from time to time, usually in connection with plantation business.

"You buy our cotton," she said to Rand.

"Some of it," he acknowledged, "some of the time. I deal in whatever happens to have the best market."

"Rand is an importer," her father explained. "He buys raw materials from us in exchange for finished goods from Europe and the North."

"How disagreeable for you that we are producing more and more of the goods we need right here," she said sweetly.

His eyes glittered with amusement at her barbed tone. "Not at all. I'm delighted to see the South give up its strict reliance on agriculture and branch out into other areas. That makes you all the stronger economically, which means you become a better customer."

Her father laughed approvingly. "You can't annoy Rand, my dear. We've all tried at one time or another, but his hide is simply too thick. The slings and arrows of outrageous fortune leave him unmarked."

Susannah doubted that was completely true, but she couldn't deny that the man before her appeared utterly unconcerned about what anyone might think of him. Amid such proper surroundings, he looked suitably civilized, but there was an aura of ruthlessness about him that suggested he lived by no one's standards except his own. Susannah tried hard to ignore the ripple of purely feminine excitement that raced through her in response to the male challenge he silently issued. Tried but did not succeed.

Distantly she became aware that the music had begun again. Rand noticed it, too. He held out a hand to her as he addressed Jeffrey. "With your permission, sir."

Her father hesitated a split second. He cast a look at Susannah, giving her the opportunity to refuse. When she did not, he apparently decided that he had no objection. "Of course," he said, stepping aside.

Snapped out of her preoccupation, Susannah had no choice but to comply. Not that she completely regretted it. The tension that had built while she waited to speak with Lee, and that would linger so long as his letter remained in her possession, made her welcome the distraction Rand Cabot represented. In his arms, it might be possible to pretend that she was just a young girl enjoying herself at a ball.

For so large a man, he was extremely light on his feet. But then she had expected that, sensing that whatever Rand Cabot did, he would do well. He held her at precisely the prescribed distance as they moved together to the jaunty strains of a reel. She was dimly aware of other people watching them, but her attention remained fixed on the bronze-faced man who held her with such skillful ease and who, she was quite certain, was finding the situation oddly amusing.

That irked her. She was accustomed to receiving admiration from men, not amusement. The urge to take him down a peg or two proved irresistible. "Is something funny?" she asked.

"No more than usual," he replied mildly.

"Are you always so easily diverted?"

He laughed softly, a deep, caressing sound that reverberated through her. "On the contrary, I suspect I'm harder to please than most. But," he continued as he drew her a fraction closer, "you will admit there's humor to be found here."

Her slanted eyebrows rose. Even a stranger would have recognized the danger signals flashing in her emerald eyes. "How so?"

His hand tightened a fraction on her waist. She realized that, far from finding his touch unpleasant—as she had with Thurston—she was inclined to enjoy it. His conversation, however, was another matter entirely.

"To begin with, there's you. A hot-tempered little Southern girl who's careless of proprieties forced to dance with the nasty Yankee rather than disappoint her father."

Susannah's chin tilted upward. "What do you mean 'careless of proprieties'?" she demanded.

Rand looked steadily down at her. Absently, she noted that he was no longer smiling. "First, you were talking with a group of married men instead of properly entertaining the young bucks who were trying to win your attention."

"I didn't notice them."

"My point. Second, you addressed me before we were introduced. Most improper." Susannah sniffed but didn't deny it. "Third, you deliberately challenged me."

"How?" she asked mildly, but with an undertone of curiosity that admitted she wasn't going to try to deny it.

"About business, no less. Don't you know women aren't supposed to be concerned with such things, or at least not admit to it in polite company?"

The implication that she was not what a woman should be stung more than she would ever admit. She said icily, "I beg your pardon. Obviously, I've offended you. Under the circumstances, why are we dancing?"

"Because you're beautiful and I'm in the mood for a diversion."

Her breath caught in her throat. Such audacity was a match for her own. Momentarily at a loss for a response, she stared straight ahead at the broad expanse of his chest. That was a mistake. It made her acutely conscious of his size and strength, of the differences between them, and of the strange melting sensation within her.

Susannah was accustomed to brazening her way out of most situations, but she was at heart a young, untried girl. Instinctive fear of her own feelings gripped her. "Don't look to me to provide that diversion," she said tartly. "Oh, I admit you have the virtue of being different. Disarmingly frank, I suppose you could call it. Tell me, does this tactic work with Northern ladies?"

Again, he laughed, and again, the sound sent a shiver of pure pleasure through her. "I wouldn't know," Rand said equably. "I've never tried it before." At her disbelieving murmur, he said, "No, really, I haven't. Something about you provokes me."

Her gaze swept upward, past the hard, square line of his chin to his firm, chiseled lips. She had a sudden, almost irresistible urge to press her mouth to his, to taste him in a way she had never done any man. A rush of blood warmed her face as she looked hastily away.

"How fortunate then that we are unlikely to have anything to do with each other once this blasted dance is over."

Rand laughed, loudly enough to draw the attention of several couples. Susannah frowned censoriously, wishing she could feel the thorough disapproval she partly feigned. He was an arrogant, rude, presumptuous Yankee, she told herself, and the sooner she saw the back of him, the better.

But the banter between them excited her as much as the sensations triggered by his physical presence and touch. She, who was so accustomed to men who tripped over themselves to please her that she no longer even noticed them, suspected that with Rand she had more than met her match. Not, of course, that she was about to let him know it.

"Has anyone ever told you," she asked in honeyed tones, "how rude you are?"

"One or two people might have mentioned it. But please don't you say it. I would be wounded to the quick."

Despite herself, Susannah felt a twinge of amusement. On a rising note of excitement, she took a deep breath, savoring the faint but tantalizing scent of him, compounded of a subtle sandlewood aftershave, excellent cigars, and something else—pure, healthy, virile man.

"Liar," she murmured huskily. "It would take a blunderbuss to wound you."

Rand was regarding her through half-hooded eyes. A

pulse beat in the shadowed hollow of his cheek, but his tone belied any intensity of feeling. "A nasty and outdated weapon, certainly never to be found in your lovely hands."

"For which you should be grateful." On impulse, she added, "I sense you would be vulnerable."

For an instant, the studied amusement slipped from Rand's gold-flecked eyes, replaced by surprise and wariness. "Perhaps, but not to pretty little Southern girls."

Susannah's temper flared, coming hard on regret for having spoken so daringly. The last thing she wanted was to provoke this man further. Daring she might be, but never reckless. "Might I ask why not?"

"You won't like my answer."

"Try it anyway."

He sighed and made a show of summoning his patience. "Have you ever been to France?"

"What has that to do with anything?"

"In France the pastry chefs make a concoction of meringue that can be shaped to resemble anything they desire—a castle, a swan, an entire city, if they wish. It all looks quite substantial but—"

"Surely you aren't comparing . . ." Susannah began.

Unperturbed, Rand continued. "But bite into it, and—"

"Your point is made," she said grimly. The music had stopped, and with relief she stepped beyond his touch. A lesser man would have feared frostbite from her glance. "There is certainly nothing more we need to say to each other. Kindly return me to my father."

For a moment, she thought she saw regret in his eyes, but she instantly dismissed that notion. He was about to oblige when their path from the dance floor was suddenly blocked by Thurston.

"Cabot," he said with the barest inclination of his head, "Miss Fitzgerald has promised me the next dance."

In fact, Susannah had done nothing of the sort, but just then she was glad of any excuse to be parted from the insufferable Yankee. The smile she gave Thurston was

nothing short of dazzling. "I'm so glad you remembered."
She held out a hand to him even as she glanced dismissively
at Rand. "Such a pleasure talking with you, Mr. Cabot,"
she said in a tone that indicated it had been anything but.
"We must do it again some time."

As Thurston led her away, she thought she must be
mistaken about Rand's response. Surely he couldn't have
murmured, "I'm tempted, Southern girl."

"What did he want?" Thurston demanded as the music
began again.

"Who?"

"Cabot, of course. You know perfectly well who I
mean."

"Oh, him. I have no idea."

"He must have wanted something."

Susannah glanced into the middle distance, her eyes
blank with disinterest while her mind was ticking away.
Rand Cabot had insulted her, no question about it, but she
couldn't seem to muster any true anger—perhaps because
his impression of her was so far from being accurate. All
she felt was a vague sense of hurt and a wistful yearning
that things might have been different.

"Pardon me?" she asked, aware that Thurston was still
waiting for an answer. "Oh, I suppose he wanted to
dance, that's all."

"He didn't . . . ?"

Thurston had a habit of not finishing his sentences.
Susannah hated it. "Didn't what?"

"Say anything improper."

For a moment she was tempted to see how much she
could provoke him, but she fought the impulse. With
wide-eyed innocence, she said, "Oh, for heaven's sake,
Thurston, I haven't the faintest idea what you mean."

"It's only that you're so beautiful and . . ."

There he went again. "And what?"

"There are men who might try to take advantage of
that." He got the words out all in a rush, as though they

were so distasteful that he could not bear to linger over them.

Susannah looked up at him through her lowered lashes. Doing so had a tendency to strain her eyes and make her slightly dizzy, but a woman did what a woman had to do. "Isn't it fortunate then that I have Father to look after me? And you, too, of course."

Thurston beamed at her, overwhelmed. She so rarely said or did anything of which he could wholeheartedly approve. "Thank you for including me. You know there's nothing I . . ."

"You . . . ?"

"Wouldn't do for you, if only you would allow me, Susannah."

That was dangerous ground. With footwork that would have done a tigress on a tree limb proud, she backed away. "Now, Thurston, let's not be swept away by the moment. It isn't proper."

The notion that he might inadvertently speak or act with the slightest impropriety genuinely horrified Thurston. "I'm sorry," he said quickly. "I don't know what came over me."

"Don't give it another thought." Indeed, she fervently hoped he would not. "Hasn't this been the loveliest evening?"

"Oh, yes, very nice. The surroundings . . ."

"You had a hand in selecting the plans for the new Capitol, didn't you? I'd be fascinated to know how you came to a final decision."

Thurston proceeded to tell her, in exquisite detail and lengthy sentences. He was in his milieu, declaiming on style and taste, and the battle he had waged against the boorish notions of lesser men. Susannah listened with half an ear as they continued their passage around the dance floor. At one point she caught sight of Rand grinning at her sardonically, but she absolutely refused to meet his eyes.

For the remainder of the evening she did her level best to forget the overbearing Yankee and keep her mind on the far more important matters at hand. Her major purpose in attending the ball had been to deliver the letter to Lee and receive his reply, but she also found such occasions useful for picking up information. After several hours of good food and wine, men were known to speak more volubly than they should.

She had paid another visit to the ladies' cloakroom, this time without incident, and was returning when she noted a group of planters speaking with several British officers. The official British presence in Richmond was limited to a small diplomatic legation, but lately there had been pressure to expand it. She would have dearly liked to know exactly what the men were saying, but caution forbade her to join them. The best she could do as she passed by was take note of a snatch of conversation about the clipper *Essex*, which would be arriving the following week with special cargo. She made a mental note to try to find out more, though she knew the chances of doing so were slim.

A short time later her father indicated that he was ready to leave. She went with him gladly, absently aware that neither Lee nor Rand Cabot was in sight.

Susannah slept late the following day. It was almost noon before she awoke to find Sukie opening the curtains to let the bright sunlight stream in.

"Rise and shine now, missy," the maid said. "Got a beautiful day waiting for you."

"Oomphf," Susannah murmured. "Sleepy." She burrowed farther under the covers, doing her best to remain oblivious to Sukie's blandishments, but the black woman didn't give up easily. She set a tray of tea and toast on the table beside the bed, fetched a robe from the nearby closet, and yanked the covers off Susannah's recumbent form.

The girl lay on her side, demurely garbed in an ankle-length nightgown of white batiste and silk, her knees drawn up almost to her chin and her eyes stubbornly closed. Her ebony hair tumbled over the pillow. She had neglected to braid it before retiring, and in the course of a more than usually restless night, it had become badly tangled.

"How did you get to bed like that?" Sukie demanded as she all but hauled Susannah upright and waved an irate finger under her nose. "Look at these tangles. Take me all afternoon to get them out."

Susannah forbore mentioning that Sukie had, as usual, been sound asleep when she returned home. Tired as she was, she simply hadn't had the stamina to do her own braids.

She was still groggy when she crept from the bed and sat down at the dressing table. She winced as a hairbrush was dragged mercilessly across her scalp, then sighed resignedly and submitted herself to Sukie's ministrations.

An hour later, clad in a riding habit of gray tweed over a silk waistcoat, she sped lightly down the stairs. Her neatly arranged hair was concealed beneath a jaunty top hat, around which was wrapped a tulle veil. She had on one gray leather glove and was about to don the other when she caught sight of her father emerging from his study.

"Awake at last?" he said with a fond smile, kissing her cheek lightly. "Sukie said you were sleeping so soundly she didn't know whether or not to rouse you."

"Don't you believe her," Susannah said. "She delights in dragging me out of bed. It pays me back for all the times I woke her as a child."

Her father's expression was faintly quizzical. He wasn't certain when his eighteen-year-old daughter had said farewell to childhood—or, indeed, if she had. Certainly, he still tended to think of her as the same beguiling little girl she had always been.

"Have you eaten?" he asked, aware that he was fussing but unable to stop himself. She *was* his only child, after all.

"You're more of a mother hen than even Sukie is," she told him teasingly. "I've slept, I've eaten, and now I'm going for a ride. Care to come with me?"

"I'm sorry," he said, genuinely regretful, "but I must meet with our factor this afternoon. We have business to discuss."

Susannah was about to say she would gladly give up her ride to stay with him and hear what was said, but she stopped herself. While it seemed perfectly logical to her that, as Jeffrey's only child, she should be trained to take over his businesses, she knew her father did not see things that way. He considered it highly improper for any woman to be involved in trade, and he looked forward to the day when Susannah would have a husband to spare her any such necessity.

Susannah did not share his anticipation. She viewed marriage with a full measure of dread, knowing how much it would restrict her cherished liberty. But, of course, she said nothing to her father. Instead, she raised up on tiptoe, gave him a fond kiss, and took herself off.

In the stables adjacent to the Fitzgeralds' town house she told a groom to saddle a horse for her. There were several mounts to choose from, but she had no particular preference. Some two years ago the beloved mare she had raised from a filly had died, and Susannah had not yet been able to bring herself to acquire another horse she would think of as truly her own. Yet she was more and more tempted to do so and had actually begun to seek out ads placed in the Richmond papers by those with horses to sell.

With the groom mounted and following a discreet distance behind her, Susannah left the mews and trotted toward the wide, linden-lined boulevard that led to a pleasant park. There she enjoyed an hour's exercise before signaling to her groom that she intended to dismount and walk for a while. As he held the horses, she strolled beside a small but elegant lake, in which were reflected the few fleecy clouds that dotted an otherwise clear sky.

She had gone only a short distance and was still within sight of the groom when she appeared to drop her gloves near a flowering bush. As she bent to pick them up, she slipped her hand into the pocket of her riding habit. A moment later, she straightened with the gloves, leaving behind in a hollowed-out log the canvas wrappings that held Lee's reply.

3

W e have made substantial progress," said the tall, gaunt-faced man as, with some difficulty, he sat down in the chair across from his guest. "President Lee has agreed that the announcement should be made on July Fourth. He will make it in Richmond, of course. It remains for us to persuade President McClellan to do the same in Washington."

"McClellan is a fool," Rand said after he had removed his cigar from between his teeth. Lincoln's doctors had long since forbidden him to smoke, but he still enjoyed few things as much as the smell of a good cigar. Rand took pleasure in obliging him. "He is also a procrastinator. If he can find some way to delay, he will."

Lincoln's characteristically gentle expression became fierce. A hint of the steel that had carried him through a turbulent and, some would say, tragic life rang in his voice as he said, "Leave McClellan to me. What is most important is that matters continue to move apace in the South. I am very concerned by the report you've brought."

"So am I," Rand said. Both men were silent as they pondered what should be done. The parlor in which they sat was warm, but not unpleasantly so. Windows with white lace curtains stood open to admit what breeze there was along Springfield's quiet streets.

Lincoln had lived in the simple, two-story house since returning from Washington in disgrace. Impeached and convicted by the Senate for the loss of the South, he had been expected to fade away into shamed obscurity. Instead he had continued to practice law and to write, though in truth no major cases ever came his way and his writings were more often published abroad than at home.

"Our information definitely indicates that something is amiss in Richmond," Lincoln said slowly, "and it appears to be aimed at stopping our efforts. Beyond that, nothing is clear."

"At the moment," Rand replied, "we cannot let matters rest. I must return and determine exactly what is going on."

"I couldn't agree more," Lincoln said. "We have an opportunity right now that will not come again. Once Lee and I are gone, there will be no one on either side who knows and trusts each other well enough to make this attempt."

Rand hesitated for a moment, wondering if for once in his life he should rein in his curiosity and err on the side of tact. Instinct and habit won out.

"Forgive me for saying so, but I've always found your friendship with Lee difficult to understand. Not," he hastened to add, "that I'm suggesting there's anything wrong with it. Only that, under the circumstances, it was . . . unlikely."

Lincoln smiled as he reached for the glass of barley water on the table at his side. He hated the wretched stuff, but his wife Mary insisted he drink it and he found it more prudent to comply than to risk upsetting her.

"You wonder," he said after he had taken a sip, "why I have such regard for the man who destroyed both my presidency and the Union I so desperately wanted to preserve?"

"Exactly."

"There's nothing very complicated about it. Lee always behaved honorably. Always. In peace and in war, above all in victory. Do you have any idea of how few men that can be said?"

"Very few, I'm sure. That explains why you respect him, but I sense genuine friendship. A friendship he seems to fully reciprocate."

Lincoln nodded as his deep-set eyes shone with warm reminiscence. "We got to know each other very well while I was Lee's prisoner. After the Union's defeat at Antietam and the fall of Washington, I was captured along with most of the cabinet. We were held first in Richmond, then later on a plantation nearby. Throughout my incarceration, Lee did his utmost to insure that I was treated with consideration and dignity. But more than that, he saved my life."

This was the first Rand had heard of any such thing. He leaned forward intently.

"You may know," Lincoln said quietly, "that I have been prone to attacks of melancholia, which, try though I do, I have a great deal of difficulty throwing off. During such times, everything appears extremely dark and hopeless to me. There have even been periods when I have contemplated ending my own life."

Rand listened in silence. He knew that Lincoln was taking him into his confidence, and he both respected and appreciated that. He also knew that any comment he might make would be superfluous at best. Having never experienced anything remotely like what Lincoln was describing, he could only marvel at the courage that had enabled Lincoln to keep going in the face of such a disability.

"One such period descended on me shortly after the fall of Washington. I bitterly regretted the loss of lives, which had been for naught. At night, when I tried to sleep, I imagined that the dead rose from the battlefields and attacked me for sending them to their doom. Within a very short time, I could not eat, and the mere act of rising each day was all but beyond me. Pride forced me to keep going, but it would have been only a matter of a few weeks before it became impossible to carry on."

"What happened?" Rand asked.

"Lee was already in the habit of paying me frequent visits. How he fit them into his schedule I don't know, since he was the guiding light behind the Treaty of Richmond, which was then being worked out. At any rate, he sensed my deep trouble and did everything he could to ease it. We fell into the habit of visiting together almost daily. He kept me apprised of everything that was happening, treating me with the courtesy and respect due a national leader rather than a defeated enemy. He solicited my suggestions regarding the treaty and even incorporated many of them into the final version. He also made certain changes in my situation which greatly improved my outlook."

"I agree that Lee behaved most honorably," Rand said, "but there is another side to the coin. His contact with you gave him the benefit of your great intelligence and insight. It was as much to his advantage to consult with you as it was to yours."

Lincoln's smile deepened. He ran a hand over his bearded jaw as he said, "That's precisely what he replied when I thanked him for his consideration. He said that had our roles been reversed, he had no doubt I would have treated him with equal honor. I must say that when the time came to return to Washington, not all my regret at leaving Virginia stemmed from what I knew I would face in the capital. I was truly sorry to be parted from the man who had become my good friend."

Rand's mouth tightened as he thought of what had lain ahead of Lincoln when he rode out of Richmond shortly after the peace treaty between the two nations had been signed. Although the loss of the war should have been laid at the door of incompetent Union generals, Lincoln bore the full brunt of the blame himself. A virtually hysterical Congress, scrambling to protect itself from the outrage of the people, had offered him up as a sacrificial goat.

Rand still felt a deep surge of anger whenever he remembered the impeachment proceedings against Lincoln. He had witnessed part of them, had seen the tall, somber figure called to defend himself from the Senate floor, then not permitted to do so as he was interrupted again and again by hoots and catcalls.

Lincoln's conviction and removal from office had surely been one of the darkest days in the nation's history. Darker even, Rand believed, than the actual destruction of the Union at Antietam. The Union could be rebuilt, but nothing could ever wipe out what Lincoln had been forced to suffer.

Yet when he said so to Lincoln, the former president merely shook his head. "I have no interest in vindicating myself," he said. "If I wanted merely to prove that North and South belong together as one nation, I would have only to sit back and allow present developments to follow their natural course. But that I cannot do. Far too many have already perished. Further violence would be nothing less than an obscenity against both God and man."

"Then we must move quickly to prevent that violence," Rand said. He stubbed out his cigar in the ashtray beside his chair, then remembered how Mary Lincoln felt about smoking and tossed the remains in the fireplace instead. He rose to take his leave.

"I'm returning to Richmond directly. Whatever the source of the rumors we're hearing, I intend to get to the bottom of them. The July Fourth announcement must go ahead as planned. Nothing can be allowed to stop it."

"Be careful," Lincoln advised. "My instincts tell me there are dangerous forces at work here. With so much at stake, men may not be overly scrupulous about what they do."

"I know how to look out for myself," Rand assured

him with a smile. "And I'm not about to trust anyone south of the Mason-Dixon. You can be assured of that."

As the two men shook hands on the front porch, Rand looked directly at Lincoln. The two were of similar height, but there the resemblance ended. The former president seemed even older than his sixty-seven years. His narrow face, rail-thin body, and stooped shoulders were eloquent testimony to all he had lived through. Yet there was a strength about him Rand could not ignore. He thought he would do well to find such steel within himself.

He had untied the reins of his horse from the post in front of the house and was preparing to mount when Lincoln called after him. "Have a safe journey, my friend. Oh, and one other thing. I understand your comment about not trusting anyone in the South, but there may come a time when you will have to. Keep an eye out for the butterfly."

"Butterflies, sir?"

"Butterfly. Singular." Lincoln's mouth curved in response to some secret source of amusement. "Very, very singular. And absolutely trustworthy."

"Sir?"

Lincoln waved and turned back to the house, leaving Rand to ponder his puzzling advice.

The journey from Springfield to Richmond required five full days. It should have taken less, but because of the heavy reparations paid by the North after the war for damage done to Southern properties, there had been little money to maintain or expand the railroads. Rand's train creaked along as best it could, finally reaching Washington in a welter of coal dust and weary travelers.

Some thirteen years after the official ending of the war, there was still no direct railroad contact between the Confederacy and the Union, so Rand had to change trains in order to complete the last part of his journey. By the time he reached Richmond late in the day, he was tired, dirty, and interested in very little save a large whiskey and a clean bed.

The Broad Street Hotel provided both. The desk clerk remembered Rand from his previous stay and made a show of welcoming him back. He was given a large, quiet room on the second floor toward the rear where the noises of the busy street did not reach.

A young, uniformed Negro took Rand's bags up to the room for him. As Rand handed over a tip, the black man looked him directly in the eye, smiled, and thanked him.

By that, Rand inferred that the man was one of the increasing number of freed slaves to be found throughout the South. Those still in bondage tended to be far more withdrawn, to keep their eyes downcast, and, if at all possible, to avoid contact with whites. The contrast between the two groups was marked, and growing ever more so.

As he removed his travel-stained suit and laid it aside to be cleaned and pressed, Rand reflected on the irony of the changes occurring in the South. For a people who had fought so fiercely to retain their cherished way of life, the Rebels certainly hadn't shown much inclination to hold onto it once they had gone their separate way.

It was scant comfort for those in the North—among them Lincoln—who had claimed that slavery was an obsolete system destined to die out to see their prediction coming true. If current trends continued, there would be no slaves left in the South by the turn of the century.

Rand regretted that it was taking that long, but he thought it better that such an abomination be allowed to fade away naturally than be artificially maintained as a few Southerners argued should be done.

A twinge in his tired limbs turned Rand's attentions to less philosophical concerns. Among its many amenities, the Broad Street Hotel had the distinction of being the first in Richmond to install hot and cold running water in all its rooms. Rand gave a deep sigh of pleasure as he sank into the tub and prepared to scrub away the grime of the road.

He lay back, a cigar between his teeth and a glass of whiskey balanced on his bare chest. Tall as he was, his feet had to be propped on the far rim of the tub. He let his thoughts idle and was ruminating vaguely about how difficult it might be to get a large enough bathtub for the house he intended to build some day when his gaze happened to fall on the painting that hung on the wall in front of him.

Because the Broad Street Hotel was situated conveniently near the Capitol, it catered almost exclusively to male travelers. Few of the gentlemen who called there were accompanied by their families. For that reason, the place had a distinctly masculine air, which Rand appreciated. It also permitted such touches as the painting he was looking at.

The naked, cavorting nymphs and satyrs at play in a bucolic setting amused Rand. They also served to remind him how long he had been without a woman. He took a long swallow of his whiskey, glanced again at the nymphs' pink bottoms and bouncing breasts, and decided it had been too long. When he rose dripping wet from the tub, there was a definite gleam of anticipation in his eyes.

One of the aspects of Richmond that made Rand grateful that the city had not suffered the vicissitudes of war was its civility. Its wide streets lined with elegant shops, its harmonious buildings, and its beautifully landscaped parks made it an excellent place in which to live. Yet it also accommodated shipping and industry, doing a bustling business in both. It boasted churches, schools, theaters, and even, its most recent addition, an opera house.

A man could settle down in such a place and live comfortably all the years of his life, not least because, away from its fashionable sections, down twisting back streets, Richmond provided less public—but still essential—masculine amusements. And it provided them with nothing less than a full measure of Southern warmth and gentility.

The Bagatelle Club was a case in point. No sign proclaimed its name, and it was not included in any listing of the city's businesses, yet it was as well known to the gentlemen of Richmond as the finest dressmakers and jewelers were to the gentlemen's wives.

It was no exaggeration to say that certain activities that transpired at the Bagatelle Club resulted in substantial business for those same dressmakers and jewelers as husbands sought to assuage their guilty consciences through openhanded spending.

Rand had no such moral qualms. As he stepped from the carriage that had brought him to the club, he was looking forward to nothing more complicated than an evening of pleasure, with the possible added attraction of a useful business dealing. As soon as he passed beyond the front door into the opulent main room, he knew he would not be disappointed.

Some might consider the Bagatelle Club's strenuous reliance on red brocade, crystal chandeliers, and gilt wall fixtures a trifle garish. But they would miss the essential function, which was to arouse the senses while providing a suitable backdrop for the young ladies strategically draped at intervals around the room.

Among the many bawdy houses that crowded certain districts of Richmond, the Bagatelle Club stood at the top of the heap, a fact attested to in a recent anonymous publication that was currently causing a stir. A group of gentlemen who preferred, for obvious reasons, not to make their identities known had compiled a listing of the bawdy houses, complete with comprehensive ratings.

Published as a small paperbound book with a red cover, the *Guide to the Shrines of Aphrodite in Fair Richmond* was sold surreptitiously by hotel clerks, barbers, bookmakers, and the like, who took a nice profit on it. There was talk that the idea would be expanded to include other cities to which discerning Southern gentlemen were likely to travel.

According to the guide, the Bagatelle was renowned for its elegance, discretion, and choice of entertainment. No rum-sodden doxies were employed there, only lovely young women who, given the proper clothing, could have passed for the sisters and daughters of the men who patronized them. When those gentlemen wanted to go further afield, there were plenty of dens and warrens to oblige them. But at the Bagatelle, they were expected to behave properly.

While all manner of wine and spirits were liberally available, an inability to hold one's drink was a definite mark against a man at the club. Even worse was brawling, which was an automatic reason for expulsion.

On the other hand, payment did not always have to be prompt, a rarity for such establishments. It was possible to open an account, a monthly statement of which was sent to the gentleman's office under the heading "Forcourt & Blakeston, Gentlemen's Apparel."

Thanks to such niceties the Bagatelle had become the traditional place of initiation for Richmond's young men, who were brought there by their fathers and remained to, in turn, introduce their own sons.

Barely had Rand taken a step inside than several of the scantily attired young women who were so essential a part of the decor noticed him. They would have descended en masse were they not warned off by the slightest gesture from the woman who took it upon herself to welcome him personally.

Lillie Dumont was past the first bloom of youth, yet she was still a stunningly attractive woman. She was, in fact, forty-six years old, but no one, including Rand, would have guessed that. Her luxurious golden hair was swept up in a mass of curls, several of which trailed artfully over her bare shoulders. She wore a gown of burgundy velvet that left absolutely no doubt as to the ampleness of her charms. A rosy hint of her nipples peeked above the extreme décolletage. She was wasp-waisted, chalice-hipped, and long-limbed, being only a few inches shorter than Rand himself.

She was also an excellent judge of men, an absolute necessity in what had been her lifelong profession. She took one look at Rand and gave him a blinding smile.

"How nice to see you again, Rand," she murmured in her rich, throaty voice, which some took for affectation, but which was in fact the result of near strangulation by a client back when she had been a destitute young girl working the streets of New Orleans.

"It's nice to be back, Lillie," he said, returning her smile. Rand liked Lillie. He felt comfortable with women who didn't pretend to be other than what they were. In her case, that meant realistic, resourceful, and damn good at her particular calling. He kissed her cheek lightly as he breathed in the seductive aroma of her perfume. His awareness of the scantily draped young ladies hovering nearby began to fade.

"Business?" she murmured.

"I'm afraid so."

"Pity. You look as though you could use a bit of pleasure instead."

His tawny eyes darkened as he smiled ruefully. "As a matter of fact . . ."

Lillie turned slightly and gestured to the lovely young ladies. "You know you can have your pick of any one of them."

He raised his eyebrows and pretended to be surprised. "Only one?"

His hostess gave him a gently chiding look. "The boy speaks, not the man. However . . ."

Rand raised his hands in surrender. "Never mind. You're quite right—more than one would be definitely overdoing it."

"Take Chandra, for instance," Lillie said, indicating a

pretty brunette who smiled at him enticingly. "She's very
. . . inventive."

Rand wasn't totally disinterested, but he shook his head
and lowered his voice as he murmured, "A bit plump for
my tastes."

"Tessie then." With a wicked smile, Lillie added, "She
used to be with the circus."

He raised his eyebrows in mock dismay. "Thanks, but
I'd like to be alive in the morning. Besides," he added,
looking directly at Lillie, "I prefer a woman who's a bit
more mature. Seasoned, as it were."

Her cheeks flushed becomingly. They had been coming
to this moment for some time, in a casual, roundabout way
that put no pressure on either of them. All that mattered
was that they enjoy themselves, which was fine with Lillie. She cherished her independence far too much to be
interested in a permanent relationship. That did not, however, prevent her from looking forward to the next few
hours with an anticipation she had not felt in many years.
As she tucked her arm through Rand's, she smiled up at
him. "I believe I have exactly what you want."

Several hours later, as he lay in bed beside Lillie, Rand
decided that she had been right. He stretched out his long,
lean body beneath the cool sheets and took a deep, reviv-
ing breath. Every bone and muscle were relaxed, but his
mind was, if anything, working overtime.

As he reached for his silver cigar case beside the bed, he
said, "Anything interesting going on, Lillie?"

Stretched out next to him on her stomach, she propped
herself up on her elbows and gave him a slow smile. Her
hair had come undone and tumbled over her shoulders and
back. Her large brown eyes glowed with a rarely seen
light, and her full mouth was slightly swollen. It had been
a long time since Lillie had felt compelled to take any man
into her bed. She was more than glad that she had made an
exception for Rand. "You mean besides right here?"

He laughed appreciatively as he struck a match and held

the flame close to the tip of the cigar. "You could put it that way. The information you had last time turned out to be accurate. It's causing us a great deal of concern."

Lillie ran a hand over the contoured muscles of his chest, her fingers tangling in the golden whorls of hair. Her body stirred, but she ignored it. Pleasure had received its due. Far more important matters must occupy them now.

"I'm sorry to hear that," she said. "I'd hoped I was wrong."

Rand took her playful hand and raised it to his lips. It was a tender salute, one Lillie appreciated, yet his thoughts too were elsewhere. "Unfortunately not. Lincoln sent me back here to get further information on exactly what's going on. All we know for sure so far is that there's a plot afoot to prevent the July Fourth announcement, but how they intend to do that, or indeed who 'they' are, I have yet to discover."

"I have a bad feeling about this," Lillie said slowly. "I can't explain it exactly since, if anything, I know less than you do. But I sense undercurrents of anger and even violence that trouble me."

Rand frowned. He was not one to denigrate the special perceptions of women. Lillie's concerns—however ill-defined at that moment—troubled him deeply.

"If you had to guess, what would you say is going on?" he asked.

Lillie hesitated. Her eyes became unfocused, as though she was looking deep into herself. Softly she murmured, "There are people who genuinely believe that North and South should never again be united; intelligent, honorable people. I have no quarrel with them. But there are those who found that victory in the war didn't turn out to be everything they thought it would be. They thought it would assure that nothing could ever change here, but exactly the opposite has happened."

As he nodded thoughtfully, she went on. "The Negroes

are winning their freedom. Industry is coming in. Why, even women have started speaking up and demanding something better for themselves. It's as though history moves inexorably in its own direction no matter what we do. These people can't stomach that. It enrages them and they need to lash out at someone because of it. I'm afraid Lee may be the most tempting target."

"But can they afford to attack him directly?" Rand asked. "He's the most beloved man in the Confederacy, a virtual icon of everything the South honors and values. Logically, Jefferson Davis should have been able to continue as president after the victory, but instead Lee soundly defeated him the first time he ran in sixty-four. And he's won again every time since. Even his opponents in the Congress are careful how they voice their opposition for fear of angering the populace that reveres him."

"I know you're right," Lillie said. "It's all but unthinkable that anyone would seriously consider trying to prevent what will surely be Lee's greatest accomplishment. Yet I'm still concerned. . . ."

"So am I, more now than ever. Somehow, we've got to clarify these rumors."

"You must realize that if I'm at all correct, the situation could become extremely dangerous."

Rand shrugged his broad shoulders. "Lincoln already pointed that out. This is hardly the first time I've faced long odds. But I can't remember any other occasion when so much was riding on the outcome."

He was silent for several moments before he added slowly. "Somehow I'm convinced that the British are the key. I need to find a way to get to them."

Lillie sighed and rolled onto her back. She studied the ceiling absently. "Major Kidderly is hosting a poker game here tonight. Perhaps you would like to sit in."

"Kidderly, the British adjunct?"

Lillie nodded. "'He fancies himself a brilliant player.''

Anticipation flickered in Rand's eyes. "Is he?"

Lillie gave a small laugh. "He cheats, clumsily."

"Then how has he managed to keep from getting caught?"

"The men he plays with are even less skilled."

"You mean the men he usually plays with."

Across the rumpled sheets, their eyes met in perfect understanding.

4

The back room at Lillie's was furnished with heavy mahogany tables and chairs, large ashtrays and spittoons, and a substantial bar containing the finest liquors, which were served in oversized glasses. The room backed onto a private yard surrounded by a high brick wall, but the windows were nonetheless covered by thick shades over which heavy velvet drapes had been pulled.

A white-jacketed waiter stood by to take orders from the four men still seated around the largest table. Earlier there had been an even half dozen, but two had already withdrawn. That left Rand, Major Kidderly, and two Virginia planters visiting the city on business.

Rand appeared to be studying his cards. In fact, he was watching the man seated directly across from him. Major Arnold Kidderly was a red-faced, beefy fellow of about thirty with small eyes, a pudgy nose dotted with the spidery webs of broken blood vessels, and a perpetually compressed mouth. He had a double chin, soft fat hands, and bad teeth. He also had a very large pile of chips in front of him.

Rand gave a chagrined smile and threw down his cards. "I'm afraid you win again, Major. Lady Luck isn't with me tonight." As he spoke, he pushed a stack of chips across the table.

Kidderly scooped them up greedily, his small eyes gleaming. "Nonsense," he murmured with a singular lack of conviction. "The cards have merely been running against you. Play a few more hands, and I daresay you'll even the score."

"I doubt that," Rand said, "however . . ." He let the other man dangle a bit, feeling his eagerness, before he went on. "I'd be a poor sportsman to pull out now, wouldn't I? Back in New York it's considered the height of bad manners for a gentleman to leave the table before either he's busted or everyone else is."

"A very enlightened city, New York," said Kidderly, who had never been there.

The man to his left disagreed. "That might be fine for Yankees, but this game's gotten too rich for my blood." He tossed down his cards with a regretful frown. "I'm out."

"So am I," said the fourth man. "Your luck's simply too good, Major."

"Luck has very little to do with it," Kidderly pontificated. "Skill's the thing. Nothing in life's worth doing unless it's done well, what?"

"I couldn't agree more," Rand said as he selected a fresh deck from a supply on a silver tray near the table. The deal was to him. With his thumbnail he broke the seal, then he disposed of the wrappings and began shuffling the cards. This last part he did adequately, but not well.

Nothing in his actions revealed that in his earlier years he had, in certain quarters, earned the sobriquet "Handy Randy" for the dexterity with which he could scramble a deck of cards without ever once losing sight of exactly what was on the top, on the bottom, in the middle, and just about anywhere in between.

But those were other days, this was now, and he had Major Kidderly to reel in.

The cards they had been using were marked. It had taken Rand no more than the first five minutes of play to figure out how. The technique was a familiar one to anyone who had spent much time in the saloons of New York's sporting districts, but Kidderly apparently thought he was on to something unique. Rand judged it time that he learned otherwise.

He finished the deal, picked up his cards, studied them for a moment, and smiled. "What do you say we up the ante?"

Kidderly looked at him suspiciously. "How much?"

Rand shrugged. "Say . . . a hundred or over."

The minimum bid up to that point had been fifty dollars, and Kidderly had already won close to a thousand. The Englishman stared down at his pile of chips, licked his lips, glanced at his hand, and jerked his head. "All right. A hundred it is."

They played for another half hour, during which Kidderly continued to win. Only then did the tide begin to turn. Rand took the next hand and the next. He shrugged almost apologetically and called for a fresh deck. Soon after it had been dealt, by Kidderly, Rand won again. And again.

The Britisher began to sweat. He took out a handkerchief, mopped his brow, and glanced toward the bar. "Boy," he called to the aged black man standing there, "another whiskey, and do more than wet the glass this time."

The man obeyed, glancing at Rand as he did so. They exchanged an imperceptible nod. The play continued. Rand kept winning; Kidderly kept sweating. He was far too compulsive a gambler to stop when losing, yet he was also plainly terrified of what was happening, with good reason. Within two hours, the large pile of chips that had been in front of the major lay in front of Rand.

"It's your bet," Rand said quietly, reminding the other

man that he had already placed his own bet on the present hand and was waiting for Kidderly to respond.

The major stared at the table in front of him and shook his head dazedly. "I . . ." He looked up at Rand's imperturbable face, and his bewilderment increased. "I'm . . . afraid you have me . . . old man."

Rand raised his eyebrows in surprise, as though he had just noticed that Kidderly was busted. He smiled apologetically. "Surely that isn't a problem. After all, we are both gentlemen. I take it as given that your credit is good."

Kidderly relaxed slightly. A ray of hope shone in his eyes. "I say, that's awfully decent of you."

They continued to play. Rand continued to win. The two men who had dropped out of the game came back to the table to watch. Several other men, alerted to what was happening, drifted into the room.

Kidderly called for another whiskey and drank it down in a single gulp. He patted his forehead with the crumbled handkerchief and loosened another button of his regimental jacket. Rand guessed that he had all but lost count of the total amount of IOUs lying on the table, but Rand himself had not. Kidderly was now in his debt to the tune of almost five thousand dollars.

"Your deal," Rand said with a smile.

The major's hands trembled. He fumbled with the deck, dropped it, and had to start over. When the cards had been dealt, Rand paused before picking his up. He laid a hand over the cards, looked at Kidderly, and said, "I'll tell you what. It's getting late, and we're all tired. Suppose we make this double or nothing?"

"D-double or . . ." Kidderly stuttered.

"Nothing. I win, you owe me double whatever's on the table. You win, and you walk away with your notes, the chips, and the same again in cash from me."

Any sane man faced with such a proposition would have run in the opposite direction. But the Britisher was beyond any such instinct for self-preservation. He hesitated a moment, then agreed.

The men watching the play moved closer. Kidderly's confidence grew with the flow of the cards. He bounced up and down in his seat, impatient for Rand's every move, alternately mopping his forehead and gulping his whiskey. "Come on, come on. You're in or you aren't. Which is it?"

Rand affected a small sigh. "I'm afraid you may be too good for me after all."

Kidderly all but exploded with delight. He slammed down his cards. "Flush! Beat that if you can!"

He was reaching for the pot when Rand slowly laid his cards down face up. "It looks as though I did. Unless I'm very much mistaken, that's a full house."

Kidderly had to be helped over to the couch. He was weeping hysterically, declaring that he was ruined, and blaming Rand for tricking him. Embarrassed by such carryings-on, and eager to spread the story, the other men hurried from the room. The Negro bartender was the last to go. Before he did so, Rand slipped him two folded notes of a very large denomination, his thanks for the bartender's switching the marked decks for similar ones Lillie happened to have on hand that only appeared to be marked.

That done, Rand sat down beside Kidderly on the couch, put an arm around the other man's shoulders, and proceeded to tell him what he would have to do to erase the enormous debt he owed Rand.

Several hours later, as dawn was turning the sky over Richmond a rosy pink, Rand left the Bagatelle Club. Lillie herself saw him to the door. Despite the late hour, she still looked delightful.

"I suppose you have to go," she said regretfully as she handed him his hat and gloves.

"I'm afraid so. There's a great deal to be done."

"Will Kidderly come through?"

Rand shrugged. "He doesn't have many alternatives. He can't pay the amount he owes, and I doubt he's the type to take the honorable way out and put a bullet in his brain. No, he'll cooperate, thanks to you." He put a hand in his pocket and removed a sizable sheaf of bills, his cash winnings from the game. "I believe these are yours."

Lillie looked at the money, then at him. "That isn't necessary."

"No, but I'd prefer it." He gave her a light, teasing smile. "It makes me nervous to carry a lot of money around."

When she saw that he was determined, she took the bills. They felt very heavy, as did her heart as she watched him stride away.

Rand returned to his hotel, took another bath, had breakfast, and then slept for six hours. When he woke up, it was early afternoon. His dealings with Kidderly were all very well and good, but he had never been one to put all his eggs in one basket. Rising, he decided to go down to the waterfront and see what he might turn up.

First he remembered that he had a personal errand to perform. His sister, Bethany, was having a birthday in a few weeks. In all likelihood, he would not be there to celebrate with her, but at least he could send an appropriate present.

Broad Street featured an array of shops that would have done London or Paris proud. With the conclusion of the war and the prosperity that had resulted from the South's victory, many of the most fashionable European establishments had opened branches in Richmond. The great French couturier, Frederick Worth, had sent some of his most able modistes to dress the ladies of the Confederacy. In addition, the legendary jewelry houses of Cartier and Tiffany were on hand, as were the finest perfumiers and purveyors of virtually any other luxury the ladies might covet.

Nor were the gentlemen ignored. Superior English tailors could be found cheek by jowel with hatmakers, bootiers, even a shop that specialized in nothing but canes. Next door to it was an establishment that sold firearms. Rand paused to glance in the window, his attention momentarily drawn by a pair of Collier flintlock revolvers dating from the early part of the century.

He was still studying them when he noticed the reflection in the window of a young lady alighting from a carriage on the opposite side of the street. Turning, he observed Miss Susannah Fitzgerald accompanied by a large Negress entering the establishment of "Mlle. Mimi, Maker of Fine Ladies' Bonnets."

Rand hesitated, torn between the desire to see Susannah again and the prudence that cautioned against such an encounter. He was by no means a self-indulgent man; far more times than he could remember he'd curbed his desires or altogether ignored them in pursuit of a larger goal. But he was also not overendowed with prudence. He crossed the street.

A brass bell jangled above him as he opened the door and stepped inside. Unlike the somber, clublike settings of the shops catering to gentlemen, Mlle. Mimi's was unabashedly feminine. Several ladies sat on white wicker settees, considering the bonnets that attentive salesgirls presented to them. Others sipped tea beside potted palms or looked at themselves in the numerous gilt-framed mirrors. The pleasantly soft sound of feminine conversation mingled with the murmur of overhead fans turned by small black children dressed in satin breeches and frock coats.

Rand had the briefest opportunity to observe the scene before it changed, subtly but perceptibly. A male, any male, intruding into so purely female a sanctuary was bound to be immediately noticed. Conversation was interrupted, then resumed with a different, more cautious tone. A salesgirl vanished swiftly behind a curtain, to return a moment later with a stout, tightly corsetted woman whom Rand presumed to be Mlle. Mimi.

"M'sieur," she said, scanning him with an assessing

glance that instantly gauged his financial status, social position, and even sexual preferences. Whatever she saw must have pleased Mlle. Mimi because she favored him with a warm smile. " 'Ow may I be of azziztanse?"

"I'm . . . uh . . . looking for a gift for my sister. A birthday present, actually. She'll be eighteen shortly, and I wanted to give her something appropriate."

In fact, he had not until that moment thought that he might find a gift for Bethany at Mlle. Mimi's, but he had to give some explanation for his presence there and he was not inclined to admit he had followed Susannah. She was standing to one side, holding a millinery concoction that seemed to consist of ostrich plumes and bits of fruit, and observing him with what could only be described as mingled surprise and apprehension.

"We 'ave many zings, monsieur," Mlle. Mimi was saying, her spurious French accent thickening in response to the presumed size of his billfold. "If you vill pleaze to 'ave ze seat, I vill personally show you—"

"Miss Fitzgerald," Rand interrupted with what was admittedly an expression of relief, "how fortunate to find you here. As you may have heard, I'm looking for a gift for my sister. Might I impose on you to be of assistance?"

Ignoring Mlle. Mimi, whose scowl indicated she did not take lightly to having so plum a customer or so attractive a male removed from her grasp, Susannah smiled. In the fortnight since the Capitol ball, she had done her best to put Rand Cabot firmly from her mind, with mixed results. His sudden reappearance in such unexpected surroundings took her aback, and she felt compelled to resort to the ingenuous charm that served her well on so many occasions. Yet she could not resist adding a special bite to her honeyed tones.

"Why, Mr. Cabot," she said, "how nice to see you again. I had heard you left Richmond and thought perhaps you didn't plan to return."

Rand's eyes gleamed as he studied her. She was prettily

outfitted in a white-and-blue organdy day dress with a wide skirt worn over a crinoline and petticoats. Lacy ruffles decorated the bodice as well as the cuffs of her wrist-length sleeves. A pale ivory cameo on a slim black velvet band graced her throat. Her ebony hair was covered by a beribboned straw bonnet tied under her chin. All in all, she looked delightfully fresh, frivolous, and feminine.

"Why, Miss Fitzgerald," he said indulgently, "whatever could have given you that impression?"

Susannah shrugged her slim shoulders as though she couldn't quite remember and wasn't going to strain herself trying. She smiled distractedly, revealing charming dimples on either side of her soft, full mouth.

"Oh, never mind. Do you like this hat?" She held up the concoction she'd been examining, all but ramming Rand in the nose with an ostrich plume.

He instinctively backed away. "It's very . . . ambitious."

"Ambitious?" An enchanting giggle escaped her. "What an idea. Of course, the last thing I would ever want would be an *ambitious* hat."

"I meant there seems to be a great deal going on on it." Indeed, a veritable horn of plenty seemed to be tumbling about the hat's broad rim. He noted silk cherries, apples, pears, and, he thought, a pineapple before Susannah sighed and tossed the hat aside.

"Pooh," she said. "I thought it had a certain élan."

Pooh? The word resounded in Rand's mind. He had never before actually heard a woman use it, though he supposed it was the kind of thing Southern ladies said. At least very young, very pretty ladies who had nothing on their minds except outrageous hats.

Gallantly he said, "Don't be dissuaded by me. I'm sure the hat would look lovely on you."

The large Negress who had been hovering nearby snorted. Susannah glanced at her and laughed. "Sukie thought it looked like an overturned fruit basket, and I have to agree with her. Anyway, I already have more hats than I know what to do with. But you were saying about your sister . . ."

"Oh, yes, Bethany's birthday. I thought she might like something . . ." He spread his hands in typical male helplessness. "Something pretty and feminine. After all, she isn't a child anymore."

"What a lovely idea," Susannah said. "How lucky Bethany is. But you realize, of course, that you can't just pick out any hat for her. You must consider her personality, her likes and dislikes, where she goes, what she does, and so on."

Rand gave her a dubious look. "Does it have to be that complicated?"

"Only if you want to choose correctly."

With an inner sigh he yielded. "By all means. Let it never be said that I gave Bethany less than the best."

Apparently delighted, Susannah took him in tow. They were shortly surrounded by hats—small ones, large ones, felt ones, straw ones, silk ones, with plumes, with fruit, with small stuffed birds, with veils and without, in all conceivable shapes and colors. His head spinning, Rand finally called a halt.

"Surely," he said, glancing at the hat-strewn tables, "we can find something among these."

"Well . . ." Susannah put a finger to her chin. After a while, she said, "What does Bethany like best of all to do? Her absolutely favorite thing?"

"Read," he replied without hesitation. "She loves to read, especially poetry."

"Oh." Susannah looked around again, considering all those hats and what if anything they had to do with a girl who liked best of all to spend her time reading. Finally she tilted her head to one side, gazed at Rand through her thick lashes, and said, "Perhaps you should get her a book instead."

"A book?"

"Of poetry. Shelley, perhaps, or Byron."

"Oh, I don't know about Byron." Rand thought the broody-eyed British poet about whom such scandalous rumors had swirled was too risqué for his tender little sister. But Shelley would be eminently acceptable.

"Oh, wait," Susannah said. "I have a better idea. Elizabeth Barrett Browning. I'm sure Bethany would adore her. They have a wonderful collection of her poems at the bookstore not two doors down." Her gaze softened and took on a faraway look as she murmured, " 'How do I love thee, let me count the ways . . .' "

Sukie coughed. Abruptly recalled to herself, Susannah flushed. "Never mind. It's the perfect gift. You must inscribe it, of course. 'To Bethany on her eighteenth birthday from her loving brother.' Something to that effect."

"I believe I can manage that part," he said dryly, thinking that she looked even more beautiful when she was flustered, if that was possible. How unfortunate that for his peace of mind, not to mention the success of his mission, he had to forgo the pleasure of dallying with her any further.

"Thank you for your help," he said when they were both back on the street in front of the hat store.

Susannah gave him her hand and regarded him gravely. "Not at all, Mr. Cabot. I think it's very sweet that you care enough for your sister to want to give her something she'll truly enjoy."

Susannah's approval was every bit as disconcerting as her ire. Rand wasn't at all sure how he felt about it. But he did know that he was not yet ready to part from her. "I wonder if you wouldn't mind accompanying me to the bookstore. You might see something else Bethany would also like."

Susannah hesitated. Common sense told her to refuse. For all her tender years, she had already learned that when she felt an impulse to prove something and acted on it, trouble resulted. That comment Rand had made at the ball about meringue still rankled. Though she went to great pains in her day-to-day life to appear exactly as he had described her, she wanted him to know she was a good deal more. Why his opinion mattered so much she could not imagine, much less admit even to herself.

"I really should be getting back," she said, equivocating.

"Ain't no need to rush," Sukie interjected. She gave Rand a benign smile. "Nothin' need doing at home that I knows of."

Rand knew an ally when he encountered one. He returned Sukie's grin and said, "I won't keep Miss Susannah long, and, of course, you're welcome to accompany us."

"Fact is," Sukie told him, "I gots some shopping of my own needs doing."

"You didn't say anything about that before," Susannah murmured. She didn't precisely object to what Sukie was up to, but she was concerned about the possible consequences. Not enough, however, to try to avoid them.

"Slipped my mind," her maid informed her. To Rand, Sukie added, "After all, ain't like the old days anymore. Nothing wrong with a young lady and a gentleman taking a stroll together, 'specially not right out in public. Don't need no watchdog trotting after you, do you?"

"I don't believe we do," Rand murmured, trying without success to repress a smile.

Sukie nodded firmly. "That's settled then. I'll meets you back at the carriage, Miss Susannah, say in 'bout an hour?"

"I'm glad somebody's asking me something," Susannah muttered. At Sukie's silent reprimand, she added, "An hour will be fine."

"Be okay if you're late, honey." With a glance at Rand, Sukie amended that slightly. "Not too late, course. Don't want to have to do any explaining to your daddy."

Having left them properly admonished, she hurried down the street with her rolling gait, leaving a bemused Susannah staring after her. "This really isn't like Sukie. She takes her responsibilities very seriously, sometimes too much so.''

"She can hardly be blamed," Rand said. He appropriated her hand, placed it on his arm, and turned toward the bookstore. Tongue in cheek, he asked, "After all, where could she find someone more trustworthy than myself?''

"In the tiger cage at the zoo?" Susannah ventured.

"Now, now, none of that. We were getting along so well, let's not spoil it.''

A small sigh escaped her. She kept silent as they entered the bookstore. A slight, gray-haired man looked up and smiled. "Miss Fitzgerald, how nice to see you again. Are you enjoying the Twain?''

"Very much, Mr. Dudley. This is Mr. Cabot, by the way. He's looking for a birthday gift for his young sister. I suggested a collection of Elizabeth Barrett Browning.''

"Excellent idea," the bookseller said. "Let me see now . . .'' He wandered toward the shelves while Rand glanced around the store.

"This is larger than I expected, and better stocked.''

"Southerners do read," Susannah said. "In fact, I daresay we are probably more literate than Yankees, who seem to spend all their time figuring out better ways to make money.''

"I don't believe it's possible to generalize about either group," Rand replied, chiding her gently. He sensed that she was very much on the defensive with him and didn't really blame her for that, especially since he felt much the same way about her.

"I suppose not," Susannah said grudgingly. She had detached her hand from his arm and was looking at a table of recently published books. "Oh, look, Mark Twain has a new book out.''

Rand picked it up and examined the spine. "*The Adventures of Tom Sawyer.* Is this what you're reading now?''

Susannah shook her head. "I've only just started *The Gilded Age.*''

"That's a rather serious work, isn't it?"

"Have you read it?"

"Not yet, but I intend to. Are you very interested in the economic and social development of our age?"

She gazed innocently up at him. "Is that what it's about? Oh, my, no wonder I'm finding it such heavy going."

Rand frowned. He had the distinct impression she was deliberately evading his questions and, in the process, pulling his leg. But he had no idea how to get her to admit it. He was still mulling over his thoughts when Dudley returned with a slim, leather-bound volume. "There you are, sir. *Sonnets from the Portuguese*. I'm sure your sister will enjoy it."

Rand paid for the book. While he was waiting for it to be wrapped, he asked Susannah, "Is there anything else you'd suggest?"

She thought for a moment, then smiled. "Well, I do have a favorite book, but it's generally considered to be for children, so perhaps Bethany wouldn't appreciate it."

"What is it?" Rand asked.

"Lewis Carroll's *Through the Looking Glass*. I loved *Alice in Wonderland*, but I think this one is even better."

"We have it, sir," Mr. Dudley interjected, "if you would care to take a look."

Rand did and was shortly laughing, along with Susannah, over the antics of Tweedledee and Tweedledum. "If this is for children," he said, "I guess you can count me among them." He handed the book to Mr. Dudley. "I'll take this as well. Bethany will love it."

He and Susannah left the bookstore a few minutes later. They still had half an hour or so before she was due to rejoin Sukie. Rand was loath to part with her any sooner than he had to, and he cast about for some means of keeping her at his side. On the opposite corner was a small shop offering tea and ices served at outdoor tables under a canopy. Nodding in that direction, he asked, "Would you care for some refreshment?"

Susannah pretended to ponder the matter for a moment before she said primly, "That would be very nice."

They had to wait to cross the street until a break occurred in the line of carriages. Rand placed a hand on her elbow, as was only proper. Her bones felt very delicate beneath his fingers. He glanced down at her, noticing the slenderness of her shoulders, the slimness of her arms, and the narrowness of her waist, in such sharp contrast to the soft fullness of her breasts. The feelings she sparked in him were uncomfortably contradictory. He wanted to possess her with such completeness that she would never truly be apart from him again, yet he also felt driven to protect her, even from himself.

Such a dilemma vexed him. He was frowning as they found a table beneath the canopy and sat down. A waiter approached. Susannah toyed with the idea of an ice, which was what she really wanted, but decided she would look too childlike eating it in front of Rand. She settled instead on a sarsaparilla. In the absence of a cold beer, Rand did the same.

It was pleasant to be seated in the shade, watching the passing parade of pedestrians and carriages. A light breeze blew from the river, and in the distance they could hear the whistles of passing ships. For a time, both were reluctant to break the silence between them.

Eventually, Susannah got up her nerve to ask what was uppermost on her mind. "Are you going to be staying in Richmond very long this time?" She hoped he wouldn't infer from her question any eagerness on her part to continue seeing him, even though any such inference would have been perfectly correct.

"That depends. I'm not sure exactly what my plans will be."

"I see . . ."

She didn't, of course, but Rand hardly felt able to

correct her. He was too busy grappling with his own
resentment of the duties that kept him from giving her his
full attention. He would have liked to linger in Richmond,
paying court to Miss Susannah Fitzgerald and seeing where
fate chose to lead them. At the very least, it would make
an amusing interlude in a life that had notably lacked such
episodes.

Realizing that he had to say something to explain the
uncertainty of his plans, he said, "The nature of my
business is such that things are constantly changing. I'm
never certain exactly where I will be from one week to the
next."

"That must make it difficult for you to have any sort of
stable life."

"To say the least. But then, I consider such an existence
highly overrated."

Well, Susannah thought, that was putting the cards on
the table. If she had been nurturing any ideas of Rand
Cabot as potential husband material, he had just quashed
them. Not, of course, that she had even considered such a
notion.

To make that point clear, she said, "How I envy you. I
would like nothing better than to simply pick up and go
wherever I liked without the entanglements of a house or
family. Independence, that's the thing. Don't you agree?"

He took a sip of his sarsaparilla, decided that it no
longer tasted as good as it had when he was seven years
old, and put the glass back down on the table. "That's an
unusual attitude for a woman."

Susannah shrugged lightly. "I don't see why. If anything, women have more reason to want independence
than men do. A married man with children can still find at
least some time to himself to pursue his own interests,
whereas a woman in the same condition is truly trapped.
She's fortunate if she has five minutes in a day for herself."

"Yet most women don't seem to mind."

"Oh, of course they do. They just don't say so in front of the men."

"I see," Rand murmured thoughtfully. "You don't seem to subscribe to that view."

"Only because I tend to be outspoken. Does that offend you?"

"No, although I admit the idea that your life would be better if you never married or had children takes me aback. What would you like to do if not those things?"

Susannah evaded his eyes. She had never intended the conversation to take such a turn, particularly since the impression she was giving him was not accurate. Pride had led her into a narrow, twisting maze of half-truths and untruths. She saw no way out but to continue in the same direction. "Oh, I'd be perfectly happy going to parties, traveling, meeting interesting people. When I got bored, I would just move on."

Rand could not suppress a twinge of disappointment. He could have lived his life in exactly the fashion Susannah was describing, but he had chosen not to. "I can think of nothing more arid or purposeless," he said bluntly.

She shrugged. "What is it the French say? *Chacun à son goût?*"

"I have no objection to each living according to his own taste," Rand agreed. "But if you prefer that sort of life, why aren't you pursuing it?"

"What do you mean?"

"Just what I said. Your family is wealthy, your father clearly indulgent. If you want to live as you've described, why aren't you doing so?"

"It isn't that simple," Susannah murmured, casting about for some explanation. She could hardly tell him that while being free to go where she chose and do as she wished was a favorite daydream of hers, she was far too wise not to know that it would quickly grow tiresome and meaningless. Beyond that, she had serious responsibilities that counted for far more than her own gratification and about which she must say nothing.

Fortunately, he didn't press her. They both caught sight of Sukie returning to the carriage and looking around for Susannah. With a wry smile, Rand tossed a bill on the table and rose. "It looks as though I must return you."

Susannah hid her regret well. Though her conversation with Rand troubled her, she had never before spoken with a man other than her father who seemed genuinely interested in her thoughts. The experience was such a novelty that she hated ending it.

Sukie, however, was growing impatient. "Thank you for the refreshment," Susannah said when she and Rand reached the other side of the street.

"It was a small token of appreciation in light of your help," he replied, bowing graciously.

Their meaningless courtesies chaffed both of them unbearably, though neither showed it. Susannah merely smiled and allowed Rand to assist her into the carriage. Sukie followed. The driver leaped into the box and took the reins.

Susannah leaned toward the window, her smile still in place. "With your plans so indefinite, I suppose I should say good-bye."

Rand's tawny eyes met hers as he, too, smiled. "You can if you wish, but I don't promise not to turn up again."

She shrugged as though it didn't really matter to her one way or the other. "Oh, well then . . ."

Her hand rested on the sill. He took it and dropped a light kiss above her knuckles. "Thank you for your help, Susannah. It was very kind of you."

She flushed slightly and reclaimed her hand. "It was nothing at all."

"Nonetheless, I appreciate it."

They continued to stare at each other until Sukie took matters into her own hands and rapped on the carriage roof. Hearing the signal, the driver chucked the reins. As the wheels turned, Susannah looked back out the window at Rand. He stood very straight and tall in the afternoon sunlight, easily the handsomest man she had ever seen— and the most disturbing.

She was still thinking about him when the carriage turned a corner and he disappeared from sight. With a sigh, she leaned back against the leather seat and gazed into space, unmindful of Sukie's broad smile or the occasional bobs of the maid's head as she nodded to herself and chuckled.

5

That was a lovely meal, my dear," Jeffrey Fitzgerald told his daughter. He smiled fondly at her across the snow-white linen that covered the large mahogany dining table brought from France at the turn of the century. The table could be expanded to seat fifty comfortably, and there was ample china, crystal, and silver for that number in the chinoiserie cabinets that graced the elegant, high-ceilinged room. But on that particular night, only two dozen guests were gathered at the Richmond town house.

Seated next to Susannah was Thurston Sanders, who was attending with his uncle. Damien Sanders was no more than fifty but looked considerably older due to his perpetually pinched expression and his penchant for wearing outmoded frock coats and pantaloons that dated from a quarter of a century before. He was thin, balding, and stoop shouldered, and his sallow complexion suggested ill health, although there were those who said he merely ate poorly. He had been known to claim that there was no point serving beef when oatmeal was every bit as filling.

Thurston complained about him incessantly, though never to his face. Damien was the guiding light behind the enormous expansion of the Sanders' business interests following the war. He held immense power not only in

Richmond but throughout the South and far beyond. Moreover, he did not hesitate to use it.

Next to Damien sat Miriam Fitzgerald, Aunt Miriam to Susannah. She was a plump, comfortable-looking woman who joked about her chronic inability to tolerate tight stays and made no attempt to hide her healthy appetite. Miriam had been married to Jeffrey's brother, Charles, who had died at Antietam. Childless herself, she had taken a great interest in Susannah, becoming a major influence in her life.

The remainder of the guests were longtime friends and neighbors in whose company Jeffrey could relax and enjoy himself. That was important to Susannah, who was becoming increasingly concerned about her father. She had thought for several weeks that he was working too hard. He had always put in long hours, but without their seeming to affect him as they did now.

Though he might look fit enough to the untutored eye, Susannah, who knew and loved him, saw the weariness evident in his manner. Despite his praise for the dinner, he had barely picked at it. Yet when she assured him that the meal had all but created itself, he laughed so robustly that she wondered if she wasn't mistaken.

"You are too modest, daughter," he said. "With no disparagement to the other ladies present, I believe our home is the most smoothly run in Richmond. No mean feat, if you ask me, for a young woman of such tender years."

Susannah stifled a sigh. Much as she loved her father, she found his accolades embarrassing, particularly since she suspected them to be as much for Thurston's benefit as her own. At least Damien didn't seem to take them too seriously.

"If you ask me," he said, snorting, "this new generation of Southerners—men and women alike—is too soft. Look at all the things they think they need: telegraphs, indoor plumbing, electrical lights. Poppycock! Country's going to hell—excuse me, ladies—in a hand basket and no one seems to want to do anything about it. Next thing we'll be hearing about is votes for women.''

"It's done in England," Susannah said quietly. She thought Damien Sanders was an old hypocrite. He might not indulge in such innovative luxuries himself, but he certainly didn't hesitate to make money from them. Only the other day Thurston had told her that his uncle was investing in Mr. Edison's company to make electrical lights available to everyone. Still, that was his own business, and she felt no need to comment.

Suffrage, however, was an entirely different matter. Ignoring her father's mildly repressive look, she went on. "Women in Britain have been able to vote in municipal elections since 1869, and it doesn't seem to have done that country any harm."

Damien scowled at her from behind his wire-rimmed glasses. "What do you expect of a place where the ruling monarch is a woman? Thank heaven we had the sense to unbuckle ourselves from them when we had the chance."

"Hear, hear," Jeffrey murmured as he again signaled to Susannah with his eyes. This time she could not ignore him.

With a sigh she rose, as did the other ladies. "We'll leave you gentlemen to your port and your politics. But please don't linger. Madame Farragamo is going to sing for us this evening. I'm sure you'll enjoy her."

There was only the merest hint of maliciousness in her smile. She knew perfectly well that Thurston, in particular, despised what he referred to as ''opera twaddle.'' But in order to appear cultured and refined—two very important considerations with him—he would endure the evening's entertainment. She hoped it would dissuade him from lingering very long afterward.

Having led the ladies to the parlor, she took her place on the couch before a low table where Ezekiel had placed the silver tea service. Susannah poured gracefully and handed the cups around. To her relief, that was the extent of her hostessing duties. The guests all knew each other well; they easily resumed their conversations, which never really seemed to end, continuing from one get-together to the next.

Amid the chatter about marriages and illnesses, servant problems and children, Susannah let her thoughts stray. She looked attentive enough, but her mind was far from the gaslit room with its elegant marble fireplace, wainscoting, and Louis Quinze furnishings. She was thinking of Rand, remembering their encounter that day, when Miriam gently interrupted her.

"You look very pensive, my dear," her aunt said as she reached for another of the mints set out in crystal dishes. She had joined Susannah on the couch where they were a little apart from the other ladies. The swirl of feminine chatter formed an effective screen around them.

"Forgive me," Susannah said with an apologetic smile. "I was woolgathering."

"There's nothing worrying you, I hope?"

Susannah knew her aunt's question was not a casual one, for all that Miriam appeared completely relaxed. Her attentive eyes missed little, her sharp mind even less.

"Everything is fine," Susannah assured her. With a quick glance to make sure that the other ladies were still thoroughly occupied with each other, she added, "I'm continuing work on my little project. I hope to make some progress soon."

Miriam nodded. Her manner continued to be perfectly in keeping with her surroundings. She looked exactly like any Virginia matron enjoying a bit of chatter with her favorite niece, but her voice dropped slightly as she said, "I do hope you haven't bitten off too much, dear."

"I don't think so."

Miriam sighed. She took a sip of her tea and eyed Susannah thoughtfully. "So troublesome, these rumors we hear."

Anyone who might have looked her way would have seen Susannah smile brightly, as though they were discussing the latest Worth creation, as indeed several of the other ladies were doing. "What rumors?"

"Our friends in London are predicting that our July Fourth celebration will not go off as planned."

"Troublesome, indeed," Susannah murmured. She needed little imagination to understand what her aunt was telling her. July Fourth was the date on which Lee was supposed to announce that talks would begin with the North regarding possible reunification. The friends Miriam mentioned were agents who monitored developments in England that might have some bearing on the Confederacy.

Every major country resorted to such agents to gather information that was often more accurate than that available through more aboveboard channels. The fact that Great Britain was at least nominally an ally of the Confederacy made no difference. There were always special factions that needed watching.

"What do they say will happen to disrupt it?" Susannah inquired softly.

"They don't, at least not directly. But the *Essex* has come up again."

"Again," Susannah repeated, remembering the snippet of conversation she had overheard at the Capitol ball regarding some sort of special cargo being carried by the British clipper. "Has she docked yet?"

Miriam nodded. "This morning. She was delayed for a week by that storm off Cape Hatteras but apparently took no damage."

"The manifest?"

"I've made arrangements to see it, but—" Miriam broke off abruptly as she noticed one of the other ladies glancing their way.

"More tea, Mrs. Harrison?" Susannah asked cordially.

"Thank you, my dear," a tightly laced matron said. Several more ladies indicated that they, too, would not be averse to another cup. Susannah returned to her hostessing duties and did not have an opportunity to speak further with her aunt. But she didn't really need to; she had already decided what to do.

Susannah's expectations regarding the evening's entertainment were proven correct. By the time Madame Farragamo had finished singing the aria from Guiseppe Verdi's *Aida*, Thurston—and for that matter, everyone else—was more than ready to depart. She stood at the door with her father to see them off.

When the last carriage had rolled away, Jeffrey patted his daughter's arm affectionately. "Nicely done, my dear. But I hope you won't take it amiss if I mention that the entertainment was a bit . . . enthusiastic."

"She does sing loudly, doesn't she?" Susannah commented as she plucked a drooping blossom from the arrangement of lilies on the hall table. A glance in the mirror above the table showed her that she was beginning to wilt herself. No one else, of course, would have thought so, but Susannah was virtually impervious to her own beauty.

"I suppose," Jeffrey ventured, "that such is the nature of opera."

Susannah shrugged. "It seems so. Now, if you'll forgive me, I'm off to bed. You should do the same."

"I will," he promised. "I just have a bit of paperwork to get through first."

"Couldn't it wait until tomorrow?" she asked with a frown.

Her father shook his head. "I'm afraid not, but it won't take long."

Susannah hoped not, on two counts. Her father needed his rest, and she needed a dormant house. Leaving him with a kiss, she went upstairs, where Sukie was waiting to help her get ready for bed.

Half an hour later, the light in Susannah's room went out, followed shortly thereafter by the lights in the servants quarters on the floor above hers. For another hour or so a lamp burned in her father's study before that, too, was extinguished.

A short time afterward, a slight figure in a homespun shirt and trousers, with a cap pulled low over its eyes, slipped from the house and headed south toward the river.

In the shadow of the railroad bridge, Tad untied a low skiff hidden in the reeds, boarded it, and paddled rapidly away. As usual, several boats rode at anchor along the river, their hulls creaking softly as they rose and fell with the eddying current. The skiff made good progress, and before long, Tad was tying up again beneath a wharf that served one of the numerous warehouses in the Rocketts section of the city.

A mist was rising off the river, wreathing the wooden piles and blurring the sharp edges of the buildings. Tad paused in the shadow of one of the warehouses and looked around. From a nearby doorway flowed light and noise. Raucous shouts mingled with earthy feminine shrieks, the cacophonous din of an out-of-tune piano, and the strum of a fiddle.

Tad smiled to himself. With the good weather and the earlier hour, Rocketts was even busier than on his last visit. That was fortunate, since it made it easier for him to remain inconspicuous as he slipped down the street, passed the flash house, and headed on toward the docks.

The *Essex* rode low at anchor which meant her cargo had not yet been unloaded. Tad knew at least some portion of her crew would have remained on board to guard whatever they had brought across the Atlantic. Crouched behind an empty wagon that had been left on the pier, cautiously he surveyed the clipper's deck. As he watched, a figure moved close to the gangway, paused, then moved on.

Small white teeth chewed at a soft lower lip as Tad considered his predicament. He had to find out what was on board the British ship. After several more minutes of contemplation, when he was certain he had taken every possibility into consideration, he rose and walked a short distance farther down the pier to where he had noticed a stack of discarded crates. A glance back at the *Essex* showed the guard near the gangway again. Tad took a deep breath, shoved over the crates, and as they fell with a clatter, screamed, "Help! Help! Somebody help me!"

The high, feminine voice drew the guard's notice immediately. He leaned over the railing and peered into the darkness as he tried to see what was happening. "Ho, down there. What're you about?"

Tad's only response was to slam and kick several of the crates, all the while continuing to scream.

The guard hesitated. He had been joined near the gangway by several other men. They debated what to do as the screams grew more and more desperate. Finally, they could stand no more. As a body, they raced down the gangway.

As soon as they neared the end of the pier, Tad crouched low in the shadows and raced for the gangway. A moment later, he was on board the *Essex,* scrambling down a ladder toward the lower deck.

The ladder led into stygian darkness. With the danger of fire so great on the wooden ship, no lamps had been left burning. Tad had to feel his way along the narrow passageway until he came at length to a door that, thankfully, opened.

Stepping inside, he found himself in a small but well outfitted cabin, which apparently belonged to the captain. The cabin had several portholes that admitted enough moonlight for Tad to see the nautical charts left out on a table along with the ship's log.

A quick look through the portion of the log dealing with the current voyage revealed nothing except a cryptic remark to the effect that the *Essex* had been delayed a day in departing while waiting for a certain passenger, "Mr. Burke," to come on board.

Tad left the cabin and continued cautiously down the

corridor, keeping both hands against the wall until his fingers at last encountered the rim of another doorway. Opening the door, he discovered a cabin similar to the captain's. For the first time since coming on board, a spurt of hope lightened the nervousness that had been coiling painfully in his stomach.

Whoever occupied the cabin was extremely neat. The only signs of habitation were a man's velvet dressing gown left hanging on a hook near the single bunk and a valise on the floor not far away. A glance at the valise revealed the initials S.R.M.

Tad attempted to open the valise, only to discover that it was firmly locked. He continued looking around the cabin. Two of the built-in drawers beside the bunk were filled with neatly folded men's undergarments and nightshirts. A dressing table near one of the portholes held a basin and pitcher, a boar's-bristle shaving brush, a straight razor, and a bottle of witch hazel. There was a book on the shelf above the bed titled *A Victorian Gentleman's Adventures in the Sultan's Harem*, author Anonymous.

Under other circumstances, Tad might have taken the opportunity to expand his literary horizons, but sounds from the upper deck alerted him. The men he had lured away had returned. He had hoped to have a little more time, possibly even enough to get off the boat before they came back. With the gangway closed off to him, he would have to find some other means of escape. Only one possibility presented itself.

Glancing out one of the portholes in S.R.M.'s cabin, Tad noted a guide rope running nearby between the ship and the pier. Closer study confirmed that, while the opening would be a tight fit, it would be passable.

With a rueful thought for a cream puff enjoyed earlier that evening, Tad opened the porthole, hoisted himself up, and began the difficult process of trying to wiggle his way through. He had to twist his shoulders this way and that before they would emerge, but the rest of his body as far as his hips followed swiftly.

And there he stopped. Suspended in midair above the dark, lapping water, clinging to the outer rim of the porthole while attempting to reach for the guide rope, he also had to extricate hips whose dimensions he was having to reconsider in light of his present predicament.

A predicament that took a major step closer to disaster when, directly above his head, he heard the voices of crew members. "I'm telling you," one of them said, "it was a trick, it was. We all run off the ship, didn't we? Somebody wanted us off so as he could come aboard."

"And do what?" another man challenged. "Tot off that fancy furniture we're hauling or them casks of port? Take a whole crew of thieves to do that."

"What about that Mr. Burke, then?" the first man challenged. "Capt'in made a point of telling us to be on watch for him. Got to be a reason for that. Somebody could be nosin' round, tryin' to find out."

"You're the one what's nosin'. If you've got any sense, you'll keep it to yerself. That there's a bad one, he is."

The first man seemed to take the warning to heart, for he offered no response. After a while, they walked away, their footsteps dying slowly on the swaying deck.

Tad exhaled sharply. He had been virtually holding his breath, afraid that the slightest sound would give him away. The closeness of his escape and the imminent danger that the men would return at any time drove him to redouble his efforts. Through prodigious wiggling and straining, he was at last able to wrench himself free.

Tad was sliding down the guide rope toward the pier, almost daring to think himself safe, when there was a sudden warning shout. "Halt there, you scurvy thief! After him, boys. Don't let him get away!"

Tad hit the pier with a thud, scrambled to his feet, and took to his heels with the men from the *Essex* in hot pursuit. He got as far as the end of the wharf and was heading for the shadows behind a warehouse when a large, muscular figure stepped out of the darkness and collared him.

"What's this then?" the stranger demanded, lifting Tad off his feet and holding him dangling in midair as he shook him. "A little thief, are you? What's he stolen, boys?"

"We don't know, Mr. Burke," one of Tad's pursuers said, "but he was trying to sneak off the *Essex*."

"Could be a stowaway," another suggested. "Capt'in goes hard on them. Makes 'em work passage back to England, then turns 'em over to the magistrate. You'll do hard time in Tyburn, boy," the grizzled seaman told Tad gleefully. "They like tender little chickens like you."

Tad was not predisposed to hear more. While the men were still discussing his likely fate, and Mr. Burke continued to stare assessingly at him, he took a deep breath, called on all his strength, and dealt his captor a kick that threatened to break his own toes. Far more important, it had the desired effect of forcing the burly man to double over in pain, emitting a stream of curses most of which were, thankfully, unintelligible to Tad.

Tad took off running. With the element of surprise on his side, he got fully half a block farther, and might have escaped altogether, if he hadn't run smack up against a large, rock-hard figure. The thought that this was becoming an unfortunate, if not dangerous, habit flitted through his head, but Tad knew he had little time in which to bemoan his bad luck before his pursuers caught up with him and he was neatly trapped between them and the new arrival.

"What's this all about?" a deep, calm voice demanded as Burke made to recover Tad.

At the sound of that voice, Tad went cold, realizing that even worse luck had just befallen him. The man who held him so effortlessly was as roughly dressed as the sailors, in contrast to Mr. Burke's more elegant attire. His golden hair was disheveled, he sported at least a day's worth o whiskers, and he smelled of the raw ale served in the flash houses up and down the wharves. But when he spoke, his voice was cultured, authoritative, even faintly amused— and exactly like Rand Cabot's.

Tad shut his eyes, wishing he could similarly close his ears, and prayed that the whole miserable business was only a nightmare. Lifting his lids again, he peered from beneath thick lashes and saw that it was not.

"The boy's a thief," Burke said. "That or a stowaway. Either way, he belongs back on the *Essex* for the captain to decide what to do with him."

"The *Essex*," Rand repeated slowly. "That's a British ship, isn't it?" Nothing in his tone revealed his intense interest. He had been making the rounds of the docks in search of information about the *Essex*, but had been able to turn up little, despite his obvious willingness to pay.

Several of the pickpockets, cutpurses, and screwsmen to whom he had made known his curiosity had clearly wanted to oblige him. One or two had even tried to invent information, but even the screwsmen—those picklocks and safe-crackers who were the elite of the Rocketts underworld —lacked either the imagination or the credibility to do so.

"What difference does that make?" Burke demanded belligerently. His attempts to stare Rand down and other-wise intimidate him weren't succeeding. On the contrary, the more he glared, the more impervious the other man appeared. Burke's beefy forehead knit with fury as he slipped a hand into his jacket pocket. It emerged holding a .45 Adams revolver, one of the deadliest of the new model handguns. Excited by the scent of violence, the sailors moved closer, pulling out knives and small clubs.

Rand stepped back a pace, taking Tad with him. He smiled pleasantly as he said, "If the boy was trying to steal, or if he is a stowaway, he's under Confederate jurisdiction and will have to appear before a judge here."

"That isn't necessary," Burke snarled. "Give him over."

"Well, now, gentlemen, I don't deny that I'd like to be

of assistance to you. However, it seems to me that the odds are a bit unfair here.''

Burke's teeth glowed in the moonlight. "That's how I like them. Do as you're told and you won't be hurt.''

"And the boy?''

"That's for us to decide.''

Rand appeared to think it over for a moment while Tad stared from one man to the other with terror-filled eyes. The consequences of Rand Cabot's discovering his identity were grim, but grimmer still was his fate should he fall into Burke's hands. Caught between two highly unpleasant alternatives, he could only pray for divine intervention.

It came in the unlikely form of a drunk who, staggering from one of the nearby flash houses, all but fell into the road, jostling Burke and momentarily knocking him off balance.

Rand didn't wait for a better chance. He pushed Tad to the side even as he directed a hard, sharp kick straight at Burke's hand. The gun flew from Burke's grasp, landing on the cobblestones a little distance away. Stunned at having been taken by surprise twice within so short a span, Burke gripped his hand, groaned, and fell to his knees. The sailors, their confidence badly shaken, hesitated.

"Come on,'' Rand goaded them. "I'll take you all at once or one at a time. Doesn't make any difference to me.''

The men's faces reflected their indecision. They didn't like the look of any man who appeared utterly fearless, despite his lack of a weapon. Each had sailed long enough to have heard tales of men trained in mysterious methods of death using only their bodies. They saw no particular reason to discover the truth behind those tales.

One by one they faded into the darkness, dragging Burke with them. Rand sighed with relief and was congratulating himself on a job well done when he turned to find that the boy he had rescued had picked up Burke's gun and was holding it on him.

"Now, wait a minute," Rand cautioned. "There's no need for that."

"Keep back," Tad said, gesturing with the gun. It felt heavy and cold in his hand, and he had to fight to hold it steady.

"You've nothing to fear from me," Rand said. There was a look of genuine sympathy in his tawny eyes. The boy was small and slender; his clothes were roughly made, and his face under the low cap appeared unusually pale. He had undoubtedly had a hard life and was unaccustomed to being gently treated by anyone. But Rand truly meant him no harm, though the longer that gun was pointed at him, the more likely his noble intention was liable to change.

"I'm sorry," Tad said, "but I don't have any choice. I have to get away."

"All right," Rand murmured soothingly even as he struggled to reconcile the waif's rough appearance with his soft, melodic voice. Something itched at the edge of his mind. Caught up in his thoughts, he took a step forward, inadvertently forcing Tad back against the wall.

"I'm sorry," Tad said again as he lifted the gun and fired.

The bullet ricocheted off the opposite wall, carrying splinters of brick with it. Barely had the reverberations begun to echo up and down the narrow street than Tad dropped the weapon and ran. A stream of fluent curses erupted behind him.

He hesitated, glancing back over his shoulder. Rand was still standing, but he rocked slightly on his feet and one hand grasped his other arm. Even in the dim light, Tad could see blood seeping from between Rand's fingers.

Bile rose in Tad's throat. He had aimed carefully and had thought there was no possibility of hurting Rand, but he hadn't considered the splintering stone. No longer concerned with his own safety, he thought only of trying to remedy the injury he had done.

Until he realized that Rand could not possibly be badly
hurt—at least not judging by the speed with which the man
took out after him. Only the swiftest of reflexes saved Tad
then. He dodged from Rand's grasp and raced down the
street. Rand was directly behind him and closing quickly
when Tad darted into a narrow alley, sprinted to the end of
it, and clambered over a high stone wall to drop onto
another road.

There he crouched, hardly breathing. He could hear
Rand directly on the other side, hear his angry exclamation
as his wounded arm prevented him from scaling the wall.
After a few moments, he called out, "You'd best be long
gone, you loathsome brat. If I ever come across you again,
you'll rue the day you were born."

Tad believed him. He remained huddled against the
mist-slicked stones until he was absolutely certain Rand
was gone. Only then did he rise and with great caution
make his way back to the river and his skiff.

6

That's what I get for trying to help someone," Rand said with a grimace. He leaned against the tufted velvet couch, closed his eyes, and assumed an expression of stoic endurance.

"Stop exaggerating," Lillie said. "It's only a scratch." She patted the bandage on his shoulder, gave him a tolerant look, and splashed whiskey into a crystal tumbler. "Here, drink this."

Rand tossed the whiskey back, eyeing her over the rim of the glass. Upon reflection he admitted, "If he was trying to kill me, he's a lousy shot. Not that that excuses him. The little bastard took off without waiting to see what harm he'd done."

"It sounds," Lillie said, "as though he was very frightened."

Rand supposed that was true. He was a worldly man, hardly ignorant of what the life of a young boy living on the docks must be like. It would be impossible for such a child to trust anyone and survive. Still, he didn't take kindly to being shot at, purposefully or not. If he met up with his assailant again, he'd make sure the boy understood that.

Meanwhile, he had other things to think about, begin-

ning with the beefy man on the dock. In the dim light, it
had been impossible to be sure, but the fellow had looked
familiar. Something about his square, gnarled face rang a
bell. Rand tried to put a name to the face, but memory
remained elusive. He gave up after a few moments and
smiled at Lillie.

"I appreciate the first aid, but I'd better be getting back
to the hotel." He wanted to slip inside before dawn,
thereby minimizing the chances of being seen in his shabby
attire, which though unorthodox for the Broad Street Hotel,
had been de rigueur for the dockside dens he had been
frequenting all night.

Lillie wrinkled her nose as she caught a whiff of the
rough wool trousers and knit shirt he had just pulled back
on. The garments were virtually indistinguishable from
those worn by any of the hundreds of sailors who regularly
visited Richmond. But nothing could hide Rand's unusual
size and strength, even among men who made their living
with their muscles; moreover, everything about him spoke
of a rare intelligence and taste, despite his earnest efforts
to the contrary. Lillie's nose wrinkled again as she asked,
"What have you been rolling in, by the way?"

"Ale, I think, though it could be something worse. I've
lost track of the number of holes I've been in tonight."

"Did your tour serve its purpose?"

"I'm not sure," he admitted. "I picked up some information but nothing detailed, and the amazing lack of it has
made me more certain than ever that trouble's brewing."
He took a final sip of whiskey and rose to go. "I'd
appreciate it if you'd keep your eyes open for a fellow off
the *Essex*, a passenger most likely." He gave her a brief
description of Burke, concluding with, "He dresses like a
gentleman but doesn't talk or act like one, and I've got a
feeling he enjoys roughing people up."

Lillie's mouth tightened. "If he tries that with any of
my girls, he'll regret it."

Rand believed her. Lillie ran the most orderly of the

so-called disorderly houses in Richmond. She made sure her girls were clean, poured an honest drink, and didn't keep too close an eye on the clock when a customer was enjoying himself. Her fairness made her an upstanding citizen to Rand, who had long ago run out of patience with hypocritical townspeople.

As he headed back to the hotel, he amused himself by thinking of Lillie circulating in proper Richmond society. She would be a standout, all right: beautiful, vivacious, an excellent hostess, and certainly no stranger to the people she would be meeting. She was already known to half of upper-class Richmond, the male half, and he was willing to bet that more than a few ladies had heard of her as well. He pictured himself at a fashionable ball, introducing the lady on his arm, only to break off when he realized that it was no longer Lillie he was thinking of but a certain impertinent miss with ebony hair and saucy green eyes.

Why Susannah should be on his mind at that particular moment he couldn't imagine. She kept floating into his thoughts at the most unexpected times. He had even caught himself thinking about her for an instant as he grappled with the boy on the pier.

Remembering that episode brought his mind back to the *Essex* and the rumors he had heard about her reasons for being in Richmond. As he reached his room, he glanced at his pocket watch. He had time to shave and change before paying Kidderly a prearranged visit at the Planter's Club, a popular watering hole for upper-class, male Richmondites.

Kidderly was there at the appointed hour, leaning against the long, marble-topped bar with what was clearly not his first drink of the day. He was in uniform, one of a dozen or so similarly garbed men. Rand frowned as he glanced at them, registering the fact that the British presence in Richmond was suddenly on the rise.

There could be a simple enough explanation for the increase in their usually modest number. Perhaps several British naval vessels had put in at the same time. But he hadn't noticed any such activity at the docks. With the exception of the *Essex,* all the other vessels tied up at the Rocketts wharves were American. Nor did he think it likely that they had arrived on a single ship. That would have excited considerable comment.

The more he considered the possibilities, the more likely it seemed that they had arrived in small groups, not more than two or three at a time, probably spaced out over several months. It was only now, when their number had reached a certain level, that they drew any attention.

Aside from the British, the bar was crowded with the usual complement of white-suited planters in straw hats and more formally dressed city businessmen, bankers, and the like. The conversation centered on the prices of cotton and tobacco in the major markets; the likelihood of a record harvest of both; and the latest mechanical wonder, a steam-powered plow that some people thought might actually catch on.

Rand joined Kidderly where he stood a little apart from the others. The major's already flushed face further darkened. "Cabot," he muttered.

"Afternoon, Major," Rand said cheerfully. He raised a finger to the waiter, ordered a beer, and propped himself comfortably against the bar. "Lovely day, isn't it?"

Kidderly was not in the mood to be sociable. He reached compulsively for one of the links of hard sausage set out in bowls along with pickles of all descriptions, hard-boiled eggs, and biscuits, the so-called free lunch every bar provided for its patrons. The victuals at the Planter's Club were noted for being particularly good, but Kidderly seemed barely to taste the sausage as he crammed it into his mouth and swallowed. A sheen of grease appeared on his chin. His chubby hand reached immediately for another sausage. "What do you want?" he demanded.

Rand shrugged. He found the major abhorrent, but no hint of his feelings showed as he nodded to the barman in thanks, then took a sip of beer. Quietly he said, "Information, of course."

"I've been thinking it over. I don't think I can—"

"Do you have the money?"

"M-money . . . ?"

"The ten thousand dollars you still owe me. Do you have it?"

Kidderly stuck a finger under his collar. He was sweating but seemed unaware of it. His small eyes darted back and forth as he said, "You know I don't."

"Then it's fortunate, isn't it, that I'm willing to accept another form of payment." Rand smiled cordially, relishing the game of skill involved in getting people to do as he wanted. Kidderly was an easy enough type to handle: weak, venal, and fundamentally afraid. Rand's intuition and experience told him there was nothing to which the major wouldn't stoop, provided he was assured of not being caught.

"After all," Rand said casually, "it's simple enough for you. All you have to do is listen. The usual mess hall chatter will tell you what you want to know and, if by any chance it doesn't, surely a man of your . . . sophistication will know what questions to ask and of whom."

"I can't be too obvious," Kidderly protested. "People are on their toes these days."

That information alone was interesting to Rand, though he merely smiled, took another swallow of beer, and signaled the waiter for another round for them both.

Kidderly was drinking mint juleps, a concoction Rand disliked intensely. In his opinion, the only people who should be permitted to drink them were the planters who could rightly claim them as a part of their heritage, and even they should confine their indulgence to warm summer nights on the veranda where they could sweat the sweet bourbon out of their systems instead of letting it fester, as in Kidderly, here.

"I'm sure you'll be discretion itself," Rand said. "All I

want to know is the identity of a man called Burke, who arrived on the *Essex,* and why he has come.''

Kidderly crammed a hard-boiled egg into his mouth, swallowed it in a single gulp, and belched. Rand backed discreetly away from the suddenly ripe air. "I don't know . . .'' the major said.

Rand was running out of patience. His shoulder throbbed, and he was tired. But more than that, a certain grimness completely out of keeping with his character was beginning to seep into him. Generally speaking, no matter what the circumstances, he maintained an even temperament and a basically optimistic outlook. Without knowing why, he was feeling increasingly worried and depressed.

Impatient with himself as much as with Kidderly, Rand said, "I'm not going to argue with you, Major. Either you live up to our bargain, or I make known your failure to pay your gambling debts.''

Kidderly blanched. He didn't have to be told what the consequences of such publicity would be. At the very least, his access to the proper sporting life of a gentleman would be abruptly severed. More likely, he could expect to be cashiered from the army and sent home in disgrace.

"I'll do what I can,'' he muttered, then felt compelled to add, "but it won't be easy.''

Rand finished his beer and turned to go. "Don't take too long. I need the information promptly.'' He left without giving Kidderly a chance to respond, confident that he'd made his point.

Outside in the sunlight he paused for a few moments, watching the crowds moving along Broad Street. After a while, he became conscious of the fact that he was hoping to see Susannah. With a softly uttered exclamation of contempt for his own waywardness, he strode briskly away. The time had come, he decided, to make some sense of what was going on at the British embassy.

*   *   *

Susannah climbed the ancient oak tree outside her bed-room and crept in through the window, all the while shaking so wildly that she marveled she could move at all. The scene at the docks the instant she had pulled the trigger was imprinted on her mind. She had only to close her eyes to replay it again in all its horrifying entirety.

In retrospect, she could not understand what had been in her mind when she pulled the trigger. Some idea about distracting Rand enough to allow her to escape, undoubt-edly, but even so . . .

Her thoughts trailed off, too painful to contemplate. She would gladly have looked down the barrel of a gun a thousand times rather than risk hurting him, yet she had done exactly that. That single, backward glance that had revealed his injury was burned into her brain. She gave a low sob as she dropped into her room, falling to her knees beneath the window, where she remained for some time before the worst of her trembling ceased.

He was alive; for that, at least, she could be thankful. That he was also furiously angry and undoubtedly contem-plating vengeance did not lessen her gratitude in the slight-est. Remembering her panic at the thought that he might recognize her, she climbed slowly to her feet and went to peer in her dressing table mirror.

The face that looked back at her appeared small and pale. With her hair still twisted up under the cap and even her lips blanched white, she might have been exactly what she sought to appear—a young, harmless boy. Except that her feelings were purely female. Only the absolute impor-tance of keeping her identity secret had stopped her from rushing to Rand's aid. Above all, she could not risk being discovered at so critical a time, when the fate of not one but two nations hung in the balance.

With a deep sigh, she pulled off the cap and let her hair fall in an ebony wave around her shoulders. Quickly, she removed her Tad clothes and bundled them into their hiding place at the back of the closet, then sat down at the dressing table and began methodically to brush her hair.

She tried hard to keep her mind on what she had learned that night, but despite her best efforts, her thoughts kept straying to Rand. She kept remembering how his body had felt against hers when he held her away from Burke; how the rough timbre of his voice had oddly soothed her at a moment when she should have known only fear; above all, how he had looked at the instant when she fired.

Her stomach heaved. She staggered to the bed and sank down wearily, only belatedly remembering to pull the covers over herself. Her last thought before falling into blessedly dreamless sleep was that perhaps she should make an effort to remember she wasn't quite as strong as she liked to think herself.

Despite the unpleasantness of the last few hours, Susannah slept well and would have slept longer had she not had the misfortune to have a maid who believed that to lie in bed much after dawn was to miss the better part of the day.

"Rise and shine," Sukie chirped as she drew the bedroom curtains open. "Got ourselves another beautiful day. Be a shame to waste it."

"Just a little longer," Susannah pleaded even though she knew she was wasting her breath. In all the years Sukie had cared for her, the maid had never let her stay in bed once she thought it time for Susannah to get up. Unless, of course, Susannah was sick. Briefly she toyed with the idea of claiming a stomach upset or something similar, but then Sukie would dose her with the vile brown liquid she dispensed for all matter of illnesses. Rather than risk such a fate, Susannah dragged herself out of bed.

"Mister Jeffrey's been asking for you. He's going to see some British man 'bout a horse and thought you might want to come along."

Her father had tentatively mentioned the idea to her the day before. He knew she longed for a horse that would be special to her, but he had not pushed her into making a selection. Susannah, however, thought the time to do so had come. "Oh, yes, I do. Please, Sukie, run down and tell him I'm almost ready so he doesn't go without me."

"He won't do that, child."

"Please. He might, and I just couldn't bear it."

Sukie went off with a long-suffering sigh. Barely had the door closed behind her than Susannah reached into the back drawer of her dressing table, took out a sheaf of paper, and penned a quick note to Aunt Miriam. A short time later, after a hurried toilette, she joined her father in the breakfast room, where he was finishing his coffee.

"Good morning, my dear," he said, rising as she entered. "Sukie tells me you want to come along to see that stallion I'm thinking of buying."

"I'd like nothing better," she told him gaily as she helped herself to the scrambled eggs, ham, and biscuits set out on the breakfront. "It won't take me any time at all to eat, and then we can be on our way."

Her father gave her a bemused smile. "I never fail to be amazed at how a young girl of your size can put away as much food as you do without showing it."

Susannah widened her eyes and pretended to be shocked. "Why, Father, what a positively ungenteel thing to say. Don't you know you're never supposed to comment on a lady's eating habits?"

"Forgive me, sweetheart. I don't know what got into me. There's nothing I'd like less than one of those fragile flowers who's forever taking the vapors and engaging in other such nonsense."

Susannah hid a smile. She appreciated her father's sentiment but very much doubted he meant what he said. Certainly if he knew precisely how far from a fragile flower his own daughter was, he would have had a fit.

But then, he had absolutely no idea what she was involved in, and she intended to keep it that way. As she finished her breakfast, she leaned across the table and gave him a quick kiss. "You really are a dear, you know, to wait for me like this. I just need to run upstairs for a moment, and then I'll be ready."

When she returned, her father was pacing in the hallway. She thought he looked very handsome in his new plaid waistcoat and told him so. He brushed off her compliment, but was clearly pleased. On her way out the door, Susannah left the note for her aunt in the brass box where their mail was deposited and collected twice each day. Miriam should receive it within the hour and, with luck, Susannah would have a response by that afternoon.

The horse her father had in mind for her was stabled near the British embassy. The Prussians were a few doors down, not far from the French, and the Russians were catty-corner from them, next to the Spanish.

The demand for residences close to the Capitol and suitable to prestigious foreign delegations far outweighed the supply, with the result that the Richmondites on Franklin Street were getting quietly rich by renting out their spacious homes. There was talk of renovating parts of the city along the river in an effort to ease the shortage, but so far nothing had come of it.

Susannah and her father chatted as they strolled up the street, nodding to friends and pausing to glance in shop windows. At length, directly across from the French tricolor, they came to the British embassy, a graceful Greco-style structure with an entrance flanked by fluted columns supporting a shallow portico that provided welcome shade as they waited for the major domo to admit them.

The spacious entry hall with its marble floor and ornately carved ceiling was pleasantly cool. Several officers resplendent in scarlet uniforms were passing on their way to various offices on the first and second floors. To a man, they cast appreciative glances at Susannah, glances she discreetly ignored.

They were joined a few moments later by a tall, slender man in his early forties who, in contrast to the uniformed officers, was dressed much like Jeffrey Fitzgerald in a morning coat, ascot, and trousers. As he came down the wide, curving staircase, Peter Beaufort's usual expression of solemnity vanished.

With a natural, courtly air, he bowed over Susannah's hand. "May I say, my dear, that you are as radiant as sunshine. There were some rather gloomy clouds drifting around my head just now, but you've banished them most effectively."

"How kind of you, Lord Beaufort," she replied, showing her dimples. "Gloomy thoughts are absolutely not allowed on such a lovely day."

The Britisher smiled. His narrow, rather austere face was transformed by a hint of gentle mischief. "I quite agree. Jeffrey, do I take it you've decided to look at Rosinante?"

"I could hardly stay away after the reports I've heard. May I ask why you're interested in selling him?"

They left the residence and walked around the corner to the stables as Beaufort explained. "The problem is that my duties as ambassador leave insufficient opportunity for anything so pleasurable as riding. Rosinante, on the other hand, is accustomed to a great deal of exercise. Of course, the grooms take him out daily, but he needs more than that. I'd like to see him settled with someone who will give him affection as well as routine care."

Susannah lifted her skirts as they stepped into the stables. Several horses were in their stalls, eating placidly from bags of oats. At the far end, separated by several vacant stalls, stood a huge black stallion. He was fully half a dozen hands larger than the other animals and, unlike them, did not stand quietly. His polished, muscular body appeared ready to spring into motion as he jerked his head in their direction, rolled his large eyes, and snorted through distended nostrils.

Jeffrey frowned. He put a hand on his daughter's arm,

halting her before she could get any nearer. "A magnificent animal, but I'm afraid not quite what I had in mind."

"Oh, Father, don't say that," she pleaded. Before he could stop her, Susannah slipped from his grasp and went directly to the stall. Without hesitation, she raised a hand and held it out, fingers down, to the horse. Rosinante started, snorted again, then sniffed at her. A low whinny broke from him as he rubbed his muzzle into the palm she offered.

"See how gentle he is," Susannah exclaimed. "Why, he's just a little pussycat. Aren't you?" she crooned as, with her other hand, she lightly scratched the horse behind an ear.

Lord Peter smiled as he watched the slender, laughing girl in the sunlit dress, the ribbons of her picture hat trailing down her back. "It appears Miss Susannah has made a conquest, Jeffrey."

"But then, she has something of an unfair advantage, hasn't she?"

The two men turned to the newcomer who had just entered the stables. Rand stood in the dust-swirled light filtering through the open doorway. He was dressed as elegantly as Jeffrey and Beaufort, but to Susannah's eyes the similarity in outward trappings only emphasized the differences between them.

She tore her attention away from the horse and instantly found her gaze locked with his. The shock of that contact made her start. She seemed destined to be forever surprised by him. Merely to see him made her feel as though he had reached out and touched her. Even more, it was as if she had welcomed his touch and returned it.

To hide the blush that suddenly flamed her cheeks, as well as her confusion, she turned back to Rosinante. As lightly as she could, she said, "Why, Mr. Cabot, whatever brings you here?"

He raised a hand to withdraw the cheroot he was smoking, and her attention was drawn unwillingly to his shoulder. She thought she could detect a slight hesitation in his movements and the padding of a bandage there, but was uncertain. At any rate, the wound seemed to trouble her more than it did him. A lump rose in her throat at the thought of hurting him, however inadvertently.

"The horse," he said, improvising rapidly. "I'd heard you had something special for sale, Beaufort, and thought I'd take a look."

"By all means," the Englishman said, a shade stiffly. "However, Miss Susannah seems as taken with him as he is with her."

"I still think . . ." Jeffrey began as he eyed his daughter dubiously.

Determined to ignore Rand, she put on her most cajoling manner. "Please, Father, don't say he's too big or dangerous. He's just the sweetest thing." Over her shoulder, she gave Lord Beaufort a dazzling smile. "Would it be asking too much to take him out for a bit?"

"You're hardly dressed for it," her father objected.

"Nonsense, I can manage fine."

"I don't imagine there could be any harm," Lord Beaufort ventured. "Rosinante really is as gentle a horse as anyone could want."

Rand did not feel called upon to comment. He merely stood back and watched, a sardonic smile playing about his chiseled mouth. Within minutes, two willing grooms had fetched a sidesaddle and secured it on Rosinante's back. They then led the steed into the yard in front of the stables. Susannah followed eagerly and was about to step onto the mounting stool when Rand appeared at her side. "Allow me," he said softly as he bent slightly and cupped his hands together.

The last thing she wanted was to accept help from him, but the alternative would be to appear rude. Steeling herself, she placed her small foot in his hands and allowed him to boost her up smoothly. His strength was such that

she might have been weightless. In an instant, she was
settled in the saddle and looking down at Rand.

"Thank you," she murmured, trying not to notice the
light of mischief dancing in his golden eyes.

He grinned as he took in the picture she made perched
on the huge horse, one hand holding her hat in place, the
other securing the reins. The disparity between her size
and Rosinante's made her seem even more delicate and
vulnerable than usual. Yet in the confidence of her bearing
he sensed a spirit that moved him at least as much as her
beauty.

Rand had decided as soon as he met Susannah that
he could not afford the distraction she represented.
Yet each time they met, his will to resist her eroded
further. That made him feel threatened in a way he had
never experienced before. He was frowning deeply as
he stepped away.

She dug her heels into the horse's side and sent him into
a gentle canter around the yard. Watching her, slender and
erect in the saddle, her glistening ebony hair cascading
down her back and her moist lips parted in a smile of sheer
delight, Rand felt his body harden. Unwelcome desire
challenged the self-discipline and rationality upon which
he had based his life.

"She seems to be managing quite well," Jeffrey said,
with a note of pride.

Beaufort agreed. His admiring gaze followed the horse
and rider. "I can think of no one who could manage
better, including myself."

"That isn't all she manages well," her father murmured
dryly. "I daresay that if I fail to buy him now, I will never
hear the end of it."

"Surely not," Beaufort protested, looking genuinely
taken aback. "Your daughter is a gentlewoman in every
sense. I'm certain that whatever you decide, she will
accept."

If the Englishman heard Rand's disparaging snort, he

gave no sign of it. Jeffrey, however, could not resist a wry smile. Beaufort's interest in Susannah had not escaped him. Had the Englishman been a few years younger and not likely to return eventually to a homeland thousands of miles away, Jeffrey might have considered him a suitable match for her. As it was, he thought it best to spare the ambassador any disillusionment.

"Susannah's forbearance aside, I'm inclined to make you an offer. However," he added, "I don't wish to deny Mr. Cabot the same opportunity."

Rand, who had been following the conversation with half an ear while watching Susannah, shook his head. "Unlike Lord Beaufort, I am not inclined to risk the lady's wrath. Please feel free to conclude the matter."

Jeffrey thanked him and named a figure that Beaufort readily accepted. The amount was fair, but Beaufort was far less concerned with profit than with securing a good home for Rosinante.

Susannah's pleasure more than matched Beaufort's when she returned from her brief ride to learn that her father had purchased the horse. She slid from the saddle without waiting for assistance and gave him a hug. "Thank you, Father. I promise you won't regret it."

"The only way I would," he told her, "is if you came to some injury on that big brute, but you've managed to convince me that you won't. However, you should also thank Mr. Cabot since he stepped aside in your favor."

Susannah hesitated. She hated the mocking light in Rand's eyes, hated even more the idea that she was beholden to him in any way. Yet short of disappointing her father, she had no choice.

"Thank you," she murmured, scuffing a toe in the dirt under the cover of her skirt and hoping no one would notice.

"What was that?" Rand asked.

She shot him a quelling look, only to realize that he had

no intention of relenting. More clearly, she said, "Thank you. I appreciate your action."

"Oh," he said, waving a hand, "it was nothing. Don't mention it." With considerable difficulty, he suppressed a laugh. If looks could kill, his life would be in serious jeopardy. As it was, he didn't doubt that to goad her any further would be ill advised.

Jeffrey, however, was blissfully unaware of the currents of tension running between them. In perfect innocence, he said, "We would be pleased to have you join us at the theater this evening, Cabot. I believe Lord Beaufort is already planning to attend, isn't that correct?"

The Englishman nodded. "I'm a fan of Mr. Booth's. Whenever he plays here, I make an effort to see him."

"You must, too," Jeffrey told Rand. "As our guest. We're having a small supper party afterward that you might also find enjoyable."

Aware of Susannah's slanted brows knitting together in irritation, Rand made a show of great cordiality. "I can't think of anything I would rather do." He held out his hand, and she was obliged to offer him hers. Bending, he touched a light kiss to her gloved knuckles. "Until this evening, Miss Susannah."

The response that sprang to her lips was unutterable. She could do nothing except smile frostily and curse her own powerlessness where he was concerned.

7

Susannah prepared for the evening with as much enthusiasm as she could muster. After she returned
from seeing Rosinante comfortably settled in his new
home, she found a note from Aunt Miriam saying that she
would not be able to join them at the theater as Susannah
had hoped. She would, however, be at the supper party.
Anxious as she was to see her aunt, Susannah's nerves
were further strained by the delay.

A hot bath helped. After soaking in a jasmine-scented
tub, she suffered Sukie to wash her hair in a tisane of
marigold before drying it between lengths of silk.

Wrapped in a dressing gown of frothy white lace, she
sat at her dressing table while Sukie concocted a pretty
confection of curls and ringlets from her ebony hair. As
Sukie worked, Susannah buffed her nails to a pearly sheen,
rubbed almond cream on her face and throat, and applied
the lightest dusting of powder to her nose.

The gown she had chosen to wear was in the daring new
mode introduced by Worth, which banished crinolines and
hoops in favor of a tightly sheathed silhouette. The heart-
shaped neckline and tiny pouf sleeves gave way to a
snugly fitted bodice of jade silk that emphasized the slender contours of her waist while drawing attention to the

graceful curve of her hips. The lavishly draped overskirt revealed an underskirt of darker velvet trimmed with lace. It in turn yielded to a bustle of embroidered silk that flared out at her ankles into a so-called mermaid's train meant to be reminiscent of that mythical creature.

Looking at herself in the full-length mirror, Susannah was relieved that she would not be doing any dancing. It would require much practice in private before she felt any degree of confidence in managing so confining a skirt. Sighing inwardly over the vagaries of feminine fashion, she thanked Sukie for her efforts and went downstairs to join her father.

The carriage deposited them in front of the theater, which was a scant block from the Broad Street Hotel. Visitors to the city, as well as numerous residents, who had learned of Mr. Booth's appearance, were arriving on foot and by carriage. A steady stream of people entered through the wide double doors and made their way to seats in the orchestra or, for the more fashionable set, up the curving staircase to the private boxes that the leading families leased by the season.

The Fitzgeralds' box was close to the center in deference to Jeffrey's insistance on good sight lines, a minor consideration for those who were less concerned with their view of the stage than that of their fellow theatergoers. Lord Beaufort, who, like Jeffrey, actually desired to see the stage, was in the box next to theirs. He was already seated when they entered, but rose when he caught sight of Susannah and bowed courteously.

They chatted briefly across the brass railing separating the boxes. Several British officers were with the ambassador, including a beefy, florid-faced fellow who Lord Beaufort introduced to her as Major Kidderly, and who seemed particularly uncomfortable. Susannah gave him a cursory glance before her attention was diverted by Rand's arrival.

As on the night of the Capitol ball, he was impeccably dressed in evening clothes, but this time Susannah was even more vividly aware of the aura of strength and determination lurking immediately beneath the civilized exterior. Compounding the effect of his magnetic presence on her overloaded senses was her continued anxiety over the shooting.

As Rand took her hand, a wave of heat washed over her, blocking out everything else. The world narrowed down to Rand and herself, alone in a realm where nothing more existed. She was appalled that only one rational part of her protested her own foolishness, but like it or not, she was unable to steel herself against him.

The brush of his lips against her fingers sent a shimmering jolt of pleasure through her. It was all she could do not to make some sound that would have given away her feelings. As it was, Rand seemed well aware that she was not as immune to his charms as she was so desperately pretending. He smiled sardonically as he took his seat beside her, his gaze steady and confident.

For a moment, their eyes met. Hers were wide and stormy, and he noticed the faint glimmer of fear in the emerald depths. His smile faded, replaced by a sudden tenderness that fairly took her breath away.

After the lights had dimmed and the play began, she remained acutely aware of his presence at her side. She had to drag her attention back to the stage, but was quickly rewarded for the effort. She had never seen John Wilkes Booth before, but knew of the actor's extraordinary reputation. In his youth, he had been considered something of a firebrand, impetuous and even given to violence. But time had smoothed the rough edges of his character while adding depth to his talent.

His evocation of King Lear was nothing short of astounding and captivated even those members of the audience who would normally have been unattentive. By the time the curtain rang down for the intermission, the only sound in the theater was thunderous applause.

A liveried waiter brought Susannah a glass of lemonade

and, for the gentlemen, something stronger. She sipped her drink absently while affecting not to study Rand. He looked the perfect picture of the elegant, sophisticated gentleman with nothing more serious on his mind than his own enjoyment. But there was something about his manner that didn't quite ring true.

Annoyed by her own heightened perception where he was concerned, Susannah excused herself. She was returning from the ladies' cloakroom when she noticed that Rand had stepped into the hallway running behind the private boxes.

He was speaking with the beefy British major who was one of Lord Beaufort's guests. Rand's back was to her, and the major was too involved in whatever was being said to notice her. As she neared them, she heard the officer murmur, "He was sent from London, but no one is saying for what purpose. His name isn't Burke though. That's an alias. More than that I can't tell you."

"That isn't good enough," Rand said. "I need to know who he really is, who's responsible for his being here, and what they plan."

Kidderly's voice rose slightly, taking on a shrill edge. "I tell you that's impossible. I've done all I can to get this much for you."

Susannah stopped, uncertain what to do. Eavesdropping was repellent to her, yet the mention of Burke stopped her in her tracks. She stiffened and pressed against the wall as the men continued to speak.

"That's too bad," Rand said. "I made it quite clear when we spoke before that your debt will be canceled only when I have the information I need. How you get it is strictly up to you."

The major mopped nervously at his forehead. "*I can't*. They'd be on to me in a shot if I started asking too many questions. Then what do you think would happen?"

"You tell me," Rand said imperturbably.

"Nothing good. You've only to look at him to know

that Burke's a killer. He won't stand for anyone getting in his way."

Rand was silent for a moment before he said, "Then don't. But find out what I want to know or I'll have to insist on more orthodox repayment, in cash."

"Why, you—"

Rand raised a hand, forestalling the threat. He was taller than Kidderly and all hard muscle where the major was lard. In any contest between them the outcome would be inevitable. "None of that now. The last thing you can afford is a scene, isn't that right, Major?"

The glare the officer sent Rand suggested that he was tempted to forget his own helplessness whatever the consequences, but the implied threat was empty. He was at root a coward and would do whatever he had to in order to save his own skin. "I'll see what I can do," he mumbled.

The two men parted. Susannah waited a discreet interval before returning to her box. She gave Rand a cool smile, bestowed a warmer one on her father, and resumed her seat.

To the best of her knowledge, Booth's performance after the intermission was as riveting as it had been before, but not even he could hold her attention in light of what had just transpired. Though she appeared to watch the action on the stage, her mind was full of the conversation she had overheard in the hall.

She could come to no conclusions about why a Northern businessman would be interested in the mysterious Mr. Burke, especially not to the extent of blackmailing a British officer in order to get information about him. The implications of Rand's involvement troubled her deeply. She was still worrying about them when the play ended and they returned to the town house for supper.

Aunt Miriam was already there when they arrived. "I'm so sorry I missed the play," she said after being introduced to Rand, "but I absolutely had to straighten out a little problem." Her hazel eyes gleamed brightly as she glanced from one to the other of them. "Was it wonderful?"

"Superb," Jeffrey assured her with a smile. Rather to Susannah's surprise, he added, "We missed you."

Surprise was heaped on surprise. Miriam, normally the most composed of women, flushed. With the pleasure of a young girl, she said, "Why, thank you, Jeffrey. Now I'm even more regretful that I wasn't there."

A lingering look passed between them before Miriam remembered herself. "You must excuse us for a few moments," she said, taking Susannah's hand. "We both need to freshen up before the other guests arrive."

With a quick tug she directed her niece into the hall. Upstairs in Susannah's room, Miriam assured Sukie that her assistance wasn't needed. When they were alone, she said, "I really am sorry I wasn't able to join you sooner, dear, but I'm afraid there was a problem."

From the dressing table, where she was absently smoothing away a few loose wisps of hair, Susannah asked, "What happened?"

"Zachery Banks is dead."

The breath caught in Susannah's throat. She stared at her aunt in shock. "Dead? But how?"

Miriam sighed. She sat down on the edge of the bed and wearily rubbed the back of her neck. "He was found shot near the warehouse. Naturally, word was brought to me at once. I've been making cautious inquiries through the usual channels, but so far there is little to go on except that he was deliberately murdered."

She paused for a moment, looking at her niece. "The police seem to think he may have been involved in a dockside pilferage ring, thieves working the cargo ships, that sort of thing. Their theory is that he crossed some of them, and they killed him for it."

Susannah put down her comb and thought for a moment. "You know, there's a chance they could be right."

Miriam nodded. "Of course. I never had any illusions

about Mr. Banks, which was why I was so concerned about your working with him.''

"He never knew who I really was. In fact, I'm quite sure he never even guessed that I wasn't a boy. Besides, he was extremely well positioned for receiving and sending messages between here and the North."

"Fortunately we have an alternative now. I also received word today that Lincoln has sent his most trusted agent here. Once we've made contact with him, we should be able to communicate far more smoothly."

"Do you have any idea who he is?"

"Unfortunately no. I'm sorry to say that while Lee and Lincoln are able to trust each other, the same cannot be said for their respective organizations. We've always been reluctant to make ourselves known to the Northerners working for reunification, and they feel the same way about us. It's an old and a very bad habit."

"That will have to change," Susannah said softly. "I understand that the lack of trust dates from the war years when we were enemies, but now that we're working toward the same objective, we have to be willing to help each other."

"I agree. Contact must be made and soon, or our goal will be seriously endangered."

"I have some information," Susannah said. She hesitated before adding, "I've been on board the *Essex*."

The color fled from Miriam's cheeks. "Oh, my dear, I specifically told you not to do any such thing."

"I know, but it seemed our best chance to pin down these rumors we're hearing, since they all involve the *Essex*. Anyway, there's no harm done." She had absolutely no intention of letting her aunt know how close she had come to being captured, nor what she had been forced to do to escape. Miriam worried about her enough as it was. Not, she admitted, without reason.

"Unfortunately," she continued, "I'm not sure I did much good either." Briefly, she mentioned the passenger named Burke. "He's definitely an unpleasant sort, but whether or not he has anything to do with this, I can't say. I never did get as far as the hold to find out what the *Essex* is carrying. I heard the sailors say furniture and port, but, of course, they could be mistaken."

Miriam nodded. "We've speculated that the cargo is weapons, to arm an insurrection against Lee should he announce the reunification talks. Nothing else seems to make sense, yet I have to admit there are a few holes in that theory as well."

"The principle one being that there's no need to import arms for an insurrection when there are already ample arms available right here."

"Exactly," the older woman agreed. "Yet our informant in London is adamant that the *Essex* is carrying something dangerous to us. Did you see anything else at all?"

Susannah thought for a moment before her mouth twitched. "Only a book about adventures in a sultan's harem."

"Where on earth was that?"

"In a passenger's cabin. Not Burke's, though, because there was a valise in it with the initials S.R.M."

Miriam sighed and stood up. "We will simply have to persevere, but for the moment we'd best get back downstairs."

"Wait," Susannah said, "there's something else. At the theater tonight I overheard Rand Cabot talking with a British major. Mr. Cabot is trying to get information about Burke. He's blackmailing the Englishman to do it."

"Cabot?" Miriam said. "Why would he be interested in Burke?"

"I have no idea. But I admit, it troubles me."

"I think I will make some inquiries myself about Mr. Burke," Miriam said. "It's just occurred to me that we've been presuming all along that the *Essex* is carrying some-*thing* dangerous to us. Perhaps it's some*one* instead."

"Burke? But what threat could he pose?"

"That's what I intend to find out. Mr. Cabot's interest also needs to be explained. It's possible that he . . ." She trailed off, pondering the problem. The two women looked at one another as the same thought occurred to them both.

"Could he be Lincoln's agent?" Susannah asked incredulously.

"He's here in Richmond, he's interested in Burke, and, unlike either of us, he's the sort of person you'd expect to find in this type of activity."

"Oh, I don't think so . . ." Susannah began, flustered. The idea that Rand might be other than what she had presumed disturbed her greatly.

Miriam seemed to sense Susannah's disquiet and raised her eyebrows. "You'd rather he was simply one more brash Yankee businessman concerned solely with profit?"

"No, of course not, but—"

"But," her aunt finished for her, "we can be reasonably certain that Mr. Lincoln would not have sent anyone down here without giving him at least some clue as to the identity of a contact. Lincoln's knowledge of our organization is limited, so whom do you suppose he would mention?"

Susannah closed her eyes as a heartfelt groan was wrung from her. "Oh, no."

Her aunt laughed softly. "You are the only one of us whom Mr. Lincoln knows directly. He may suspect my involvement, but he can't be sure. I wonder," she said as she turned toward the door, "what Mr. Cabot thinks of butterflies."

"He probably collected them as a boy," Susannah speculated. "Trapped them in a net, killed them, and pinned them on display boards. Ugh." She shivered in distaste.

Miriam laughed gently. "Somehow I don't think so. Mr. Cabot may be a very large and undoubtedly strong man, but he doesn't strike me as the sort who would ever deliberately hurt anything."

"He hurt me," Susannah murmured, "when he called me a meringue."

"A what?"

"Never mind, it's a long story and, as you said, we'd best get back." With a deep sigh she glanced at herself one more time in the mirror, decided that she looked passable enough, and stood up. "Of course, I will have to find some way to discover whether or not he is Mr. Lincoln's agent."

"Be careful," her aunt advised. "If we're wrong and he guesses who you are, the consequences could be unpleasant. Under no circumstances are you to reveal yourself to him before you are absolutely certain of who he is."

Susannah nodded but said nothing more. She knew Miriam was not speaking only of the possible consequences to Susannah herself. Far too much time and effort, not to mention loss of life, had been given to the cause of reunification to allow anything to prevent it from proceeding. If Rand Cabot stood in the way, he would be dealt with speedily and decisively.

By the time the ladies returned to the parlor, several other guests had arrived. Susannah left her aunt to see to her duties as hostess. She greeted Thurston and his uncle, noting that Damien was as sour as ever. He glanced at the sumptuous buffet, muttered something about foolish extravagance, and made haste to load his plate. As he was doing so, Thurston drew her to one side. "I'd like to call on you tomorrow," he said solemnly.

Distracted by the flow of guests, Susannah nodded. "Of course. You know I'm at home on Fridays."

He frowned. "Actually, I hoped for some time alone with you."

A warning bell sounded in Susannah's mind, but she managed to maintain her smile. "Why, Thurston, whatever for?"

"You know perfectly well."

She fluttered her fan, glancing around the room, looking everywhere but at him. Her gaze fell on Rand, who was observing the scene. His obvious amusement irked her. "Do I?" she murmured.

"Susannah, you really are the limit sometimes. I've hardly made a secret of my f——"

"Oh, there's Mrs. Carlisle. I absolutely *must* speak to her. Do excuse me, Thurston."

Before he could attempt to stop her, she sailed off in the direction of a plump dowager who was pleased, if a bit puzzled, by her effusive greeting. From the corner of her eye, Susannah caught Rand laughing. She glared at him, but his smile merely deepened.

Supper was winding down when Susannah slipped into the garden for a few moments of fresh air. She genuinely enjoyed most parties, but her lack of sleep the night before was catching up with her. Her head ached, and her shoulders drooped with weariness. The effort to appear lovely and vivacious when she felt only fatigue was taking its toll.

It was warm in the garden but not unpleasantly so. She breathed deeply, inhaling the scent of mimosa mingled with that of the roses she herself had lovingly planted. A night bird called softly from a nearby tree.

She sank onto a stone bench near a fountain and gazed up at the sky. A full moon garbed in wisps of clouds sailed across a sea of stars. As she watched, one star fell. Quickly, without thinking, she whispered a wish.

"Care to tell me what it is?" Rand asked.

Susannah jumped. "You're always doing that," she blurted.

"Doing what?" he asked as he stepped from the shadows. The tip of the cheroot he held in his hand glowed red. Its smoky scent was an odd but pleasing counterpoint to the flowers' perfume.

"Sneaking up on people. You did it the first time we met, then again in the stables, and again now. It's a very bad habit."

"I'm terribly sorry," he said gravely. "It must be my Cherokee upbringing."

Susannah's eyes widened. She welcomed any opportunity to learn more about him, but the idea of such an exotic origin enthralled her. "Really? You're part Cherokee?"

For a moment he looked tempted, then he laughed and shook his head. Sitting down on the bench beside her, he said, "Not unless some of them made it to Ireland a couple of hundred years ago. That's where my mother was from."

"What about your father? Was he Irish, too?"

"Perish the thought. He was blueblood English and never let anyone forget it."

"But he married an Irish woman. How romantic . . . ."

"No, he didn't."

"Didn't . . . ?"

"Marry her." He gave her a sardonic look. "Does that shock you, Miss Fitzgerald?"

"Not particularly. I'm well aware that such things happen. But it must have been difficult for your mother. Is she still alive?"

"As a matter of fact, she is. When I was about ten she married a merchant, Harry Cabot, whose name I took. They live in New York with my four sisters."

"Four? But I thought you only had one, Bethany."

"She's the oldest. After her comes Colleen, who's thirteen, Gwendolyn, who's eight, and last but not least, the baby, Heather, who's five."

"It makes my head reel," Susannah declared.

"What does?"

"Thinking of you with four younger sisters. Do you love them all dearly?"

"Yes," he admitted with a smile that reached all the way to his golden eyes. "I do, even though they can be a handful."

"Of course, they're all wild about you, aren't they?"

His smile deepened. "I seem to be popular with them."

"I wish I'd had a brother," Susannah admitted softly. "It's difficult growing up as an only child."

"You and your father seem very close."

"We are, in some ways. He's wonderful, and terribly good to me, but there are times—" She broke off, aware that she was perilously close to revealing too much. The heady sensations his nearness provoked were undoubtedly responsible.

Seated close to him on the bench, she was acutely aware of the contrast between his size and strength and her own delicacy. She could also hardly overlook the fact that they were alone in private for the first time. But Susannah could not bring herself to cut their encounter short, as propriety dictated.

"Times when you can't be completely forthright with him?" Rand prodded gently.

"Whatever makes you say that?"

He turned slightly and looked at her, taking in the pure lines of her profile lit from behind by the moon. Her eyes were thickly lashed, her nose turned up slightly at the tip, and she possessed a mouth he could only think of as luscious. All the evidence indicated that she was exactly as she appeared, a beautiful, flirtatious Southern belle lacking a thought to call her own.

Why that should trouble him, he couldn't imagine, except that he kept catching glimpses of something more behind the delightful facade, something that hinted at an intelligence and strength she strove to conceal. Under ordinary circumstances, Rand enjoyed a puzzle. But not in the midst of a highly critical and dangerous mission.

He reached out, cupping her chin. He caught her startled glance as he murmured, "What are you, Susannah Fitzgerald? The empty-headed belle you try so hard to appear . . . or something else?"

For an instant, the truth hovered on the tip of her tongue. It was all she could do not to blurt it out to him. The mere temptation to do so was terrifying. Her back stiffened, and before she could stop herself, she put a hand to his chest as though to push him away.

That was a mistake. The place of contact between her
hand and the hard, broad surface of his chest seared her.
She gasped even as her fingers curled into the crisp wool
of his frock coat. On a thin thread of sound, she protested,
"Oh . . ."

Rand did not have to ask what she was fighting. He felt
it, too; had felt it from the first moment he met her: the
unwelcome, unwanted, but completely undeniable attraction between them that now, at this very moment in the
scented garden beneath the cloud-draped moon, could no
longer be held at bay.

Mindlessly, he drew her close. She nestled against him
as naturally as if she had been born to do so. His arms
closed around her with gentle strength.

"Susannah . . ." His mouth touched hers, warm and
soft. Uppermost in his mind was an awareness of her
innocence, which he cherished even as he cherished the
passion he could feel coming awake within her.

She moaned softly. Heat spread from her mouth, the
sudden focus of all sensation, through her body to melt her
limbs and fill her with sweet languor. Hesitantly, with the
shyness of a doe approaching the unknown, she returned
his kiss.

Rand's arms tightened around her. His self-control was
eroding at an alarming rate. He would never have imagined that a simple kiss could provoke such wildfire desire
within him, yet as he deepened his kiss, lightly teasing her
lips with the tip of his tongue until they parted to admit
him, he was hard-pressed not to go further. The warm
sweetness of her mouth, and the tentative darting of her
tongue as it touched his, sent a bolt of pleasure through
him. His body hardened as his hands traced the curve of
her hips before pressing her more closely to him.

Susannah felt his arousal, but, lost in his kiss, needed a
moment to understand its meaning. She flushed then, as
much from her own delight as from the embarrassment she
thought she should properly feel. Her eyes fluttered shut,

concealing emotions she did not wish to acknowledge. For so long she had lived with pretense and evasion until they had become almost second nature to her. Now she determined to cast them aside and allow her true self to triumph.

She tangled her hands in his thick, golden hair. With a boldness she had not known she possessed, she drew her mouth from his and traced with her lips the hard line of his jaw. Emboldened by his response, she went further, savoring the clean, faintly salty taste of his skin until her lips brushed against a jagged pulse beat in his throat. There she lingered, fascinated to feel the rhythm of his life. It echoed within her, resonating like the high, pure sound of a single note that challenges all silence and emptiness.

A great wind drawn from their twin souls buffeted them. Susannah bent before it, pliant as a sapling, shorn of even the thought of resistance. The sudden snap of a branch some distance away abruptly punctured their intimacy with the force of a rifle blast.

Shocked as much by her own emotions as by the sudden sound, she jerked away from him. For an instant, his arms tightened around her, compelling her back into his embrace. But, as she continued to resist, she was abruptly released.

Rand was not inclined under any circumstances to hold a woman against her will. The mere idea appalled him. He was also, and far more intensely, shaken by his response to her. Hardly a stranger to the pleasures found in a woman's arms, he had nonetheless been stunned by the sensations Susannah provoked in him. With her he had sensed something never before glimpsed, something that went vastly beyond mere physical ecstasy into a realm he had never visited. In that regard, he was as much an innocent as Susannah herself.

In an effort to hide his discomfiture, he spoke more gruffly than he'd intended. "I'd better get you back inside, before I forget that I'm your father's guest and do something unforgivable."

Susannah stiffened. To her, it seemed he was mocking, belittling what had happened between them. Moreover, he seemed to be suggesting that she was his for the taking; that only his restraint, his self-control, his morality, stood between her and seduction.

Angrily she said, "I am perfectly capable of getting myself inside, thank you very much. As for the rest, I assure you I would not forget who and what you are, not for an instant."

She turned abruptly and would have stomped off had not Rand taken hold of her arm. Ignoring the rage spitting at him from emerald eyes, he said softly, "What am I, Susannah?"

"A . . . a Yankee. A brash, arrogant, presumptuous Yankee who thinks he can take anything he wants." Heedless of what she was saying, she rushed on. "We showed you once that doesn't work, but since you seem to need a reminder, I'll be happy to show you again." She tore herself free, and an instant later, she was fleeing up the path to the house, tight skirt be damned.

Rand stood motionless behind her. Only his eyes moved to follow the vanishing girl, his expression surprised and thoughtful.

8

"I still don't understand," said Thurston, "what you were doing in the garden with Cabot."

Susannah stifled a sigh. They were riding through the park, normally a favorite activity of hers, but Thurston's presence spoiled her pleasure. He had arrived toward the end of her "at home" afternoon, as she was visiting with half a dozen callers, both male and female. When he loitered past the correct hour, she had realized she was not going to be easily rid of him.

But, with a faint glimmer of hope, she had remembered that Thurston hated to ride, even though he would never admit his dislike because it was considered the height of ineptitude for a Southern man to be less than fully competent on a horse. So, she had suggested a ride and was surprised when he agreed.

His mount was bad tempered and given to suddenly shying, so that Thurston had to cling to the saddle from time to time. Susannah suspected the horse of misbehaving deliberately and found herself in sympathy with Thurston. She prayed, for both their sakes, that the ride would be a short one.

Rosinante, on the other hand, behaved impeccably. He pranced along, thoroughly enjoying himself and giving her no trouble. As he tossed his proud head toward a pretty mare, Thurston scowled.

"What was your father thinking of to buy that brute for you? It was unconscionable for Beaufort to pass him on to you."

"On the contrary. He's a wonderful horse and I'm delighted to have him." She leaned forward and patted Rosinante's mane. "Don't listen to him, sweetheart. He doesn't know what he's saying."

"Oh, for heaven's sake, you're talking to—" He broke off, belatedly aware that he had wandered from a subject of far greater interest to him. "Never mind. You still haven't explained to me about Cabot."

Susannah prided herself on a more than ordinary measure of self-control, but there were limits to what she would put up with. Thurston's self-centered, boorish behavior grated on her. Not even for her father's sake could she meekly pretend that she was not annoyed.

"Is there any particular reason I should explain about Cabot?" she challenged.

"What do you mean?" Thurston demanded, startled.

"Only that I don't see why I should have to account for his presence in the garden yesterday evening."

"But I saw you, sitting on that bench together."

"So?"

"So what were you doing there, the two of you alone? I must tell you, Susannah, that it appeared most improper."

"I'm sorry to hear that, Thurston," she murmured without the slightest hint of contrition. Had he arrived a moment earlier, he would have seen precisely how improper they had been, but she wasn't about to tell him that. Thanks to his clumsy snapping of a branch, he had no idea of what had actually transpired.

He did, however, have his suspicions. "Mind you," he said stiffly, "I'm not making any accusations. But you are a very young girl and Cabot . . . well, frankly, his reputation isn't the best. Much as I hate saying this, I'm afraid he's the sort who would take advantage of a woman, even a lady."

Susannah sighed. All unknowingly, Thurston had put her in a position where she felt called upon to defend Rand. Smiling inwardly at the irony, she said, "I really don't think that's the case."

"You are hardly a fit judge. I'm beginning to regret not bringing the matter to your father's attention. I held my tongue only because I was confident you would give me some explanation, but . . ."

Thurston's threat banished any temptation she might have felt to be conciliatory. "You may feel perfectly free to tell my father what you saw," she said. "So long as you tell him the truth."

Thurston drew himself up in the saddle with an expression of extreme offense. "Surely you aren't suggesting that I would lie."

"I'm suggesting nothing. I am saying, quite clearly, that you are taking a great deal upon yourself. I am not a member of your family; you have no right to monitor or criticize my behavior."

He was clearly taken aback by her reprimand. She glanced at him from the corner of her eye as they continued riding. His narrow face looked first puzzled, then pensive. A sinking sensation appeared in her stomach when he suddenly gave her a sly smile.

"Forgive me, Susannah. I'm not usually so dense. Of course, your point is well taken. At the moment I have no right to instruct you in proper behavior. However, I don't need any urging to correct the oversight." His smile deepened, taking on a predatory glimmer.

Susannah felt a tremor of unease. She had the distinct impression she had just managed to neatly box herself in.

"Let's not be precipitous," she said hastily. "After all, I'd never want you to feel you'd been pushed into anything."

"Still, there comes a time when—"

"And then, of course, there's my father to consider.

He's so accustomed to there being just the two of us. Certainly he could manage well enough, but I dread his having to do so.''

''But surely he wants only your happiness?''

''Oh, surely,'' Susannah agreed. ''As I want his. If only my mother were still alive, or if Father had remarried. But the thought of leaving him alone is simply too painful to me.''

''It's not as though you would be going any great distance,'' Thurston pointed out.

''What does physical separation matter when the spirit is apart?'' Susannah emoted. She wasn't absolutely sure that what she had just said made any sense, but she was comforted to see that Thurston was at a loss as to how to respond.

She took the opportunity to distract him. A party of half a dozen red-coated horsemen was riding toward them. Susannah recognized the beefy major who had shared Lord Peter's box at the theater. Beside him was another, older man whom she did not know. The riders drew rein as they came abreast. Six pairs of eyes scanned her. Six plumed hats were lifted in salute.

''Thurston, old chap,'' said the beefy major, his gaze still on Susannah. ''Nice to see you out and about, and in such lovely company. I don't believe I've had the pleasure, though you were at the theater last night, weren't you, Miss . . . ?''

Stiffly, Thurston made introductions all around. Most of the men's names eluded Susannah, but she took note that the beefy major was Arnold Kidderly and that the tall, gray-haired man at his side was Captain Edmund Fortescue of Her Majesty's Royal Navy, commander of the clipper ship *Essex*.

Struggling to hide her excitement, Susannah held out a hand to the captain as she gave him a charming smile. ''Welcome to Richmond, Captain. I hope your voyage was safe and successful.''

His pale eyes were shuttered, though he replied cordially enough. "Be assured of that, Miss Fitzgerald, if only because it has provided me with the opportunity to meet the fairest flower of the South."

She flushed becomingly and managed an ingenuous laugh. "Why, I declare, Southern gentlemen could take lessons in cordiality from Queen Victoria's faithful sons. Present company excepted, of course," she added for Thurston's benefit.

Rosinante snorted and shied beneath her. She tightened the reins in gentle reprimand, and he immediately grew quiet, though she sensed his impatience to be gone. Thurston, however, was disposed to linger.

"How are things in London, Captain?" he inquired. "We hear a great deal, but it isn't always possible to sort truth from fiction."

"There are complex forces in motion, Mr. Sanders. In my opinion, we stand at a watershed in history. It is a time for strong men to seize the initiative."

"I couldn't agree more," Thurston said a bit pompously. "What we do today will shape the future."

Susannah could hardly think of a more ponderous non sequitur, but Captain Fortescue seemed pleased by it. He smiled at Thurston and the two of them exchanged meaningful looks.

"My, how serious you both sound," Susannah said airily. "And on such a lovely day, too."

"Please forgive us, Miss Fitzgerald," Fortescue replied. "Such conversation must be boring for a lady. May I induce you to ride along with us if I promise to discuss nothing more serious than the latest court gossip?"

Even as she simmered inwardly, Susannah held on to her temper. Experience had long since taught her that men were far more likely to reveal vital information in front of a woman they thought could not possibly understand it. Her wide-eyed guilelessness was therefore her best weapon.

"Well, now, Captain," she said sweetly, "I can't ex-

actly admit to enjoying gossip, now can I? But I won't
turn my ears away either.''

The gentlemen laughed approvingly as they fell in together. Susannah found herself at the center of attention,
surrounded by the British officers, several of whom were
undeniably attractive and all remarkably gallant. She pru-
dently reserved her attentions for Captain Fortescue, however, who gave every appearance of appreciating them.

His approval did not completely distract from Kidderly's
more cautious appraisal. She was aware of him watching
her with a hint of wariness and suspected that he might
have remembered seeing her in the corridor of the theater.
If so, he was undoubtedly wondering how much she had
overheard of his conversation with Rand. In that case, it
was all the more important for her to appear utterly harmless.

By the time the officers had escorted both her and
Thurston back to the stables, Susannah was convinced she
had succeeded in directing suspicion away from herself. In
the process, she had also learned that Captain Fortescue
was well connected in London, particularly among the
more conservative members of Parliament.

He made several allusions to men Susannah knew to still
nurture dreams of bringing the former colonies back under
British sway. Men who, while outwardly opposing the
North's incursions into Canada, quietly approved of them
with the expectation that they would raise the ire of Queen
Victoria to a point where anything might be possible.

She made a mental note to discuss all this with Aunt
Miriam as she bade the gentlemen farewell. Thurston saw
her to her door, but she did not invite him to linger,
fearing a resumption of their earlier discussion.

As she entered the house, she was surprised to find Lord
Peter and her father emerging from her father's office. The
two men wore somber expressions, which they quickly
attempted to disguise.

"Did you have a pleasant ride, my dear?" Jeffrey asked
as he lightly kissed her cheek.

"Very nice," she murmured, concerned by the pallor of his skin and the shadows beneath his eyes. "Is something wrong?"

The two men glanced at each other. "No, of course not," her father said quickly. "Lord Peter and I were just having a little chat."

"I met a compatriot of yours in the park," Susannah told the Englishman. "Captain Fortescue. He was regaling me with the latest news from London."

"Was he?" Lord Peter set his mouth in a hard line. Her mention of the other man appeared to further darken his mood. He exchanged another glance with Jeffrey before bowing to Susannah. "I must be going. Jeffrey, I'll be back in touch with you as soon as I have anything further."

"Fine, Peter. I'll see you out."

Susannah stepped aside. She put a foot on the stairs, intending to go to her room to rest and freshen up before supper. On impulse, she glanced back over her shoulder at the men. They were standing on the stoop, visible to her through the etched glass in the door, and she could see that they were in deep conversation. As she watched, the two men nodded, shook hands, and then the Englishman took his leave.

Susannah was still pondering the reasons behind their meeting and subsequent actions when she came down to supper a short time later. For a change she and her father were dining at home. They enjoyed a simple meal together and afterward played a few hands of piquet. Susannah went to bed early, glad of the rest.

Her sleep, however, was not as undisturbed as she would have liked. Images of Rand floated through her dreams, making her toss and turn across the rumpled sheets. She felt again the tantalizing touch of his mouth, the strength of his arms, and her own fiery response. The sound of her own soft moan woke her, and she sat bolt upright in bed.

Something was wrong. She couldn't place the source of

her conviction but was no less certain of its rightness. Susannah leaped from the bed in a tangle of white lace and cotton and rushed into the hallway. It was dark and quiet. She stood, barely breathing, straining to see or hear something that would explain what had awakened her.

From the far end of the hallway, in the direction of her father's room, she heard a low groan. Running quietly and swiftly on bare feet, she reached his door, paused, then knocked softly. There was no response. She hesitated for a moment, torn by uncertainty. In all likelihood her father was simply asleep. He needed his rest so badly that she was loath to disturb him unnecessarily. On the other hand, she was deeply worried that he might be in danger.

Another groan reached her through the thick wooden door. Pushing her doubts aside, she opened it a crack and peered inside. Her father lay half out of the bed, slumped on his side. His arm was extended toward the bell pull, which he had not been able to reach.

Susannah yanked frantically on the bell pull while struggling to ease her father back onto the bed. When she had managed her task, she lit the gas lamp on the table nearby with hands that were trembling so badly she could barely strike a match.

By the glow of the lamp, she could see that her father's face was gray and his breathing labored. He was clutching the collar of his nightshirt as though he had been trying to loosen it. She tried to rouse him but without success. At that moment Zebediah poked his head into the room to see what all the commotion was about.

"Oh, miss!" he exclaimed when he took in the scene, "what's happening here?"

"I don't know," Susannah whispered brokenly, "but Father is very ill. You must send for Dr. Smithers at once. Tell him it's an emergency."

Zebediah wasted no time on further questions. He hurried away, calling to several other servants, who rushed in to see if they could be of help. Susannah sent them away, aware that nothing could be done until the doctor arrived. She knelt beside her father, clutching his hand in hers, her lips moving in a silent prayer that her father would be well.

Dr. Smithers was a portly, middle-aged man with silver sideburns and a ponderous manner. In his youth he had been a surgeon on the battlefields of the War of Secession and he had not lost his ability to heal or to respond quickly and effectively. Barely had he arrived and heard Susannah's choked summary of what had happened than he dispatched her from the room and set to work.

Sukie was waiting for her in the hallway. The large black woman took one look at Susannah's stricken face, put her arms around her, and rocked her gently. "There, there, sweetheart," she murmured. "Your daddy going to be all right."

"Oh, Sukie, if anything happens to him . . ."

"I know, honey, but he's a strong man. He's just been working too hard. The doctor set him right on that, and he be better than ever."

"He has to get away from here," Susannah said as Sukie led her back to her own room. "There's something preying on his mind, worrying him so much he can't rest. I just know it."

"You could be right, child. He been mighty thoughtful lately. Best thing for him be to go home to Belleterre."

"That's it," Susannah agreed. "Once he's home, I'm sure he would feel better." She thought of their sprawling plantation home with longing.

Dr. Smithers agreed with their assessment. A short time later, as the eastern sky was lightening, he sat with Susannah in the parlor. She had dressed hurriedly, not bothering to do anything with her hair except tie it back with a ribbon. Her apricot-colored day dress of softest voile was trimmed with tea-dyed lace. She wore no jewelry except her mother's watch, which was fastened to her bodice with a gold pin. As she sat across from the doctor, her green eyes wide with apprehension, she looked younger and more vulnerable than her eighteen years.

"Now, don't worry, my dear," he said gently as he set down his teacup. "Your father will be fine, but this episode must be taken as a warning. He's been pressing himself much too hard, and that has to stop."

"What exactly happened to him?"

"He had a mild heart seizure, one that shouldn't leave any permanent damage provided he follows my advice, which is that he get more rest and maintain a calm frame of mind."

"Do you think it will be possible for him to do that here?" Susannah asked.

"Frankly, I have my doubts. When would you normally return to Belleterre?"

"In another month or so. Certainly before the worst of the summer heat hits the city."

"I recommend that you leave sooner than that. The city becomes unhealthy as the weather warms. For a man in your father's condition, it would be unwise to linger."

"I assure you, Doctor, that we will make speedy arrangements to close the Richmond house and return to Belleterre."

As she saw him out, she was already making a mental list of everything that needed to be done before they could depart. At the top of it was getting in touch with Aunt Miriam.

Once she'd dispatched a note, Susannah mustered all the servants and set them to packing. Trunks and valises were pulled from storage as piles of clothing, books, and other belongings were assembled.

Sukie's son, Walter, was sent to the steamboat office to book passage for them all the following day. He was also told to stop by the stables and warn the grooms that Rosinante had to be ready to travel. Dust cloths were thrown over the furniture. The window awnings were folded, and the outdoor shutters of the rooms that would not be in use again were closed and secured.

In the midst of all the chaos, as Susannah was standing in the hallway dispatching servants hither and thither like a commanding general, Miriam arrived. She took one look at her niece and shook her head ruefully. "I rushed over to help, but I can see it wasn't necessary."

"On the contrary, I need all the assistance I can get. But first we must talk."

Drawing her aunt into the parlor, she shut the door behind them and took a deep breath. The ceaseless activity since dawn had kept her anxiety at bay, but the moment she paused, it came back in a rush.

"Oh, Aunt Miriam," she murmured softly, "I'm so sorry about this. I feel absolutely terrible, but I don't know what else to do. Father was taken ill last night, and the doctor says we must leave Richmond at once."

"Sit down," the older woman urged her gently. "Tell me exactly what happened."

When she had heard Susannah's account, Miriam nodded firmly. "You're doing the right thing, dear. There can be no question of that. Jeffrey absolutely must rest, and you know as well as I do that unless you move quickly, he'll find some excuse to stay here. You know how stubborn he can be."

"I think that's where I get it from," Susannah said with a smile. Talking to her aunt always made her feel better. There had never been a problem she couldn't bring to Miriam. "But I wish there was some alternative. This is the worst possible time for me to be leaving."

"Actually, I think it may be the best time." Her aunt patted Susannah's hand gently. "To tell you the truth, I've never been happy about your involvement in this matter, and in recent days I've been more concerned than ever. The sooner you're out of Richmond, the happier I'll be."

"You shouldn't feel that way," Susannah told her. "I made my own choice. It's true that I was influenced by you, but that doesn't mean you're responsible for my decision.''

"I'm not so sure of that," Miriam said. "When you were a child and I would come to visit, we always talked so much. You were so bright and curious, and, oh, the questions you asked." She shook her head ruefully. "You wanted to know about everything, but especially about people. Why they did the things they did. Why some were free and others were slaves. I tried my best to explain in ways that your father wouldn't object to, but I think that in the process I passed many of my values and beliefs on to you.''

"There was nothing wrong with that," Susannah said. "You raised me to believe in what is right."

"But with no clear understanding of where those beliefs would lead you." She smiled chidingly. "You can be very stubborn, my dear. I should have refused the moment you said you wanted to join the reunification underground. In fact, I should have denied knowing anything about it.''

"That would hardly have been possible," Susannah reminded her gently, "after I overheard you talking with another agent. Besides, you'll admit I've been of *some* use.''

"Considerable use," Miriam corrected her. "But when I think of what your father would say . . .''

Susannah paused to consider that her aunt seemed preoccupied with her father these days. An unlikely possibility that Miriam's and Jeffrey's feelings might have become something more than mere friendship occurred to her, only to be dismissed. Nothing would have pleased her more than for the two people who had formed the foundation of her life to have come to love each other, but that was a topic for another time.

"Then it's fortunate that Father doesn't know, isn't it?" Susannah finally responded.

"I suppose. Still, you must do as the doctor recommends. I will keep in close touch, but you must promise me not to worry about what's happening here. Concentrate on helping your father get well.''

Miriam left a short while later, after promising Susannah again that she would stay in touch. The hurried packing continued with only a break for a cold supper. Susannah was rooting in a trunk when Sukie poked her head into the room to tell her that her father was awake.

Jeffrey Fitzgerald was sitting up in bed with a bemused expression on his face and a faint look of disbelief in his eyes, as though he was trying to recollect what had happened to him. He had been staring off into space, but as soon as Susannah entered, he focused his attention on her. "Dr. Smithers was here last night, wasn't he?" he asked.

She shut the door behind her and said softly, "You were very ill."

Her father considered her words for a moment, his brows drawn together as though he still couldn't quite believe that anything had gone amiss in the body that had served him so well for such a considerable number of years. "I seem to remember him telling me something about my heart."

Susannah sat down on the edge of the bed and took her father's hand in hers. His complexion was still pale, but the awful grayness of the night before was gone. Nevertheless, she did not doubt for a moment that he was still seriously ill. "The doctor says you had a heart seizure and that if you aren't to have another, one that could do serious damage, we must leave Richmond at once. This warm weather is dangerous to you. You will be far more comfortable and safer at Belleterre."

"I really don't think—" Jeffrey began.

"You've been feeling poorly for some time, haven't you?" Susannah broke in.

Her father smiled wryly. "I wouldn't go that far. The fact is I'm not a young man anymore, and I can't expect to feel like one."

"There's a difference between simply growing older

and actually being ill. Dr. Smithers made it clear that you've passed over the line. Please, Father," she continued when he still looked doubtful, "I've never been so frightened in my life as when I came in here and saw you nearly half dead. Surely, you don't want me to go through that again?" She had no qualms whatsoever about so blatant an appeal to his parental love. She was determined to do anything she had to in order to make him behave sensibly.

"I'm sorry I put you through this," he said softly.

"That isn't important. What counts is that you get well. Oh, think of it," she said, jumping up. "It's beautiful at Belleterre this time of year. We'll open the house early, watch the garden bloom, and when you're feeling better, we'll have parties."

"It does sound lovely," he admitted. "But you realize that I will also have to do some work."

"But why? Surely there isn't anything so urgent that you can't let it go for a while."

"I'm afraid that isn't quite the case. But don't trouble yourself, my dear," he reassured her. "The business matters that require my attention are perfectly straightforward. In fact, if you'll bring me paper and pen, I'll start organizing them right now."

Susannah complied, then sat down again at his side as he wrote a quick note. As he was signing his name, she said, "I could help, if you'd let me. You only need to tell me what has to be done."

Her father eyed her tenderly, clearly not taking her suggestion seriously. She was, after all, a woman and therefore not remotely suited to such an undertaking. Still, he was far too kind to reject her offer entirely. "To begin with, you can see to it that this note reaches Rand Cabot. He's stopping at the Broad Street Hotel."

"Rand . . . ? But why?"

"We're negotiating for the sale of this year's cotton. I can hardly break our talks off now. Fortunately, we can continue as easily at Belleterre as we can here, so I'm suggesting that he come with us.''

"Oh," Susannah murmured, hoping fervently that her dismay did not show on her face. Her encounter with Rand in the garden had convinced her beyond the shadow of a doubt that he was a danger to her. She seemed to have absolutely no willpower where he was concerned. Her safest course by far was to stay away from him. But now, if he accepted her father's invitation, they would be thrown into even closer contact.

Fighting a sudden rush of anticipation, she took the note and promised that she would see to its delivery.

9

The Belleterre plantation sprawled over some two thousand acres dotted with several dozen buildings in which more than a hundred people lived and worked. The heart of Belleterre was the gracious white columned mansion that had been home to the Fitzgeralds for almost a century. A long gravel drive shaded by ancient oak and pine trees led past carefully tended flower beds and rolling lawns to the house itself, which seemed to slumber beneath the late spring sun.

The carriage carrying Susannah and her father had barely rumbled to a stop before it was surrounded by servants. A gentleman who looked remarkably like Zebediah, and who was in fact his twin brother, hurried out to greet them.

"Welcome home, Mr. Fitzgerald, Miss Susannah. We sure are glad to see you. Come right on in now. It's too hot outside to be lingering. You children shoo."

Jeffrey climbed the few steps to the veranda. Susannah watched him carefully and was relieved to note that her father managed them without any outward sign of difficulty. She had been extremely concerned about his making the trip so soon after his attack, and had endeavored to assure his comfort in every possible way.

Her efforts, however, had not been a great success.

She'd tried to get him to spend the river portion of the trip in a shaded cabin where he could lie down, only to be met with a short and outright refusal. He had, instead, sat on deck, where he always did, watching the banks of the James slip by and sipping a bourbon and soda. Yet the trip hadn't seemed to do him any harm. He already looked better than he had in weeks.

"Everything in order, Jedediah?" he asked with his usual confidence.

"Everything's just fine, sir," Jedediah assured him. "We weren't expecting you so soon so we're still laying in supplies. Supper might be a little simple tonight. Hope you won't mind."

"Not at all," Susannah said. "I'll check with Hattie about what's needed, but there shouldn't be any problem. We won't be doing very much entertaining."

"Who says we won't?" her father asked. He gave her a stern look that lost much of its impact because of the twinkle in his eyes. "Don't expect me to take to my bed and play the invalid, daughter. I'll admit I was glad to shake the dust of Richmond off my feet, but now that I'm here there's no reason for us not to carry on as usual. Of course we'll be entertaining."

Susannah stifled a sigh. She had been a little surprised by the ease with which she had convinced her father to comply with the doctor's instructions. It was unrealistic to expect that he would go along with everything else that was good for him. Still, she hoped . . .

Catching sight of herself in the mirror that hung over a Louis Quinze side table in the entry hall, she grimaced. The curls beneath her bonnet were wilting, and she had a smudge of dust on her nose. Her gray travel dress was crushed in places, and its narrow skirt made her lower limbs feel as though they were encased in lead. Though she had sensibly neglected to wear a corset, she was still uncomfortable and growing more so by the moment.

"First things first," she said. "I'm going to freshen up,

then I'll speak with Hattie. Father, I will be in your
everlasting debt if you would refrain from riding over the
fields today.''

"I think I'll be able to restrain myself," he answered
dryly as he headed toward his study. "Jedediah, tell Johnson I'll meet with him in an hour to go over the account
books.''

Upstairs in her room, Susannah removed her bonnet,
pulled the pins from her hair, and shook the ebony strands
free. She bathed her face in cool water and patted it dry
with the towel Sukie handed her. "It is good to be home,"
she said with a sigh.

Sukie undid the buttons of Susannah's dress, which
reached all the way down the back. Susannah slipped off
the dress and wrapped herself in a soft silk dressing gown.
She sipped from a glass of iced tea as she sat wearily on
the edge of her canopied bed. "I can't understand why I'm
so tired.''

"You been under a bad strain," Sukie replied, "and
you hardly had any rest in days. Why don't you lie down
now and take a nice nap?''

"I really shouldn't. Hattie—''

"She can wait," Sukie said firmly. She took the glass
from Susannah and gently urged the girl back against the
pillows. "You go to sleep now, honey. We'll all keep an
eye on your daddy.''

"Maybe I will just shut my eyes.''

"That's fine now," Sukie murmured. She laid a light
cover over Susannah and tiptoed from the room. Susannah's eyes fluttered open as she heard the door creak shut.
A moment later her thick lashes drooped and she slept.

When she awoke it was early evening. A lark was
singing in the branches of the tree outside her windows.
She sat up and rubbed the sleep from her eyes. Her
stomach rumbled, and she realized she had not eaten since
early that morning.

She jumped from the bed and to avoid bothering Sukie,

dressed herself in a simple violet silk dress she ordinarily wore during the day but that she thought would be fine for an informal supper at home. She left her hair down, pausing only long enough to tie it back with a bow that matched her dress. The nap had done her a great deal of good; her eyes sparkled, and her cheeks were slightly flushed as she hurried down the curving marble staircase.

She heard voices coming from the study and she frowned, wondering if her father was still with Johnson. The plantation manager was an intelligent and hardworking man, but he had a passion for detail shared by his employer. The two of them could talk for hours about the most minute aspects of seeds and crops.

Except that it wasn't Johnson's voice she heard. Coming to a stop before the open study door, she drew a sharp breath. Rand was sitting on the couch directly ahead of her. He had one long leg crossed over the other, his tie was undone, and he looked perfectly relaxed. In one hand he rotated a snifter of brandy that glowed golden in the soft gaslight. In the other he held a cheroot, the faint scent of which made Susannah's nose twitch. Jedediah had just lit the cheroot for him. It was Rand's thanks she had heard.

At first he did not appear to react to seeing her, but instead moved with a slow deliberation that imprinted itself on her mind. First, he placed the snifter on the table next to him and rested the cheroot on the rim of a large leather-and-glass ashtray. Then he stood up, unfolding his long body in a fluid motion.

"Susannah," he said softly, his tawny eyes gliding over her.

"I didn't . . ." Abruptly aware that her voice was reed thin, she cleared her throat and tried again. "I didn't expect to see you here."

His eyebrows rose in gentle mockery. "You weren't aware that your father had asked me to come?"

"Yes, actually, I was." Feeling foolish to be still standing by the open door, she came farther into the room, only to realize that, except for herself and Rand, it was empty. "Where is Father?"

"He was feeling tired and went to bed."

She was instantly alarmed. "Is he . . . ?"

Rand stepped forward and laid a hand lightly on her arm. "All right? Yes, he certainly seemed so, only weary as should be expected under the circumstances. He was apologetic, but I assured him I didn't require looking after. However," he added with a slight smile, "now that you're here, I've changed my mind."

His touch, light though it was, sent a wave of heat through her. It made her feel acutely self-conscious, as well as rebellious. She had been thinking about him almost continually despite everything else going on around her. Her feelings had alternated between determination to stay as far away from him as possible, elation at the mere thought of seeing him again, and underlying all, a deep resentment at his ability to affect her so powerfully and with such apparent casualness.

Determined to give him a taste of his own medicine, she removed his hand from her arm and said coolly, "Please don't feel you have to put yourself out on my account. If you'd prefer to dine alone, I have no objection."

He shook his head, the amusement in his eyes deepening. "And deprive myself of your company? Impossible." Behind his mocking words was a more serious note. He had noticed the shadows in her eyes and the brittle tension in her manner, which suggested she was even more deeply anxious about her father than he had guessed. It even occurred to Rand that Susannah might be worried about more than Jeffrey Fitzgerald's health.

"I'm afraid I won't be a very entertaining hostess," Susannah continued, unaware of his scrutiny. "After all, you came here to discuss business with my father, didn't you? I know nothing about that."

"Good," Rand said decisively. "Discussing business over dinner gives me indigestion."

Jedediah, who had been watching their exchange with great interest, looked from one to the other and smiled. "Supper, Miss Susannah?"

"Yes, please. Oh, and have you settled Mr. Cabot in?"

"Certainly, miss. He's in the Lincoln Bedroom."

"The what?" Rand asked after the elderly servant had departed. "Did I hear him right?"

"It's the room President Lincoln used when he stayed here," Susannah explained as they crossed the entry hall to the dining room. The rooms were similar to the ones in the house in Richmond, but larger and furnished with a greater variety of styles, some dating from the previous century. Once in the dining room, Rand held out a Colonial rail-back chair for her.

"I had no idea Lincoln was ever here," Rand said as he took his own place. Jedediah proffered a bottle of wine for Rand's approval.

"It was right after the war," Susannah said, glad of any subject that would keep her mind off Rand. It was difficult enough to be seated so close to him, with only the width of the table between them, and not remember every moment of the episode in the garden. But she was determined to ignore the unsettling emotions caused by his nearness. "You know that Lincoln was captured when Washington fell?"

"I had heard that," Rand murmured as he set down his glass after tasting the wine and nodding his approval.

"Well, he was brought back to Virginia. He stayed in Richmond for a while and then he came here."

"Don't you mean that he was imprisoned here?"

"Strictly speaking," she admitted. "Though we never thought of his situation in that way."

"We? Oh, yes, of course, you would have been a little girl then."

"I was five." Despite herself, she smiled. "I remember hearing people talk about him before he came. The way they spoke of him, I couldn't figure out whether he was an angel or a devil."

"I guess that must have depended on whom you were
listening to."

"That's true. To our neighbors he was the incarnation
of their worst fears. To the slaves, he was that greatest of
rarities, a white man they trusted and loved."

Rand cast her a swift, appraising look. "I thought all
Southerners liked to believe that their slaves loved them."

Susannah shrugged. Jedediah had returned with the first
course. She glanced at the soft-shell crabs and smiled.
They were one of her favorite dishes. "There's a difference between what people want to believe and what's true.
I can't imagine any slave loving his master. The very idea
rings false."

"Then you must value freedom very much yourself."

She took a forkful of food, savoring the delicate taste on
the tip of her tongue, and swallowed slowly, aware that
Rand was watching her intently. "Surely that's a dangerous attitude for a woman," she said at length.

"Oh, I don't know. There are people who believe that
women should have more freedom, that they're really as
capable as men and should be accepted on those terms."

Susannah glanced at him from beneath the thick fringe
of her lashes. Cautiously she said, "Are you one of those
people?"

Rand laughed. He sat back and regarded her across the
table, aware of how extremely young and innocent she
looked, yet also conscious, as always, of a sense of great
strength where he would have expected none. "Would it
shock you very much if I said I was?"

"Shock isn't the right word. I would, however, be
surprised."

"What's the distinction?"

"Shock suggests a degree of disapproval. I happen to
think that women *should* have more rights, including the
right to vote. But in my experience, few men concur."

"Well, you've met one of them who does. I accept the
fact that men and women are different. In fact, I applaud

that difference. But I don't believe women are inferior. As you said, the mere idea rings false.''

"How extraordinary,'' Susannah murmured. She took a sip of wine and regarded him closely. She couldn't help but wonder how he had come by his very unusual attitude—if he was telling the truth. "What led you to this conclusion?''

"My knowledge of my mother and sisters, as well as certain other women.'' He was silent for a moment, returning her steady gaze, before he added, "I have the distinct impression that one more may be added to their number.''

Susannah laughed, more from nervousness than amusement. She was so accustomed to playing a role that the thought of exposing her true self to anyone was frightening. Yet she seemed on the verge of doing exactly that with Rand. Aunt Miriam's warning echoed in her mind. Until she knew exactly who he was and what he intended, she could not risk revealing herself to him.

"What a notion,'' she said with a breezy giggle. "Aren't you the gentleman who called me a meringue?''

"Anyone can make a mistake,'' Rand murmured.

"Oh, but you didn't. That's exactly what I am.''

"And pigs fly.''

"Pardon?'' Susannah said, certain she couldn't possibly have heard him right.

"Pigs, up in the sky. I'm not sure what you are, but *meringue* definitely doesn't fit. Have you ever been to France?''

Susannah shook her head, surprised but not troubled by his sudden change of subject. Whatever difficulties he caused her, keeping up wasn't one of them. "I've hardly been out of Virginia. That's one of the reasons I'm so unsophisticated.'' It shocked her to realize she was actually beginning to enjoy this game. Rand's chiding look almost made her laugh, though she managed to hold it in.

"I spent a couple of years in Paris,'' he said. "I didn't have much money at the time, so when I did get a chance to eat well, I tended to take advantage of it. For various reasons I won't go into"—memories of a lovely if insatiable comtesse flitted through his mind—"I attended a rather elaborate affair at Versailles. One of the courses was a goose stuffed with a chicken, stuffed with a duck, which in turn was stuffed with chestnuts. I forget what they called it, but it was the most elaborate creation I've ever eaten."

"Did it taste good?"

"Oh, yes, it was superb. You see, they deboned each of the birds so that they could slice straight through them. Each bite therefore contained a great variety of flavors and textures which went very well together."

Susannah lowered her eyes. Being compared to a multi-layered but tasty entrée had to be one of the odder compliments she had ever received. Still, she couldn't deny that it teased her fancy. "It sounds fascinating, though a great deal of work. I would hate to suggest that Hattie do it."

"Is she the rather ample person who was introduced to me as the housekeeper?"

Susannah nodded. "Hattie actually runs Belleterre, the house at least. She tolerates my attempts at management but doesn't take them too seriously."

"It sounds as though you and she get along very well."

"I respect her, and all the other people here. They were all slaves at one time or another, and they all had unpleasant if not outright terrible experiences before they came here. Yet they remain strong, capable, caring people."

Rand heard her out in silence, watching candlelight dance over her delicate features. He caught the faint scent of jasmine clinging to her and remembered breathing it when he had held her in the garden. At that unbidden recollection, his body instinctively hardened. He smothered a curse at his susceptibility and tried to turn his attention elsewhere.

"You were saying about Lincoln . . . ?"

"Oh, yes, before he came I was rather afraid of him.

But he hadn't been here very long before we became the greatest of friends.''

Rand knew very well that Lincoln loved children. His own sons were the joy of his life and had remained close to him despite everything that had happened. Rand could well imagine the defeated, sorrowful president and the small, bright-eyed girl Susannah must have been. She must have been a godsend to him.

"Didn't your father object?" he asked.

"No, of course not. My father had, and still has, a great deal of respect for Mr. Lincoln. That's part of the reason Lee brought him here.''

"I see," Rand murmured. Jedediah had arrived with the second course, a filet of beef in mushroom gravy flavored with parsley and thyme. He murmured apologies for its simplicity as he portioned it out, then refilled their wineglasses and withdrew.

"Does that mean," Rand continued, "that your father agrees with Lincoln's principles, those he continues to write and speak out about?"

"He isn't published in the South," Susannah said, hedging, "and his speeches are never reported in the papers here.''

"Still, I would hazard a guess that your father knows that Lincoln has never stopped arguing for reunification."

Susannah's fingers tightened on her fork until the knuckles showed white. Of all the topics they could possibly have gotten into, reunification was far and away the most dangerous. Yet she couldn't resist the opportunity to learn Rand's views on the subject.

"What do you think about it?" she asked innocently. "Do you believe North and South should be one country again?"

Rand hesitated. He was well aware that there was no more volatile subject so far as the Confederacy was concerned. Unlike the Union, which, by virtue of being the loser, could see reunification as a restoration of lost honor, the Confederacy had fought for and won what it believed was right. To turn away from that victory after the fact threatened to diminish the enormous sacrifices that had been made to achieve it in the first place. Not even the question of slavery could bring tempers to a boil more quickly. Which was why only Robert E. Lee had the necessary stature to guide his fellow Southerners through such rocky emotional and political waters.

Neither could Rand forget Susannah's comment in the garden about his being a Yankee, one of those who had believed they could get anything they wanted. In the context in which she had spoken, she had seemed to suggest that she thought the South was better off on its own. It was also possible that he was misinterpreting the comment of a young girl who had been caught unawares by her own feelings. Unsure of which was the case, he felt compelled to tread warily. "I believe that together we would form a greater and stronger nation than we can ever hope to achieve separately."

"It was tried once before," Susannah reminded him, "and didn't work. North and South were simply too different to get along."

"I'm not sure that's true. It seems to me that influential people on both sides decided that they were not going to compromise in any way. I think they wanted a war, and by God they got it."

The bitterness with which he uttered those last few words made Susannah wonder. Softly she asked, "Were you in it?"

"Oh, yes. From the beginning right through to the end. I was very idealistic, you see. When it started, I was twelve years old, but that didn't stop me from regarding it as a great adventure. I was big for my age, so there was no problem claiming to be sixteen. I joined the Twelfth New York Militia in April of sixty-one, got shipped out in time for Bull Run, and finally ended up at Antietam."

"My father was there," Susannah said softly. "With the First Virginia Cavalry. That's where his leg was injured."

Rand nodded. "He and I have talked about it. My unit went up against the Virginians near Dunker Church. I was also wounded."

Susannah couldn't help but wince. Though her father had told her little about Antietam, believing the story unfit for a young lady's ears, she had heard from other sources of the great climactic battle that had brought the War of Secession to an end and had established the independence of the Confederacy. It had been a horribly bloody encounter waged back and forth over the space of an entire day until, toward dusk, the Confederate forces broke through the Union lines and carried out a pincer movement that effectively trapped the enemy in a vise from which there was no escape.

Afterward stories were told of already wounded Union soldiers killed in cold blood on the battlefield, and of acts of great kindness and compassion by Confederate soldiers who carried their fallen foes to medical tents. Those were the two sides of human nature, nowhere more in evidence than on the battlefield.

"Were you seriously hurt?" she asked in a small voice.

He shrugged. "Not compared to some of the others. But I was lucky. Somebody, I've no idea who, brought me to one of the field infirmaries, and a Confederate doctor took care of me. It was a time of great confusion, but most of the doctors on both sides were taking care of the most gravely wounded first, regardless of which side they were on. I spent about six months afterward in a prisoner of war camp, then got repatriated home."

"I'm surprised you weren't left with some bitterness toward the South. Or were you?"

"Maybe at first, but only briefly. The South won fair and square. You had the better generals and the more determined soldiers. Understand, I think that if the war had gone on past sixty-three, it would have been a different story. In the end the South couldn't have stood against the sheer industrial power of the North. But you struck hard and fast, and were rewarded with a quick victory."

"My father says the same thing. He also believes that if the war had dragged on we would have lost. I think that's one of the reasons he opposes reunification. He fears that the South could be dwarfed by the North again, and made vulnerable to it."

Rand shook his head. "There's no chance of that, not since the Confederacy has industrialized the way it has. You're more than a match for us now."

"Which, of course, explains the interest in Canada." Abruptly aware of what she had said, Susannah broke off. She made a show of suddenly focusing on her food.

Rand wasn't fooled. "I wasn't aware that little Southern girls kept up with political talk, much less understood its significance," he murmured.

"I must have heard some gentlemen talking. Anyway, it's really all very boring, don't you think? I'd much rather hear about the latest fashions up north, or better yet, the theater. You still have far better theater than we do, you know, although we are improving. Why, just the other day I was saying—"

"Susannah," Rand interrupted firmly, "why do you do this?"

"Whatever do you mean?" she murmured, stooping so low as to actually flutter her eyelashes.

"Pretend that you don't have a brain in your beautiful head when I'm convinced the opposite is true."

Nervously she picked up her wineglass and took a sip. "What a thing to say. I suppose I should be insulted since everyone knows men don't like brainy women."

"Is that so? Actually I find them refreshing. It's a relief to be able to talk about something that is neither frivolous nor malicious."

"Is that what you think women talk about? Running on about fashion or running down their neighbors? What a dreary picture."

"Isn't it true?" Rand inquired with a faint smile. "If a woman isn't allowed to exercise her mind, what else is she going to talk about?"

Susannah agreed completely, but she couldn't risk saying so without revealing far more of herself than she could afford. As she grappled for a reply that was safe, Rand said inexorably, "We were talking about Canada."

With a sigh she accepted that there was no easy way out of the trap she had neatly stepped into. "All right, I am interested in more than who's marrying whom and whether or not we'll be wearing bustles next year. The idea of the North's trying to take over Canada fascinates me. Do you think you'll succeed?"

"Please," Rand said, throwing up his hands, "don't involve me in that insane venture. It's strictly McClellan's doing, his and that band of incompetents he calls his cabinet."

With a faint smile Susannah asked, "Do I take it you are not a supporter of the Union's noble president?"

"I don't trust any politician. They're all alike in the final analysis. As far as Canada goes, there is no possibility of the North's seizing it from the British. They simply won't permit it."

"They didn't have much choice when we declared our independence," Susannah pointed out.

"That was a different matter. There's no reason to believe Canadians have any interest in cutting their ties to the mother country. On the contrary, they've made it eminently clear that the Union's advances are most unwelcome. They'll fight to preserve their present status, and the British will fight with them."

"Then surely the Union will be defeated."

"As things stand right now," Rand agreed. "But should the Union and the Confederacy reunite, and turn their sights together toward Canada, it would be an entirely different matter."

"I imagine," Susannah said quietly, "that it would therefore behoove the British to do everything possible to prevent reunification."

Grimly Rand nodded, thinking of the *Essex* and its

mysterious cargo, of the rumors of a plot to derail the reunification talks before they even began, and above all, of the disturbing news he had received from Kidderly immediately before leaving Richmond. News that was, in fact, his primary reason for being at Belleterre. Jeffrey Fitzgerald's request that Rand join him there had been merely a welcome coincidence. Or at least Rand hoped it was, though he acknowledged that Jeffrey might have ulterior motives for the invitation.

He had difficulty imagining that a man of Jeffrey's sensibilities would be involved in any way with Damien Sanders. Still, he couldn't help but recall that Jeffrey seemed amenable to Thurston as a suitor for Susannah. The mere thought of Thurston's hands on her made Rand's temper flare. He got a firm grip on himself and glanced toward the French doors on the other side of the dining room.

"It looks like a pleasant evening. Perhaps you'd join me for a walk when we finish here."

Susannah hesitated. She had no business going any-where alone with Rand, yet she was sorely tempted. The memory of how his mouth had felt on hers almost destroyed her resolve. With a great effort of will she managed to shake her head. "I'm afraid not. I really must get to bed early so I'll be fresh tomorrow and able to cope with Hattie."

Rand was tempted to try to change her mind but thought better of it. Much as he would have liked to believe he could walk with her alone in a scented garden merely to continue their dinner table conversation, he admitted that wasn't true. He'd been honest when he'd told her that he approved of women with keen minds; part of her attraction for him was that he could discuss all sorts of matters with her.

But his appreciation of her intellect in no way lessened the intensity with which he was drawn to her in a sensual way. He wanted to make love to her, was sorely tempted to do so every time he looked at her. His chances for a restful night's sleep would hardly be aided by another frustrating bout of foreplay.

He smiled at her mention of Hattie. Not for a moment did he doubt that Susannah could handle just about anyone or anything she chose to, whether she had slept soundly or not. From her refusal to meet his eyes and the slight flush warming her cheeks he concluded that her feelings were not all that different from his own. That realization comforted him somewhat so that when she bid him good-night, he raised her hand to his lips, kissed it gently, and said, "Sleep well, Susannah. I'll look forward to seeing you in the morning."

Before she could think better of it, she murmured, "And I you, Rand."

Then she was gone, in a swirl of skirts, leaving only the slight fragrance of her perfume behind her.

Rand sat up in the library, sipping a brandy and leafing through Walt Whitman's *Leaves of Grass*, a copy of which he had found on the amply stocked shelves. It was getting on toward eleven P.M., according to the clock on the mantel, when Jedediah put his head in the door to ask if Rand required anything else.

"I'm fine, thanks," Rand assured the elderly man. "After I finish this nightcap, I'll turn in."

"You should be very comfortable, sir. President Lincoln's room is one of the nicest in the house."

"I'm sure it is. By the way, Jedediah, were you here when Lincoln stayed here?"

"Oh, yes, sir, I sure was. I remember him well."

"Miss Susannah speaks very highly of him."

Jedediah laughed. "She just adored that man, and he thought the world of her. Once he was feeling better, they went everywhere together. There was a guard of sorts, but that didn't amount to much. Everybody trusted Mr. Lincoln. He had the run of the place. Wasn't a day in good weather that he and Miss Susannah weren't out in the gardens or down to the river."

"It was generous of Mr. Fitzgerald to allow that."

"Oh, he wanted Mr. Lincoln to be content, no doubt about that. But it was Miss Miriam who really put them together. She's a kind lady, she is, and she knew they'd be good for each other." Jedediah smiled, his wizened face aglow with memories. "You know what Mr. Lincoln called Miss Susannah? He said she was just like a little butterfly flitting here and there, wanting to see and do everything."

"Mr. Lincoln has an affinity for children. He—" Rand broke off abruptly as shock roared through him. Lincoln had told him to keep an eye out for the butterfly. For a moment, Rand was tempted to believe that the former president had been engaging in a little matchmaking, but that would have been completely out of character. No one knew better than Lincoln the enormous seriousness of the challenge they faced. If he wanted Rand to meet Susannah, it was for reasons other than personal attraction. "Butterfly, you say?"

"Oh, yes," Jedediah confirmed, nodding. "That's what we called her for the longest time after. Still suits her, if you ask me."

Rand thought so, too. He thought so very much, and he was determined to find out if he was right.

10

Susannah spent most of the following morning clois-
tered in the kitchen with Hattie. Strictly speaking,
her advice wasn't necessary, but she enjoyed the
housekeeper's company as well as the warm, homey aromas
that filled the small building set a short distance from the
main house, to which it was linked by a covered walkway.

Gingham curtains fluttered at windows that looked toward
the river. One wall of the building was made of brick
and contained a beehive oven where bread and rolls were
baked. Across from it was an immense cast-iron stove that
was regularly blackened and polished so that not a smudge
could be seen on it. Tall mahogany-and-glass cabinets held
an assortment of cooking tools, everyday china, and
condiments.

Two large iceboxes contained the perishables. Twice a
week, blocks of ice stored in the plantation icehouse were
brought in by one of the huskier workmen. The slow,
steady dripping of the ice into the tin catch pan beneath it
was a familiar sound to Susannah. She listened to it absently as she sat at one of the long oak tables, snapping
green beans and chatting with Hattie.

"We sure do miss you when you're away, child," the
housekeeper said. "Personally, I wouldn't give a sniff for

Richmond, but everyone to their own tastes, I always says.''

"Belleterre is far nicer," Susannah agreed, "but city life can be exciting. Didn't you ever want to go there, meet handsome young men, have a good time?"

"Good time, indeed. People living cheek by jowl just ain't natural. I prefer to spread out." She patted her ample hips and smiled. "Fact is, I gotta."

"Oh, Hattie, you never change, and I hope you never will." On impulse, Susannah leaned over and gave her a hug. "Remember those ginger cookies you baked for me when I was a little girl?"

"What you talking about? I bake them for you every time you're here. I never saw anybody go through so many of them as you do, and you still a little wisp of a thing."

"But I haven't had any in ages, Hattie. Not in absolutely *ages*. Fact is, I've practically forgotten what they taste like. Maybe they aren't really as good as I remember."

Wise to Susannah's ways, Hattie merely laughed. "Maybe they ain't, but I'll still fix up a batch for you today. How would that be?"

"Wonderful. I'll eat them all, spoil my dinner, and have a wonderful time."

"You get sick and that Sukie will have my head."

"Get sick on your ginger cookies? It couldn't happen. I'll stay and help you bake them if you like."

Hattie cast her a puzzled look. "What you want to be inside for on a day like this? It's about the prettiest we've had so far. That new horse of yours is probably itching to go for a nice ride." With a teasing glimmer in her eyes, she added, "Why don't you ask that Yankee who's visiting to go with you? You could show off Belleterre to him."

"Not in a million years!" Susannah blurted. Recovering herself, she added, "He and Father are discussing business. I couldn't interrupt them." The truth was, she wouldn't. During the night her resolve to avoid Rand had hardened into absolute determination.

Now that she had left Richmond, she was effectively out of whatever plots were brewing. Frustrating as that might be for her, she had to be sensible. Whoever Rand was, he would undoubtedly not be staying long. She would simply keep out of his way until he left.

"Suit yourself, missy," Hattie said, "but if you ask me, that Yankee's about the best-looking man to come through these parts in quite some time."

"Why, Hattie, I didn't think you noticed things like that."

"Girl, the day I stop is the day you can bury me. Now get yourself out of my kitchen. I got cookie baking to do."

Susannah grabbed a handful of carrots on her way out the door, then went up to her room and changed into her dark green riding habit. Rosinante was pawing the ground in his stall when she arrived. He had already been out for a run with one of the grooms, but the moment he saw her he was eager to go again. Patting his nose gently, she laughed as he wolfed down the carrots.

"Come on, sweetheart," she murmured when he was saddled, "let's see how much dust we can kick up."

The groom eyed horse and rider with respectful caution as Rosinante pranced out of the stable yard. Everyone gave them a wide berth, which Susannah found amusing. The stallion's sheer size led people to presume much about his character that wasn't justified. But Susannah didn't mind. She had few qualms about riding around Belleterre on her own, nor did she have any objection to being on a very large and, at least to other people, intimidating animal.

The fields of cotton, wheat, and tobacco sprouting in the golden sun flowed past on either side of her as she gave Rosinante his head. They thundered along the narrow dirt road that circled the plantation. Susannah crouched low in the saddle, her hair streaming from beneath the confines of her wide-brimmed hat and her skirts fluttering about her. The sheer, heady exhilaration of the ride made her laugh with delight. Her emerald eyes sparkled, and a healthy glow lit her cheeks before she finally drew rein beside a small stream.

Having dismounted, she led Rosinante to the water and watched to make sure he drank slowly. When he was settled munching grass nearby, she sat down beneath a willow tree, eased off her boots and socks, and wiggled her toes in the grass.

She remembered her father telling her when she was a little girl that the fairies came out at dawn to collect the dew in golden pails. Several times she had tried to wake up early enough to see them, but she had never managed it. Smiling at her own whimsy, she leaned her head against the trunk of the tree and closed her eyes.

Rosinante wandered some distance away. She glanced at him through her lashes, saw that he was behaving himself, and closed her eyes again. A bee buzzed past her, and she fluttered her hand to keep him moving. The sweet scent of sun-warmed grass surrounded her. She was almost drowsing when a sudden sound brought her upright.

Rand stood over her. His face was obscured by shadows, but she thought he was smiling. Seeing that she was awake, he knelt down beside her, and she saw that he was indeed smiling.

"You make quite a pretty picture when you're asleep, Miss Susannah," he said softly.

Heat stained her cheeks. The unwarranted intimacy disturbed her. She looked away while trying to collect herself. "What are you doing here?"

Rand laughed. He stretched out beside her, ignoring her startled glance. "That's what I like about you. You get straight to the point."

Susannah only wished that she could. She had never before been so close to a man in a position of such intimacy. The warmth of his body seemed to reach out to engulf her own. She was acutely aware of the tantalizing scent of him, the faint shadows in the hollows of his lean cheeks, the slight nick on his chin where he had cut

himself shaving that morning. In a desperate effort to
distract herself, she murmured, "I didn't mean to sound
rude, but—"

"But you'd still like to know why I wasn't wherever it
was you expected me to be, instead of turning up here to
disturb your solitude."

"Since you put it that way . . ."

"My business with your father is more or less concluded." He cast her a teasing look from the corner of his
eye. "I'm sure you'll be relieved to hear that your cotton
went for a good price. You'll be able to afford all those
little fripperies you'd have me believe are so dear to your
heart."

Susannah shrugged. She had never doubted what the
outcome of their negotiations would be. "We look to bring
in a bumper crop this year, but a lot of other planters
aren't doing as well. So, of course, ours will go dearly."

"How do you know that?" Rand asked with deceptive
mildness.

She frowned slightly and sat up, slowly so as not to give
the impression that she was in any way discomfited by his
nearness. Better that he should think being so close to him
had no effect on her at all. Warily, she cast him a sidelong
glance to see if she had managed to convey the desired
impression. His long body was stretched out, the collar of
his shirt open and his arms folded to form a pillow for his
head. As she cast her glance along his supine length, she
couldn't help but notice the snugness of his riding pants
over a certain portion of his anatomy.

Susannah flushed and looked hastily away. She was
enormously annoyed at herself for her own wayward
thoughts, and equally relieved that Rand had apparently
not noticed. Stiffly she said, "Know what?"

"About the crop—that it's bigger than your neighbors',
and that such a difference means more money for you."

"It simply stands to reason."

"If you say so," he said skeptically.

She waited a moment to be sure he wouldn't press the issue, then said, "Since you've concluded your business, I presume you'll be leaving shortly."

He opened one eye to look at her. "Anxious to be rid of me?"

"Certainly not," she said firmly. "It makes no difference to me whether you go or stay."

"Not even when you take into consideration how well I've entertained you?"

Her eyes widened. She had not imagined that he would speak of what had passed between them, even obliquely. It simply wasn't done. Still, there was a certain excitement to treading on dangerous ground, however lightly. "Whatever do you mean?" she murmured.

He had shut his eyes again. His lashes struck her as being absurdly long and lush for a man. Nothing else about him, however, was in the least womanly. She was conscious of a sudden, irksome sense of confinement in her riding habit, an irrational desire to throw it off and be free in both body and soul. Even the thought was dangerous. She pushed it aside relentlessly.

"It's only that I get the impression you find most people, not to say life itself, fairly predictable," he said equably. "It probably does you good to encounter someone occasionally who shakes you up."

"And you do?" She managed to sound appropriately disbelieving.

His lips quirked in a teasing grin. "If you deny it, I'll just have to try harder."

"No," Susannah said quickly. "You've already taught me quite enough about Yankee brashness. Oh, I admit that when you're gone, life will be a tad less amusing, but that's fine with me."

"Is it?" He moved so swiftly that she had no warning. One moment his lean, hard body was stretched out beside her, the next she was lying on her back with Rand above her, his face close to hers. Save for the sudden intake of her breath, silence reigned between them. She was aware of the soft murmur of the water as it flowed nearby, of the swish of their horses' tails as they companionably munched grass, of the far-off cry of a whipporwill seeking its nest.

Sunlight filtered through the leafy bower above her head to reflect molten gold in his eyes. His skin was lightly burnished, and every plane and hollow of his rugged features stood out clearly. Her lips parted. Unable to resist, she raised her hand and pressed a finger to his mouth.

"Rand . . ."

Her voice was only a breath, no more, but the sound was ample to his needs. He bent his head, holding his weight on his braced arms, and slowly, gently, tasted her, savoring her lips until their pleasure became mutual. They played with each other, tenderly, unabashedly, delighting in their discoveries, at once innocent and sensual, without shame or regret.

His mouth slipped from hers to search out the scented hollow between her collarbones. As he found it, she dipped her head back and moaned softly. Her hands clenched on his back, feeling the play of steely muscle through the thin linen of his shirt. He was all sun-warmed strength and mounting tension, a tension that spiraled upward in her, too, carrying them both to an unknown but longed for conclusion.

The moment in the garden was eclipsed, surpassed by a passion to which had been added the grace of slowly growing familiarity. They hung in the misty, indeterminant stage between strangers and lovers. Neither regretted the need to pass through levels of intimacy. Neither wished to rush the culmination. Without speaking, and, for Susannah at least, without truly knowing, neither doubted the outcome of what was happening between them.

When he raised his head at last and smiled at her, a soft sigh escaped her slightly swollen lips. "What is more dreadful?" she asked. "To break a rule and feel guilty, or to break it and be glad?"

He laughed softly, taken aback by her train of thought—or, more correctly, that she was capable of any thought at all. He had hoped, indeed believed, that the kiss had affected her sufficiently to at least temporarily halt the restless questing of her mind. Wryly he realized that he should have known better. "Guilt," he assured her, "is highly overrated. I can't believe anything good has ever come of it. In fact, its very anticipation has led to more twisted and warped behavior than any other emotion."

Susannah swallowed with some difficulty. Her heart was still beating so rapidly as to be painful, and an odd, melting sensation permeated the center of her being. She had a sudden, all but irresistible urge to cast aside reason, caution, even common sense, and yield completely to him. Desperately she scrambled to retain a fingerhold on rationality. "Nonetheless, everything I've been raised to believe tells me that this is wrong."

He sighed and rolled onto his side, drawing her with him. Strands of ebony hair mingled with gold. "Why?"

"It's . . . unchaste."

"We have a way to go before that."

She propped herself up to look at him. "Isn't the intention the same as the deed?"

"Not quite. Intention is never irreparable, only action. Besides, I don't consider you unchaste."

"I don't have to point out," she said, "that you have a vested interest in saying that."

"It's still the truth. This idea that has somehow gotten about that women shouldn't feel passion is a terrible distortion and burden. It robs men as well as women of much of the beauty life offers."

"I agree with you in theory," Susannah said. "Yet you must acknowledge passion is dangerous."

Rand laughed softly and touched the back of his hand to her cheek in a gentle caress. "Oh, yes, it is that. Rarely has my peace of mind been under such attack."

The corners of her mouth lifted slightly. "Should I apologize?"

"Oh, no, never." He regarded her tenderly. "If it makes you feel better to try to reason all of this out, go right ahead. But I will tell you"—he smiled in self-mockery—"from the vaunted position of my greater years that it won't work. What's happening between us has nothing to do with reason. In case you have any remaining doubts about that . . ." His hand cupped the back of her head as he slowly drew her to him again.

Their lips had only begun to touch when a distant sound made Susannah pull away from him and look in the direction of the river.

"What's that?" she asked, as much to herself as to him.

"What?" Rand glanced to where she was looking. On the other side of the stream, a party of three riders, one slightly built, another bulky in form, and the third somewhere in between, was passing. Instinctively Susannah stiffened. She was taken aback by the sudden intrusion of others into so private a scene, but more than that, the identity of the riders appeared significant.

The slightly built man was Damien Sanders, not completely a surprise because he owned the plantation adjoining Belleterre. She had thought he was still in Richmond, but there was nothing untoward about his being on his own land whenever he chose to be.

It was, however, a shock to realize that his fellow riders were Captain Fortescue and the man she knew as Burke. Straining her ears, she struggled to hear a snatch of conversation from the threesome, but they were too far away. The rush of water obscured whatever they might be saying, though she could see clearly enough that they were talking. Their conversation appeared animated but not heated. They seemed to be in a uniformly excellent mood, laughing and smiling as they rode.

She waited until she was certain they had passed. Only then did she disengage herself from Rand and stand up. He had remained motionless, his eyes hooded as he observed both the riders and Susannah's reaction to them. Now he also rose and regarded her closely. Softly he said, "You're upset," though whether her mood resulted from the passion of their kiss or what had happened afterward he wasn't sure.

"What? Oh, no, I simply must get back." She called softly to Rosinante, who came quickly at her summons. Rand's horse followed as promptly.

"Who was that with Sanders?" he asked as he helped her to mount.

Susannah hesitated. He must have recognized Burke, since he had also seen him on the docks, yet she could hardly remind him of that meeting without revealing her own unfortunate involvement in the incident. Yet she had to wonder why he was asking her what he already knew, as though the question was a test of some sort.

"Guests of his, I suppose," she hedged, once again aware of his proximity. Sweet, languorous warmth still suffused her body. The fragrant grass on which they had lain beckoned almost irresistibly. She had to exercise all her strength of will to turn away.

"You seemed surprised to see them," Rand said gently. "And now you seem to feel that you have to run off."

Susannah settled the reins in her hands and gazed down at Rand from the safety of Rosinante's broad back. "I am not running," she said stiffly. "It is simply past time for me to go home."

He laughed, clearly unconvinced, but mounted as well. The moment he was seated, she dug her heels impatiently into Rosinante's side. Both horses broke into a canter. Susannah would have liked to gallop home, but she could hardly do so without further arousing his suspicions. Instead, she forced herself to smile and look unconcerned.

"It hardly matters to me who Damien invites," she said, "though I must say he isn't known for his hospitality. Still, I suppose even he has his moments."

"I suppose . . ." Rand repeated thoughtfully.

They were silent much of the way home. In the stable

yard Susannah handed Rosinante to a groom. As quickly as she could, she took her leave from Rand and hurried upstairs to pen a note to Miriam. Her aunt had to be informed of Burke's whereabouts, and of Sanders's involvement. She was almost grateful for both, since they distracted her from more personal considerations. Eventually she would have to think about what had happened between her and Rand, but for the moment she was glad to have something else demand her attention.

Rand, however, had other ideas. He was not one for putting off what was best dealt with at once. So Susannah discovered a short time later when she came downstairs with the sealed note in her hand. Rand was lounging against one of the pillars that framed the entry hall, his very posture declaring that he had been waiting for her. He took in her rumpled hair, her flushed face, and her general air of urgency with a quick, perceptive glance. "Something wrong, Susannah?"

Taken aback by his sudden reappearance, she shook her head. "Wrong? Why nothing, of course. I just remembered that I had a letter to send, and I don't want to miss the afternoon boat." The paddleboat would be putting in at the Fitzgeralds' dock within the next half hour or so. She needed to find a servant and dispatch him with the letter. "If you'll excuse me . . ."

"Running off again, Susannah?"

Her soft, full mouth thinned. With hindsight she realized it was only natural that he interpret her sudden withdrawal as a reaction to him. But she also suspected he was trying to provoke her. Unfortunately, he was succeeding. "Why, Mr. Cabot," she drawled, "whatever would I want to do that for?"

He took a step toward her, looking down at her from the considerable difference in their heights. Her riding boots made her slightly taller than she would be in dancing slippers, but his sheer size still made her feel smaller than she truly was.

"I can think of several reasons," he murmured.

Daring greatly, she smiled at him. "I wonder what they could be?"

His tawny eyes narrowed slightly. "When you were a little girl, did you play with fire?"

"Of course not. I was a very well behaved child." Actually she had been a little hellion, but she saw no reason to tell him that.

She didn't have to; he had already guessed it. "Liar," he said softly as he bent his head to hers. She could have stepped back, or even darted around him, but instead she remained absolutely still, knowing what was going to happen and powerless to prevent it.

His lips were firm and cool against hers. His hands rested lightly on her shoulders as he drew her to him. She felt the rough texture of his jacket against her cheek, the warmth of his body reaching out to engulf her, and the welcome strength of his arms as they closed around her narrow waist. Beside the river she had felt passion. Now she felt that passion plus a deep sense of rightness, startling in its incongruity.

Every particle of common sense that she possessed told her what she was doing was wrong. Aside from the whole issue of being involved with him, they were standing in the entry hall, for heaven's sake, where anyone might see them. But that was an inconsequential consideration when compared with the awakening demands of her body—and her heart.

In the last moment, before her mind shut down entirely, she consoled herself with the thought that with Burke and Fortescue in the neighborhood, she was back in the game. She therefore had a duty to get to know Rand better in order to discover his part in whatever was going on. Aunt Miriam would undoubtedly disapprove of her methods, but she needn't know of them.

Such was the power of that rationalization that Susannah was able to relax completely and give herself up to Rand's caresses. The now familiar taste and feel of him evoked tremors of sensual pleasure deep within her. She twined her arms around his neck, which pressed her breasts even more closely against him. His hold on her tightened. She was bent back slightly as his mouth claimed hers completely.

Slowly, with more uncertainty than reluctance, her lips parted. His tongue slipped lightly past to tease and cajole hers. Susannah gasped at such intimacy even as she discovered that it delighted her, as did the warm strength of his arms which held her to him, the gentle but insistent stroke of his hands down the slender line of her back, the hardness of his masculinity through the layers of their clothing, clothing which at that moment was unbearably restrictive. Susannah shuddered against him, overwhelmed by the desire to feel his body against her own, as it had been by the river, only this time with no barrier between them, not even her own fears. So powerful was that need that she lost all sense of time, place, and reason, yielding to him with a passion that matched his own.

Long moments later, Rand raised his head and laughed shakily. "I have to be out of my mind."

Susannah gazed up at him, uncomprehending for a moment. Slowly she drew away. Her breath was labored, and her lips felt unusually tender, acutely sensitive, and quite bereft. She inhaled raggedly as his words sank in. With stark honesty she murmured, "I should say the same thing. This is absolutely insane."

Rand recognized her sincerity at the same moment that he realized the full extent of their danger. Until just then he hadn't understood how much he was relying on her own innocence to protect them both. Now, knowing that she wanted him as much as he did her, respecting the proprieties was going to be well nigh impossible. Still, they both had to try.

As calmly as he could manage, he said, "It must be the full moon."

"It's daylight."

He shot her a quick, chiding grin. "Don't split hairs. How old are you—eighteen? I'm ten years older." He stepped slightly back without releasing her. A derisive smile played about his firm mouth. His tawny eyes were shadowed with self-contempt. "I'm a rough-edged Yankee practically old enough to be your father, while you're—"

"Now wait just a moment," Susannah interrupted. Her gaze had turned dark and stormy, much like her temper. He was being insufferably patronizing, and she was not about to let him get away with it. "I can do arithmetic as well as you can. For you to have fathered a child my age, you would have had to have made medical history, not to mention been extremely careless."

Rand's eyebrows shot up. It wasn't often that anyone managed to genuinely shock him, but Susannah had a rare talent for it. "Careless? What do you know about—?"

"Never mind. As far as what you think of me, I don't want to hear it. You've already made your feelings clear." She was recalling his infamous meringue comment, not easily forgotten. Why she should care for this man was absolutely beyond her. He was insufferably arrogant in his presumptions about her. Tears stung her eyes. She turned quickly away, but not before he had seen them.

"Susannah," he murmured, reaching out a lean finger to touch the sudden moisture on her cheeks. "Don't . . ." His voice had gone suddenly soft and almost unbearably tender. Instinctively he began to draw her closer, only to stop abruptly. "Damn it," he murmured. "Since when did I become so susceptible to a woman's tears?" Stung by his own vulnerability, he added, "You probably learned in your cradle how to turn them on and off at will, and I fall for it. I can't believe I'm that—"

"That what?" Susannah demanded furiously. For just a moment, she had felt a glimmer of genuine understanding between them, only to be denied it by his insistence on seeing her as a manipulative, scheming creature out of his own fantasies.

Pure, wholesome rage swept through her. She stamped her foot so loudly on the marble floor that the entry hall rang with the sound. Through gritted teeth she said, "You are the blindest, the dumbest, the most stubborn man I have ever met in my entire life. If you think for a moment that I have the slightest interest in you—"

Rand had just opened his mouth, undoubtedly to reply, when a voice behind them derailed whatever intentions either might have had. "Susannah! What on earth—?"

Turning, the guilty pair confronted Jeffrey Fitzgerald emerging from his study, his face blank with surprise at the tirade he had just overheard. He looked in bewilderment at his daughter, who still stood within Rand's embrace. "Have you taken leave of your senses?" he said.

His gaze shifted to Rand with more than a hint of suspicion. "I think you had both better answer that question. Rand, you're my guest. I like and respect you, but I would hate to think you could take advantage of my hospitality."

Rand's face darkened. He had no doubt about what Jeffrey Fitzgerald meant, any more than he doubted that he had come perilously close to doing exactly what the older man feared. Embarrassment swept over him. Genuine manners and a high standard of morality, as opposed to hypocritical posturing, were the foundation of his life. He had never before come close to violating the principles by which he lived. The realization that he had done so now truly dismayed him.

"Jeffrey," he said swiftly as he stepped away from Susannah, "I'm truly sorry. Please believe me, I mean no disrespect to either you or your daughter. But Susannah is . . . a very lovely young lady."

"I thought I was a spoiled brat," the lady in question muttered.

"We were having a slight disagreement," Rand explained, somewhat lamely.

Jeffrey's mouth twitched. He looked from one to the

other of the pair as his anger died away. He remembered
all too well what it was like to be overwhelmingly at-
tracted to a woman. Nothing else was so guaranteed to
turn even the most sensible and honorable man into a
blithering idiot. "It sounded as if you were having a
full-blown battle," he commented.

His daughter tossed her lovely head and looked unperturbed. "Don't be silly, Father. What would Mr. Cabot
and I have to argue about?"

"I have no idea," Jeffrey said blandly. His tone nonetheless made it clear that he intended to find out. "However, to move on to a more appropriate topic for the
moment, Damien Sanders has left the city early. It seems
he removed to Five Oaks several days ago. I've invited
him to supper." With a meaningful glance at his daughter,
he added, "Thurston will also be coming."

"Wonderful," Susannah murmured under her breath.

"What was that, daughter?"

"I said I really must speak with Hattie about the menu."

"Then may I suggest that you do so now?"

Susannah knew a dismissal when she heard one. She
also suspected her father wanted to talk at greater length
with Rand. The idea of the two men discussing her was
provoking, to say the least, but there was nothing she
could do to prevent it. She went off in a mutinous mood
with a glance over her shoulder that spoke volumes of
what she would do if their conversation took an untoward
turn.

Hattie had finished the ginger cookies, which were cool-
ing on the table near the windows. Susannah plopped
herself down, put a cookie into her mouth, and asked,
"What's for supper?"

"Don't talk with your mouth full," Hattie said automatically. Upon closer inspection she added, "What hornet's
nest did you sit on?"

"No such thing. I've just decided that I absolutely
cannot abide men."

Hattie gave a deep, wheezing chuckle. "This wouldn't have nothing to do with that Yankee, would it?"

"He's insufferable. As bullheaded as they come."

"Speaking of bullheaded . . ." Hattie said with an affectionate if pointed smile.

"I admit to being a shade strong-willed, that's all."

"Mmmm. And a mule's just a sweet little critter what'll do anything you want him to."

Susannah finished her cookie, leaned forward, and cupped her chin in her hand. "Am I really mulish, Hattie?"

"No such thing, child. You've just got a mind of your own, and there ain't nothing wrong with that. After all, ain't that how Miss Miriam wanted you to be?"

"Yes, but probably my father wouldn't have approved, if he had realized the ideas I was picking up."

"Is that what worries you? Child, don't you know that your daddy understands you better than anyone else? That's what love does for a person. Oh, I know there's lots of stuff you keep to yourself, but he knows you for the person you are and that's what really counts."

"What makes you think I keep things to myself?"

Hattie cast her a speaking glance. "Sure you want to talk about that, child?"

Susannah bit her lip. She wondered how much Hattie knew, guessed it was probably more than she would have liked her to, and subsided. As Hattie suggested, some things were best left undisturbed. "We're having company for supper."

"I know. Jedediah told me."

The shortness of Hattie's response made Susannah smile. She knew the old cook had no liking for either of the Sanderses. Their reputation for being tight with their servants was well known. "Don't mix the salt up with the sugar like you did the last time when you were making those little tarts for dessert. Funny how only Thurston's and his uncle's tarts got made wrong."

"These things happen," Hattie said with a shrug. "Not

all the time, of course. Got that Yankee to think of now. Wonder if he likes seafood gumbo.''

"Oh, he does," Susannah said brightly. "But he likes it really spicy, with lots of hot pepper."

Hattie gave her a skeptical look. "You sure about that?"

Susannah took another cookie and gazed innocently back at her. "Of course. There's nothing he hates worse than bland food."

Hattie nodded in approval. "Sensible man. Bland food makes for bland people, I always says. Well, he won't have anything to complain about with my cooking."

Susannah hid a smile, finished her cookie, and reached for a third. Hattie's wooden mixing spoon caught her across the back of the hand, lightly but firmly. "I'm not sweating over a hot stove so as you can spoil your appetite. Get along now and freshen yourself up. You look like something the cat dragged in."

"Yes, ma'am," Susannah murmured meekly. She whistled softly to herself as she left the kitchen. Supper should be entertaining, if nothing else.

11

A bsolutely delicious," Rand said. He sat back in his chair, removed the napkin he had thoughtfully tucked into his collar, and grinned at Jedediah. "Easily the best seafood gumbo I've ever had. It's difficult to find it properly seasoned, but this was perfection."

"I'll tell Hattie, sir. She'll be real pleased."

Thurston rather ostentatiously took a sip from the water glass he had insisted on having refilled half a dozen times during dinner. "Personally, I prefer less potent food. No offense intended, Jeffrey," he added hastily.

"None taken," his host assured him with a benign smile. "Everyone's palate is different. I, however, enjoyed it."

Susannah stifled a sigh. The gumbo had been hotter than usual, enough so that upon first tasting it, she had presumed that a Yankee accustomed to baked beans and brown bread, or whatever it was they ate up north, would have his tongue burned off.

Rand, however, had dug in with a will, accepting a second and even a third helping. All the while he'd smiled at her across the table as though he knew exactly what she had done and was taunting her for it.

That wasn't really being fair. He'd been an exemplary

guest, though there was no indication that whatever her father had said to him had in any way dampened his spirits. On the contrary, he'd gone out of his way to be provoking by encouraging Damien to discuss his political views.

The old man was a throwback to a very different time. He persisted in referring to the blacks as niggers, insisted loudly that they'd all been better off when they were slaves, and contended that the South had been chosen by the Almighty to show the rest of the world the way things ought to be done.

Thurston had looked more bored than embarrassed by his uncle's diatribe. He had nodded in the right places, made soothing noises, but otherwise effaced himself. Susannah thought him so thoroughly under the older man's thumb that his lack of backbone sickened her. Her stomach tightened at the mere thought that her father might be serious about Thurston as a potential husband.

"Damn fool waste of money," Damien muttered as they got up from the table. Since Susannah was the only lady present, the convention of her leaving the men to their brandy had been waived. They were all withdrawing to the parlor so that the servants could clear up.

"What's that, Damien?" Jeffrey inquired mildly.

"All that seafood, expensive stuff. Ought to tell your cook to substitute something cheaper. No need for it to be fresh when it's in a stew."

"I'm afraid Hattie has her standards, Damien. She wouldn't be happy if I suggested she do anything of that sort."

"Exactly what I was talking about. Free a nigger and he gets uppity right away. Don't stand for it at my place. They toe the line or I sell them downriver."

"You really should consider manumission," Jeffrey said quietly as they took their places in the parlor. "After all, starting next year the tax on slaves is going to be prohibitive."

"That's more of Lee's doing," Damien grumbled. "Damned if I know who he thinks he is. I fought tooth and nail against that bill, but Lee had it so sewn up nothing could stop it."

"The money will be used to improve public education," Jeffrey explained to Rand, who had been following the discussion with interest. "Many of us here in Virginia and elsewhere in the South believe that universal education is essential to both a good work force and an informed electorate."

"Another damned waste," Damien scoffed. "You can't teach niggers and white trash anything except to do as they're told. And this idea that they ought to be encouraged to vote, that positively makes my blood run cold. All Lee's doing," he repeated as he snatched a snifter of brandy off the silver tray Jedediah proffered. "Man's a goddamn traitor, if you ask me."

"Isn't that rather strong language?" Rand inquired. "After all, I had the impression that Lee is still the South's greatest hero."

"In most eyes he is," Susannah said softly. "But a small number of people believe he is leading the Confederacy in the wrong direction."

"We'll see how small it is, missy," Damien said. "There's a change coming, mark my words. A big change."

"Now, uncle," Thurston said, intervening, "surely we've tried Susannah's patience quite enough with all this talk of politics." He shot a censorious look at Rand. "Perhaps it's the custom up north to impose on a lady's tolerance, but that isn't the case here."

Damien was about to respond when he apparently thought better of it and subsided. Silence reigned for a few moments before Susannah said, "What made you leave Richmond early, Thurston? I thought you'd be staying several more weeks."

He looked at a loss for an answer, leading her to conclude that he had come along simply because his uncle told him to. He would hardly be eager to admit that, though. "The city is so tiresome at this time of year," he said instead. "The heat and the flies are a danger, besides being annoying. I really think the social season should be better arranged to take those factors into account."

"That certainly is something to think about," Rand said. "Why don't you start up a movement, Thurston? You'd be the man for it, if you ask me."

Susannah bit her lip, well aware of the derision that prompted Rand's comments. Thurston, however, was blissfully obtuse. "Well, yes," he said, "I suppose I would be. I do have a certain amount of influence."

"While you're at it," Jeffrey said innocently, "something should be done about the shocking lack of organization to the social season. Someone simply decides to give a party and does so, regardless of whether or not it conflicts with another event. Some very delicate situations have arisen as a result."

"You're absolutely right," Thurston said. "There ought to be some sort of clearinghouse to prevent that sort of thing. A central scheduler"—he pronounced the word in the British manner—"to avoid such embarrassments."

Susannah lowered her eyes, certain that, if she did not, the unholy humor in them would be noticed. She had never before heard her father bait Thurston. He had always treated him kindly and with a measure of tolerance she herself thought excessive. But something had happened to change all that, much to her delight.

As Thurston rumbled on about getting the Richmond elite better organized, and Damien sipped morosely at his brandy, Susannah studied Rand as surreptitiously as she could manage. He looked very fine in his fawn gray evening trousers and darker dinner jacket. The fabric was perfectly cut to his broad, muscular form. His thick golden hair glowed in the gaslight. Shadows both obscured and highlighted the chiseled planes of his face. Her gaze focused on his well-shaped mouth. Heat grew within her as she remembered his touch.

"Susannah?"

"What—?" Abruptly returned to herself, she realized Thurston had asked her something she had failed to note. "Pardon?"

"I said, why don't we work together on this project?" Ever ready to put his foot in his mouth, he went on. "After all, it hasn't escaped my notice that you are not quite as well thought of in Richmond society as I would like you to be. This could go a long way toward improving everyone's opinion of you," he finished obliviously.

Taken aback, Susannah stared at him. Her father, however, drew the line at such tactlessness. "I've never noticed anything wrong in the way my daughter is thought of," Jeffrey said coldly. "Frankly, I'm amazed to hear you claim that's the case."

While Thurston fumbled for a reply, Damien laughed wheezily. "They're jealous of her. So long as she's footloose and fancy-free, there isn't a mama in Richmond's elite who'll think well of your Susannah."

"Then that's their loss," Jeffrey replied, "not Susannah's. I cannot imagine why she should be expected to court people who are so petty minded to begin with."

"I assure you, sir," Thurston sputtered, "I didn't mean that she—"

"If you don't mind," Susannah interrupted firmly. "Since this matter does concern me, I would prefer to speak for myself. It's true that I'm aware of not being universally liked by our social circle, and I'm sorry about that. But I don't lose any sleep over it. Other things are far more important to me."

"I can't imagine what," Thurston said. "The esteem of our peers is essential to a happy life."

"That's true," Susannah agreed. "But it all depends on who you consider your peers to be. The people whose

opinions matter to me have never given me any reason to
believe that I disappoint them.'' As she said this, she
looked boldly at Rand, daring him to contradict her.

Instead, he smiled and inclined his head graciously. "Of
all the many words I can think of to describe you,
disappointing is not among them."

Susannah's cheeks warmed, but for once she didn't
mind if he saw. He made her feel very daring, very feminine, and above all, very excited. If she hadn't known
better, she would have almost thought she was falling—

Susannah broke off that thought abruptly. It was absolutely unthinkable that she should be having tender feelings for Rand. Nothing was more unlikely, foolhardy, or
inappropriate. Granted, he aroused in her a certain . . .
agitation. But that was merely something any healthy,
normal young woman was liable to feel for an extremely
handsome, dashing, challenging, frustrating man.

Putting on her most ingenuous smile, she murmured,
"Really, Mr. Cabot, how very gracious of you."

He inclined his head gravely. "Why, Miss Fitzgerald, I
thought we had established that I was the furthest thing
from gracious."

"You have your moments, Mr. Cabot."

"How nice of you to say so, Miss Fitzgerald."

"Not very often, of course."

He laughed softly, his gaze intent. "I would never wish
to be thought predictable or tedious."

Susannah took a deep, sustaining breath. Once again she
had the odd but not at all unpleasant sensation that the
world had narrowed down to just the two of them. She was
vaguely aware of her father's listening to them with a
bemused smile and of Thurston's scowling, but nothing
mattered except Rand and the light dancing in his amber
eyes. "I can assure you, Mr. Cabot, you have absolutely
nothing to fear in that direction. In fact . . ."

"Pray continue, Miss Fitzgerald."

She hesitated, aware that she was treading on dangerous ground and not quite certain how she had gotten there. There was a hint of desperation in the glance she shot at her father.

Seeing her confusion, he said gently, "It might be better for you to favor us with a tune, my dear. You and Rand can always continue this fascinating conversation at another time."

Susannah breathed a palpable sigh of relief not untinged by a lingering hint of regret. Much as she appreciated her father's intercession—had, indeed, asked for it—she would have liked to have been able to deal with Rand on his own terms. At the moment, however, she did not feel up to them.

"Of course," she said softly, "if you'd like." She rose gracefully, crossed the room, and took her seat before the piano, all the while aware that Rand was watching her. Her back was very straight, her head high, as she rifled through the pages of music before her and decided on a selection.

Moments later the pure notes of a Bach cantata poured from her fingers. Susannah played very well, not only with mechanical dexterity but with an intensity of feeling and a sensitivity to the music itself that could not be taught. She lost herself in the flow of dazzling passages conceived by a genius who seemed to speak to her directly.

Her personal concerns dissolved, replaced for at least a time by a sense of oneness with a higher vision. Her slender body swayed slightly as she moved to the music. Her emerald eyes glowed with her inner pleasure. All unaware, she made an exquisite picture of feminine grace and strength.

Rand was enthralled. He was already becoming accustomed to the idea that Susannah would always surprise him, but he was still unprepared for this latest insight into her character. His own standards for musical excellence

were very high; he had expected her to be merely competent and had feared she might be less.

Whichever had been the case, he would have sat through
the performance politely and found something nice to say
at the end. Now he didn't have to try. He was as captivated by the music as she herself; even more so, he was
enchanted by the depth of emotion he felt in her.

He forgot where he was, who he was with, everything
except Susannah and her music. Nothing else existed.
Without knowing that he did so, he leaned forward intently, his gaze locked on her.

For a moment after she finished, neither of them moved.
Susannah remained still, her fingers lingering on the keys,
slowly coming out of what had almost been a trance. Rand
hung suspended for an instant on the last pure note of
sound. Then, with complete sincerity, he stood up and
applauded.

"Bravo, Susannah," he said. "That was magnificent."

She turned to him and their eyes met. False modesty did
not become her. "Thank you, Rand," she said, and inclined her head graciously.

He had come up to join her at the piano, standing at her
shoulder. Her skin was very white in the gaslight, all the
more so in contrast to the rippling darkness of her hair
falling over her shoulders. She made him think of deep,
hidden places, forest glens and shadowed grottoes. She
was part wild thing, part angel, all woman. And he could
no more hide his fascination for her than he could deny his
own existence.

Unbidden the thought rose of what he suspected about
her. Looking at her as she was just then, he found it even
more incredible that she might be Lincoln's butterfly. The
name fit, but nothing else. He was half convinced he must
be wrong. But if he was, then what reason did she have for
playing a role so at odds with her true character?

Anger at her flared through him. If she was involved in

the underground, he intended to put a stop to her activities before they could go any further. It was insane that she should so endanger herself. He would have it out with her, set her straight, make sure she understood that such a thing simply would not do. She would be perturbed at first, he admitted, but ultimately she would be grateful to him. He smiled faintly, indulging in thoughts of where such gratitude might lead.

Until Thurston interrupted his pleasant train of thought. "Very nice, my dear. Ably done."

Rand frowned. His desire to protect Susannah—with or without her approval—extended to shielding her from even the most ordinary insensitivity. Irritation shone deep in his eyes. She saw it and lightly touched his hand. Without having to speak of it, he understood. She expected nothing more from Thurston, would have been astounded if he had been capable of anything else. Moreover, his opinion was of no concern to her. She played for the music, not the audience.

Jeffrey's gaze did not leave the pair at the piano as he said, "Will you favor us with another? The Vivaldi duet, perhaps?"

Susannah looked up at Rand. "Do you play?"

"Occasionally."

She moved over on the bench. He needed no further invitation and took his place beside her. The Vivaldi was known to him; he had played it with his sisters. But never had he experienced it as he did now.

There was no awkwardness between them as they took up their parts. So perfect was their harmony that they might have spent hours practicing to achieve it. Their hands, their minds, their bodies moved in complete accord. As one, they gave themselves to the music, delighting in its playfulness, its gamboling joy in the world of light and love, even its impetuosity when passages soared to seemingly unattainable heights, only to carry them along.

When it ended finally, they looked at each other and laughed with sheer pleasure. "That was wonderful," Susannah exclaimed. "You're a fabulous pianist. I've never played with anyone so good. Where did you study?"

"In Paris," he admitted, with a slightly abashed smile. "That's what took me there."

"Did you ever think of concertizing?"

Reluctant to admit that such had once been his reigning ambition, he shrugged. "It crossed my mind. But there seem to be as many pianists as the world's stage will hold, and then some. Besides, I had to consider the practicalities of earning a living."

"What a shame," Susannah said. "I understand what you're saying, but I'm certain you would have made a great success of it."

"I didn't really lose anything," he assured her. "I play for my own pleasure and my friends'. But what about you? Did you ever think of going further?"

She glanced away, suddenly uncomfortable. "That isn't done, you know."

He did, and cursed himself for having forgotten, however briefly. Proper young ladies, particularly those from affluent families, did not go on the stage. Not for any reason or in any capacity. The fact that Susannah had undeniably extraordinary talent made no difference.

"It doesn't matter," she assured him quietly. "A long time ago I accepted what I can't change." Silently she added that she had also made up her mind to work for what change was possible. Still, it was a difficult subject for her and one she didn't want to discuss to any great extent. "Gentlemen," she said with a smile, "tomorrow promises to be a busy day. So if you will excuse me, I believe I'll retire."

Thurston's brow furrowed. He had clearly not been pleased by her closeness with Rand and was driven to return her attention to him, however inappropriately. "I hope it was nothing I said."

Susannah looked at him in bewilderment. She had completely forgotten his comments about her lack of universal approval in polite society, so little impact had they had on her. When she realized what he was referring to, she suppressed her amusement and held out a hand to him. "Not at all. Everyone is entitled to his opinion."

Thurston had barely a moment to feel the coolness of her fingers before she turned away and gave her father a light kiss. "Good-night, Papa. Please don't stay up late."

"I won't," he promised with a fond smile. "But you do the same. None of that sitting up late reading those mysteries you favor."

Susannah had a fondness for the works of Edgar Allan Poe, which many another father might have found unseemly. She was currently reading *The Murders in the Rue Morgue*, which utterly terrified her and which she found all but impossible to put down. Nonetheless, she intended to be sensible that night.

"I promise," she said. With the briefest hesitation she held out her hand to Rand.

He bent over it and touched a gentle kiss to her fingers. A tremor raced through her. Her hand lingered in his as their eyes met. Hers were dark with yearning and confusion. His were much clearer in both their thoughts and intent.

He wanted her, and he did not mind her knowing that. But he was also filled with determination to shield her even from her own desires. For all the rough edges he had spoken of, he was still very much a gentleman. He resolved that the proprieties would not be merely observed but genuinely respected. She deserved nothing less.

There was a note of self-conscious nobility in his voice as he said, "Sleep well, Susannah."

She suppressed a faint twinge of concern and withdrew her hand. The warmth of his touch lingered long after they parted. She was completely silent as Sukie helped her out

of her clothes and brushed her hair before braiding it. Her
thoughts were amorphous, wordless, yet hardly without
direction. Rand was firmly at their center—not the man
whose identity and purpose she was supposed to be discovering but the man who moved her so effortlessly with a
mere smile or touch, who had awakened her to sensations
she had never before experienced, who made a muddle of
her best intentions and a mockery of her self-control.

An impatient sigh escaped her. Sukie smiled but kept
her own counsel. Not until Susannah was safely tucked in
bed did she say, "Get yourself some rest now, child. Got
to rest if you're gonna think with a clear head. Ain't that
right now?"

"Is that what I'm going to do, Sukie?" Susannah
murmured.

"Oh, yes, child, I got no doubt about that. Now that
Mr. Cabot, he might not know just what a good head you
got on those pretty shoulders, but I gots a feeling he gonna
find out."

Susannah laughed softly. "I hope you're right. At the
moment that good head of mine doesn't seem good for
much of anything except spinning."

"Happens sometimes that way," Sukie said as she turned
to go. "Good night's rest steady you down just fine, you
see."

For once, Susannah doubted that Sukie's prescription
would work, but she wasn't about to say so. Instead, she
let her eyes flutter shut and pretended to be falling asleep
as Sukie's footsteps receded down the hallway.

An hour later, Susannah heard Thurston and his uncle's
carriage leaving. She lay awake in the darkness of her
room, listening to the sounds of the house settling down
around her.

She recognized her father's step as he passed her room,
his left leg dragging slightly as it always did when he was
tired. A few moments later, she heard a firmer tread and

held her breath until Rand, too, had passed by. Surely she only imagined that he lingered a moment outside her door.

The sky was pitch-dark when she slipped from the bed and hurried to the window. Storm clouds were rapidly gathering, and there was no moon. For a moment she debated the feasibility of her mission, then decided it could not be delayed regardless of the difficulties she would encounter. Fortunately, she knew the land around Belleterre as well as she did the contours of her own face. If she had to, she could find her way by sheer instinct.

Dressed in Tad's clothes, she eased over the windowsill, grasped hold of a branch of the ancient oak tree immediately beyond, and with a few swift, economical motions swung to the ground. In an instant she was off and running soundlessly toward the river.

A soft curse broke from her when she reached the bank and realized that the small boat she had expected to find there was unaccountably missing. With a storm blowing up, the river was higher than usual, but she had swum it so many times over the years that it did not occur to her that she might encounter any difficulty. In fact, either the current was stronger than she had expected or she was simply more tired than she'd thought. She had to pull hard to reach the other side more or less where she had intended.

By the time she dragged herself onto the shore, her heart was pounding heavily and her breathing was labored. She had to lie for some time in the cool night wind, her sodden clothes clinging to her, before she was able to go on.

The main house of Five Oaks lay a half mile from the river. Susannah followed a dirt path she knew well and reached the house without incident. Despite the late hour, several lights were still ablaze on the lower floor, in the room she knew to be Damien's study.

With the steadily increasing wind to muffle her movements, she approached the house and crouched behind a clump of bushes near the study windows. One of them was open a few inches, allowing her to hear the voices from within. By peering carefully over the sill, she also had a fairly decent view of what was happening.

Damien Sanders sat on a broad leather couch that had once been choice but over the years had become cracked and stained. He had his feet up on an equally disreputable ottoman. His tie was undone, his gray hair askew, and he looked uncharacteristically jolly.

"Fitzgerald doesn't suspect a thing," he told the other men. "I'm sure of that after this evening. His unexpected arrival needn't cause us any concern."

"You'd better be positive about that," Captain Fortescue said. He stood with his back to the anemic fire, which Damien had undoubtedly only reluctantly lit. "We can't afford any slipups at this late date."

"There won't be any," Damien insisted. "Everything is going exactly as planned."

"Fitzgerald isn't the sort for us to worry about," Thurston stated. He was leaning against the corner of a desk, looking weary and uncomfortable. Susannah guessed he would have vastly preferred to be in his bed but couldn't withdraw until his uncle gave him leave. "It's true he's generally been a supporter of Lee's, but he's also spoken out against reunification."

"That doesn't mean he'd approve of what we're doing," Burke said. He was stretched out in an oversized leather chair across from Damien. His ruddy face was even redder than usual, most likely thanks to the large glass of whiskey he held, apparently not his first. Damien was hardly the sort to pour generous drinks. Susannah wondered what it was about Burke that made his host so indulgent of him.

"I'm not suggesting that he would," Thurston said with a barely suppressed note of irritation. "Merely that we need have no fear of Fitzgerald discovering what's going on until it's far too late for him to do anything about it."

"What about that daughter of his?" Burke asked.

Thurston was clearly taken aback. "Susannah? What could she possibly have to do with it?"

Burke shrugged and took another long swallow of his drink. "Plenty of women are nosy. Why should she be an exception?"

"She happens to be a lady," Thurston said stiffly. "Not that I expect you to understand what that means."

"That's enough." Fortescue intervened even as Burke was beginning to hoist himself from his seat with a fierce gleam in his eyes. "We'd be damn fools to start arguing among ourselves when we're so near success. That's exactly what our opponents would like us to do."

For a moment it looked as though Burke intended to ignore him, but he finally subsided, grumbling. "Just don't want any loose ends, that's all."

"There won't be any," Fortescue assured him. "Not if each of us does his part."

"Have you got the statement ready yet?" Burke asked.

Damien nodded. "I've been working on it all week. We must strike exactly the right note of grief and resolution."

"Let's take a look," Fortescue said.

Rather than bestir himself, Damien gestured toward a leather folder on the desk. Thurston opened it, withdrew a single sheet of paper, and passed it to Fortescue, who read it over several times before nodding. "That seems to cover everything."

He handed it to Burke, who scanned it briefly and grunted. "Looks all right to me."

Thurston recovered the paper, replaced it in the folder, and put that in turn into one of the desk drawers. Meanwhile, Damien finished his drink and rose. "Bad night. I'm for bed."

"We all might as well get some rest," Fortescue said, "while we yet have the chance."

Susannah waited until the faint sounds of their footsteps had completely faded away. Only then did she emerge from behind the bushes and gingerly ease the window farther open so that she could slip inside. She padded quickly over to the desk, pulled the drawer out, and winced as the old wood squeaked. She didn't dare light a lamp, but the light from the fire was enough to see by. She found the leather folder without difficulty and scanned the document within. A puzzled frown creased her brow as she tried to decipher its meaning.

"Sons of the Confederacy," it began, "rally to the terrible outrage committed by our perfidious enemies. Stand tall against the forces that would destroy us. Keep faith with the sacrifices of our fathers and brothers. Special emergency meeting to be held at the Capitol, tomorrow night, seven P.M. All veterans and those willing to serve welcome. Important decisions to be taken. The Confederacy now and forever!"

"What the . . ." Susannah murmured, reading the document again. It was clearly intended to be an advertising bill, posted on walls and handed out on public wayfares. But what was the outrage it referred to and why the call to remember the sacrifices of the past?

She had no time to ponder the matter. A sudden sound from the hallway alerted her to danger. Quickly she replaced the document in the folder and put the folder back in the desk. By the time she had slid the drawer closed, she could hear footsteps approaching the study.

Hardly daring to breathe, she crouched beneath the desk, praying that she wouldn't be noticed. Burke had entered the study and was glancing around as though wanting to confirm that he was alone. He wasted no time in going to a narrow wooden cabinet that proved to contain a number of decanters. He helped himself to a generous measure of whiskey, gulped half of it down, and refilled his glass. Only then did he put the stopper back into the decanter and make his way back to the door.

His step was unsteady as he did so. He stumbled against the desk so that some of the whiskey sloshed from the glass and landed directly in front of Susannah. She held her breath, struggling against the instinct to panic, while Burke cursed softly. He weaved his way back to the cabinet, topped off his drink again, and this time managed to make it out of the room without further incident.

The moment he was gone, Susannah scrambled for the window. She slipped back outside and managed to get as far as the corner of the house when something that felt very big and very hard suddenly struck her from behind. The breath was knocked from her as the ground came up in a great rush. She had time only for a soft moan before blackness engulfed her.

12

When Susannah came to, she was lying on the ground some distance from the house. It was raining, and fat, cold drops were running down the collar of her shirt. She shivered and tried to sit up, only to be stopped by a firm hand on her shoulder.

"Take it easy," Rand said. "Jump up too fast and you'll go right back out again."

"You . . ." Susannah murmured, not so much with surprise as with resignation. Of all the people who could possibly turn up at such a time, he was unaccountably the least startling. However, she didn't mean to accept his presence without a struggle.

"What are you doing here?" she demanded, her attempt at sternness undermined by the thinness of her voice. The starch really had been knocked out of her. Moreover, it didn't seem to be in any hurry to return.

"I felt like taking a stroll," Rand muttered. Only the slightest tremor revealed the tension he had felt from the instant he had seen her climbing out the window. Tension that had increased a hundredfold since her loss of consciousness. He all but glared as he asked, "How about you?"

"Oh, the same," she said as airily as she could manage.

"It's such a lovely night." She sat up again, more slowly, and peered at him. "What did you hit me for?"

"It was the quickest way to get you out of sight. You didn't see the guard?"

"What guard?"

"The one making his rounds just as you crawled from the window. Another moment and he would have seen you." Almost accusingly, he added, "I didn't count on you passing out, much less staying that way for a while."

"What did you expect when you knocked my head off?" she demanded.

"It was a little tap, that's all," he protested. The sight of her unconscious body lying crumpled on the ground lingered in his mind with the sharpness of a particularly frightening nightmare, one from which a man might awake screaming. He had wanted only to protect her. Instead, he had turned out to be the biggest danger to her so far, more so than Burke or any of the others. He blamed himself for underestimating his own strength, and overestimating hers. But he was in no mood to admit that.

A crack of lightning rent the sky above them, bathing them in its white glow. Susannah saw the implacable strength and will in his face. Oddly, they comforted her.

Hard on the lightning came thunder, rolling toward them in a great, reverberating peal that threatened to shatter the very ground on which they sat. "Come on," Rand said, standing up and reaching for her in a single motion. "We've got to find shelter."

"There's a shack," Susannah said as the sky suddenly unloosed a torrent of rain. "Near the river."

"Let's go."

They hurried along in silence, Susannah leading the way because only she knew it. She felt unusually weak and cold, and had to force herself to keep going. Twice she stumbled over exposed roots and would have fallen if Rand hadn't caught her from behind. She heard his soft, fluent curses but could not quite make out the words.

"There," she said finally, "behind those rocks." The shack she led him to was a crude affair, a single room with a wooden floor, a brick chimney, and two small windows covered in oilskin. Some of the Five Oaks slaves used it during harvest when they were kept in the fields so late that they could not walk all the way back to their quarters. But the harvest would not come again for several months and, in the meantime, the cabin was unoccupied.

"At least it's dry," Rand said as he glanced around with a grimace. Susannah was standing in the middle of the floor. She had wrapped her arms around herself, but they could not stop the convulsive shudders that racked her uncontrollably. He frowned as he took in the wet clothes clinging to her slender body. She had pinned up her hair before leaving the house, but he could see that it, too, was drenched.

In a moment he had stripped off his jacket and put it around her. "Sit down," he said. "I'm going to look for something to make a fire with. We've got to get you warm."

"The smoke," Susannah protested. "It might be seen from Five Oaks."

"Not at night, and we'll be gone before morning." He spotted a pile of wood in a corner of the cabin. Without further ado, he built a fire with brisk efficiency, and when it was going well, carried Susannah over to it.

"I can walk," she protested against his shoulder.

"Be quiet. You are without doubt the most infuriating female I have ever encountered. If you say one more word, I will not be responsible for my actions." As he set her down, he demanded, "What the hell were you doing in Damien's study, anyway?"

Susannah pressed her lips together and remained silent. After a moment Rand realized why. "This would be the one time you choose to obey me. Talk, my girl, and make it good. I want answers and I want them now."

"I'm not sure I can provide them," Susannah said in a

small voice. She clutched his jacket to her, absorbing its warmth along with the special scent of him that clung to the fabric. A dizzying wave of emotion washed over her, leaving her feeling even weaker than before. But at least she was warm—very, very warm. The fire and the jacket must be doing their job. She was almost burning.

"Why, Susannah?" Rand demanded. His voice softened, becoming almost caressing. "Because you don't think I can be trusted with a butterfly?"

Her eyes, dark as a storm-tossed sea, widened with shock. "Where did you hear . . . ?"

"From a gentleman in Illinois."

Susannah stared at him for a long moment. He met her gaze steadily with no attempt at evasion. Slowly she said, "You're Lincoln's agent."

It wasn't, strictly speaking, a question, but Rand chose to answer it as one. "That's right, and unless I'm very much mistaken, you're Butterfly."

Susannah hesitated an instant longer before she nodded. With a soft sigh she said, "Such a frivolous term. Code names should be impressive and vaguely sinister, don't you think?"

Rand couldn't restrain a smile despite the surge of emotion her admission prompted. Until that moment, he had suspected her role without being sure of it. Now that she had confirmed her identity he was swept by a host of contradictory feelings. On the one hand, he was impressed despite himself, knowing full well how extremely difficult and complex it was to play such a part. On the other hand, he was absolutely infuriated at those who had allowed her to become involved, whoever they might be.

"Your father," he said abruptly, "does he know?"

Susannah shot him an incredulous look. "Don't be silly. Papa would have an absolute fit if he had any idea what I was up to. And not only because he opposes reunification."

"I would think," Rand muttered, his eyes sweeping over her slender form huddled within the shelter of his jacket, "that politics would be the least of his objections. You have no business being mixed up in this conflict, Susannah. No lady does."

She gave an audible sniff. "Tell that to Aunt Miriam. She won't appreciate it any more than I do. Women happen to be the mainstay of the reunification movement in the South. We know only too well the cost of war, and we're determined to avoid paying it yet again."

Rand missed the last of her laudatory sentiments. "Your Aunt Miriam? She's involved in this, too?"

His astonishment made her laugh, if shakily. She wasn't worried about revealing Miriam's part; that would have had to come out eventually anyway. Besides, she trusted Rand, so much so that her faith in him startled her. "Shocking, isn't it," she murmured, "the things women get up to?"

"Knowing you is rapidly robbing me of the ability to be shocked," he declared.

The anger behind his words abruptly dampened her spirits. She wasn't by nature a changeable creature, but her mood was fragile and under the circumstances it took little to undermine her. "You're always saying things like that," she muttered with a small sniff.

He glared suspiciously at her, fearing she was about to start crying again. That he absolutely would not tolerate. "Like what?"

"Mean things. You don't like me very much." She sniffed again and rubbed her nose with as much dignity as she could muster.

Rand muttered impatiently. "I would be curious to learn how you arrived at that conclusion." When she didn't reply, merely remained seated clutching his jacket and averting her eyes, he sighed deeply and fished in his trouser pocket. With an annoyed sound he handed her his handkerchief.

"Thank you," she said, and promptly sneezed.

Mildly let down, he murmured, "You don't sound very good."

"I'm fine. *Atchoo.*"

"Not good at all. By the way, how did you get across the river after I took the boat?"

Susannah's head shot up, and she glared at him. "You took it? I might have known. I swam, of course. How else could I have gotten here?"

The string of expletives he unleashed froze her. She stared at him wide-eyed as he demanded, "Are you absolutely crazy? There's a strong current tonight. You could have been killed."

"I happen to be an excellent swimmer."

"I don't care how good a— Oh, never mind, there's no point trying to talk to you. Here, give me that jacket."

"But I'm not dry." Surely he didn't want it back simply because he was annoyed at her.

Rand must have caught the direction of her thoughts, for he shot her a fierce scowl and all but ripped the jacket from her. He was not normally given to temper, but she made a mockery of his self-control. He found himself saying and doing things with her that he would never have believed possible.

One moment he wanted to treat her with all the tenderness and consideration he showed his mother and sisters. The next, he wanted to shake her damn, stubborn head right off her shoulders. Along with each, always and undeniably, was the desire to lay her down and make long, passionate love to her until they exploded together in the pleasure he instinctively knew they would find.

That thought in no way improved his present mood. "Your clothes have to be even wetter than I realized," he said darkly. "If you don't get them off, you'll catch your death of cold."

"Off?" Susannah squeaked. She clutched the lapels of her shirt and dared him to tell her he was actually serious.

"Off," he repeated implacably. "There are blankets in

that chest over there. You can wear one of them until
you're dry.''

"I don't care what I can wear. I'm absolutely not taking
off my clothes in front of you.''

"There's hardly any reason to stand on ceremony. The
clothes you're wearing don't hide very much.''

It was true that the shirt and trousers were plastered to
her. With the jacket gone, the high, firm contours of her
breasts, the nipples erect, could be clearly seen, as could
the tapering lines of her thighs and the soft indentation
between them.

Rand cursed again, even more fluently, when she merely
wrapped her arms around herself and made no attempt to
obey him. He rose, jerked several blankets from the chest,
and threw them over a rope line that extended across one
corner of the cabin.

That done, he seized Susannah, dragged her to her feet,
and all but tossed her behind the impromptu but effective
screen. "Strip," he ordered. "To the skin, or I'll do it for
you.''

This time Susannah made haste to do as he said. As she
handed out the clothes, including the lacy camisole and
pantaloons she had worn beneath them, she blushed crim-
son. Rand made no comment as he tossed them into a
corner near the fire.

When she emerged a moment later, wrapped toga fashion in one of the rough woolen blankets, he couldn't help
but grin at her. She had let down her ebony hair, which
tumbled in disarray around her pale shoulders. A corner of
the blanket was tucked between her breasts, and she had to
hold up the other end to avoid tripping on it.

She looked like a little girl playing dress up, except that
only a woman full grown could be so blatantly seductive.
And only an innocent could be so unaware of it. With an
inward groan, he remembered his conversation with her
father and schooled himself to new heights of fortitude.

"Sit down," he ordered, "before you fall down." Critically he added, "You look awful." This last was a gross exaggeration, not to say an outright lie. What he actually meant was that her general air of fragility distressed him. He was afraid once again that she might be becoming ill.

"I'm so sorry to disappoint you," she said stiffly, feeling unaccountably inclined to cry. Left to her own devices, she would have liked nothing better than to crawl into his arms, be enfolded in his strength, and go blissfully to sleep. But the hostility raging between them made any such possibility unthinkable.

"For heaven's sake," he muttered, "it isn't a question of disappointing. I'm afraid you may be getting sick."

The idea that he could actually feel fear for her struck Susannah. She looked at him closely to see if it could be true even as she said, "I am never sick."

"There's a first time for everything. Come over here where you'll be warmer."

With great dignity she gathered the blanket once again around her ankles and came closer to the fire. Her clothes were still lying bundled where he had let them fall. "They'll never get dry that way," she protested.

"Small loss." At her chiding glance he relented and began to lay the clothes out flat in front of the fire. As he did so, his movements slowed and he looked suddenly thoughtful. "Wait a minute. . . . These look familiar." His eyes narrowed to slender glints of golden fire.

The expression he turned on her would have made a lesser person quail. As it was, Susannah had to suppress a shudder that ran the entire length of her body. "You make a charming boy," he said slowly, his eyes never leaving her, "even if you are a lousy shot. But then I suppose I should be grateful for that."

Susannah straightened her shoulders and met his relentless gaze without the slightest outward sign of fear. "As it happens, I'm an excellent shot. I just wasn't aiming at you." More softly she added, "I'm very sorry you were hurt. That really wasn't my intention."

Still grappling with the discovery that she had been the boy on the dock, he asked, "Why did you fire the gun then?"

"To distract you long enough for me to get away. I was afraid you'd recognize me."

"I almost did, now that I think back. You smelled of jasmine."

"Thanks for telling me. I'll have to be more careful of that."

Her calm demeanor and refusal to show any sign of being embarrassed by what she had done infuriated him, not in the least because he fully understood the danger she had run.

Reaching forward, he took hold of her arms without any attempt at gentleness and yanked her to him. "You could have been killed," he snarled, a pulse pounding in the shadowed hollow of his cheek. "Or worse. Don't you know what Burke and those others would have done to you if they'd discovered you were a woman?"

"I can imagine," Susannah said, struggling against a sudden sense of breathlessness, but not against him. She remained unresistant in his arms, accepting tacitly that there was nowhere else she wanted to be. Despite his anger, his hold on her was not in any way cruel. The large, somewhat calloused hands that slid down her bare arms were infinitely gentle.

"Can you?" he demanded huskily. "Why did you do it? Surely nothing could have justified that risk."

She could have told him otherwise, could have at least attempted to explain the motives that had driven her to board the *Essex*. But just then the effort was beyond her. She was far too comfortable in his arms, so much so that the events of the last few hours were at last catching up with her. Her eyelids were leaden as she snuggled against him.

Rand stifled a groan. He was dismayed by the thought of her in such danger, but he was also rapidly losing sight of it in his increasing awareness of her. "Susannah," he murmured deep in his throat.

"Mmmm?" She was far too content to say anything else. Her body was nestled against him, her head on his shoulder and one slender hand resting on his chest. The slow, steady beat of his heart infused her with a profound sense of peace.

Rand's reaction was rather different. He took a deep breath and summoned all his finer impulses to the aid of his rapidly weakening self-control. "You don't realize . . . ."

She had a vague sense of what he meant, knew that she was causing him unease, but not for the world could she bring herself to pull away from him. Instead, she snuggled closer to him and closed her eyes.

Rand gritted his teeth. The slight weight of her against him, the softness of her skin, and the subtle but unmistakably feminine scent arising from her all conspired to set his senses whirling. Gone was the distance he had always managed to maintain between himself and those other women he had held in his arms.

The vaguely sardonic attitude he had always taken toward matters of the flesh was notably absent. Possibly because far more than the flesh was involved. The irksome, vexing hoyden nestled so trustingly against him had touched a part of him always before left pristine. Without his even being aware of it, she had insinuated herself into his heart to a degree he found astounding.

He looked down at the gleaming black hair flowing in gentle waves down her back. Against its darkness, her skin looked even paler than usual. The thick fringe of her lashes concealed her eyes. Her soft, pink lips were slightly parted. His own mouth lifted in a slightly incredulous smile as he realized that while he had been mulling over the question of their joint futures, if any, she had gone peacefully to sleep. He didn't know whether to be touched by her utter faith in him or insulted by her total unawareness of him.

With a long sigh, he laid her down gently, hesitated a moment, then stretched out beside her. If he could do nothing else, at least he could keep her warm.

Susannah could not remember ever feeling so completely at ease. She had awakened naturally from a deep sleep but had not yet troubled herself to open her eyes. Her head was lying on something hard yet comfortable, as though it had been made for precisely that purpose. A weight lay over her waist; she felt it most when she stirred slightly, yet she had no desire to free herself from it.

Slowly her eyes opened, flickered shut for a moment more, then suddenly widened to their fullest. From where she was lying, she had an unobstructed view of Rand's broad chest. His shirt was partially opened, and she found herself staring at bronzed skin, heavily muscled and overlaid with a fine dusting of golden hair.

Susannah had never seen a man's bare chest before, not even glimpsed through the lapels of a shirt. She blushed fiercely even as curiosity overwhelmed her. Tentatively she reached out and touched the tip of her finger to him.

The lack of any response emboldened her. She sat up and studied the contours of his body, noting in passing a bulge between the legs of his trousers, the significance of which did not immediately register with her.

It was very quiet in the cabin. The only sounds were the soft hiss and crackle of the fire that still burned low, the wind without, and the rhythm of their own breathing. The latter grew more urgent as Susannah brushed a hand down the length of Rand's chest, fascinated by the play of muscle and sinew she thereby discovered. He was all hard steel, this man, without even the pretense of softness.

She suspected that he must live a very rigorous life for all that he enjoyed civilization's luxuries. She could imagine him surviving very well in the wilderness, swinging an ax to clear wood, silently tracking game, returning at the end of the day to a cabin he had built himself where a woman would wait for him and . . .

Susannah abruptly broke off the direction of her thoughts. She must be a besotted romantic to spin such visions. They were not at the frontier, she was not his woman, and wresting a living from the wilderness was not their concern. Compared to their true situation, that life was hopelessly idyllic.

Her gaze flew to the window. It was still dark outside; not even a hint of light shone. With dawn would come the relentless need to go on, with who knew what consequences. It was not inconceivable that either she or Rand could be killed. They had so little time together, and so much weighing against them.

Reality or rationalization, the effect of such thoughts was the same. She drew even closer to him and, with studied concentration, touched him again. Through the thin linen of his shirt, his skin felt very warm. She was astonished to discover that his flat nipples were as hard as her own had become. The knowledge of her own arousal took her unawares. Liquid heat pooled between her thighs and deep within her. Her breasts felt swollen and ached slightly; the scratchiness of the rough wool blanket was oddly pleasing.

She moistened her suddenly dry lips with the tip of her small tongue. Beneath her hand, Rand's muscles stiffened. She glanced up and found him watching her. "Do you have the slightest idea what you're doing?" he murmured.

Susannah turned bright red. She tried to pull back, as though she had belatedly felt the singe of fire, but he would not permit it. His hand held hers firmly as his gaze swept over her heated face before drifting lower. "H-how long have you b-been awake?" she stammered.

His chiseled mouth curved in a smile that did not reach as far as his smoldering gaze. "Long enough."

"I . . . I don't know what came over me."

His eyebrows rose. "Don't you?"

"Oh, you . . . let me go!" She twisted frantically, determined to break free. Her other hand flew up to push against him, only to be captured in turn. With a swift movement, Rand turned, drawing her under him and pinning her effectively to the ground.

"Stop it, Susannah," he ordered. "Don't lie to yourself or me."

"I don't know what you're talking about." Her head thrashed back and forth, tangling her silken hair. Her fists were clenched and would have been pounding against him had he not held them effortlessly at bay.

"You're a normal young woman with normal desires. I'm flattered that I've aroused them, but—"

"*Desires?* Is that all you think . . ." At his suddenly quizzical look, she shook her head repeatedly. "Never mind. I made a mistake, I'm sorry. Now let me go."

He stared at her a moment longer, his eyes thoughtful, then slowly he, too, shook his head. "No."

"W-what did you say?"

"No. I'm not going to let you go. I don't want that and neither do you."

"But you have to. You're a gentleman."

He laughed tenderly at her innocence, at the knowledge that she was right all the same, and at the growing conviction that it still didn't matter. He had tried to write off her actions to simple desire, but the look he had just seen in her eyes had told him volumes. He was not the only one caught in Cupid's untimely web. Not for a moment would he take advantage of her, but the realization that she felt the same as he did changed matters considerably.

"I'll make you a promise, Susannah," he said as he lowered his head. "If you tell me again to let you go, I'll do it. But first I want five minutes."

"W-what for?"

"You'll see."

Or rather feel, which was all Susannah did in the moments that followed. She knew she should be outraged, should protest, should above all make some further effort to get away. But all action was beyond her. She could only lie back and luxuriate in the rush of sensations pouring through her.

Rand kissed her long and deeply, his tongue playfully stroking and teasing hers. He raised her arms above her head, then let go of her wrists so that she was no longer confined. His hands slid around her back, stroking her bare shoulder blades as he gathered her closer to him.

"Beautiful, Susannah," he murmured as he withdrew from her mouth but not from kissing her. Again and again his mouth lightly touched her, tracing her high-boned cheeks, her wide brow, the straight line of her nose, the curve of her chin.

When he at last found the vulnerable pulse point at her throat, she gasped softly. The sensation was not unlike being tickled, yet went far beyond that. She had not the slightest desire to giggle. On the contrary, as wave after wave of pleasure swept over her, she was struck with wonder.

"Rand," she whispered, her hands tangling in his golden hair, "what's happening to me?"

He raised his head and smiled down at her, his eyes gentle in the darkness. "You're learning what it means to be a woman."

"I never realized . . ."

"Wait," he bade her, "there's so much more."

Susannah didn't see how there could be. Already she felt as though she was about to fly apart into a thousand pieces. If he went any further, she would do so and then where would they be?

That consideration didn't seem to concern Rand, who returned to his perusal of her throat and shoulders. Her skin felt cool except where he touched it. There she burned.

"Rand," she gasped as he began to undo the blanket she had wound around herself, "don't . . ."

"It isn't five minutes yet," he said huskily.

Unaccountably, his words caused her to subside. After all, she thought somewhere deep in the back of her mind, a deal was a deal.

Cool night air touched her breasts as he slid the blanket to her waist. He paused then and simply gazed at her, his heart hammering against his ribs. She was easily the most exquisite woman he had ever seen. Her breasts were high and firm, the nipples small and delicately pink. They tilted upward, as though begging for his touch.

He did not hesitate to oblige. His mouth closed gently on her. She jerked in his arms, but he held her firmly, waiting until she had become accustomed to the strange sensation. Only then did he lave her lightly with his tongue and let her feel the slightest edge of his teeth.

"Oh, sweet lord . . ." Susannah gasped. Of their own accord, her hips rose, only to encounter the hardness at the center of his body. Another gasp broke from her.

"Easy," he whispered soothingly. "It's all right. I'm not going to let anything bad happen to you."

Susannah believed him, but more than that, she was honest enough to admit that they shared a common goal. The unfathomable urgency building within them demanded the release that could come only when they became truly one. She might not be absolutely clear on all that entailed, but she had a vague idea and she was not afraid.

Her hips lifted again, this time brushing deliberately against him. He groaned and, taking hold of the blanket that, with his trousers, was all that separated them, he wrenched it away. A wildness seized Susannah as she realized she was completely exposed to him. When he raised his head and gazed fully at her, she did not flinch. She was proud in her nudity, certain of her ability to please him.

She was smiling as her hands went to the buttons of his shirt. "You . . ." she murmured, finding it difficult to breathe.

He understood what she wanted. Shakily he rose and,

without taking his eyes from the naked woman who reclined at his feet, he stripped off his clothes. Susannah
watched him with unabashed fascination. As each part of
his body was revealed to her, her excitement deepened.
Until at last, when he stood before her as God had made
him, she could do nothing except hold out her arms to him
in unbridled welcome.

13

Rand had not meant to go as far as he had. He'd
thought merely to introduce her to the pleasure of
which her body was capable without robbing her of
the innocence proper society thought so essential in a
young woman of her class. But when it came down to it,
he simply could not restrain himself. The temptation she
presented proved irresistible. Every instinct he possessed
cried out at him to claim her in the most undeniable way
possible.

Slowly and with great care, he eased down on top of
her. She stiffened slightly, but made no effort to pull
away. Holding the bulk of his weight on his arms, he gazed
down at her. "Susannah, if I hurt or frighten you . . ."

"You won't." She could not say how she knew that,
but her certainty was absolute. No hint of fear marred her
joy. Her utter faith in him allowed her to relax completely
and to follow his softly murmured urgings as he led her
into realms of delight so far beyond her imaginings as to
be all but incomprehensible.

With hands and mouth he worshiped her body. She
arched beneath him, calling his name, as his lips trailed
fire from the scented cleft between her collarbones to the
crests of her breasts and beyond. He lingered over the

204

slight swell of her belly, his tongue delving into her navel while his thumbs slowly stroked the hollows formed by her curving hips. She discovered that she was particularly sensitive there, the merest brush of his lips enough to make her cry out softly.

To be caressed by him, even so evocatively, wasn't enough. She had to touch him in turn. She raked her hands down his back, feeling the fluid clenching and unclenching of his muscles as he moved. His skin was smooth and hot beneath her questing fingers, velvet laid over steel. She felt the clearly defined contours of his ribs, the narrowing at his waist, and the rock hardness of his buttocks. His body was slowly becoming known to her, as hers was to him, so that soon it would no longer be that of a stranger but rather of a lover.

The profound intimacy growing between them filled her with poignant happiness. She felt closer to him than she ever had to anyone. Not only their bodies, but their hearts and minds spoke to one another in the smoke-scented darkness of the little cabin that might, for all that they cared, have been a palace.

Yet Rand had not completely forgotten their surroundings. When the moment came when he knew he could wait no longer, he turned onto his back and drew Susannah with him. Finding herself suddenly perched above him, held there by his strong hands at her waist, she gasped and looked at him in bewilderment.

"My back is tougher than yours," he offered by way of explanation. Cupping the soft cheeks of her bottom, he gently urged her forward. "It's all right, Susannah. We'll go slowly, I promise." Even if it killed him, which he was beginning to suspect it might. If she didn't understand . . . or couldn't manage it, he would have to . . .

He gazed up into her eyes, alight with the primal fire that lurked both at the heart of emeralds and in the profound depths of the sea. His concern fled, replaced by a fascination that mercifully did not linger long. He watched

the birth of comprehension, enthralled by her awakening
awareness of her body's capabilities. She flushed slightly
but was undeniably taken by the notion that she, not he,
could be in control at this particularly crucial moment for
her.

"Are you sure . . . ?" she whispered.

In answer, he took her hand and gently guided it to his
manhood. "This is perfectly natural, sweetheart. It's as
God made us."

She hesitated barely an instant longer, then slowly lowered herself onto him. He saw her astonishment as she felt
him entering her. She tightened slightly, but in the next
moment, when he smiled at her encouragingly, she relaxed. Meanwhile Rand was grinding his teeth as he struggled to remember every technique he had ever learned for
controlling his passion. All involved thinking of something
other than her, and that was blatantly impossible. She
filled his vision and his world even as he began slowly but
inexorably to fill her.

Susannah winced. She bit down hard on her lower lip to
keep from crying out. The pain was not unexpected. She
took courage, reminding herself that she would feel it only
once.

Beads of sweat had broken out on Rand's forehead. He
knew he was hurting her and cursed himself for it. Yet
when he tried to draw back, she shook her head so that her
silken hair brushed over his chest like the warm, living
pelt of a forest animal.

"No," she said huskily, "it has to be now." Before he
could object further, she took a deep breath and moved
with stunning effectiveness to make them one. The soft
moan that tore from her ripped through Rand's heart. He
gathered her close to him, stroking her back soothingly as
he murmured reassurances to her.

Scant moments passed before the pain faded. Susannah
straightened up, her hands on his shoulders. An infinitely
female smile tilted her mouth as she began to move. Rand

gasped with surprised delight. Her audacity stunned him, but he knew it shouldn't have. Courage and the willingness to face life on its own terms were as much a part of Susannah as her astounding beauty. She was a woman in a million, and she was his.

Pure possessiveness unlike any he had ever known seized him. It was not enough that she belong to him simply for the moment. He wanted her forever, into the furthest twilight reaches of time. When he realized that he could not stop himself from making love with her fully, he had resolved to at least withdraw in time to spare her the possibility of a pregnancy. But that noble resolve did not prove strong enough to withstand far more primal urges. She was his; he welcomed anything that would make her and everyone else acknowledge it.

Glorying in her responsiveness, he managed to hold back until he felt the tidal pull of her fulfillment drawing him even deeper within her. Her head fell back, her hair brushing his thighs, as a low, keening cry escaped her.

Rand waited no longer. His hands clenched on her hips as he drove into her, at once losing and finding himself within the secret depths of her mystery.

Afterward they lay together in a tangle of limbs, touching each other softly and repeatedly as though neither could quite accept that what had happened was real. Rand gently brushed aside a stray lock of hair from Susannah's forehead, his caress lingering as he savored the infinite softness of her skin.

"So beautiful," he murmured. "So delicate . . . and yet . . ."

She smiled against the smooth rippling muscles on which her head was pillowed. His confusion did not surprise her; she felt it herself. In Rand's arms she experienced the sensation of being both infinitely fragile and cared for while at the same time discovering a completely unsuspected strength within herself. She felt oddly protective toward him, as though having taken him into her body, having cherished him in the most intimate way possible, she now wanted to go on doing so forever.

A soft sigh escaped her. Such weighty thoughts would have to wait for another time. She watched enthralled as his eyes slowly shut. Try though he did, he could not keep them open. Within a few moments his regular breathing told her that he was asleep. She stretched out more comfortably beside him, warmed by his body and by the lingering resonance of their lovemaking. Hardly aware that she did so, she followed him into dreamless sleep.

Susannah woke several hours later to an instant of confusion followed hard by memories that warmed her cheeks. Sitting up slowly, she looked around. There was no sign of Rand. The fire was out, and through the window she could see the first faint light of dawn. Moving swiftly, she discarded the blanket he had placed over her, found her clothes, and pulled them on. She was fastening the cord belt around her waist when he returned.

Smiling shyly, she murmured, "Good morning."

His only answer was a scowl. He stood, hands on his hips, staring at her as though she was something unpleasant he had suddenly stumbled over. As the silence drew out between them, Susannah became first disbelieving, then dismayed.

She had no way of knowing that she was far from displeasing to Rand; he was struggling against the urge to lay her down on the ground again and make love to her over and over. He was also fighting his own conscience, which had proved to be a singularly inconvenient companion throughout the long night.

He had awakened some time before her and had lain looking down at the exquisite shape nestled against his own, his thoughts growing progressively darker. Unbridled pleasure at the joy they had found together had given way to remorse over having taken her innocence. Conveniently he forgot that what was freely given could not, by definition, be taken. He was guiltless but could not admit it. All he could think of was bringing her back home safely, then dealing with what had happened.

"You're up," he said, not looking at her. "Good, let's get going."

His abruptness and the lack of any tender word or gesture reminiscent of the previous night struck Susannah harshly. It seemed that he was already regretting what had passed between them. That hurt her deeply. Her throat constricted as she hastily finished dressing, her eyes locked on him.

Something was obviously wrong and she was not a woman to hide from confrontation. She wanted to know what had disturbed him, if only to understand the abrupt change in him. "Rand," she said softly, "what's happened?"

He gave her a look of such blank astonishment that she might have laughed had not the circumstances been so suddenly grim. The look vanished almost at once, replaced by a blank, shuttered gaze that told her nothing. "I hardly think I need to remind you," he said stiffly. Before she could reply, he turned on his heel and walked out of the cabin, leaving her to follow.

She did so wordlessly, staring at his back as he plunged into the underbrush toward the river. He did not look at her again until they reached the bank a short time later. Rand had gone out earlier to reconnoiter as well as to round up the boat he had used. He held it as she climbed in, then followed.

They crossed the river swiftly and in silence. Once on the other side, it was only a short distance to Belleterre. Rand murmured a soft curse as he belatedly realized that even at that early hour, servants were already about. Having gotten her safely away from Five Oaks, he had thought he could relax enough to tell her what was in his mind and in his heart, but there was no chance for that now. If she was to conceal her highly irregular absence from her father, she had to get upstairs immediately.

He laid a hand on her arm, mindful of how she stiffened in response. "We'll have to talk later." Glancing at the tree beyond her window, he asked, "Do you need help with that?"

What she imagined to be coldness hurt her even more and made her withdraw from him even further. Before she would ask him for assistance, she would sprout wings and fly. "No," she said shortly. "I can manage."

He nodded, still thinking only of protecting her from curious eyes. If they were seen together at such an hour, with her so oddly dressed, questions would be bound to be asked. There was so much he wanted to say and do, but already he could hear the house servants starting about their duties. He gently touched her arm again and repeated, "Later." Then he was gone.

Susannah stared after him for a moment before choking down a sound that lay somewhere between a sob and a scream of pure rage. She was deeply wounded but also extremely angry. How dare he treat her so lightly? Did what they had shared mean so little to him?

Far in the back of her mind, she knew that wasn't the case. He was simply acting like a typically clumsy and inept male. The fact that he was neither only made his lapse all the more infuriating. She broke into a run, determined to get away from him as quickly as possible.

Susannah climbed the oak tree by instinct only, her vision blurred by tears. She regained her bedroom, peeled off her clothes, hid them in the wardrobe, and pulled on a nightgown, barely aware of what she was doing.

By the time she climbed into bed, reaction had set in, not only to Rand's behavior but also to the events of the previous twelve hours, primarily the soaking in the river. She had never felt so utterly miserable in her entire life. She was shivering all over, her head throbbed, her eyes burned, and she was very afraid that she was going to be sick.

That was how Sukie found her when she entered the

room a short time later. Susannah was curled up in a tight ball under the covers, shaking so hard that the whole bed seemed to quake. With a startled shriek, Sukie dashed to her side. "Oh, my poor lamb, whatever's happened to you?"

"Nothing," Susannah said from between her tightly clenched teeth. "I've just taken a little cold." As though to confirm her diagnosis, she sneezed loudly.

"Little . . . ? On my blessed mama's soul, that ain't no cold, little or otherwise. You've taken the ague, child, and it's all my fault." The maid wrung her hands as she looked heavenward. "What's your papa gonna think of me? Oh, blessed Lord, how could something like this happen?"

"It's nothing," Susannah croaked, secretly not displeased by the fuss. She rather thought she deserved it, although she made a valiant attempt to claim otherwise. "I'm fine."

Sukie wisely ignored her. She bustled over to the wooden chest at the foot of the bed, plucked out a down comforter, and spread it over Susannah. "Can't have too many covers when you've got the ague. Don't you move now, honey. I'll be right back with your medicine."

"Oh, no!" Half rising up in bed, all she could manage, she tried to grab hold of Sukie, only to have the maid elude her as she dashed for the door. With a groan Susannah fell back against the pillows and tried to reconcile herself to the inevitable.

Two teaspoons of vile brown liquid later, she sat up in the bed sipping a cup of tea. Sukie bustled about, laying out handkerchiefs, a hot water bottle, books, and needlework. "Everything you need's right here. No reason to be getting out of that bed."

"I can't stay here," Susannah muttered. "I've got too much to do."

Sukie put her hands on her hips and glared at Susannah. "You try getting up and see what happens to you."

Despite herself, Susannah smiled. "Will you paddle me, Sukie?"

"No such thing. Nature take care of it herself."

Sukie was right. The moment the maid left the room, Susannah put down the teacup and tried easing out of bed, only to find that her legs would barely hold her far enough to reach the bathroom. Anything more ambitious was out of the question.

Tears of frustration burned her eyes as she made her way back to bed. Barely had she settled once more against the pillows than her father knocked on the door. "Do you feel up to company?" he asked as he stuck his head in.

She gave him a bright smile that sought to belie her wan expression. "Absolutely. I'm already bored to tears."

Jeffrey thoughtfully surveyed his daughter's face but did not comment on the traces of moisture lingering on her lashes. He sat down on the side of the bed and took her hand in his. "I'm thinking of asking Dr. Smithers to come down here to see you."

Susannah made a face. She despised few things as much as being poked at by doctors, particularly one who would be feeling put out at being required to make a long trip for no good reason. "I'll be fine by the time he gets here."

Her father frowned. "Sukie says it's the ague."

"She said the same thing last year when Tessie was feeling poorly, remember?"

Jeffrey laughed. "Actually, I'd forgotten, but you're right."

"Instead of the ague, Tessie ended up with a bouncing, seven-pound boy." Barely had she spoken than Susannah flushed. All things considered, she probably couldn't have thought of a worse comparison than the young sewing maid who had turned up pregnant without benefit of matrimony.

That had been speedily rectified and the family was happily settled down now, but she most certainly didn't want to give her father any untoward ideas about what might be responsible for her illness. They couldn't possibly be correct, of course, but they struck too close to home to be comfortable. "I've got nothing more interesting than a summer cold," she went on hurriedly.

"We'll see. If you aren't feeling better in a few days, I'm sending for Smithers." When she had reluctantly accepted his pronouncement, he added, "By the way, Rand and I have concluded our business, and I've invited him to stay on for a while."

"Surely he's anxious to return to Richmond?" she ventured, knowing even as she did that such was not the case. He would remain until he unraveled whatever was going on at Five Oaks. Grimly she resolved to do her damnedest to help him, if only to see the back of him that much sooner.

"He doesn't seem to be," her father said. "On the contrary, he accepted my invitation most warmly."

Despite herself, Susannah could not restrain a spurt of curiosity. Rand had behaved so oddly when they parted that she wondered if he had continued to do so. "Was that this morning?"

Jeffrey nodded. "At breakfast. We both missed you there. Rand was as concerned as I to learn that you were indisposed."

"How kind of him," Susannah muttered. Why he should treat her with such coldness yet still appear worried over her illness bewildered her. But then who could understand the workings of a man's mind?

"He asked if he might come up and see you later today."

"No! That is . . . wouldn't it be highly improper?"

"Sukie would be present, of course. I don't think there's anything untoward about a guest paying a short call to express his hopes for your swift recovery."

"He can express them to you," Susannah said firmly. "I don't want to see him."

Her father could not conceal his surprise. "Has Rand done something to offend you?"

Susannah could not bring herself to lie outright, but she

could hardly admit the truth. Instead, she tried to parry the
question. "Why should you ask that?"

"You seem reluctant to talk about him, much less see
him."

"It's just that we don't know him very well, do we?
He's a Yankee . . . different from us. He'll be gone in a
few days, and we'll probably never even see him again. . . ."

Jeffrey's mouth twitched. "I wouldn't say that, daughter. On the contrary, I have the distinct impression that
Rand intends to be around for a while."

"Why do you say that?"

"Oh . . . just an idea I have." Her father rose to go. He
smiled at her and patted her hand reassuringly. "I'll tell
him you don't feel up to company, but in a day or two you
should see him. To do otherwise would be rude."

At least she had won a reprieve. In a day or two she
would be feeling better and would be able to face Rand
calmly. She would be as cool to him as he had been to her,
and she would make it clear that what had happened
between them was forgotten.

With that resolved, and Sukie's nostrum taking effect,
Susannah slept on and off throughout the day. Late in the
afternoon she managed a sponge bath and afterward felt
sufficiently revived to eat most of the dinner brought to her
on a tray.

Her father came by again while she was eating. Convinced that she was recuperating, he stayed only long
enough to tell her that he had received a note from Aunt
Miriam to the effect that she would shortly be joining them
at Belleterre.

Susannah made no comment, though she knew her aunt's
arrival was in response to the message she herself had
sent. She was glad to be spared the effort of reporting by
letter what she had found in the desk at Five Oaks. Instead, she would be able to tell Miriam in person, and
together they could decide what to do. Miriam would
undoubtedly want to inform Rand, since he was also in-

volved, but that would further spare Susannah any need to deal with him.

She fell asleep again, struggling against the memories of the previous night. Never before had she felt so alone and bereft. Her anger at Rand redoubled as she thought of how cruel he had been to awaken her to unimagined happiness only to snatch it away again. She wept softly even in her sleep, her pillow growing damp beneath her.

She was tossing and turning in her agitation when strong hands suddenly gripped her and she was lifted into a strong embrace. "Hush," a low, deep voice rumbled. "It's all right . . . everything will be all right."

Heedless of anything beyond her own grief, Susannah clung to the source of comfort. She burrowed her head into a broad, hard chest and held on tightly. "Don't cry," the voice continued, "please . . ." A warm, gentle hand stroked her back. She murmured and nestled closer.

Warm, firm lips touched hers lightly. Her own parted, growing soft and yielding. Rand hesitated an instant before desire won out over common sense. He kissed her long and deeply, breaking off only to rain kisses along the delicate curve of her cheek and the slender line of her throat. She felt so good in his arms, so delicate yet strong, a woman with passion to match his own. The memory of how it had been between them all but overwhelmed him. He drew her even closer.

She trembled but made no protest, until she abruptly realized exactly what was happening. *"You!"* she exclaimed as she jerked away from him. The delightful dream she had thought she was having suddenly shattered. Face-to-face with reality, she was aghast at her own behavior, and his. "How dare you come in here?"

"Be quiet," Rand said tersely. He was still holding her, refusing to let go even when she struck him with her tightly clenched hands. No pretended fury there. The little devil packed a wallop. His chest stung as he muttered, "I'd rather not bring the whole house down on us, if you don't mind."

"Oh, you wouldn't, would you? Well, I don't happen to care about that. You have some nerve coming in here. I told Father I didn't want to see you."

"Scared, Susannah?"

She stared at him in mute disbelief. Was there no end to what this man would do to provoke her? "It'll be a cold day in hell before I'm scared of you, Rand Cabot. I may be smaller than you and nowhere near as strong, but I'm twice the person you'll ever be. For one thing, I'd never, ever treat someone the way you treated me."

His smile looked pained. He'd realized that he had behaved badly that morning in the cabin. He should have been there when she woke up, to comfort and reassure her. Instead he had been grappling with his own guilt and concern about the future. He regretted it now even as he accepted that he couldn't change his past behavior. He could only attempt to improve on it.

Still holding her wrists, he lowered her back onto the pillow and gazed down at her. For a moment she thought she saw remorse in his tawny eyes, but surely she had imagined that. "It would be difficult for you to ever act as I did," he said, "since you aren't a man."

"That isn't what I meant. I'd never pretend to have feelings I didn't have. You made me think . . ." Her voice broke. She turned her head away, determined to not let him see her tears. "Oh, never mind."

"Is that what's upset you so? You thought I was pretending to care for you?"

"What else could I think after the way you acted this morning?"

"For God's sake—" He broke off, staring at her long and hard before he attempted to continue. "I was very upset this/morning," he admitted. "When I woke up and saw you lying beside me, so young and trusting, I was horrified by what I'd done. To take you like that, in a backwoods cabin, with none of the refinements you should have had." He shook his head regretfully. "I'm sorry, sweetheart, but I swear I'll make it up to you."

Susannah barely heard him. Her mind was reeling under the incredible discovery that Rand somehow believed he had wronged her. That he could even imagine that the previous night had been less than perfect stunned her. Not for a moment had she missed the so-called refinements he spoke of. They were inconsequential when compared to her feelings for him.

Rand, however, saw things in a different light. His face was grim as he said, "I've made a mistake. It must be rectified."

A terrible suspicion was building in Susannah. She wanted desperately to believe she was wrong, but she feared that was not the case. Through stiffened lips, she murmured, "What do you mean?"

"It should be self-evident. We must be married, of course, and as quickly as possible."

"Married?" The word came out in a breathless rasp, conveying both surprise and dismay.

Rand's brow furrowed. He hadn't expected her to be boundless in her joy, but neither had he anticipated this rebuff. "Surely, you must see that there's no alternative," he said stiffly.

"On the contrary," Susannah said slowly. "It is unthinkable to me that any two people should marry simply because one of them believes he has dishonored the other."

"It isn't a question of that," Rand insisted. Belatedly he realized he was handling the situation very badly, but it was too late to do anything about it. If he lingered much longer in her room, they would most certainly risk discovery. Jeffrey would consider that his trust had been betrayed, and Susannah, at the very least, would be highly embarrassed.

"I don't for a moment consider you dishonored," he said tersely. "However, the fact remains that our society does think of women in such terms. It isn't right that you should be left to face the consequences of what happened between us on your own."

"And that's why you want to marry me? Because it's the noble thing?"

"Yes . . . no . . . what difference does it make?"
Despite his best resolve, he was rapidly running out of
patience. The contrary little miss knew perfectly well that
he was right. It was past time for her to admit it. "You do
realize that you could be pregnant?" he demanded bluntly.

Susannah paled. The possibility had hardly escaped her;
she had simply chosen not to dwell on it. Now he had
thrust it to the forefront where she had no choice but to
confront it. The thought of a child of their making sent a
bolt of heat through her. She was at once delighted and
terrified of the prospect. And utterly unable to come to
terms with it.

Too much had happened in too short a time. She was
overwhelmed by her feelings for Rand and by his exquisite
awakening of her body. From that pinnacle of delight she
had plunged to a rude awakening, discovering that he felt
merely obligated to do the right thing by her. Disappointment filled her as much as joy had such a short while
before.

"I hardly think it proper for us to be speaking about
such a thing," she said as she gazed studiously over his
shoulder at some apparently fascinating spot on the wall.

It took Rand a moment to realize that she was serious.
He shook his head, bemused. "It's a bit late to be hiding
behind propriety, isn't it?"

Still not looking at him, Susannah said, "I am not
hiding."

"What do you call it then?"

"Being realistic. What happened was mistake enough.
Let's not compound our error through misguided notions
of honor."

His lean cheeks darkened. "Is that really what you
think?"

Susannah hesitated. Nothing she had ever said was more
false to her nature. She longed to recant the words but
could not. The moment she gave him such an opening he
would impose his will without compunction, heedless of

the anguish so reluctant a marriage would cause them. For his sake as well as her own, she nodded firmly. "I do, and now I really must insist that you leave."

He let go of her wrists, but made no further effort to comply. When she still refused to look at him, he caught hold of her chin and compelled her to meet his gaze. "Susannah, let's make sure there are no misunderstandings between us. I feel very deeply about you. It would not be a hardship to take you as my wife."

"How kind of you," she murmured, her lips barely moving.

Rand cursed under his breath. He was discovering in himself a hitherto unsuspected capacity for clumsiness that made a mockery of his vaunted self-control. "I'm putting this very badly, but—"

"Tell me something," she interrupted. "If last night hadn't happened, would you still be asking me to marry you?"

For Susannah that was the crucial question. It passed over the issue of honor and got directly to the heart of the matter. For Rand it wasn't so simple. He had been a bachelor for twenty-eight years, during which he had always envisioned marriage as something to do eventually in the hazy future.

His feelings for Susannah were unlike those he had ever entertained for any other woman, yet he had not reached the point of spontaneously declaring his intentions before their lovemaking had preempted such a declaration. He had, however, promised her father that he would treat her honorably, and that was exactly what he was endeavoring to do.

"Last night did happen," he reminded her gently. "It changed everything."

"Yes," Susannah said sadly, "it did."

"I'm glad you realize that." He thought he had won and was relieved enough to smile. "I'll speak to your father in the morning."

"No, don't do that." Hastily she continued, "I know I run the risk of having a baby . . . and if that turns out to be the case, I'll have to deal with it. But I've learned far too much about the unhappiness in this world to embroil myself in a forced marriage. Before I would do that, I would bear any degree of censure."

Her simple dignity astounded him so that it dawned on him only slowly that his proposal—if it could be called that—had been well and truly rejected. Her position was completely untenable, of course. She would have to reconsider, whether or not there was a baby. In the meantime, he thought he understood her refusal to come to terms with reality.

"You aren't feeling well," he said softly. "When you're better, you'll see things differently."

"I don't think so."

Rand did not press the issue. He tucked the covers around her, placed a light kiss on her forehead, and gave her a tolerant smile. "We'll talk about it later. Go back to sleep now."

Susannah glared at him. His presumption that she would come to her senses and gratefully accept his proposal stung. He had yet to learn that she was far less inclined to accept unpleasant realities than she was to set about changing them.

14

Aunt Miriam sat on a brocade chair beside the settee where her niece reclined. Though it was only the following day, Susannah was up and fully dressed, despite Sukie's dire threats. She had chosen her soft yellow day frock precisely because it detracted from the pallor of her skin. Her hair was brushed free of tangles and drawn back from her face by a matching silk ribbon. The moment Susannah had heard her aunt's step in the hallway outside her room, she pinched her cheeks and pasted a determined smile on her face. Miriam was not fooled.

"You swam the river?" she repeated incredulously. "At night and alone?"

Susannah had the grace to look contrite. "I had no choice. Having seen Burke and Fortescue, I had to find out what they were doing at Five Oaks."

The older woman shook her head in exasperation. "I was right to want you out of it, and I'm desperately sorry that you're involved once again. This is becoming more dangerous by the day."

"Even as it becomes more vital for us to discover what is afoot," Susannah countered. "The announcement I found in Damien's desk makes it clear they're planning something dastardly."

221

"Yes," Miriam agreed, "so it seems, but we're still no closer to knowing what that something is. Though I must say, I'm not at all surprised to learn that both the Sanderses are involved. Damien has hardly made a secret of his political leanings, and Thurston follows him slavishly."

Susannah could not argue with that, but she didn't want to dwell on it. Any mention of Thurston, the man she might reasonably be expected to marry, would lead inevitably to thoughts of Rand, the man she most unreasonably wished to wed. She had wasted enough time and anguish on him over the course of the long, painful night and was determined not to do so any longer.

"Let us review what we know," she suggested. "Our information from London was clearly correct; the *Essex* does have something to do with the plot against reunification. Captain Fortescue clearly knows the plan and is involved, as is Burke. That means that if the British aren't actually behind it, they are at least co-conspirators with Damien and whoever else backs him."

"But which British?" Miriam asked softly. "I have a difficult time imagining Lord Beaufort involved with the likes of Burke, or Damien for that matter."

"So do I," Susannah admitted. She paused to take a sip of the hot tea with lemon that Sukie had left beside her. It made her feel better than the vile brown liquid. "Beaufort is worried about something, though. I'm certain of that." Briefly she explained how he and her father had met the other afternoon in Richmond, and how struck she had been by the Englishman's concern.

"You say he was meeting with Jeffrey?" Miriam queried.

"Yes, but I don't know what they discussed. They've had a number of dealings together in the past, most recently Rosinante's purchase, so it could have been almost anything."

"I suppose . . ." Miriam said, her eyes thoughtful.

Reluctantly Susannah said, "More important is the news I have regarding Mr. Cabot. You were correct to wonder about him; he is Lincoln's man."

"He told you so himself?"

Susannah nodded. "He knew that Lincoln used to call me Butterfly, the code name I still use."

"Excellent," Miriam declared. "Now that we have made contact with the North's agent, everything will be so much simpler."

Susannah wished she could agree. As it was, she could think of no worse complication. Cautiously she said, "I think it would be best for you to deal with him."

Miriam did not conceal her surprise. "Why is that?"

Susannah hesitated. She could not risk raising her aunt's suspicions by pretending disinterest, but neither could she bring herself to admit the true cause of her reluctance. As independent and free-thinking as Miriam was, she would be dismayed by even the hint of an improper relationship between her niece and Rand.

"You . . . have so much more experience in these matters than I do," she said at last.

"But I can't claim to know Mr. Cabot, and you do. It stands to reason that he will be far more willing to work with you than with me."

"I doubt that," Susannah murmured.

She spoke so softly that Miriam seemed not to hear her. At any rate, she appeared far too distracted by the news of Rand's involvement. "What did he say when you told him about the announcement you found?"

Susannah closed her eyes as the realization of her own laxity swept over her. She pressed a hand to her forehead. "I didn't . . . It slipped my mind."

Miriam had been taking a sip of her own tea as her niece spoke. She coughed and set the cup down abruptly. "Slipped . . . ?"

"It's terrible, I know. I can't imagine how I could have made such a blunder." Actually, Rand had so completely dazzled her that it was a wonder she remembered anything, even belatedly.

"He has to be told," Miriam said. She waited, appar-

ently giving Susannah the opportunity to offer to speak
with Rand herself. When she did not, Miriam rose and
smoothed the skirt of her gray silk gown. "I'll speak with
him as soon as possible. He went riding this morning and
hasn't returned yet."

The thought of Rand out riding alone made Susannah
long to be with him. She yearned to show him the Belleterre
she had known and loved all her life. To share that with
him would be much like sharing herself. With a desperate
effort, she turned away from the images such thoughts
conjured up. "I think I'll nap for a while," she murmured.

"That sounds like a good idea." Miriam spread an
afghan over her niece's knees, then left the room quietly.

Susannah did make a genuine effort to rest, but the more
she tried, the harder it became. She lay with her eyes
open, staring up at the mid-afternoon shadows drifting
across the high ceiling, but seeing in her mind Rand and
herself.

She thought of how he had looked the night before
when she awoke to find him in her room. Remembering what
had passed between them, she flushed, though more with
anger than embarrassment. It still irked her that he had
simply presumed she would be grateful to become his
wife.

For a time she tried to divert herself by reading, but
when even her most beloved book, *Jane Eyre*, failed to
absorb her, she gave up. The need to lie still was beyond
her. Correctly or not, she felt as though she was trying to
hide from Rand, and that she could not bear.

With sudden decisiveness she got up from the settee
and, pausing only long enough to take a light shawl from
her closet, left the room. The house was quiet. At that
hour the servants were usually gathered in the kitchen to
chat and rest before beginning preparations for supper. The
gardeners had completed their work and departed. The
field workers had not yet returned to their quarters behind
the main house. If she listened very hard, Susannah could

hear the far-off cadence of their voices carried on the slight breeze.

She draped the shawl over her shoulders and left the house by a side door that gave directly onto a gravel path. The path led through a shaded section of the garden. Bees droned around the rosebushes, and here and there a robin darted about on the rolled lawn, searching for worms.

Susannah's spirits were revived by the sunlight and fresh air. She absolutely refused to be disheartened by her difficulties with Rand. Nothing would have been more selfish when events far beyond their own lives were unfolding in such ominous fashion.

As she walked, she set her mind to the puzzle of what Damien Sanders was up to. Nothing good, she was sure. He despised Robert E. Lee, believing himself personally injured by the president's determination to bring the South into the modern era. But that begged the question of exactly how far he would go to stop Lee. The more she thought about it, the more Susannah believed she needed to pay another visit to Five Oaks. Not, however, in the way she had the night before.

The gravel path wound from the main house to the stables. Rosinante whinnied a greeting as soon as he saw her. She patted his nose gently. "Poor thing. I'm sorry we can't go out today. But you'll get your exercise, never fear."

"Already has, miss," a young boy said behind her. She turned to find one of the junior grooms regarding her respectfully. "Name's Wilson, miss," he said, tugging off his cap. "I took your horse out this morning for a run. Hope that's all right."

"That's fine, Wilson," she assured him. The boy was small and slightly built, no older than twelve or thirteen. She was surprised he had dared to go anywhere near Rosinante, much less actually ride him.

"He's a bit of a handful, isn't he, miss?"

"Did you have a problem with him?" Susannah asked, concerned.

Wilson shook his tousled head. "Who me? Not a bit. We had a fine time, we did. Isn't that true, Rosy?"

"Rosy?" Susannah repeated, eyebrows rising.

The boy flushed. "Sorry, miss. He's got a long name, he has. I just shortened it a bit. Fact is, he reminds me of a roan I knew back in Ireland. Same kind of spirit, he has."

He looked at her so appealingly that Susannah couldn't help but laugh in appreciation of his courage.

"Have you been here long?" she asked. "I don't remember seeing you before."

The boy shook his head. "Only a fortnight, miss. I was up north before that."

"Why didn't you stay? Have you family here?"

"No, miss. No family, here or elsewheres. But I had to come." He hesitated, his wide blue eyes, set in a narrow face, studying her cautiously. After a moment he blurted, "They don't like the Irish up north, they don't. Call us micks and keep us on the run. No jobs a decent man would want and even if you can find work, there's nowhere to stay. They'll rent you a basement cubby, all right, for a king's ransom, if you don't mind the rats and the stink."

He stuck out his chin, as though daring her to contradict him. "That's not for me, it isn't. I'm for open spaces, sunlight, and a bit of pride. Not much sense to life without that, is there?"

"No," Susannah said softly, "there isn't." She thought how different her own experience had been, yet how, oddly enough, they had arrived at the same conclusions. To do right by oneself and the world, that was the thing. She was trying, but the task seemed harder than ever.

"I hope," she added, "that you like it here."

"Oh, yes, miss," he said, "this is a fine place. Mr. Johnson, now, he's a tough one but fair. Animals are all well cared for, too. Say, did you know old Lucy had kittens?"

"Lucy?" Susannah said, remembering the battered ginger cat who had arrived out of nowhere several years before and taken up residence in the stables. "I'd have thought she was past that."

Wilson chuckled. "So did most everybody else, 'cepting Lucy. Care to see them?"

"Oh, yes." She eagerly picked up her skirts. Wilson led the way. In an unused stall, in a corner strewn with fresh hay, Lucy was holding court. Five tiny, mewing kittens sprawled around her. Their eyes were still closed, and they were too weak yet to stand, but they looked healthy. Two were ginger, like their mother, but the remaining three were unremittingly black.

"How adorable," she said as she knelt before them. Lucy gave her a cautionary glance, but Susannah knew better than to try to touch such young kittens. "You've done yourself proud," she told the cat softly. "That's a beautiful family."

Lucy gave a rasping purr of agreement as she set to work licking one of her progeny. It squirmed beneath the rough ministrations of her tongue and mewed all the harder.

Susannah was laughing at the kittens' antics when Rosinante, in his nearby stall, nickered a warning. She looked up to find Rand watching her. Wilson took one look at the tall, muscular man dressed in riding clothes and jumped up. "Everything all right, sir?"

"Fine," Rand told him without taking his eyes from Susannah. In the moment before she realized he was there, her expression had held such a wealth of tenderness that the very air seemed to shimmer with it. All that feeling for newborn kittens. He found himself wondering how she would be with a child of her own. The image of her holding a baby, laughing as it chortled and kicked, sent such a pang of longing through him that he stiffened in response.

Abruptly aware that both Susannah and Wilson were staring at him, he said, "You gave me a good mount. Do me a favor, will you, and rub him down." He flipped a silver dollar to the boy. Wilson caught it on the fly and

grinned broadly. "Aye, sir, that I will." He nodded to
Susannah and took his leave.

When they were alone, Rand leaned against the stable
wall, his arms folded across his chest and a sardonic gleam
in his eye. "You seem much improved," he said.

"Tea and sympathy work wonders," Susannah said in a
voice not quite her own. She stood up carefully and brushed
the hay from her skirt. With a flash of her usual spirit she
drawled, "I do apologize for not being able to play hostess, but I trust Aunt Miriam has kept you occupied?"

Rand nodded. He came away from the wall and closed
the distance between them. "We have to talk," he said,
taking hold of her arm.

Instinctively Susannah tried to pull away, without success. She found herself being drawn along the gravel path
toward the garden. "Don't you ever think to ask permission?" she demanded.

"That doesn't seem to work very well with you."

That stymied her, briefly. By the time he had come to a
halt beside a young willow that hugged the bank of a small
pond, she had her forces in better order. Her feelings
notwithstanding, there were more vital issues at hand.
"Aunt Miriam hasn't had a chance to speak with you yet,
has she?"

"No, why?"

Briefly she explained about the announcement she had
found in Damien's desk. When she finished, she expected
him to make some scathing comment upon her lapse in
memory, but if he thought of it at all, he did not say so.
Instead he asked, "What do you make of it?"

Susannah tilted her head to one side, looking up at him
through the dappled sunlight. His expression was somber,
and she sensed a new tension in him. "The obvious, I
suppose. Damien intends to protest the reunification talks
and to try to gather people of like mind to his side."

"You think that's what the announcement means?"

"What else?"

Rand didn't answer at once. His tawny eyes looked from her across the broad sweep of lawn to the river in the distance, but she knew he was not seeing it. Less pleasant inner visions clearly held his attention. "There is an alternative, one I've begun to consider recently, one which this latest bit of news seems to make even more plausible."

"What is that?"

"Sanders might be plotting Lee's assassination."

Susannah's eyes widened. The suggestion was so outlandish that she wasn't even certain she had heard him correctly. "That's beyond belief. No one, not even the most fanatical opponent, would do such a thing."

"It's happened before."

"When?"

"There were rumors back in sixty and sixty-one that if Lincoln was elected, he'd be assassinated. To this day there are people who think John Wilkes Booth was involved in some absurd plan to prevent a war by killing the man he thought was provoking it."

"I've heard that," Susannah admitted, "but I've never believed it. It sounds like the sort of thing Booth himself would invent simply for the stir it would cause, so that he could then sit back and enjoy all the fuss."

"Perhaps . . . but there may also have been a grain of truth to it. My point is that human beings have an infinite capacity for violence. There are no depths to which our species will not sink."

The absolute certainty in his voice, as well as the bitterness, took Susannah aback. She reached out a hand to him as she said softly, "Rand, what makes you believe that?"

"Experience," he said flatly. Belatedly he saw her wince and regretted his harshness. He would just as soon have forgotten his words, but Susannah felt differently. Gently she said, "Tell me, Rand, please. I've wondered all along how you came to be involved with Lincoln and the underground, what led you to risk your life when you could have sat back comfortably. So many people never lift a finger to challenge injustice. Why have you?"

He smiled faintly, touched by her desire to understand and by his own need to speak of memories too painful to confront alone. Quietly he said, "I guess what it comes down to is that I'm offended by waste. I don't like to see lives being snuffed out, potential thrown away. I don't like the people who are willing to do that kind of thing, and most particularly I don't want to see them end up running the world."

"You must have seen terrible things during the war," she murmured.

He shrugged. "Everyone did. But a soldier in a war expects to have people trying to kill him. He has the capacity to fight back, to protect himself. Others aren't so fortunate. Innocent, helpless people are the most vulnerable."

He fell silent, his gaze turned inward on a fathomless vista she could not see. Nor was she sure she wanted to. She sensed that when he spoke of the innocent and helpless, he wasn't talking in generalities. He seemed to be thinking of something in particular that disturbed him deeply and was at the root of his determination to do everything he could to prevent the breakdown of order that led to such violence.

Quietly she said, "You really believe there may be a plot to assassinate Lee?"

It took him a moment to draw back from his inner thoughts. He nodded curtly. "The possibility exists. Damien Sanders strikes me as a man who doesn't like to lose. He hates Lee, blames him for the loss of the South that Sanders claims to love. It makes sense that he'd want revenge."

"Perhaps," Susannah said, "but I can't see him personally confronting Lee."

"No," Rand agreed, "he'd hire someone to do the dirty work."

"What amount of gold would prompt a man to give up his own life in the bargain? That's surely what would happen to anyone who tried to harm Lee. If the assassin wasn't caught immediately, he'd be a hunted animal. The entire South would rise against him."

A breeze rustled the long, golden leaves of the willow trees. Far off on the river a paddlewheeler's whistle blew long and sweetly. Rand turned to her. "To kill Lee and escape, a man would need powerful allies who could smuggle him out of the country to a place of sanctuary."

They looked at each other for a long, tense moment. Silently, her lips barely moving, Susannah mouthed the words that were in both their minds. "The British."

Rand nodded grimly. "They would have much to gain by provoking a new conflict between North and South. Their interests in Canada would be protected, and they might even be able to take advantage of the chaos such conflict would cause to try to restore their old power over us."

"That's madness. Surely Queen Victoria would never agree to—"

"She wouldn't necessarily have any idea of what was happening," Rand pointed out. "Until it was over. And then what could she do? Refuse to accept results highly favorable to Britain simply because she didn't agree with the methods by which they had been attained? I hardly think so."

"But assassination . . . do you really think . . . ?"

"I think the possibility must be laid before Lee. I would offer to do so myself, but he doesn't know me and will be more likely to dismiss what I have to say. We can't take that risk."

Susannah brushed away a stray wisp of hair that had fluttered across her furrowed brow. "But how can I return to Richmond? Whatever pretext I might invent, Father would insist on accompanying me. I must consider him as well." Her dilemma was real and without apparent resolution. While she could place herself at risk, she could not do the same to those she loved.

"Lee is planning to leave Richmond shortly," Rand

said. At her surprise he explained, "Once the Congress adjourns, he intends to travel through the South, quietly raising support for the reunification talks before announcing them in July."

"Then he might be persuaded to stop on his way."

"He might, but do we want him to? I rather think that would be akin to drawing him into the lion's den."

"You're right, of course. But how then . . . ?"

"His first stop will be Yorktown, where a ball will be given in his honor. Can you possibly convince your father to let you attend?"

"I think so," she said. "We have friends there, and it isn't as though it's very far. Certainly much closer than Richmond."

"Then I think that's our best opportunity," Rand said.

Silence drew out between them as each contemplated the most recent turn of events. Susannah could still not bring herself to believe that Rand's theory was correct, but she did see the sense of presenting it to Lee. Not, however, without further substantiation than they presently had. The problem was how to get it.

Rand had no inkling of her thoughts. He was concerned only that, with the stakes as high as they now appeared to be, he must be all the more determined to shield her.

"Once you've told Lee what you've found," he went on, "your involvement will be over."

Instinctively Susannah bristled. He sounded as though he was simply stating a fact that she could not possibly dispute. "That is for me to decide, and I will not do so unless I am convinced I can be of no further use."

Rand took a deep breath, schooling himself to patience. He had underestimated the strength of her will from the beginning, and was determined to not continue making the same mistake. As patiently as he could manage he said, "Your devotion is exemplary. However, I assure you that I will do everything on Lee's behalf that you would do."

She chose to ignore the stiff formality of his words,

which warned her that his hold on his temper was precarious. "What has that got to do with it?" she demanded.

"Surely my meaning is clear." Her expression showed it was anything but. Rand's exasperation was evident even as he struggled to appear patient and reasonable. "You can turn this matter over to me with perfect assurance that nothing will be lost in the process. That must come as a relief to you."

"Let me be sure I understand you," Susannah said carefully. "You are willing to marry me because it is the honorable thing to do. Is it also the honorable thing to take my place in the effort to protect Lee, or are you simply convinced that, as a female, I would bumble it?"

"I didn't say that," Rand shot back. "But, yes, it is the honorable thing." His temper flared despite his best efforts to contain it. "When did honor become such an ill-gotten notion with you?" he demanded.

"Never, at least not true honor, which I flatter myself is what I possess. But you—" She broke off, almost but not quite at a loss for words. "The honor you speak of is a weak and shallow thing founded on appearance rather than substance. For it, you would condemn us both to a miserable fate."

Rand inhaled sharply. He had taken her reluctance to accept his proposal as little more than a woman's natural desire to not appear too eager. He had assumed that in a few days, a few weeks at the most, she would have satisfied her sense of propriety and they would go on from there. Now it appeared he had drastically underestimated the situation. Was it possible that Susannah genuinely did not want to marry him?

"I'm sorry you feel that way," he said slowly.

Susannah bit the inside of her lower lip. Silently she reprimanded herself for succumbing to impulsiveness and an inherent tendency toward the dramatic. She had blurted out the first words that came to mind, without stopping to consider their impact. She lowered her gaze, suddenly self-conscious and uncertain. "I only meant that we always seem to be at odds with each other. I suppose that's because we come from such different backgrounds and see things so differently."

"And you believe people must be more compatible than we are in order to live together happily?"

"Oh, yes," Susannah said in perfect sincerity. "My father and mother adored each other and, from what I have heard, had the most idyllic marriage until her untimely death. But they had both grown up in the same world. They saw things the same way. It's hardly surprising that they were able to achieve such harmony between them."

"A case could be made," Rand said, "for what you have just described being a prescription for boredom, not harmony."

"As I said, we don't see anything the same way."

Feeling as though he had stepped into a rather neatly laid trap, Rand sighed. He didn't for a moment doubt that she was being forthright in stating her beliefs, but he also sensed something else at work in her. She was afraid not so much of him as of what he had awakened in her. For a moment he considered saying as much, but it required little imagination to guess her reaction. For once, he chose to err on the side of prudence.

"There will be time to straighten all this out later, after the matter with Lee is over."

Susannah did not reply. To her chagrin her brief period out of her room had left her feeling unpleasantly weak, just when she was most determined to appear strong. Her legs wobbled slightly, and her vision was somewhat unsteady. "If you will excuse me," she murmured as she tried to turn away.

Rand looked at her closely and said something under his breath. His arm lashed out, closing around her waist. An instant later she was lifted from the ground and cradled against his broad, unyielding chest. "Don't say a word, Susannah, not a word. I've already listened to more than enough from you." He strode back toward the house, no more hindered by her weight than he would have been by the air itself.

"There's no need for th——"

"Not a word," Rand repeated ominously. He glared down at her, acutely aware of the pallor of her skin, against which her eyes looked even more brilliant and fathomless. The shawl had slipped slightly, revealing the soft curve of her breasts. For an instant he was swept by the remembered taste and feel of her. His body hardened and he knew a brief, stabbing regret that they were not alone in the house.

The sound of a pianoforte being lightly played greeted them as they came into the entry hall. The door to the music room was open. Miriam sat at the bench facing them; Jeffrey was in a nearby chair. They had clearly been talking and laughing as she played, but broke off when they caught sight of Rand and Susannah.

"What . . . ?" Jeffrey said, rising from his chair.

"Oh, my dear," Miriam exclaimed. "What has happened?"

"Nothing," Susannah said.

"She overdid," Rand contradicted. Deliberately he added, "As usual."

"I had no idea you had left your room," Miriam said, hurrying to her side.

"I should have sent for Dr. Smithers," Jeffrey insisted as he studied his daughter with deep concern.

"Stubborn as a mule," Rand said. "No sense of her own limitations."

"She was always like that," Miriam replied. She led the way up the stairs after cautioning Jeffrey not to make the climb himself. "Once or twice a day is quite enough," she told him over her shoulder. "Susannah will be fine, won't you, dear?"

Before she could respond, Rand said, "I'd suggest locking her in, except I happen to know she climbs trees."

"You're learning quite a bit, aren't you?" Miriam said with a sidelong glance of amusement.

"Out of sheer self-preservation," Rand muttered.

They had reached the top of the stairs. Susannah looked down in time to see her father smiling up at them. With great dignity she said, "I'm very glad you all find this so entertaining."

Rand laughed. She felt the deep rumbling in his chest as his arms tightened around her. Miriam had gone ahead and was holding Susannah's bedroom door open. Rand carried her in and laid her gently on the bed. As he stepped back, he murmured, "Behave yourself, spitfire. At least for a little while."

Behind him Miriam said, "We'll take care of everything, dear. You just rest."

Susannah subsided against the pillows and closed her eyes. She saw no reason to tell them that she had already conceived a plan of her own. It remained only to set it in motion.

15

Rand stood with his back to the parlor room mantel, an elbow resting casually on the marble surface. His attention was focused on Susannah, who was seated on the couch across from him. The alabaster smoothness of her arms and shoulders, and the midnight darkness of her gleaming hair, were both in sharp contrast to the scarlet gown that flowed around her like the blossoms of a wild lily. She appeared to rise from its center, her back elegantly straight, her head proudly tilted, a tantalizing smile playing on her delightful mouth.

The smile was for Thurston, who sat beside her, rambling on about something or other. After every few words, Susannah nodded or deepened her smile. She appeared to find him utterly fascinating. He said something else and she laughed, looking at him admiringly.

Rand's mouth tightened. He was uncertain why Susannah was behaving in such a fashion, but he knew he didn't like it. If she had deliberately set out to provoke him—and he by no means disregarded that possibility—she couldn't have been more successful.

Thurston, meanwhile, was clearly enjoying Susannah's attentions, though it was also evident that he took them as his due. There was an almost palpable sense of satisfaction

in him, as though he believed she had finally come to her
senses and was behaving as she should. He was, after all,
the most eligible bachelor in Virginia, and he expected to
be treated accordingly.

Susannah was not disappointing him. Objectively Rand
had to admire her perfect portrayal of a flirtatious, flatter-
ing belle out to twine herself around a man's heart. Personally he was enraged by it.

His anger was made all the more threatening by the
thoroughness with which he suppressed it. No sign of his
inner feelings showed on his chiseled features. On the
contrary, he appeared mildly amused by the scene before
him.

Susannah seethed inwardly. She was acutely conscious
of Rand's sardonic regard but was determined not to be put
off by it. Let him think what he would, she was definitely
making progress with Thurston.

"I do agree with you about Five Oaks," she said eagerly. "It absolutely is the finest house in these parts. Not
that I don't love Belleterre, of course I do. But it just
doesn't have the . . . oh, you know what I mean . . . the
magnitude of Five Oaks."

"It is an impressive residence," Thurston said complacently. "My forefathers didn't believe in doing anything
on a small scale." With a cautious glance to where his
uncle was holding court, he added, "Of course, it has been
allowed to go downhill in recent years. Uncle has rather
simple tastes."

"What a shame he never married," Susannah said.
"Why, any woman would just adore to be let loose in such
a place. I declare, I'd never have another boring day if I
lived at Five Oaks." As though abruptly aware of what
she had said, she blushed prettily. "Oh, Thurston, please
don't think I'm too outspoken. Sometimes I just don't
know what gets into me."

"That's perfectly all right," he assured her. A bit awkwardly he placed his hand over hers and patted it. "I do believe we are coming to understand each other at last."

Susannah's only reply was a long, sweet smile.

Rand abruptly drained his brandy snifter. The liquid burned his throat, but he didn't notice. He was far too occupied thinking of the things he would like to do to the pair on the couch. Susannah might believe she was too old to be spanked, but he held the opposite view. As for Thurston, Rand was hard-pressed to decide a suitable fate for him, perhaps because merely being Thurston seemed bad enough.

"I was wondering," Thurston said after discreetly clearing his throat, "if you might be interested in touring Five Oaks. You've been there, of course, but I don't think you get a chance to properly see a house when a party is going on, do you?"

"Oh, certainly not. I'd adore seeing it."

"You could perhaps give me some suggestions for its redecoration. That will have to be done eventually." He glanced again in his uncle's direction, as if hoping Damien wouldn't catch him discussing plans that in all likelihood would only be carried out after the old skinflint had gone to his reward.

"I'd be delighted," Susannah said, all but clapping her hands in what to Rand, at least, looked like a badly overdone show of glee. Not that she shouldn't be pleased with herself. She had just neatly wangled an invitation to Five Oaks, where, he didn't doubt for a moment, she intended to continue her investigation.

He was determined she would not do so alone. Levering his long body away from the mantel, he walked over to where the happy twosome was ensconced. "Forgive me for eavesdropping," he said with a patently insincere look of contrition, "but I couldn't help hearing you mention something about touring Five Oaks. I'd hate to be thought overly curious, but I admit to a great interest in that house."

"You've heard of it?" Thurston asked, viewing Rand with a certain wariness.

"Of course," Rand replied. "It's quite well known up north. After all, it's one of the finest examples of Southern architecture. Possibly the finest. There is the Romney mansion outside Atlanta, which I've had the privilege of visiting, but I find it difficult to believe that it outclasses Five Oaks."

"It most certainly does not," Thurston insisted. Rand knew the Romneys and the Sanderses were longtime business rivals, and he suspected Thurston brought up the competition when trying to convince his uncle to spend money on Five Oaks. Damien, however, seemed impervious to such considerations.

"I should be very interested to hear how you think Five Oaks compares," Thurston said. "You would be welcome to join us."

Susannah had not expected him to accede so readily. She was caught short and had to hasten to catch up. "Oh, Thurston, I'm sure Mr. Cabot only wants a tiny peek while I'm just yearning to see every little nook and cranny. He'll be dreadfully bored if he goes with us."

Thurston looked hesitant. He was not a man of firm opinions, but rather more like a weather cock, liable to swing with the slightest change in the wind. "Perhaps you're right."

"I'm sure Miss Susannah means well," Rand said, giving her a chiding glance, "but she underrates my interest. I assure you I wouldn't be bored." Deliberately he looked Thurston directly in the eye and smiled. "Not bored at all."

A dull flush spread over the younger man's face. Rand watched it assessingly. He was a sophisticated man, aware of the many variations of human behavior and generally tolerant of them so long as they hurt no one. Whatever Thurston's private tendencies—and he was no more sure of them than he suspected Thurston was—Rand didn't condemn him for them.

But he did blame Thurston for thinking of marrying any woman, most particularly Susannah. She clearly suspected nothing untoward, but then how could she? For all her unusual experiences, she was an innocent about certain matters. He would just as soon she remained that way.

"My uncle has to be away on business tomorrow," Thurston was saying, more to Rand than to Susannah, who no longer claimed his attention. "That might be the best time to visit. I hope you understand . . ."

"Perfectly," Rand assured him. "Some people simply don't appreciate the importance of such things."

Thurston nodded eagerly. "That certainly describes Uncle. He has no artistic sense whatsoever. His idea of a good painting, for instance . . ."

Rand gave Susannah a cheerful grin and sat down beside her on the couch, forcing her to give way, however unwillingly. Speaking across her, as though she was no more than an inanimate obstruction, he asked, "Do you paint?"

Thurston flushed again. He moved his hands disparagingly. "A little. I would hesitate to show anyone my efforts."

This was news to Susannah, who had had no idea that Thurston possessed interests beyond charting his own genealogy and going to parties.

"Perhaps you will reconsider," Rand said. "I studied art a bit when I was living in Paris and—"

"I thought you studied music," Susannah interrupted tartly.

"I did," he said equably, "but there were times when I found it convenient to pop into a museum." With a smile that was purely for her, he said, "When it was raining, for instance."

She regretted her sharpness, wishing she hadn't needed to be reminded that affluence was a relatively new experience to him, one brought about solely through his own considerable efforts. He would not have been able to enjoy the usual refuges from inclement weather; restaurants and cafés would have been too expensive. He didn't seem to mind, though. She caught no hint of regret in him. On the contrary, his memories of that time, however difficult it had been, were pleasant.

"You lived in Paris?" Thurston broke in. "It's always been my dream to do that. Was it truly wonderful?"

"Magnificent. There really is no place like it on earth." He spread his hands, waxing lyrical, enjoying himself. "The bookstalls along the Seine, the wonderful aromas from the markets, the extraordinary blue light that comes over the rooftops in the evening."

"You really do know Paris," Thurston said admiringly. "I must hear more about it. Perhaps when you come tomorrow . . ."

"I'd be delighted," Rand assured him. He glanced at Susannah, as though vaguely surprised that she was still there. "That is, if this dear, sweet thing won't find our conversation too tedious."

The smile she gave him was no more than a baring of the teeth that, he did not doubt, she longed to sink into him. He smiled back, giving her fair warning that the battle was joined.

Susannah was not in the best of moods by the time she returned to her room. Though her cold was much better, she felt distinctly out of sorts. Rand was to blame. He had deliberately interfered with her plans, yet she couldn't manage to be angry at him, knowing as she did that he was simply trying to protect her. That she didn't need such protection didn't completely prevent her from appreciating the consideration behind his actions.

If only he weren't such an infuriating man. She understood little of what had gone on between him and Thurston. Rand seemed to know how to handle him with much less effort than she had to expend. But then, he could do more than a few things better than she could.

"Oh, no, my girl," she murmured to herself as, seated

at the dressing table, she began pulling pins from her hair. She wasn't for a moment going to think about what Rand was good at. That could lead her in only one direction, where she had absolutely no business going. It was enough that she would have a chance to look around Five Oaks. Though what exactly she would be looking for she didn't know.

Sukie bustled in a few moments later and took over the chore of untangling Susannah's hair. Afterward Susannah insisted on a bath before supper. "I'm fine now, and it's a nice warm evening. There can't possibly be any harm." Sukie grumbled but complied.

In the not-too-distant past servants would have had to cart pails of hot water up from the kitchens in order for Susannah to have a nice soak. But since indoor plumbing had been installed at Belleterre a few years before, she had only to turn the taps of her spacious porcelain tub set on elaborately carved feet.

When the tub was full, Susannah removed her ivory-and-pink silk dressing gown, hung it on a hook, and with a blissful sigh slipped into the water. Her hair was gathered at the crown of her head by a tortoiseshell clip. The tips of the long strands brushed her shoulders as she slid farther down in the tub, which was so large that, even lying nearly flat with only her head above water, she could not press her toes against the far end. She wiggled them contentedly, feeling the tension and anxiety of the last few weeks ease away.

If it hadn't been for the small clock on the table nearby, she would have lost all track of time. She delayed as long as she could, but the need to dress for dinner finally forced her to rise. Water sluiced off her slender body as she reached for a large Turkish towel Sukie had left out.

Her back was to the door when she heard a sound from the bedroom. Thinking her maid had returned, she wrapped the towel around herself and called, "You can come in. I'm drying off."

"What a shame," Rand drawled.

Susannah gasped and whirled around. Her foot slipped on the damp floor, and she would have fallen if she hadn't caught herself in time, even as Rand was hurriedly crossing the room toward her. "Oh, no," she said, holding him off with an outstretched arm. "Get back where you were. Better yet, get out entirely. What possessed you to come in here in the first place?"

"Sheer devilment," he replied cordially, his tawny eyes dancing as they swept over her barely concealed form.

"You can go to the devil," Susannah shot back. She'd had all she could take. He invaded her body—she conveniently forgot how eagerly she had welcomed him—and he invaded her privacy, as though he had a perfect right to do both.

The sudden fire in his gaze made her acutely aware of her dishevelment. Clutching the towel more firmly to her, she said, "I absolutely insist that you leave."

Rand appeared unimpressed by her firmness. "Not so fast. We've got a few things to talk about." He leaned against the side of the sink and smiled, as though perfectly content to remain there for an indefinite time.

"You can hardly expect me to . . ." she began as a warm flush suffused her cheeks. "Oh, what's the use? You've got less respect for the proprieties than any man I've ever met."

Rand appeared genuinely stung by the accusation. "I would hardly say that, considering my willingness to m——"

"Don't start that again," she warned, raising a hand. Belatedly she was reminded that she needed both hands to keep the towel in place. Grabbing the edges, she said, "At least let me put on a robe. I can't even think straight this way."

"I'm not sure that's a bad thing," Rand murmured, but he stood aside to let her pass.

In the bedroom she snatched a wrapper from the closet and disappeared behind the modesty screen. Her hands trembled as she secured the belt around her narrow waist. The robe was meant for warm weather wear in the privacy of her bedroom. It concealed little more than the towel had.

She was debating whether or not to try again to get Rand to leave, or to find something more ample to put on, when he called, "It won't do any good to keep hiding behind that thing. Sooner or later, you're going to have to come out."

The suggestion that she was afraid to face him had the desired effect. She stomped from behind the screen and glared at him. Rand had stretched out on the settee. His tie was loose, and his arms were folded behind his head. He looked insufferably at ease, as though he had every right to be there when in fact he had none.

Before she could point that out, in the most scathing terms, he drawled, "Did you really think I'd let you go over to Five Oaks alone, especially with Fortescue and Burke hanging around the place?"

"They won't be there," Susannah informed him haughtily.

His brow furrowed. "How do you know that?"

"It's simple logic, that's all. What you men are supposed to be good at. Thurston said his uncle would be away on business, but he still wouldn't have invited us if Fortescue and Burke were to be about. They must be going with Damien."

"I'd give a lot to know where to," Rand murmured, realizing that she was right. He should have thought of that, and would have if she weren't so damn distracting.

Susannah went over to the dressing table. She fiddled with a crystal vial of perfume while observing him in the mirror. "Then follow them. I'll find whatever there is to be found at Five Oaks."

Rand shook his head. "It's a tempting thought, but besides the fact that I don't want you there on your own, I'm no good at following people."

"You aren't?" she asked, startled that he should admit to not doing something superbly.

" 'Fraid not. However, I can think of somebody who might be . . ."

"Who?"

"That lad in the stables, Wilson. He's a smart boy, and I don't imagine he'd mind picking up a bit of extra money."

Susannah turned around abruptly, her hands on her hips. She was genuinely shocked. "That child? How could you even think of involving him?"

"Child? I'll bet he doesn't think of himself that way, and wouldn't appreciate knowing that you do. Besides, I'm not asking him to take any risks, just to keep his eyes and ears open."

"I don't like it."

Rand shrugged. He really didn't see what she was so concerned about. At twelve, he'd been dodging bullets at Bull Run, trying to stay alive from one moment to the next. "He can always refuse," he pointed out reasonably.

"But he won't," Susannah said. "He'll want whatever you offer to pay him, and he'll think of it as an adventure to boot."

"I'll make sure he understands he has to be careful," Rand promised her. He was touched by her concern for the boy. That was the kind of thing he associated with soft, tender women like his mother and sisters. Not like—

He broke off, suddenly confused. Susannah was soft and tender; he was absolutely certain of that. But she also had a streak of steel in her that he wasn't used to. The different sides of her nature should have been contradictory, but somehow they all seemed to fit together smoothly.

As smooth as the silken skin so lightly and enticingly covered by her robe. With a slight smile, he rose from the settee. Hardly aware of what he was doing, he crossed the short distance between them. "Susannah . . ." he murmured softly.

She loved the sound of her name on his lips, loved the

light in his eyes, loved the way his mouth turned up at the corners, loved the touch of it on her own. Gossamer light, questing, tantalizing. A low moan broke from her. She lifted her arms, twining them around his neck, and yielded to the long, passion-borne kiss.

When at last they drew apart, Rand looked tenderly down at her. Her emerald eyes were smoky with desire but also with concern. He knew she was as bewildered by what was happening between them as he was himself, and he felt driven to reassure her. "It will be all right, Susannah, I promise."

She longed to believe him, indeed almost managed to. She raised up on tiptoe and touched her lips to his once again. "I hope so, Rand. Oh, how I hope so. But . . ." She forced herself to smile. "But nothing will be 'all right' if my father finds you in here. That would be enough to start another war all by itself."

"Can't have that," he said as he gently released her and stepped back. Privately he didn't think it would be a bad thing for Jeffrey to stumble on them. That, at least, would resolve the matter of her refusal to marry him.

She saw his reluctance and guessed what he was thinking. Before he could comment further, she pushed him toward the door. "Father might not worry you, but Sukie should. She'll be in here any minute to help me dress, and if she finds you . . ."

"Heaven forbid," Rand murmured with a laugh. He was tempted to take her in his arms again, Sukie be damned, but he understood he had pushed her as far as he could. His gaze intent on hers, he said, "I'll see you downstairs, Susannah."

She nodded, watching as he opened the door, paused to glance up and down the corridor, then vanished. He went as quickly and stealthily as he had come, moving with the grace of a great hunting cat.

When he was gone, she sighed deeply and mentally shook herself. She was a fool to be so swept away by him, especially when such vital matters demanded her attention. Yet perhaps precisely because of that, she couldn't resist the urge to savor every moment they spent together and to relive them in her memory.

She was still lost in reverie a short while later when Sukie paused in the midst of brushing her hair and asked, "Somethin' on your mind, child?"

Susannah looked up, startled. "What? Oh, no, I was just thinking."

" 'Bout what?"

"Nothing special."

Sukie laughed, a warm, rich sound. "You might call him that, honeychild, but I sure wouldn't. That there's one special man, if you ask me."

Susannah's eyes met Sukie's in the mirror. "Why, Sukie," she said, "I've no idea who you mean."

The black woman laughed again. She shook her head and resumed her brushing. Susannah went on smiling.

16

"And this, of course, is the music room," Thurston said, gesturing broadly with his arm. Susannah and Rand looked around silently. It was a large, graceful space, with a high ceiling on which the original mural could still be seen, at least in parts. Flecks of it had peeled off over the years, leaving patches of bare white plaster underneath. In one corner there was a long, brown stain, indicating water leakage, possibly from one of the crumbling gutters above the windows.

A piano stood at one end of the room in front of double French doors that led to the garden. Susannah walked over to it and ran her hand over the closed lid. "Does anyone play it?" she asked.

Thurston shook his head. "I never learned, and Uncle . . ." His voice trailed off. It was hardly necessary to explain that his uncle had no time for such fripperies.

Near the piano was a harp. Rand plucked a string, and a sharp, discordant sound rang out. The strings had been allowed to loosen, with the result that the harp was badly out of tune. That didn't surprise him; rather it suited his mood. Five Oaks depressed him. He couldn't say exactly why, except that he hated all waste and this place was rampant with it. The waste of beauty and elegance sacrificed for some twisted sense of what was and was not important. It made him sad and angry. He felt an unexpected moment of sympathy for Thurston, who at least had the sense to want to restore it.

"There's a great deal you could do here," Rand said almost to himself.

Thurston brightened. He had been downcast as the tour proceeded, perhaps because Rand was paying more attention to Susannah than to him. He had no way of knowing that Rand was doing so because he suspected her of planning to slip off and conduct a search. One of them would have to, of course, but he preferred that it be him. Getting Thurston to stay with her was the problem. He had yet to come up with a persuasive enough strategy.

"What would you do?" Thurston asked, looking at him eagerly.

Rand suppressed a sigh. He could tell by the younger man's expression that he was hoping for a nice long talk about current styles of decor, of which Rand knew nothing. But the solution to Thurston's decorating problems seemed perfectly obvious to him.

"I'd leave it alone," he said. "I wouldn't make any alterations at all. It's perfect as it is. All it needs is a little cosmetic work—paint, varnish."

Thurston looked disappointed. Clearly he was itching to do far more. "I think some of the rooms are awkwardly arranged," he suggested. "This one, for example. Don't you think the ceiling is too high?"

Rand actually thought it was just right, especially for its purpose. "You have to consider the acoustics," he murmured, "at least if you're going to keep it as a music room."

Thurston regarded Susannah, still standing beside the piano, her hand resting lightly on it. He smiled complacently. "I suppose I'll have to, won't I?"

Rand's face tightened. It was all he could do not to disabuse Thurston of that notion in the most graphic way possible. Only the strictest self-discipline stopped him. He managed to shrug casually. "Shall we move on?"

They had already seen the major public rooms that took up the first floor, with one exception. "The library is through here," Thurston said as he led the way down a corridor.

Rand touched Susannah lightly on the back, urging her ahead. They exchanged looks of unspoken understanding. Despite her stated desire to see every nook and cranny, it was unlikely that Thurston's tour would extend to his uncle's office. He was too afraid of the old man to enter his inner sanctum even in his absence. Yet that was the place to start if they hoped to find anything important.

The office was next door to the library. Its door was closed. A heavy knob of engraved silver gleamed dully in the shadowed light. Susannah had to fight against the all-but-irresistible temptation to try turning it. If the door was locked, she would just as soon know now.

Thurston gave her no opportunity to find out. He stood aside at the open library door and ushered them ahead. "Some of the volumes in here are remarkable," he said. "It seems that several generations of my ancestors had a penchant for collecting. I admit I don't share the interest, but the books look nice, don't you think?"

This last part he addressed to Rand, who nodded absently. He was engaged in studying the spines of the books nearest him, noting that many were more than a century old and were rare first editions of important works.

"Very impressive," he murmured as he touched a finger to a leather binding. It came away smudged. However disciplined Damien thought his servants, they didn't seem particularly conscientious about their housekeeping. There was dust everywhere, but especially in what gave every sign of being a rarely entered room.

"The molding is Italianate," Thurston pointed out. "My great-grandfather had it brought over from some palace in Venice."

"He had good taste," Susannah said quietly, thinking

of all the palaces that must have been looted to provide
Five Oaks with its amenities. That those ornaments should
then go unappreciated saddened her.

Her gaze fell on an ivory chess board set out on a
nearby table. "Where did this come from?"

Thurston looked at it blankly for a moment. "China, I
think, or Japan. You know, I'd forgotten this was here. I
really should move it somewhere else, where it would get
some use."

"You play chess?" Rand asked.

Thurston affected a modest shrug. "Tolerably well.
You?"

"Not too badly." Rand looked at the board already set
up for a game and silently debated what to do. Clearly the
means of distracting Thurston were at hand. The trouble
was, they required him to do the distracting while Susannah did the searching. She gave him a small, triumphant
smile.

"Why don't the two of you have a game?" she suggested.

Thurston made no secret of being tempted, but he still
hesitated. "You wouldn't think it rude?"

"Oh, no," she assured him. "Not at all. I'll just wan-
der about outside. You know how I love gardens, and I've
been just itching to see what-all you have here."

In fact, Thurston had known no such thing about her,
but the promise of a chess game with Rand, and Susannah's assurance that she would not mind being on her
own, combined to make the offer irresistible.

"Well . . . if you really won't feel rejected . . ."

She beamed both men a warm smile and picked up her
skirts. "Just forget that I'm here."

Rand suppressed a groan. He had visions of the vast
mischief she could get into while he was trapped entertaining Thurston. "I haven't played in years," he said. "It's
liable to be a fast game."

"Don't hurry on my account," Susannah told him

brightly. It was all she could do to not flounce out of the
room humming a little tune.

Once beyond the door, her expression sobered. She
didn't for a moment underestimate the enormity of her
task, or the risk involved. Granted, she could count on
Rand to keep Thurston occupied. But she didn't know who
else was in the house.

There was a possibility, however remote, that Burke and
Fortescue were still lurking about. Even more important,
there were the servants to consider. They might hate Damien, but that didn't mean that if they caught her, they
would keep quiet about it. She might instead be seen as a
way of currying favor with him.

With all that in mind, she walked the few steps to
Damien's office. Her heart was beating heavily as she
turned the silver doorknob. It squeaked slightly and she
almost jumped back, but she forced herself to go on. Only
when she had turned it as far as she possibly could were
her worst fears confirmed. The door was locked.

She stood for a moment, undecided. She could always
try to enter through one of the windows. That had worked
well enough in reverse, but then she had been dressed very
differently. She pictured herself getting tangled in her
petticoats, hanging floundering from the window. It was
not an encouraging image.

If the office was no longer the best possibility, she
would just have to look elsewhere. Keeping an eye out for
anyone lurking about, she made her way back to the
central hallway. There she glanced around as she tried to
decide what to do.

The hallway rose three stories to a central dome painted
to depict the night sky over Five Oaks. Around it were
plaster medallions of the Sanderses gotten up in the guise
of Roman nobles. Their hooded eyes seemed to follow
Susannah as she turned in a full circle, her skirt fluttering
around her, looking for some clue as to which way she
should go.

The central hallway was dominated by an immense
marble-and-mahogany staircase that curved up out of sight.
Lacking any reasonable alternative, she began to climb it.
After a few steps, as she committed herself more wholeheartedly to that course, she broke into a light run that
quickly carried her to the second-floor landing.

There she paused and looked up and down the long
hallway. Closed doors led to rooms on either side. There
were a dozen in all. Holding her breath, she hastened to
the first one, turned the knob, and peered inside. A quick
glance told her she had found Thurston's room. A gray
evening coat she remembered seeing him wear hung from
a wooden valet. A chess set, inferior to the one in the
library, was set up on a table near the bed.

She withdrew immediately, convinced that there was
nothing of value there. Thurston undoubtedly knew what
was being plotted since he had been present at the meeting
in Damien's office, but she was convinced his uncle would
never trust him with anything that might betray their
intentions.

She was intent on finding Damien's own room when she
opened the next door, peeked inside, and almost immediately withdrew. The room was clearly intended for guests
and appeared to be unoccupied. Only when she paused and
took a second look did she notice that a man's hairbrush
and various other items were laid out on the bureau. She
stepped into the room, and her eyes narrowed. On the
floor near the bed was the valise she had seen on board the
Essex, the one bearing the initials S.R.M.

Yet, so far as she knew, only Burke and Fortescue were
staying at the house, not the unknown S.R.M., whoever
he was.

She was wondering what that meant when a sound from
the drive in front of the house drew her up short. She
hurried to the window and glanced out. Her hand went to
her throat as she stared down at the arriving carriage.

Barely had the carriage door opened than Damien Sanders got out, quickly followed by Burke and Fortescue.

Running for all she was worth, Susannah tore out of the room. She skittered around a corner, almost losing her balance in the process, and was about to hurl herself down the steps when she realized that to do so would bring her almost literally into Damien's lap. Instead, she looked around frantically for the back staircase. After several nerve-straining moments she found it and raced down the narrow steps. They brought her out near a side door through which she was able to reach the gardens.

She was seated on a stone bench, struggling to catch her breath, when Thurston emerged from the house. With him were Rand and an extremely irate Damien.

"Ah, there you are," Thurston said with palpable relief. "I told Uncle you had gone to inspect the gardens."

Susannah managed a smile, which wilted slightly in the face of the elder Sanders's scowl. "Don't like people wandering around," he said bluntly. "No telling what they'll get into."

Susannah ignored his rudeness. "Oh, I'm so sorry. Rand and Thurston were playing chess, and I just couldn't resist a stroll through the gardens. They're quite lovely." In fact, they were weary and weed infested, although not lacking in potential.

She stood up, relieved that her wide skirt hid her still trembling legs, and turned to Rand. "How is the game going?"

"Fine," he said, "but I think we should continue it at another time." Lying straightforwardly, he added, "I had forgotten that your father is expecting us back shortly."

"Oh, yes," Susannah murmured, "that's right." To Damien, she said, "You know he hasn't been terribly well lately. I don't like to be away from him for any length of time."

As she spoke, she began moving toward the door, Rand at her side. Thurston still looked intensely uncomfortable, and Damien continued to scowl suspiciously at them. Susannah glanced up for a moment and noticed the half-hidden form of a man in a second-story window. Someone else—Burke or Fortescue, possibly both—was watching them.

She shivered inwardly but managed to maintain a smile. "Thank you so much for letting us drop by, Thurston."

"It was nothing," he muttered, clearly wishing he'd never invited them. Little imagination was required to envision the dressing down he was about to receive from his uncle. She almost felt sorry for him before she remembered he had himself to blame for being Damien's toady.

"I'll see you out," Thurston offered, as if eager to avoid being left alone.

"That isn't necessary," Rand said. He took Susannah's arm. "We know the way."

Damien raised a thin, blue-veined hand. Instantly Thurston stopped and stood resignedly in place. The elder Sanders did not offer them the courtesy of a farewell. He merely stared after them as they withdrew, his rheumy eyes boring into their backs.

When they had regained the outer courtyard, Rand murmured, "Don't say a word. Just pretend that everything is normal."

"I'm trying," Susannah whispered back. "It isn't easy. Why did they return so suddenly?"

"I've no idea," he said, then fell silent as they came upon the carriage. The rains of a few nights before, added to the earlier effect of the spring thaw, had swelled the river to bursting. The levees were threatened from Richmond all the way through the Tidewater. Susannah and Rand had promised Jeffrey they would not cross by boat. They had agreed instead to take the longer way around, using a bridge that crossed some five miles downriver.

A servant opened the carriage door, then stood aside as Rand helped Susannah in. Both were still conscious of being watched as they took their places and the door was closed. Not until the wheels were rolling and they were on their way down the drive did they both breathe sighs of relief.

"That was close," Rand said. "Where were you when you realized they had returned?"

"In a guest room on the second floor." She paused to withdraw a lacy handkerchief from a hidden pocket of her dress and touched it lightly to her brow. Ladies might not sweat, but she was certainly doing something suspiciously close to that. And she didn't blame herself a bit.

"I couldn't get into Damien's office," she explained. "The door is locked. So I went upstairs to see what I could find. A funny thing happened. In the guest room, I came upon a valise that I saw on board the *Essex*."

"What's odd about that?" Rand asked, his tawny eyes watching her closely. He understood that she'd had a fright, but she was handling it extremely well. Only someone who truly knew her, as he was beginning to believe he did, would have noticed her agitation. Even so, she looked remarkably lovely. Her color was high, her hair slightly disarrayed, and her breasts moved enchantingly with each breath she took. He smiled wryly, chiding himself for being so easily distracted at the same time that he knew she would always have that effect on him, no matter what the circumstances.

"There are initials on the valise," Susannah was explaining. "S.R.M. Doesn't that mean it can't belong to either Fortescue or Burke?"

"One would think so," Rand agreed thoughtfully. "Is there someone else involved whom we know nothing about?"

"That appears to be the case, unless . . ."

They stared at each other. Softly Susannah said, "Unless Burke is S.R.M. That would explain what the valise was doing on the *Essex* as well as here."

Rand nodded. "It fits, but then the question is: Who is S.R.M.?"

Neither of them had an answer to that. They returned to
Belleterre in silence, each occupied with private thoughts.
Susannah was, of course, deeply worried about what was
going on at Five Oaks, but she hadn't completely accepted
Rand's view that an assassination plot was in the works.
That idea still seemed so outlandish that she could barely
conceive of it.

Perhaps in reaction to her near apprehension a short time
before, she shied away from thinking about the situation.
Instead, she became absorbed in more personal matters.
But as hard as she tried to prevent it, her gaze kept
returning to Rand.

He was seated across from her, his long legs stretched
out in front of him, his arms folded lightly over his chest.
He was dressed casually in the customary summer apparel
worn by planters, a white cotton shirt left open at the
collar and ivory-hued linen trousers, and he looked perfectly at home in his garb. His skin was bronzed by the
sun, which had also lightened his hair. It was growing too
long; she smiled secretly to herself as she considered what
his response would be if she offered to trim it for him.

The idea of performing such a wifely task for him both
pleased and dismayed her. She had hardly forgotten his
ill-phrased proposal. It continued to rankle deep within
her, and if she thought about it too much, her composure
would threaten to crack.

Afraid of the direction of her thoughts, she forced herself to turn away from Rand and stare out the window
instead. They were passing through an area of flat green
fields planted with cotton slowly ripening in the sun. The
carriage wheels creaked rhythmically in the dirt ruts deepened by recent rains. The river ran nearby. She could see
that it was still high, the water frothing as it washed high
up along the banks. A shiver ran through her as she stared
into its ominous depths.

Rand saw her tremble. He put out his arms in invitation
and she went to him. She nestled against him, her head on

his chest. They shared a brief interlude of peace and contentment that endured until they drove up the drive to Belleterre.

Glancing out the window, Susannah saw Aunt Miriam standing on the veranda. The older woman's face was white and strained, her hands clasped tightly in front of her to control their shaking. As the carriage rolled to a stop, she hurried toward them.

"Oh, my dear," she said as Susannah leaped out, not waiting for Rand's assistance, "I'm so sorry. Your father . . ."

Susannah heard nothing more. She picked up her skirts and ran into the house, leaving Miriam and Rand staring after her.

17

All this fuss," Jeffrey said, "and over what? I admit to a slight feeling of indisposition, but really, Miriam, that was no reason to become so upset."

Whatever sting there might have been in his words was erased by his tender smile. He reached out a hand to Miriam, who quickly took it and came closer to the bed.

"I'm sorry, Jeffrey," she said softly. "But when you suddenly became so pale and lost consciousness . . ."

"I most certainly did not," he insisted stoutly. "A momentary dizziness, perhaps, but no more than that. At any rate, whatever it was hasn't lingered. I feel fine now."

"Nonetheless, sir," Rand interjected smoothly, "you might be well advised to rest a bit longer. After all, there's no point in upsetting the ladies, is there?"

As Jeffrey hesitated, Susannah added her own plea. "Say you'll rest, Father. Aunt Miriam and I are both terribly worried. So is Rand. None of us wants anything bad to happen to you."

"And nothing will," he said with a hint of irritation, "provided I'm allowed to go about my business. This idea of keeping me in bed, coddling me like an invalid, even sending for that quack Smithers—"

"Quack?" Susannah echoed. "You were all for getting

him down here to see me, and your condition is far more serious.''

''It's nothing of the sort,'' Jeffrey insisted. Yet despite his protests he made no attempt to leave the bed. Lines of weariness radiated from around his eyes and mouth. Though his color had returned, he still looked badly strained. Susannah could well understand why her aunt had become so concerned.

Just then, however, Miriam appeared more angry than worried. ''Very well, Jeffrey,'' she said stiffly, ''please yourself. You've always made it clear that you need no one's assistance or care. Go your own way, keep right on with what you've been doing, just don't expect to live very long.'' Her voice broke. She turned away abruptly and hurried toward the door.

Susannah and Rand exchanged startled glances, which deepened as Jeffrey raised himself and called out, ''Miriam, I'm sorry. Come back here.'' When she hesitated, he added softly, ''Please. You're quite right, I've been behaving like a boor. I do need to stay here, at least for a while. It's just that I hate to admit it.''

Her face softened as she turned back to him. ''I understand that, Jeffrey. You're used to being in perfect health, and you will be again. You simply need a little time.'' She glanced at Susannah and Rand as she added, ''And freedom from the strain you seem to be under lately.''

''That will pass,'' he murmured, but without conviction.

Miriam hesitated, clearly wrestling with herself. After a while she said softly, ''Jeffrey, you received a letter this morning. I believe you were reading it when you were stricken. Did its contents cause you some concern that might have brought on the attack?''

Susannah watched, fascinated, as her father stared at Miriam for a moment in surprise, then flushed and looked away. ''Nonsense. The letter had nothing whatsoever to do with it.''

''The letter was brought by private messenger,'' Miriam

said gently. "What was so urgent that it couldn't wait for the usual mail service?"

Concerned by her father's growing agitation, Susannah felt compelled to intervene. "Do we really have to discuss this now? Surely Father should be resting."

"I agree," Miriam said softly, "but I'm afraid there may not be time to delay. I could, of course, simply find the letter—I believe it's still lying on the floor in the library—and read it for myself, but I'm loath to do that." She looked at Jeffrey, who was regarding her with puzzlement.

Quietly he asked, "Why is it so important for you to know what's in that letter?"

"For two reasons," she replied. "I believe the news it contains was responsible for your attack, no matter what you say. I also think it is possible that it concerns us as well as you." With a nod to Susannah and Rand, she explained, "I caught a glimpse of the envelope. It bears Lord Beaufort's seal."

Susannah inhaled sharply. Rand took a step closer to the bed. He fought to contain himself, wanting to do nothing that might upset Jeffrey, but like Miriam he believed they had stumbled onto something that could prove vital. "Sir," he said, "if the British ambassador has communicated something of importance to you, it would be well advised of you to tell us."

Jeffrey looked from one to the other of the group gathered around the bed. His frown deepened. "Why? What possible interest could you have in my dealings with Lord Beaufort?"

"Perhaps none," Rand acknowledged. "But I believe there is a possibility that you and he are engaged in a matter which also—" He paused, looking at Miriam and Susannah. They both nodded imperceptibly. "Which also," he continued, "has our attention. A matter involving . . . President Lee."

Jeffrey stared blankly at them. For a long time his face

revealed nothing, then slowly it reflected surprise and growing awareness. "How," he asked softly, "did you know that?"

"I didn't," Rand admitted. "It was simply a guess. You've been under an enormous strain recently, far greater than your business dealings could account for. And you've been in close contact with Lord Beaufort. I believe he called on you shortly before you left Richmond."

Jeffrey's gaze shifted to his daughter, who flushed slightly. "Papa, if you have learned something concerning President Lee, you must tell us."

"Us?" he repeated, looking from her to Miriam, who was flushing darkly. "Not Rand alone, but all of you?"

The two women glanced anxiously at each other. "I'm afraid so," Miriam said finally. She sat down on the side of the bed and took Jeffrey's hand once again. "My dear, I'm afraid you aren't going to much like what we have to tell you. I would do anything to postpone this moment, but it simply can't be done. Lee is arriving in Yorktown tomorrow and—"

"That's just as well," Jeffrey stated quietly. "The sooner he's out of Richmond the better. His life is in danger there."

The three exchanged startled glances. With some difficulty Susannah asked, "How do you know that?"

Jeffrey released a deep sigh. "I may as well tell you. It will have to come out eventually anyway. Some time ago Lord Beaufort came to me with a matter that deeply concerned him. He had begun to hear rumors that there would be an attempt to reunify the Union and the Confederacy, to make them one nation once again. Further, he had been given to understand that there were powerful factions in both Britain and the South that were sworn to prevent it. Lately, there have been indications that they were willing to resort to violence in order to achieve their ends."

"I understood, sir," Rand said carefully, "that you yourself oppose reunification."

"I do," Jeffrey said bluntly, "but that doesn't mean I think men should be killed in order to prevent it." Quietly he added, "Especially not one particular man. Robert E. Lee has been the cornerstone of the Confederacy. It is no exaggeration to say that I not only respect but also genuinely love him. However I may disagree with him on the question of reunification, I am unalterably opposed to any attempt to silence him."

"Silence," Susannah repeated. "Do you mean assassinate?"

Jeffrey hesitated. "Yes, I'm afraid that's exactly what I mean." He sat up farther in the bed, impatient with his own weakness. Now that the truth was out, he could no longer contain the secret worry that had plagued him for so many weeks.

"Lord Beaufort and I both became suspicious recently that an assassination plot might be in the works. We've been doing some discreet checking on our own to discover whether our fears were well founded. The letter I received contained the news that a British ship which recently arrived in Richmond—the *Essex*—carried a passenger traveling under an alias. His real name is Seamus Rufus McMahon. He's known to be a paid killer wanted for murder in Britain and on the Continent."

"Burke," Susannah said, so softly that her father did not hear her.

"He's in Richmond now," Jeffrey went on. "Beaufort believes he's been smuggled in to kill Lee, and I'm very much afraid he's right. If he succeeds . . ."

"He isn't," Rand interrupted. "That is, Beaufort may well be right, but McMahon isn't in Richmond."

"He's right here," Susannah said. "At Five Oaks."

Her father's eyes narrowed speculatively. "Would you mind telling me how you know that?"

"We saw him," Susannah explained, "just a short time ago when we were visiting Thurston. He's there with the captain of the *Essex*."

"I can understand your being able to recognize Fortescue," Jeffrey said, "since you've encountered him at social functions, but how did you put this man Burke together with McMahon?"

Susannah hesitated, at a loss as to what to say that would not send her father into a rage and perhaps further threaten his health in the process. Sensing her quandary, Rand said, "It's a complicated story, sir, and unfortunately we don't have a great deal of time. Would it be possible to postpone explanations until a more opportune moment?"

Jeffrey gave him a hard, steady stare. "Ordinarily I would not even entertain that notion, young man. However, under the circumstances . . ." He cast a quick glance at Susannah, who stood with her eyes downcast, looking uncharacteristically subdued.

"It appears to me," Jeffrey said slowly, "that the forthcoming explanations will be very interesting." He let that sink in before adding, "In the meantime I will take it as given that you recognized McMahon at Five Oaks. But why would he be there?"

No one had to answer the question for him; he did it himself. "To be closer to Yorktown and Lee. To lay their final plans." He uttered a low, explicit curse that wrung shocked looks from both Miriam and Susannah. "Damn Damien Sanders and all those like him. The insufferable arrogance of the man, thinking he can enforce his will over that of the people."

Jeffrey's face darkened as he slammed a fist into the palm of his hand. "We didn't fight and die for our freedom to lose it to a man of Damien's stripe. Misguided though Lee may be, he has the right to state his case unmolested. By God, I want to see him get that chance."

"Then he must be warned," Rand said quietly. "He has to be convinced to take precautions to protect himself."

"A letter," Jeffrey suggested. "I'll write it immediately explaining what we've learned. Rand, if you would be good enough to carry it to Yorktown for me . . ."

"I would be delighted," Rand assured him. "However, I'm not certain such a letter would have the impact you desire."

Jeffrey frowned as he considered that possibility. "Lee is hardly a foolish man . . ."

"But he knows you oppose his goals," Rand interjected. "While he may not suspect you personally of trying to trick him into believing there is danger where there is none, he may consider the possibility that you yourself are being used. No, if our information is to have the necessary impact, it must be brought to Lee by someone he trusts implicitly." Meaningfully he glanced at Susannah.

Jeffrey followed Rand's gaze, his eyes dark with surprise and speculation. "More of those explanations that will be forthcoming?"

"Yes, Papa," she said softly.

He was silent for what seemed to them all like a very long time. Finally he sighed deeply. "I don't believe I've ever before been asked to take so much on faith, but it seems I have no choice. All right, Susannah, you have my permission to go to Yorktown, provided, of course, that Rand accompanies you."

"That's wonderful, Father," she exclaimed. "Thank you—"

"Not so fast," Jeffrey admonished. "I expect you to speak with Lee, explain what's happened, then return here at once. You are not to linger there a moment longer than necessary. Is that understood?"

She hesitated, biting her lower lip, but finally she nodded. "Yes, I understand."

"Good. Rand, I expect you to keep a very close eye on her. Very close. Not, mind you, that I'm suggesting Susannah's word is less than her bond. However, she is inclined on occasion to be . . . overly enthusiastic. I am depending on you to protect her from that tendency."

Rand took a deep breath, thinking this was no time to dwell on how singularly ill-equipped he was to cope with

Susannah's enthusiasm, not when he had been on the receiving end of it himself and longed to be again. However, honor demanded that he live up to Jeffrey's trust in him.

"I'll do my best, sir," he promised.

Jeffrey appeared satisfied with that. He relaxed somewhat as Miriam said, "Where will you stay on such short notice? With Lee coming and the ball scheduled, Yorktown is bound to be crowded."

Susannah thought for a moment. With some reluctance she said, "What about Cousin Julia? She would put us up, don't you think?"

"Cousin Julia," Jeffrey repeated with thinly veiled distaste. He was the most chivalrous of men; it wasn't in him to speak ill of any woman, but he came very close when he considered his Yorktown relation. She was a thin ratchet of a woman, forever given to interfering in other people's lives. For years she had been trying to pair him with her numerous female acquaintances, all equally unappealing. Moreover, she and Miriam did not get along well.

"Are you sure you want to do this?" he asked.

"I'm afraid I don't see any alternative," Susannah admitted.

Jeffrey sighed. "All right, I'll send a message to her at once to tell her you're coming. Remember, Rand," he added, "I'm counting on you to be responsible for Susannah's safety."

"And I'll be responsible for his," she chimed in before Rand could reply. Enormously relieved to have her father's permission, she wasn't even particularly irked by his reminder that young ladies weren't considered capable of looking after themselves. Still, she couldn't resist teasing as she jumped up and kissed Jeffrey's cheek. "I'll be sure to give Cousin Julia your love."

"Spare me," he said with a wan laugh. "I wouldn't want her getting any ideas." Glancing at Miriam, he added, "Especially now."

As her aunt blushed prettily, Susannah looked from one
to the other with unfeigned interest, until Rand's discreet
cough reminded her of her manners. She glanced away
then, but not without a sense of relief that at least for her
father and aunt happiness seemed possible. For her and
Rand there could be no such assurance.

A short while later, after speedily completed preparations, they were back in the carriage and rolling down the
gravel drive. Susannah was silent at first, her thoughts on
her dual worry for her father and Lee. Rand saw the
shadows in her eyes and put an arm gently around her.

"Don't worry," he murmured, "Jeffrey will be fine and
we'll get to Lee in time."

She sighed deeply and let her head rest against his
shoulder. "I hope so. It's bad enough that my father's
health should be affected, but the situation with Lee is
nightmarish. That anyone should even think of killing
him . . ."

Rand didn't share her genuine shock at the idea of an
assassination plot. He had a great deal more experience in
the ways of the world and knew far better than she what
people were capable of. For that reason alone he was
determined to protect her whether she wanted him to or
not.

Yet he was also a prudent man who learned from his
mistakes. While his genuine respect and admiration for
Susannah might cause him to try to explain exactly why he
thought she needed to be protected, sheer practicality
weighed against such a course. He had no doubt that were
he even to broach the subject, the snuggling kitten in his
arms would promptly turn into a spitting cat.

Rand was no more enamored of trouble than any sensible man. He warred only briefly with his conscience before settling back against the leather seat. Let her think
what she would until they got to Yorktown. Soon enough
she would find that he had absolutely no intention of
allowing her to endanger herself.

Having decided that, he felt more at ease. Susannah, however, did not. He could hear the worry in her voice as she said, "Even if Lee does believe there is a plot to assassinate him, he may refuse to change his schedule. Certainly he will still want to appear at the ball."

"Probably," Rand agreed. "We will have to deal with that as best we can. In the meantime it would be a good idea for you to get some rest."

She saw the sense in that and agreed. They passed the remainder of the journey in silence. Susannah slept, cradled in his arms. Rand was content simply to gaze at her, marveling at the delicacy of face and form that hid such strength, such stubbornness. A rueful laugh broke from him, quickly stifled when she stirred and murmured in her sleep. He gathered her closer, his head resting on her hair, and fought against the wish that their journey might go on forever, that there might never be anything except the two of them safe from all the rest of the world.

Susannah awoke as the carriage came to a halt in front of the Costain residence—Cousin Julia was a Costain by marriage. Her husband was a sea captain who was rarely home. Susannah sometimes wondered whether he had chosen his occupation before or after his marriage.

As Rand was helping Susannah from their conveyance, the front door was thrown open and a tall, thin woman, incongruously dressed in a frilly, beribboned frock that would have better suited a young girl, emerged and strode toward them.

"There you are," she said, her voice pitched at a note intended to be high and fluting but that succeeded only in being shrill. "I've been looking out the window every five minutes since your father's messenger arrived. Where is the dear man?"

"Father remained at Belleterre," Susannah said. "Surely he explained that he would be doing so in his note?"

"He did," her cousin acknowledged, her small eyes

focused on Rand. She stared at him down her beaked nose and sniffed audibly. "But I didn't credit it. What could he be thinking of, allowing you to run around the countryside unchaperoned?"

Far from appearing perturbed by the woman's rudeness, Rand beamed at her warmly and reached out to take her hand. "Only that Susannah couldn't possibly have been safer, Mrs. Costain. And may I say how much I appreciate your hospitality? It isn't often that a traveler is so warmly welcomed, but then, that is the Southern tradition, isn't it?"

Susannah could barely avoid choking as Rand kissed her cousin's beringed hand. Cousin Julia clearly remained unconvinced, but she was weakening.

"In my day," she said as she led the way up the front steps and into the house, "there was such a thing as propriety. A young girl didn't just decide to go where she pleased when she pleased." With a censorious glance at Susannah she demanded, "Why didn't you let me know sooner that you planned to attend the ball?"

"Actually," Susannah murmured, "I didn't know myself until quite recently. Mr. Cabot is staying with us, you see, and I thought he would enjoy it."

Putting the onus on Rand had the effect of redirecting her cousin's attention to him. She stared up at the tall, tawny-haired man with the lion's eyes, and shrugged. "Well, you'll raise a few eyebrows, that's for sure. At any rate, I've no time to waste worrying about it. Did you know the president is going to be there? There's so much to be done. I don't have a moment to spare. Jameson," she called, "Jameson, where are you?"

A tall, somber man with a long-suffering air appeared. "Here, madam. May I be of some assistance?"

Cousin Julia waved a hand in their direction. "Guests," she said succinctly. "They need looking after. See to it."

So saying, she bustled away, leaving them to the butler's care. He sighed and cast a dubious eye at their sparse luggage. "If you would come with me."

He showed Rand to a small room on the first floor toward the back of the house; Susannah was given a room above and in the front. Cousin Julia could not have contrived to put more distance between them unless she had put one in the backyard gazebo. Susannah didn't doubt the possibility of doing just that had occurred to her cousin.

Once upstairs, Susannah quickly unpacked with the help of a small, silent maid. She had decided in consultation with Aunt Miriam to leave Sukie at Belleterre. While neither remotely questioned the servant's trustworthiness, they thought it best not to involve anyone else in a potentially dangerous mission.

As the maid put away the contents of the small trunk, Susannah surreptitiously slid a small leather satchel to the back of the wardrobe. She then returned to the main floor, hoping to find Rand without bumping into Cousin Julia, and was rewarded when she saw him emerging from his own quarters. "I have to go out for a short time," he said. At her inquiring glance he added, "To see if I can get more accurate information about when Lee will be arriving."

She frowned, surprised by this sudden turn of events. "How do you plan to do that?"

"I . . . uh . . . have friends here who may prove helpful." He was not about to explain further. There was no need for Susannah to know that the Bagatelle Club had its summer quarters in Yorktown, where many of its most faithful patrons fled to escape the worst of the heat. Lillie had long since decided that there was no reason for them to be deprived of her services in the process. She had left the city a few days before and should be nicely settled in by now.

"Do you have any idea how long you'll be gone?" Susannah asked worriedly, even though she sensed he would tell her nothing more.

Rand shook his head. "Can you make an excuse for me at supper if need be?"

"I'll come up with something." Her eyes met his. Softly she added, "Be careful."

"You, too," he murmured. Without bothering to look around to see if anyone was watching them, he bent his head and kissed her gently. "Stay put until I get back."

Susannah muttered something that might have been taken for agreement. She watched as he let himself out the front door and closed it quietly behind him. She was fighting against the urge to go after him, to share whatever danger he might confront. Only with a great effort was she able to restrain herself and, like a dutiful guest, go offer her presence to Cousin Julia.

After two long, strained hours of listening to her cousin expound about everything that was wrong with all her neighbors, not to mention Susannah herself, while ostensibly tying up favors for the ball the following night, Susannah was more than willing to return to her room to change for a late supper.

She had alerted her hostess to Rand's absence, saying he had an ill friend in town he felt obliged to visit. Whether Cousin Julia believed her or not wasn't important; the woman's nose was put out of joint at the mere idea that anyone sleeping under her roof should choose to be elsewhere.

She said as much when Susannah reluctantly rejoined her and the two sat down together to a meal of chicken and salad. Susannah suffered through the meal and was on her way up to bed, thinking about Rand and wondering what was keeping him, when she heard a faint knocking at the back door. The servants were in the kitchen belowstairs, finally having their own supper. Unwilling to disturb them, Susannah answered the door herself.

18

L ord, miss," Wilson exclaimed, "am I ever glad to see you. I been worrying all the way here that I wouldn't be able to find the place."

"Come in," Susannah said as she stood aside for him to enter. She was equally relieved to see the young boy whose safety had greatly concerned her. Putting a finger to her lips, she cautioned him. "The servants are below and my cousin has retired for the night, but we must be cautious. It would be difficult to explain your presence."

"That it would, miss," he whispered, "and I won't linger." He took a deep breath and explained quickly, "They said at Belleterre that Mr. Cabot had come here with you. Can I speak with him then?"

"I'm afraid not," Susannah answered. "He went out some time ago and hasn't returned. But you can tell me whatever you would tell him."

The boy hesitated, then made up his mind. "I been watching Five Oaks, miss, since I followed the three gents back there. They met somebody on the bridge, you see. Whatever he told them made them turn around again. Anyway, I knew from talking to Mr. Cabot that something might be up, so I figured to stay around and see what happened.

"I saw you and Mr. Cabot leave," he went on, "then I settled back to wait. Soon as it was full dark, they came out, they did, all three of them. Mr. Sanders the elder and Mr. Thurston got into a carriage. That fellow Burke was on horseback. I didn't know what to do then, but I remembered Mr. Cabot had told me to watch out for Burke in particular, so I figured I'd best follow him."

He paused for a moment, then continued. "I'd brought Rosy with me, miss. I hope you won't be minding, but he's the best horse in the world and I figured if I was needing a mount, he'd be the one to have. He seemed to know something was up, kept ever so still. Anyway, I got up on him and away we went after Burke. Kept well back, we did. I'm sure he never got a clue that he was being followed. Tracked him to a house down by the docks right here in Yorktown."

"Whose house?" Susannah asked anxiously. The news that both the Sanderses had left Five Oaks was ominous enough, but the fact that Burke was in Yorktown on the eve of Lee's arrival filled her with dread.

"I don't know, miss," Wilson said. "It's not a proper place, but good enough for a fellow who wants to lie low for a bit."

"I see . . . Well, wherever he is, you're absolutely right, he must be watched. Give me just a few minutes and I'll come with you."

"You, miss? Oh, no, I'm sure Mr. Cabot wouldn't want that. It's him I have to find."

"But you can't," she reminded him. "Not unless you give up watching Burke altogether and go in search of him, which would hardly be prudent. No, there must be two of us." With a smile she added, "I'm afraid you'll just have to put up with me."

"It's not that, miss—" he began to protest as she raised a hand and gently silenced him.

"I know this offends your sense of propriety, Wilson,

but I'm sure Mr. Cabot would be the first to tell you that propriety is often overrated. Besides, there's no choice.''

Mollified by the assurances that the man he had so quickly come to admire would understand his predicament, Wilson agreed to wait with Rosinante in the shadows behind the garden. Susannah ran back upstairs, where she found the maid nodding in a chair. She woke her hurriedly and sent her off to bed, insisting that she could manage perfectly well on her own. The girl was tired and over-worked; she went with only a token demurral.

Once she was alone, Susannah wiggled and wrestled her way out of her gown and stays, then quickly burrowed for the leather case at the back of the closet. Within moments she had thrown on her Tad clothes. Feeling far more free and buoyed up by her excitement that, for the moment at least, blocked out her fears, she returned swiftly to join Wilson.

Rosinante nickered her a welcome but otherwise re-mained calm as she and the boy scrambled up on his broad back. Within moments they were cantering through the silent streets on their way toward the docks.

Wilson, meanwhile, having overcome his shock at seeing Susannah in boys' garb, expressed second thoughts. ''You've got to understand, miss,'' he ventured, ''where we're going is a very rough part of town, it is. Burke's no proper gentleman. He probably feels more at home in such places than anywhere else. But you—'' He broke off, clearly at a loss as to what he could say that would get his point across without offending her delicate sensibilities.

''It's all right,'' Susannah murmured. ''I understand.''

''No, miss,'' he manfully persisted, ''I don't see how you could. There's things a lady doesn't know about.''

She took a deep breath and decided that the best way to quiet the boy's anxieties was to give him a dose of candor. ''He's holed up in a flash house, is he?''

''Flash—? Where did you ever hear about them?''

''I know about a lot of things, Wilson,'' she told him.

"You'd be surprised. At any rate, let me assure you that I
realize where we're going and I'll be very careful. I hope
you'll do the same."

Perhaps not so much reassured as stunned, Wilson subsided into silence. They had left the pleasant part of
Yorktown and were entering a section of the town Susannah had never seen before. It was not, however, all that
strange to her. It reminded her on a smaller scale of the
Rocketts area of Richmond.

As they rode along, going deeper into the narrow streets
that twined around the docks, a plop of rain splattered
against Susannah's back. Another followed, and another.
She looked up at a sky that had turned leaden and ominous. "Another storm," she murmured.

Wilson followed her gaze. "Been having a lot of rain
lately," he said. "River's sure running high."

Susannah nodded and drew her collar up around her.
"Perhaps this won't amount to much." Even as she ventured that hope, the sky opened and unleashed a torrential
downpour. Within moments they were both soaked. The
road before them, already dark, became rapidly obscured.
Susannah tightened her grip on the reins as Rosinante
carefully picked his way along the cobbled streets.

"Down there, miss," Wilson said as they came to a
corner. "That's where he is."

Susannah glanced around and noticed a small shed standing up against a derelict building. She quickly motioned
Wilson to get down and led Rosinante over to the shelter.
The animal protested being left there, but she soothed
him gently, and after a moment or two he quieted.

When she emerged again, it was raining even harder.
Wilson gave her a look that spoke volumes about her
bedraggled state, and murmured, "Mr. Cabot isn't going
to like this."

"We'll worry about him later. First let me see where
Burke is staying."

Reluctantly Wilson led the way to a building at the far

end of the street. Its door was closed against the rain, but the windows stood open. Through them came raucous music and loud voices.

"They rent rooms out," Wilson explained. "He took one for tonight only. Told the man who runs the place he . . . uh . . . only wanted to be left alone." What Burke had in fact said, as Wilson had learned moments later from the flash house owner, was that he wanted the room only, not the doxy who usually went along with it. That was odd enough for the owner to note and to repeat—goaded by the incentive of Rand's gold, which Wilson had been careful to apply.

"Did Burke come directly here?" Susannah asked.

The boy shook his head. "Rode around a bit down by the Civic Hall, like he was looking the place over."

When she heard this, Susannah grew even more tense. Burke's interest in the site where Lee would be the following evening convinced her once and for all that their worst fears were justified. She put a hand on Wilson's arm. "Do you have any idea where Mr. Cabot could be? Any at all?" He hesitated long enough for her to add, "He was going to see a friend in town, someone he thought might have useful information, but he didn't mention the gentleman's name."

"Could be anyone, miss. Yorktown's a fair-sized place."

"I know," Susannah said regretfully. "If only I'd thought to ask him." She was blaming herself for that omission, not having expected that he would be gone so long or that she would need to get in touch with him suddenly. "There must be someone here who has some idea of where he might have gone."

Wilson evaded her gaze. He was thinking of the gracious residence he had happened to pass while following Burke, noting as he did so that it was once again occupied. Although he had never been inside, he had heard enough about the legendary Bagatelle Club and its proprietress to suspect that Rand might not be a stranger there. The only problem was that he couldn't bring himself to mention the possibility to Susannah.

"There is a place . . ." he murmured reluctantly.

"Where?" she demanded. "How quickly can we get there?"

"That wouldn't be a good idea, miss," Wilson hedged. "Better for you to stay here while I— No, that isn't good either. If Burke comes out again, you'll take after him, and the Lord only knows where that would lead."

"Make up your mind," Susannah ordered in exasperation. "Either I stay here and watch Burke or I find Rand. We don't have all night to argue about it."

"I don't mean to be stubborn, miss, only—"

"Only what?"

The boy took a deep breath and seemed to hold it as he blurted out, "It's a long shot, miss, but there's a . . . a lady here in town who might have some idea of where Mr. Cabot's gone. She . . . uh . . . knows a lot of people. Gentlemen, that is. I mean to say—" He broke off, blushing fiercely.

In the dim light, Susannah did not notice his discomfort. Urgently she asked, "Who is this lady?"

"Lillie Dumont, miss." Wilson waited, half tensed, expecting an eruption.

The name meant nothing to Susannah. "I'm not acquainted with her."

With the utmost reluctance Wilson said, "I'm not surprised, miss. She . . . uh . . . runs a business in Richmond."

"She does?" Susannah repeated, impressed by the idea of a woman's being so independent. "Then I would like very much to meet her. What sort of business is it?"

Wilson reddened further. He hopped from one foot to the other and for a moment looked as though he was choking. Finally he blurted out, "She's a madam, miss. The most famous in Richmond, probably in all of Virginia. She owns the Bagatelle Club, and she moves it over here for the summer."

"The Bagatelle . . . ? A madam—? Oh . . ." It was Susannah's turn to blush. "I see," she murmured, though she didn't see at all. For all her experience in areas young ladies of her sort were supposed to know nothing about, she felt decidedly out of her depth. "Do you, by any chance, know where this Bagatelle place is?"

"You aren't thinking of going there, miss?" Wilson exclaimed. "Surely now that I've explained you understand why it isn't possible."

"I understand," she said quietly, "that we face exactly the same situation we did a few moments ago. This is no time for squeamishness. I will go there, find out if this Miss Dumont has any idea of Mr. Cabot's whereabouts, and then go in search of him. Meanwhile, you will remain on watch here, ready to follow Burke again should that prove necessary. Nothing could be simpler."

She didn't believe that for a moment, nor did Wilson, but neither of them saw any alternative. With the utmost reluctance he gave her directions. Susannah's eyes widened. "That's one of the best sections of town."

"Yes, miss."

She mulled that over, wondering how she could have been oblivious to such things all these years, then straightened her shoulders. "Keep a careful watch, Wilson. I will be back shortly with Mr. Cabot."

He nodded as if he shared her confidence, though his worried look said otherwise. Susannah wasted no time, but ran back up the street to where she had left Rosinante. She patted his muzzle reassuringly. "You stay here, boy, in case Wilson needs you. I'll be back soon."

The huge horse whinnied softly, for all the world as though in warning.

The summer location of the Bagatelle Club was a large, three-story house set amid rolling lawns on the outskirts of Yorktown. It was surrounded by a high iron fence and reached by a driveway guarded by ancient oaks. As Susannah hurried up, all but breathless in her rush to get there, a burly young man emerged from the shadows near the door and blocked her way.

"What are you wanting here, boy?"

Mindful of the need to preserve her disguise, Susannah pitched her voice as low as she could. "I need to see the . . . uh . . . lady of the house."

The guard laughed disbelievingly. "Go on with you, runt. Come back when you've started shaving."

Susannah realized the futility of arguing further. She pretended to turn away, then darted around the man and ran up the steps.

"Hold on," he yelled, even as her foot was on the first step leading to the porch. "Just what in hell do you think you're doing?"

Susannah ignored him. She thrust the door wide and darted inside. Instantly a wave of music and laughter struck her. She paused for a scant second, but long enough for the guard to catch up with her.

He dropped a heavy hand on her shoulder and was about to pull her away when a door at the side of the entry opened and a woman emerged. She was tall and lushly curved, dressed in a gossamer silk gown that left little to the imagination. Her eyebrows rose as she regarded Susannah.

"What's going on here, Samuel?" she demanded of the guard.

"Little squirt tricked his way in here, ma'am. I was just removing him."

"Wait!" Susannah cried as the hand tightened further on her shoulder. "Are you Miss Dumont?"

Lillie nodded cautiously. Her gaze flicked over the disheveled creature before her with mingled disdain and amusement. "Who might you be?" she asked.

Susannah gathered all her courage and blurted, "A friend of Rand Cabot's. I've got to find him and I'm hoping you can help."

Lillie's face froze. She gestured to the guard, who

abruptly released Susannah. As she stumbled forward, Lillie said, "What makes you think I know Mr. Cabot?"

"I heard . . . that is, a friend suggested you might, but if you don't . . ." Susannah wasn't sure which she would have preferred. She was truly desperate to find Rand, yet she was hardly happy with the idea of his being acquainted with such a woman. Getting a grip on her emotions, she told herself to be reasonable. He was a man, not a monk. It was only to be expected that he would be known in such quarters.

"That will be all, Samuel," Lillie said suddenly. She gestured again, beckoning Susannah to follow her. The room they entered was easily the most feminine one Susannah had ever seen. It was decorated entirely in blue, white, and gilt with an airy, floral design wallpaper, matching fabrics on the couch and chairs, and, set in one corner, a magnificent Louis Quinze marquetry desk.

Lillie leaned against the desk and regarded Susannah speculatively as she asked, "Is Mr. Cabot expecting you?"

"Expecting? Uh . . . no . . . not exactly." A most unpleasant suspicion was beginning to dawn on Susannah. She steeled herself against it and resolutely concentrated on the matter at hand. "I have news for him of some importance."

"I see . . . this seems to be his night for it." Lillie smoothed the skirt of her peony red gown and straightened. Susannah could see that the other woman was of moderate height, no taller than Susannah herself, and amply endowed. She carried herself gracefully, with an unfeigned confidence that was rare in any woman.

Lillie strolled over to a mahogany escritoire and opened its double doors to reveal an array of crystal decanters. "Would you care for a drink?"

Susannah shook her head. "Ah, no, ma'am, thanks all the same." The mere thought of swallowing anything, much less hard liquor, made her stomach tighten. She shook her head again to emphasize her refusal. "About Mr. Cabot, ma'am."

"My, you are in a rush. That isn't a good thing for a young boy. How old are you, by the way?"

Susannah swallowed hard, struggling for patience all the while she was aware of time ticking away. "Eighteen, ma'am."

Lillie's laughter rang out. "You haven't seen sixteen yet." She finished pouring her drink and came closer. Lifting a hand, she let her long, painted nails scratch lightly over Susannah's cheek. "Beardless, a child still." Her voice dropped to a low purr. "Or are you?" She took a step closer, and her hand slid downward toward the joining of Susannah's thighs.

Before Lillie could touch her there, Susannah jumped back, her eyes wide with shock and bewilderment. Seeing the expression in them, Lillie tossed back her head and laughed. "You've got nerve, I'll say that for you. But don't you think it's time you dropped the masquerade?"

Aware that nothing was going as she had expected, Susannah stared down at the carpet. Thanks to the rain outside, she was dripping water onto it. Automatically she murmured, "I'm sorry."

"Well brought up, too," Lillie said as she returned to her desk and propped herself on a corner of it. "Who are you?"

"I told you, ma'am—"

"Stop it," Lillie ordered. "You're a girl who for some reason has chosen to dress as a boy. You come in here looking for Rand, making it clear that it's urgent you see him. That would be unusual under any circumstances, but tonight—" She broke off, clearly reluctant to say too much. Resolutely she said, "I must know who you are and why you are here, or you have no possibility of seeing him. Do you understand?"

Susannah nodded. She had accepted that Rand was some-where in the building but entertained no hope of finding him on her own. She would be stopped before she got more than a few feet beyond Lillie's office.

Softly she asked, "Are you really his friend?"

Lillie's face softened a fraction. "Who told you that?"

"He did. He said he was going to see a friend, to get some information we both needed."

"I see." Lillie stared at her nails for a moment, then abruptly came to a decision. "Yes, I am his friend. Now who are you and why are you here?"

Equally decisive, Susannah cast doubt aside. "I'm Susannah Fitzgerald. Rand and I are working together on the matter that brought him here tonight."

Again Lillie's penetrating eyes looked her over. "How nice for you," she murmured. After a moment's further thought, she said, "Have a seat, Miss Fitzgerald. I'll let Rand know you're here."

As she swept out of the room, Susannah subsided onto the nearest chair and drew a deep, shaky breath, attempting to master her myriad emotions. She'd made little progress in that direction when the door abruptly banged open and Rand strode into the room. He stopped, hands on his lean hips, and stared at her. "I thought Lillie had to be joking. I couldn't believe even you would pull a stunt like this."

"I had no choice," Susannah said as she stood up quickly. His show of temper provoked her own, but she fought it down determinedly. "McMahon is here. He's looked over the Civic Hall where the ball is to be held, and now he's holed up near the waterfront."

Rand's mood changed abruptly. "Damn it," he muttered. "I was hoping we had more time."

"So was I," Susannah agreed. "Damien and Thurston have gone elsewhere. Wilson had to choose between following them or Burke, so we have no way of knowing their whereabouts."

"Far from here, I'm sure," Rand said grimly as he ran a hand through his tawny hair. "Though close enough to get the news when it comes. They wouldn't care to be anywhere near the scene of the crime. We'll worry about them when the time comes. Right now we've got to get to McMahon before he can move against Lee. The presidential party is due here before noon."

As he turned toward the door, she followed. Out of the corner of her eye she caught a glimpse of Lillie watching them go. The older woman smiled faintly and raised a hand in farewell.

Outside, at the front of the house, Rand quickly unhitched one of the horses that had drawn their carriage. He vaulted into the saddle and reached a hand down to Susannah. "Come on."

He hoisted her up in back of him with a smooth, effortless movement, and they set off at a brisk trot. If anything, the rain had grown heavier. The horse's hooves sent up showers of water in their wake.

"Where are we going?" Susannah demanded. "This is the wrong direction."

"I'm taking you back to your Cousin Julia's. You'll tell me where Wilson is and I'll find the place, but you're out of this as of now."

"The hell I am," Susannah muttered loudly enough for him to hear. "I haven't come this far to be packed off now."

"Don't be ridiculous. You must realize how dangerous—"

"You're wasting time we don't have," she interrupted.

"Of all the . . . Oh, all right, have it your own way. But that's an end to it. You'll keep your head down if I have to knock it down for you."

"So chivalrous," she muttered again, this time prompting only a snort.

Turned in the right direction, the horse made good time despite the rain. During the time she'd spent waiting in Lillie's office, Susannah had begun to dry off somewhat. Now she was soaked again, as was Rand. Clinging to his narrow waist, she closed her eyes for a moment and did

her best not to think about what the next few hours would
hold.

As they left their mount with Rosinante in the shed, she
turned to Rand. His features were obscured by the darkness, but she could feel the rock-hard determination ema-
nating from him. "What are you going to do?" she asked.

"What I have to."

She made no further comment, realizing the implacabil-
ity of his will as well as the lack of any alternative. Her
stomach clenched painfully, but she ignored it as they
reached the corner where Wilson waited. He saw them
quickly and beamed a smile of relief.

"He's still in there. Leastways, he sure hasn't left by
the front."

Rand nodded. "You'll stay here." Looking at Susannah, he added, "Both of you."

She laid a hand on his arm. "Rand, for God's sake be
careful. The man is a killer."

He said nothing, only kissed her and was gone.

"He'll be all right, miss," Wilson said. "I'm sure of it.
Don't be fretting."

"I can't help it," Susannah murmured. She pressed
against the wall of the building opposite the flash house,
her eyes on the door through which Rand had just disappeared. In her mind, she followed him into the dark and
stinking den, imagined him exchanging a few words with
whoever ran the place, passing a coin or two, and then
starting up the steps to McMahon's room. Her heart ham-
mered painfully as she envisioned the confrontation between the two men.

"I'm terribly afraid," she whispered, "that something
is wrong. I don't know what, but I can't stop thinking
that."

"It's natural, miss. But Mr. Cabot's a right smart gent.
Knows how to take care of hisself, he does."

"I suppose." She shivered and turned up the collar of
her shirt. They subsided into silence, broken only by the

splatter of rain against the cobblestones and the low but ominous sound of water sloshing against the nearby piers. Susannah closed her eyes in weariness. When she opened them a moment later, she thought she saw a flicker of movement to one side of the flash house.

"What was that?" she whispered.

"What?"

"I thought I saw someone moving."

Wilson peered through the darkness, straining to see. He shook his head. "I don't see anything, miss."

"No, perhaps I didn't either."

She closed her eyes again, but an instant later her lids snapped open. Beneath the sound of the rain, she thought she had heard something else. A sharp, metallic sound. "What was that?"

"I don't know. It sounded almost like a bolt being shot."

Thinking quickly, Susannah asked, "Is there anything behind the flash house?"

"I don't know . . . could be. A stable, maybe."

They looked at each other with alarm. Susannah held her breath. She leaned forward, straining to hear. There was nothing at first, then a sound, followed by another: horse's hooves leaving the stable.

"It might not be him," Wilson murmured.

"But we can't be sure. Wait here and watch." Without another word she ran on tiptoe, making no sound, to where Rosinante waited. She was in the saddle in an instant. Leaning forward on his broad back, she patted his mane to keep him silent. The hoofbeats could be more clearly heard now. They reached the street and turned in the direction of the river. Susannah waited through the space of several heartbeats, then urged Rosinante on.

She drew rein beside Wilson. "It was him, miss! You were right. He went off that way."

"Go inside," Susannah instructed urgently. "Find Mr.

Cabot and tell him what's happened. I'm going after McMahon.''

"No, miss, you can't!"

Susannah didn't bother to argue. She pressed her heels into Rosinante and took off in McMahon's wake.

They were nearing the river; she could see its broad, turbulent swath only a few yards off. Not far away was the landing where Lee would come ashore in a few hours. Susannah had been there herself when she and her father had come to Yorktown directly from Richmond via the paddlewheeler. She remembered that the landing faced a semicircle of warehouses and other buildings that would offer ample cover for a would-be assassin.

All along they had presumed that McMahon would strike at the ball, but in fact there was no reason to think that. Once he reached the buildings and hid himself, anyone trying to find him would be at a great disadvantage. He was undoubtedly armed and wouldn't hesitate to shoot whoever came near. He would have to be stopped while he was still in the open.

Susannah searched frantically for a better alternative but could think of none. She took a deep breath, tightened her hold on the reins, and leaned far over. "Now, boy!" she said in a harsh whisper and dug her heels hard into the stallion's sides.

Rosinante sprang forward. All the powerful, superbly trained strength of his muscled body hurled him on, and Susannah with him. McMahon had barely a moment to see them coming before the stallion slammed into the other horse, knocking its rider from the saddle.

More quickly than she would have thought possible, McMahon was on his feet. He stood panting, rainwater streaming from him, as he glared at Susannah with reddened eyes. "You little bastard," he snarled. "Come after me, will you. I'll make you curse the day you were born."

He came toward her, his face distorted with rage and blood lust. For a brief, crucial instant Susannah was frozen

with fear. In that tiny expanse of time, McMahon's hand
lashed out, closing around her leg. She screamed and tried
to pull away, but without success.

Even as she felt herself being dragged from the saddle,
Susannah was aware of a sudden change in Rosinante. His
mighty body tensed, and his nostrils flared. The night air
was suddenly torn by a high, piercing shriek, the cry of a
stallion aroused to fury.

Before Susannah could make a move to prevent it,
Rosinante reared back, his huge hooves slashing directly at
McMahon. Instinctively the man raised his arms to protect
himself, thereby releasing Susannah. As the stallion's cry
resounded again, McMahon stumbled backward. He took
two steps, then a third, when suddenly he lost his balance.
As Susannah's eyes widened with horror, he fell backward
into the raging river and disappeared from sight.

19

An extraordinary story," Lee said thoughtfully. As he sat back in his chair and regarded the two people before him, a slight smile lifted the corners of his mouth. Rand and Susannah were both bedraggled and weary, yet there was about them an ineffable sense of strength and beauty. Even in her outlandish garb, Susannah was lovely. She had discarded her hat, and her ebony hair tumbled around her pale face. Her shirt and trousers were still slightly damp, emphasizing the slenderness of her form. Beside Rand she appeared small and fragile, yet Lee did not for a moment underestimate her resolve.

Her emerald eyes flashed. "Sir, if you don't mind my saying so, you don't seem to be taking this matter very seriously."

Lee's smile deepened. He regarded her affectionately before turning his attention to Rand, who sat beside Susannah on the couch. His golden hair was windblown and tangled, his clothes as damp as her own and stretched over his muscled breadth. Rand's tawny eyes were shadowed with concern as Lee asked, "Do you agree with that, young man?"

Rand nodded. "If I had just been informed of a plot against my life, I doubt I'd be in such good humor, sir."

Lee stood up and walked over to the window, looked
out at Yorktown's rain-swept streets. Thanks to the inclement weather, the pomp and circumstance surrounding
his arrival had been mercifully cut short. He'd said only a
few words before withdrawing to the shelter of his hotel,
where he would shortly receive various dignitaries. They
were waiting for him even now, undoubtedly wondering
what was keeping him.

"Ah, but you see," he said as he turned back to his
visitors, "what you've informed me of is a plot against my
life that has apparently failed. That is hardly bad news."

Rand and Susannah exchanged glances. They had both
been concerned that such might be Lee's response. "Sir,"
Rand said carefully, "there is a possibility—however
remote—that McMahon could still be alive."

Lee's snow-white eyebrows rose slightly. "Didn't I understand you to say that he fell into the river?"

Susannah nodded. "Yes, sir, he did." She suppressed
the image of that terrible moment, telling herself she should
feel no regrets over what had happened. McMahon had
clearly deserved to die. She only hoped he had in fact done
so.

"Considering the way the river is running," Lee said,
"do you really believe he could have survived?"

Susannah shifted slightly on the couch. "It's unlikely."

"So much so," Lee said, "that I see no reason not to
regard the threat as past. Of course, the Sanderses remain
to be dealt with, as well as whoever else was involved
with them." He looked as though he relished that prospect. "However, I fail to see how they could still be an
immediate threat."

"They aren't," Rand agreed. "At least not for the
moment. But McMahon—"

"Would have to either be part fish or have the devil's
own luck to have survived," Lee interrupted. "I fully
expect his body to wash up in another day or two."

Susannah flinched. Her always vivid imagination seemed

to be working overtime, undoubtedly the by-product of fatigue and shock. She trembled and wrapped her arms around herself.

Instantly Lee was contrite. "I'm sorry, my dear. I've kept you both here quite long enough. You need to rest and put all this behind you."

Their dismissal, however gracious, was clear. Reluctantly Rand stood up and held out a hand to Susannah. She took it gladly, grateful for the support that was missing from her own wobbly legs.

"Mr. President," Rand said as they walked together to the door, "I fully appreciate your desire to close the book on this matter and get on with your work, but I feel compelled to caution you again that it may not be over."

Lee looked at him directly, his gaze clear and untroubled. "A wise friend of mine once said that there comes a time in every man's life when he must accept the fact that his fate is not in his own hands. It is ruled by a higher power whose purpose we cannot always understand."

Rand suppressed a sigh. He recognized the words as Lincoln's and knew he could not argue with them. There were times when he, too, had taken a fatalistic approach to events. Invariably things had worked out for the best.

"I understand what you're saying, sir," he told Lee. "I hope you'll understand that I still intend to keep a close eye on you. Our mutual acquaintance would not take kindly to my failure to do so."

Lee laughed. He held out a hand to Rand and gave Susannah a fond smile. "I'll look forward to seeing you both this evening. In the meantime, if there's anything you need"—he opened the door, gesturing to the young aide who waited immediately beyond—"Soames here will assist you."

"That's very kind of you, sir," Susannah murmured.

As Lee returned to his office, the young man glanced at them with surprise and a faint touch of nervousness. She could hardly blame him. Her own appearance was hardly calculated to inspire confidence, while Rand's rough-hewn looks and assertive manner tended to make other men ill at ease.

She managed a light, reassuring smile. "We won't trouble you. We're staying with my cousin and she is undoubtedly wondering where we've gotten to."

"She can keep on wondering," Rand said bluntly. Addressing the aide, he added, "Get us a couple of rooms here. Send someone over to the Costain residence to pick up our bags. Also, there's a young lad waiting down in the lobby, name of Wilson. He'll need a room as well."

Soames pursed his mouth in distaste. He did not take kindly to being ordered around by an unkempt, overly large Yankee. Haughtily he said, "I really don't think it will be possible to accommodate you here. The hotel is full."

"Obviously," Rand said, "you weren't listening when President Lee said you should assist us in any way."

The young man turned an unattractive shade of red. He stumbled slightly as he said, "Perhaps I should have phrased that differently. While I would certainly like to help, I'm afraid it simply isn't possible. The hotel really is fully booked."

"Unbook it," Rand said. "Yourself, for instance. I presume you've got a room?"

"Yes, but—"

"Clear it out, double up with somebody. Get a few others to do the same thing. While you're at it, we could both use a hot bath and a meal. The same goes for the boy."

The young man's mouth tightened even further. He cast a glance toward Lee's door but apparently decided that no help would come from that quarter. As coldly as he dared he said, "If you would follow me."

Half an hour later, Susannah lay soaking in a scented bath, idly watching fingers of steam rise toward the ceiling. She sighed contentedly and tilted her head back against the tub's rim. The dank coldness that seemed to have pervaded her very bones was at last disappearing. Inch by inch she could feel herself relaxing as tension eased away.

She took a deep breath and let it out slowly. So much had happened in the past day that she could barely keep everything straight. It seemed like such a short time since she had been at Five Oaks with Rand and Thurston, yet in the intervening hours the plot against Lee truly seemed to have unraveled. She told herself yet again that McMahon must be dead. There couldn't be anything more to fear from him. As for the others, they would be rounded up quickly enough.

She had dispatched a note to her father and Aunt Miriam explaining what had happened. With the danger apparently past, she had said, she hoped they would understand her desire to remain in Yorktown at least long enough to attend the ball. She didn't for a moment think her father would not be aware of the same possibility that Rand had raised, namely that McMahon might still be alive. She could only hope he would discount it as Lee had.

With a frown she reached for the soap on the edge of the tub and began lathering herself. The ball raised certain problems she was reluctant to mention to Rand. He would undoubtedly think her frivolous for being worried because she had nothing suitable to wear. But when she had thrown a few things into a bag before leaving for Yorktown, she'd had no expectation of being there long enough to attend the ball. All she had with her was a change of underwear, a robe, and a simple day dress.

That would simply have to do. She was hardly so vain that she couldn't bear to be less than spectacularly attired. Nonetheless, she couldn't suppress a twinge of regret that Rand would not see her at her best.

A short time later, after noticing that her fingers and toes were beginning to wrinkle, she rose from the tub. As she wrapped a towel around herself, she remembered a similar action interrupted by Rand. A quiver of desire rippled through her.

With a soft, barely perceptible sigh she went into the bedroom. It was a pleasant, nondescript room showing no sign of its previous, brief occupant. Her own bag was laid on a stand near the bed. While she was bathing, it had arrived from Cousin Julia's. Susannah smiled as she considered her relative's reaction. Undoubtedly Julia was agog with disapproval and curiosity.

Grateful that she would not have to deal with either emotion, at least for a while, Susannah took her robe from the bag, put it on, then sat down at the dressing table. She was brushing her newly washed hair, struggling to get the tangles out, when there was a knock at the door.

Expecting Rand, she was surprised and a bit taken aback by the lovely, statuesque woman who smiled hesitantly at her. "I hope I'm not disturbing you, Miss Fitzgerald," she said. "If I've come at an inconvenient time—"

"Not at all," Susannah assured her. She stood aside as Lillie Dumont swept into the room with a rustle of silk and the scent of roses. Her costume was properly high-necked and appropriate to the time and place, but it was also exquisitely feminine and in the height of fashion. She moved gracefully to a settee, but waited to be invited to sit down.

"Please," Susannah said, indicating that her guest should make herself comfortable. As she resumed her seat on the dressing table bench, she regarded Lillie cautiously. Such women were completely outside her experience, yet she couldn't bring herself to condemn someone who appeared strong, courageous, and intelligent. Softly she said, "We left so abruptly last night that neither of us had a chance to thank you for your help."

"That isn't necessary," Lillie said. "Rand and I have been friends for a long time. I was glad to do anything I could to help."

Susannah flushed. Part of her longed to know exactly

how far that friendship had gone; another part shied away from any such revelation.

Lillie seemed to recognize her quandary. She smiled gently. "Rand is an unusual man, a rare combination of passion and discipline. When he commits himself, it's wholeheartedly, with nothing held back. That makes him rather vulnerable."

"Yes," Susannah murmured softly, "I imagine it does."

"We've had some good times together," Lillie went on. "But that's in the past. When he came to see me last night, it was clear that you were uppermost in his mind, even more so than Lee. He mentioned you several times with a certain . . ." She spread her hands evocatively. "How shall I put it? A certain intensity I've never seen from him before." Wryly she added, "He also made it clear that what once existed between us is over. Oh, not the friendship—I hope that will always continue—but anything else is finished. I accept that because I genuinely care for Rand and want him to be happy. What I'd like to know from you is whether or not he's going to be."

"I want him to be," Susannah answered, her hands clasped in her lap. She looked down at them as she added, "But I'm not sure I hold the key to his happiness. No relationship founded solely on adherence to duty can possibly be happy."

"Duty?" Lillie said, puzzled. "What are you talking about?"

Susannah flushed, then raised her eyes, not realizing that her heart was in them. Lillie stared at her for a moment, then laughed softly. "I think I understand. Rand is being noble, is he?"

"I'm afraid so," Susannah murmured.

"How tiresome of him. Especially when what you want is to be swept off your feet, overwhelmed by passion, and carried off into the sunset."

"When you put it that way, it sounds foolish."

"No," Lillie said gently, "it's not foolish at all. You

have every right to want Rand to love you as you do
him.''

"I don't—'' She broke off, unable to utter so blatant a
falsehood. Instead she asked wryly, "Is it that obvious?''

"No more so than the nose on your face.'' With a smile
Lillie rose to go. "You've greatly reassured me, Miss
Fitzgerald. I'm glad I stopped by.''

"I don't see that I've said much to comfort you,''
Susannah ventured. "So long as Rand thinks it's his duty
to marry me, there's no future for us.''

"That would be a pity,'' Lillie murmured as she turned
to the door. Her gaze fell on the day dress laid out on the
bed. "There's a ball in Lee's honor tonight, isn't there?''

Susannah nodded. "Rand and I will be going, if only to
keep an eye on things.''

"Very wise.'' She held out her gloved hand. "Well,
thank you again. I do apologize for dropping in unannounced.''

Susannah assured her there was no reason to do so. She
watched her visitor depart with regret, wishing she would
have stayed longer. She would have liked to have asked
her about Rand, but wasn't sure she would have had the
nerve. With a faint shake of her head, she considered the
irony of her being able to face down a man like McMahon
but not being able to confront her own emotions.

She was still dwelling on that when there was a sudden,
sharp rap at the door, utterly unlike Lillie's polite knocking. "Who is it?'' she called.

"Open up,'' Rand demanded. The moment she did so,
he strode into the room, looking at her narrowly. "Why
aren't you at least lying down? I have to find out from
Lillie that you aren't feeling well. You should be in bed.
You should—''

"Lillie?'' Susannah repeated. "She told you I was ill?''

Rand nodded curtly. "She stopped by my room for a
moment after seeing you.'' As if realizing how that might
sound, he went on hurriedly, "Susannah, you have a right
to know that Lillie and I were . . . close at one time. But

that's over now. She's only a friend, a good one. I'm glad she thought to tell me you were ill. It's no wonder considering everything you've been through."

Without giving her the slightest chance to reply, he caught her up in his arms and carried her to the bed. "You'll stay here while I get that idiot Soames to send for a doctor." As he lowered her gently onto the mattress he added softly, "I'll never forgive myself if anything happens to you, Susannah. When I think of coming upon you just as McMahon went into the water . . . If he'd gotten his hands on you—" He broke off, his throat suddenly too constrained to allow for speech.

Stunned by the depth of his emotion, Susannah raised a trembling hand to his face. She touched his lean cheek lightly, feeling the roughness of a night's growth of whiskers that he had not yet had a chance to remove.

"It's all right," she murmured softly. "Rosinante protected me."

Against her throat, he said, "I should have been there. I shouldn't have let you out of my sight for a moment. You're too beautiful, too precious . . ." He drew her closer, cradling her against him. His big hand stroked her hair as his mouth found hers in a searing, evocative kiss. They clung together, swept by passion that overwhelmed all else, until finally Rand raised his head.

Shakily he said, "I have to be crazy to be doing this. You aren't feeling well."

"I'm fine," Susannah said when she was able to get her breath sufficiently to speak. Gently she added, "Lillie is a better friend even than you know, to both of us."

His eyebrows rose. "Are you suggesting, Miss Fitzgerald, that I was lured here under false pretenses?"

"Exactly, Mr. Cabot," she said with a soft laugh. Raising herself slightly, she ran a fingertip over his lower lip, tugging at it gently. His tender concern coupled with the passion that sparked so effortlessly between them filled her with heady confidence. She wondered dazedly why it had taken them so long to understand what Lillie had seen at once.

"I suppose," Rand murmured reluctantly, "that I should leave."

"Hmmm," Susannah whispered, her arms reaching up to twine across his broad back. "Eventually."

He looked down at her, his golden eyes smoky with desire so intense that it might have frightened her if she hadn't welcomed it wholeheartedly. "Susannah," he said with mock sternness, "let us be sure we understand each other. I will absolutely not let you take advantage of me again in this shameless manner and then refuse to do the honorable thing."

She laughed softly, her lips caressing the taut column of his throat. "That would be churlish of me, wouldn't it?"

"Incredibly," he agreed. Her lips moved again, finding the particularly sensitive spot near the lobe of his ear. As she licked at it delicately, he groaned deep in his chest.

Abruptly the world shifted. She was laid flat on the bed, his weight pressing her down, not uncomfortably but with a firmness that suggested his desire for the upper hand. His smile was utterly male, and extraordinarily provoking, as he undid the belt of her robe and gently laid it open.

As her body was revealed to him, his eyes narrowed, their golden gaze rippling over her like a strong, hot wind, "I want to cherish you," he said huskily. "I want to adore every exquisite inch of you. The first time was magnificent, but I want this time to be even better." He raised his gaze, looking deeply into her eyes. "Will you let me, Susannah? Let me love you completely without restraint, as I want you to love me?"

She swallowed thickly, feeling herself sinking into a sea of enchantment from which she doubted there was any rescue. Not that she wanted any. Without hesitation, she arched slightly, enough for her bared breasts to press against his chest. The smooth cotton of his shirt tantalized her unbearably. Her nipples were hard and full, begging for his touch, as she whispered, "No restraint, Rand. No misunderstandings or doubts. Whatever happens, let's at least have this time together."

That wasn't quite what Rand wanted to hear. He wanted to believe that everything was settled between them, that no further shadows lay over their future together. But deep inside he sensed that wasn't the case. Like it or not, the world beyond them still existed, still had to be confronted. But not just then.

This was their moment, however brief and elusive it might prove to be. As his hands slid over her body with exquisite gentleness, he resolved that whatever happened next, she would not leave this room without knowing how thoroughly and completely he loved her. Never had he set himself a more enticing task, nor one he could savor more fully. A wry smile lit his eyes as he gave himself up to the incomparable enchantment of the woman who was his heart and soul.

20

You look exquisite," Rand said gently as he reached out a hand to Susannah. Drawing her to him, he gazed down at the picture she made in the lovely, ivory silk dress that had appeared unexpectedly a short time before, just as they were preparing for the ball. In the height of fashion, it fit Susannah to perfection and looked as though it had been made for her.

"This was very kind of Lillie," she murmured. "She has superb taste." With a teasing smile she added, "Though I admit when I realized who had sent it, I was expecting something a bit more daring."

Remembering the gown Lillie had been wearing when he first met her, Rand laughed. "My guess is that Lillie had to search high and low to find something this proper." Even so, Susannah looked so enthralling that he was tempted to strip the gown from her and tumble her back onto the bed they had so recently left. Only the knowledge that Lee would shortly conclude his private conversations with the various dignitaries and be once again in a position of potential danger stopped him.

Regretfully he offered Susannah his arm. They left the room and went downstairs to the hotel lobby, which they found in a swirl of activity. Lee was about to depart for the

Civic Hall. He glanced their way, looked again, and smiled indulgently.

"I trust you had a good rest, my dear," he said to Susannah.

She flushed but managed to meet his gaze unflinchingly. "It couldn't have been better, sir."

"Excellent. Then I'll look forward to a dance. That is, if Rand doesn't object." He chuckled softly at their surprise. Before they could speak further, a gentleman appeared at Lee's side, murmuring that it was time to go.

Susannah and Rand followed in another carriage. They were close at hand when Lee stepped in front of the hall, waved to the crowd gathered there to greet him, and proceeded inside. Both noticed with some relief that security around the president had been increased. Although Lee had minimized the remaining threat in his conversation with them, it was clear he had not dismissed it altogether. For that they were both grateful.

Inside, the Civic Hall was ablaze with lights. Several hundred planters, merchants, and their families were on hand to welcome the president. He received a heartfelt cheer as he entered. The orchestra struck up a stirring rendition of "Dixie," which brought further cheers.

When the noise had died away, Lee said a few words, then concluded, "Let us dispense with formality tonight, my friends. Yorktown is famous for its hospitality. I intend to enjoy it fully and hope that you will do the same."

No one, Susannah and Rand least of all, believed Lee meant to do no business that evening. He had come to Yorktown for a particular purpose, to begin politicking for reunification. He would devote the next few hours to that task, but quietly, subtly, in the behind-the-scenes way most likely to be effective.

An hour later, as Susannah stood next to Rand at the refreshment table, she thought that perhaps Lee had been right after all. The ball could not have been going more smoothly. Everyone seemed to be having an excellent time, and there was no sign of trouble brewing.

When she said as much to Rand, he was forced to agree. Nonetheless he cautioned, "I won't be completely satisfied until we know McMahon's fate for certain. Once that happens and the Sanderses are apprehended, then I'll believe the threat is truly over."

She was about to reply when the orchestra struck up a waltz. With a smile Rand led her onto the floor. As they danced, both kept an eye on Lee. He was standing off to one side, chatting with a group of men who were intent on his every word.

"He has to succeed," Susannah murmured. "We can't let anything stop him."

"We won't," Rand assured her. He wished he felt as confident as he sounded. An odd sense of apprehension was growing in him: not the continued concern he had that McMahon might have survived, but something at once less well defined and more immediate. He had experienced nothing like it since his days on the battlefield. He could well remember the same tensing of muscles, the lifting of hair on his nape, the conviction that something just out of his reach was warning of danger.

He shook himself slightly, trying to clear his head, but the feeling persisted. As the music stopped he was frowning.

"Is something wrong?" Susannah asked.

He looked blankly down at her for a moment. "What? Oh, no, everything is fine."

He looked again at the group around Lee. Nothing appeared to be amiss. The security men he had spotted earlier were well positioned. Dressed in plain clothes, they blended well with the guests. Only the most careful eye would note their watchful vigilance, which set them apart from the others. McMahon was an experienced assassin; if he did still live and nurtured any remaining hopes of carrying out his mission, he would surely reconsider upon seeing the security around Lee.

Yet Rand could not shake his growing premonition of danger. It plagued him particularly because his concern involved not only Lee but also Susannah. If trouble suddenly did erupt in the ballroom, he could be certain she would be in the middle of it. After a while he drew her off to one side. "Will you wait here for a moment? I'll be right back."

"I'll come with you," she said promptly.

He had been prepared for that. With a perfectly straight face he said, "I'm afraid that would be most improper, my dear."

When she understood him, Susannah flushed. "Oh," she murmured, "I see . . . Well, in that case . . ."

He maneuvered her adroitly toward a chair in a secluded corner of the room and set her down. Cautiously he repeated, "I'll be right back."

Susannah got the message. He did not want her to go wandering off. As though that were likely. "I'll keep an eye on Lee," she assured him.

He nodded, though he still looked doubtful. A moment later he was gone. Susannah sighed, not all that sorry to be sitting down. She was tired, but pleased that everything was going so well. Lee was laughing at something one of the men had said. He looked very confident, with nothing whatsoever on his mind except his politicking.

Susannah was just beginning to relax when out of the corner of her eye she suddenly noticed Cousin Julia barreling through the crowd in her direction. No great effort was required to imagine what the older woman must think of Susannah's all-night absence. Confronted with the prospect of an imminent tongue lashing, Susannah briefly debated what to do. The security men were all in place, watching Lee and anyone who might come near him. Surely there could be no harm in her momentarily slipping away.

Directly behind her was a brace of French doors leading onto a veranda. She darted through them and quickly concealed herself behind a large stone urn. Cousin Julia poked her head out, glanced back and forth, and muttered to herself. After several minutes of futile looking, she drew back inside, undoubtedly intending to confront Susannah later.

Breathing a sigh of relief, Susannah emerged from behind the urn, knowing she should return to the ballroom promptly. Rand would be extremely concerned if he discovered her missing. She was turning toward the doors, her attention focused on the music and laughter beyond, when there was a sudden movement in the darkness behind her.

She jerked her head around to see what was happening, just as a brutal hand closed over her mouth. Even as she struggled to escape, she was yanked back against a burly form. "Bitch," a voice rasped in her ear. "Thought you were finished with me, did you? You shouldn't ride around on that fancy horse if you don't want to be recognized. Now you'll pay for what happened on the dock, but first you'll watch me finish this job."

Frozen with horror, Susannah was dragged back into the shrubbery beyond the veranda. McMahon threw her roughly onto the ground, keeping a hand over her mouth as he pulled a dirty handkerchief from his pocket and fashioned it into a crude gag. The cloth bit into her cheeks, but her discomfort mattered nothing compared to the terrifying realization that the danger was not over. The killer still lived. Lee was in mortal danger. Worse yet, he had no way of knowing it.

She struggled vainly, trying desperately to scream, but without effect. McMahon merely laughed at her efforts. "Thought you were so smart, did you? You and that fine gentleman friend of yours. Thought you could outsmart me, but I outfoxed you both. Your fine friend'll dance to my tune if he wants to keep you alive."

At Susannah's wide, bewildered stare he said, "I'll trade you for Lee. All he has to do is get him out here, away from that crowd and his guards. Shouldn't be hard for him. Lee'll trust him right enough." He laughed hoarsely. "Be the last mistake he makes."

Horror burned through Susannah. Staring into McMahon's reddened eyes, she remembered what Lee had said about his needing the devil's own luck in order to survive. At that moment she believed Lee had been right. The burly face was livid with bruises undoubtedly taken during his pounding by the river, but his strength was in no way diminished. Nor was his cunning. He would be presenting Rand with an impossible choice: the life of the man he was sworn to protect or that of the woman he loved.

She shut her eyes, desperately wishing she would open them again to discover that the whole terrifying scene was no more than a nightmare. Beside her McMahon stiffened. "Get up," he ordered, grasping her arm, "somebody's coming."

Dumbly she obeyed, a leaden sense of hopelessness settling over her. She fought against it instinctively but without success. No matter which way her mind turned, she could think of no way to thwart McMahon.

He muttered under his breath when he saw that the new arrivals on the veranda were only a couple intent on dalliance. Susannah watched with growing despair as the man drew the woman into his arms and kissed her tenderly. She thought of the all-too-brief interludes she'd shared with Rand. Tears stung her eyes as she wondered if she would ever feel his touch again.

"Can't be much longer," McMahon muttered. "He's got to be wondering where you've gone to."

In fact, Susannah was surprised Rand hadn't already come in search of her. She was trying to figure out what might be keeping him when McMahon said, " 'Less he's been hunting greener pastures. I watched the two of you in there. You looked pretty chummy, but maybe I was wrong."

"No," a low, steady voice suddenly said behind them, "you weren't wrong, McMahon."

The killer whirled, yanking Susannah around with him. She had a momentary glimpse of Rand standing straight and tall in the moonlight, a look on his face such as she had never seen before and hoped never to see again.

Taken by surprise, McMahon loosened his grip on her. In that instant Rand moved. Susannah was knocked to one side. She landed with a jolt that knocked the breath out of her in a clump of bushes. By the time she managed to straighten up enough to see what was happening, the two men were on the ground, struggling fiercely. She wrenched the gag off and screamed as McMahon yanked out a knife and moved to thrust it into Rand's side.

Rand only just managed to evade the thrust. He got a hand on McMahon's wrist and gripped it hard enough to force him to release the knife. It fell with a dull thud. McMahon made a desperate lunge for it even as Rand kicked it out of reach.

Frantic to do something, anything, Susannah tried to reach the knife but could not. Her desperate gaze fell on a dead tree branch not far from where she stood. She grasped it tightly and was advancing on the men when the sharp crack of a gunshot suddenly ripped through the night. McMahon jerked, and for an instant she thought he had been hit, but he'd merely been stunned by the sound. That was enough, however, to give Rand a momentary advantage. He reared back, closed his fist, and delivered a blow to the other man's jaw that sent him sprawling.

As McMahon collapsed unconscious, Lee and half a dozen security guards ran up to surround the would-be assassin. Rand got to his feet. His frock coat and shirt were torn and streaked with dirt, and his features still bore the stamp of rage and brutal determination that had sent him hurling at McMahon. But his golden eyes glowed with tenderness as they settled on Susannah. He looked from her stained face and bedraggled hair to the tree limb she still grasped. A gentle, teasing smile curved his mouth.

"If you'll put that thing down," he said, "I'll show you how glad I am that you're all right."

Instantly she complied. Rand laughed softly as he advanced toward her. "That's a change," he murmured. His arms felt blessedly strong and solid as they came around her, and she sighed in utter relief and yielded to them. Rand held her tightly as they clung together. Long moments passed before either could give any thought to the men who were regarding them with mingled surprise and curiosity.

Only Lee was unperturbed. "Well, my friends," he said calmly, "it appears you were right to suspect the worst. However, I believe it's safe to say that we have nothing more to fear from Mr. McMahon. These gentlemen"—he gestured toward the officers—"will take care of him." His eyes twinkled as he added, "And I'm sure I can count on you, Rand, to take care of Susannah."

"I certainly hope so, sir," Rand murmured, gazing down at the tousled head nestled against his shoulder. She lifted her gaze, meeting his. He saw the relief shining in her eyes, as well as the passion. But beneath both was a hint of challenge that momentarily gave him pause.

Lee noted the sudden flash of concern that tightened Rand's rugged features and laughed softly. "If worse comes to worst, my boy, I have a certain amount of influence with the lady. Isn't that true, Susannah?"

She lowered her head, her thick ebony lashes shielding the glow in her eyes. "Indeed, sir," she murmured prettily, "but in this particular case I don't believe it will be necessary."

Epilogue

Richmond, Virginia
July 4, 1876

Sunlight sparkled over the broad swath of lawn in front of the Capitol. Groups of elegantly dressed men and women clustered about, sipping champagne and chatting gaily. Earlier there had been speeches and a parade. Shortly after nightfall there would be fireworks. The Centennial celebrations were proceeding very nicely, if with a surprising degree of calmness.

Susannah and Rand strolled arm in arm, smiling and nodding to their acquaintances. He looked dashing in a gray morning coat and trousers, his golden hair neatly trimmed and his burnished features alight with gentleness as he gazed at the woman by his side. Susannah wore a high-necked dress of white silk and lace that matched the parasol she twirled over her shoulder. Beneath a frilly white picture hat, her ebony hair was caught in a soft twist. She smiled up at him, her emerald eyes gleaming with remembered passion. They had left their bed late that morning after a protracted bout of lovemaking, the effects of which still resonated within them.

"I rather thought," she murmured, "that Lee's speech

308

would arouse more comment. People didn't seem at all surprised when he announced the reunification talks. More to the point, they didn't seem displeased.''

"There'd been rumors for weeks about what he was going to say,'' Rand reminded her. "I don't think anyone was truly taken unawares. As for anyone's being displeased, Lee's popularity has never been greater. He could have announced just about anything this morning and people would have cheered.''

Susannah laughed softly. Damien and Thurston had both been arrested the night of the Yorktown ball, as they were attempting to board the *Essex* to flee to England. Captain Fortescue had been apprehended along with them.

"Making Lee even more popular was hardly the effect Damien and the others were aiming for,'' Susannah said, "but that's just too bad for them. The news that they conspired to try to kill Lee aroused such outrage that it was a wonder they weren't lynched.''

"Their trial should be interesting,'' Rand murmured absently as he watched the play of light and shadow over her delicate features. "Lord Beaufort will testify that Damien had an arrangement with the renegade British factions opposing reunification. In return for his assistance, they would grant him extraordinary trading rights throughout the Empire. That would have enabled him to parlay an already considerable amount of wealth into an immense fortune.''

"While also destroying a man he feared and hated,'' Susannah added softly.

"Instead, he'll be the one who's destroyed. Any doubts that might have remained about the Sanderses' involvement will be erased by McMahon's testimony.''

"Can you blame him?'' Susannah asked. "Ever since they implicated him in the murder of Zachery Banks, he's wanted revenge. While also claiming, of course, that they're lying.''

"In this case,'' Rand said thoughtfully, "I think the

Sanderses are telling the truth. Banks did try to betray you
and the rest of the underground for his own gain. In the
process he stumbled across the plot against Lee and tried
to blackmail McMahon. He was an opportunist, a man
who looked out strictly for himself. That, as much as
anything, is what got him killed.''

Despite the balmy day, Susannah shivered. She thought
again of how close they had all come to disaster. It was
difficult to believe, given all that had happened since that
night in Yorktown.

"There's Father," she said as she caught sight of him
standing in a small group talking with Lee. He looked
extremely well, showing no lingering effects from his
illness. Susannah gave full credit to Miriam for that. The
two were planning to be married the following month. No
one looked forward to that event with greater pleasure than
Susannah herself.

"I'm glad he accepted Lee's invitation to sit on the
reunification committee," Rand said. "Even though he
still thinks it's a bad idea, he'll make an important
contribution."

"So will you," Susannah said softly. Rand had been
surprised by his own appointment to the committee and
had felt some reluctance to accept it, until Lincoln pointed
out the importance of younger men helping to shape the
reunified nation that they would inherit.

"I'll try," Rand said quietly. "There are bound to be
difficult times ahead. What we're attempting won't come
easily. That's one of the reasons Lee wanted your father to
serve. We all felt the need for someone of unusual tolerance and patience."

He grinned down at her. "Of course, even Jeffrey has
his limits. I did notice that when he found out for sure
what you'd been up to, he was only too happy to pack you
off into my loving care."

She shot him a frosty look from beneath her slumberous
lids. "That is not precisely how I would have put it.

Although," she admitted, "he did say he didn't see any reason to delay our marriage."

He stopped and turned, stroking a finger lightly along her cheek. "Did you?"

"No," she admitted readily even as a soft blush appeared. He laughed softly and, heedless of anyone who might be watching, dropped a gentle kiss on her upturned mouth.

"What would you think," he murmured, "if I told you I'd recently been in touch with Damien?"

"Whatever for?" she asked, surprised by the very notion.

"He expects his legal expenses to be extremely heavy," Rand explained. "He still can't bring himself to believe he'll be convicted, so he wants to hold onto his businesses. However, he's willing to sell Five Oaks."

Her eyes widened. In the weeks since their marriage, they had made no definite plans as to where they would live. She had more or less presumed that their home would be in the North, but now it seemed there was an alternative possibility.

"Oh, Rand," she breathed softly, "if we could . . ."

Rand smiled tenderly. "We will," he murmured. "We'll fill Five Oaks with our love and with our children. When the time comes, we'll cherish Belleterre as well. We'll make them both part of all the good things to come."

Susannah gazed up into his tawny eyes darkening with passion. She felt the strength and courage in him, a match for her own. And she knew that he had seen the future they would share.

The Timeless Romances
of New York Times Bestselling Author
JOHANNA LINDSEY

DEFY NOT THE HEART   75299-9/$4.50 US/$5.50 Can
To save herself from the union being forced upon her, Reina
offered to become her kidnapper's bride, but the nuptial bed
was not part of the bargain.

SILVER ANGEL   75294-8/$4.50 US/$5.95 Can
Kidnapped and sold into slavery, Chantelle Burke swore she'd
never surrender to her ruthless master. Yet the mysterious
stranger ignited the fires of her very soul.

TENDER REBEL   75086-4/$4.50 US/$5.95 Can
Insisting on a marriage in name only was something Roslyn
quickly grew to regret as she dared to trust her new husband
with her life...and her love.

SECRET FIRE   75087-2/$4.50 US/$5.95 Can
From the tempestuous passion at their first meeting, theirs was
a fever that carried them to the power of undeniable love.

HEARTS AFLAME	89982-5/$4.50 US/$5.50 Can
A HEART SO WILD	75084-8/$4.50 US/$5.95 Can
WHEN LOVE AWAITS	89739-3/$4.50 US/$5.50 Can
LOVE ONLY ONCE	89953-1/$4.50 US/$5.50 Can
TENDER IS THE STORM	89693-1/$4.50 US/$5.50 Can
BRAVE THE WILD WIND	89284-7/$4.50 US/$5.95 Can
A GENTLE FEUDING	87155-6/$4.50 US/$5.50 Can
HEART OF THUNDER	85118-0/$4.50 US/$5.50 Can
SO SPEAKS THE HEART	81471-4/$4.50 US/$5.95 Can
GLORIOUS ANGEL	84947-X/$4.50 US/$5.50 Can
PARADISE WILD	77651-0/$4.50 US/$5.50 Can
FIRES OF WINTER	75747-8/$4.50 US/$5.50 Can
A PIRATE'S LOVE	40048-0/$4.50 US/$5.50 Can
CAPTIVE BRIDE	01697-4/$4.50 US/$5.50 Can

AVON BOOKS